DAWN RISING

A Story of Extraordinary Love

MARY ELLEN FERON

White Dawn Rising
Copyright © 2013 by Mary Ellen Feron
All Rights Reserved

ISBN-13: 978-1484982488
ISBN-10: 1484982487
Also available in eBook publication

Note to the Reader:

White Dawn Rising is the third and final book of the *Extraordinary Love Trilogy*, the story of Meg and Tom Phalen and their family. Like the first two books, *A Tent For The Sun* and *My Tears My Only Bread*, *White Dawn Rising* is set in the west of Ireland and traces the powerful and enduring love of a family destined to survive against incredible odds.

In *My Tears My Only Bread* we left Meg, Tom and their family, starved and grieving. Already having lost two children and everything but the rags on their backs they are forced to leave their home on Achill Island.

They pick up the threads of their lives in *White Dawn Risin* after being rescued by their friend Duffy McGee and offered a chance for survival as servants at Browne's Inn in Westport, Co. Mayo.

They do adapt well and begin to thrive as the hunger continues to plague all but the wealthy they must serve. The work is very hard and the indignities many but they do have food and a place to live at a time when friends and neighbors are dying every day.

Things look like they may settle down into a routine when Meg's past threatens to disrupt the very heart of her marriage. At the same time, deep political subterfuge swirls around them as the powers of oppression and rebellion prepare to clash violently, threatening them, their children and their beloved friend Duffy.

Mr. Robert Gilchrist chases them down, involving not only Meg and Tom but their eldest son Denny in a critically dangerous situation. Both Tom and Meg are forced to make terrible, life changing decisions that could destroy everything they've built between them.

As the story of the Phalen family's survival and perseverance continues, they once again meet overwhelming challenges and egregious injustice with grace, faith and honor. Against all odds, they come to the end of their journey with their dignity valiantly preserved and their love unscathed by the fires that threaten to consume them.

A Story of Extraordinary Love
Told in Three Installments

A Tent for the Sun
My Tears, My Only Bread
White Dawn Rising

Dedication:

For Helen Casey Zimmer, my Grammie;
from beginning to end, this is for you.

Acknowledgements:

I wish, with a full heart, to acknowledge all those who made this book possible.

First, and without a doubt, foremost, my beloved husband and long-standing supporter, Ed. Without you, I would never have been able to write a single word. Ever since you put my very first essay in the mail, when I was too shy to do so myself, I have trusted your advice and relied on your support. Thank you. I love you.

Secondly, my sons, Francis and Paul whose personalities and traits, experiences and journeys are infused into some of my characters in ways so intimate and complex that only I, as your mother, can tell. You both are so very precious to me.

I need to say thank you to many friends, who over the years of writing, listened and supported my work. Thank you to the first reader of my first chapter, Meg Stoll; my colleagues in the Labor and Delivery Unit at Sisters of Charity Hospital, who allowed me to read a chapter to them one rare, quiet evening and offered some of the most solid encouragement I ever received and didn't take: the suggestion that I quit nursing and just write. I cannot number the times I remembered that advice during the course of this creation. Even before that, I thank my fellow nursing students at Sisters of Charity School of Nursing for appointing me editor of our senior yearbook and giving me the opportunity to hone my skills. I want to thank Tim Denesha, dear Old Bud that he is, for ever so gently nudging me throughout the years, sharing his own wonderful stories and poetry, always turning me forward; always believing.

I must credit the leaders of the many writers groups I worked with: Tom O'Malley of Canisius College in Buffalo,

New York; Kathryn Radeff of the Just Buffalo literary group; my dear friends and fellow writers, Dianne Riordan, Patty McClain and the late Grace McMeneme. I learned so much, writing with you. Dianne, you have been beyond supportive and I am so grateful.

I chose certain individuals to read my manuscript with the clear goal of editing and winnowing, correcting and critiquing. I thank my friend, Ann Szumski for starting me off on the right path; Karol Morton, a writer herself, read the book with a red pen. I thank her for her honesty and holding me to the integrity of the story; Bev Malona and my mother, Joan Feron read the manuscript before it was finished and lovingly badgered me to keep writing once they had reached the end of the pages; my friends Lynn Dulak and Elise Seggau, former editor of "The Cord" at St. Bonaventure University; my sisters, especially Kate, who many times kept me from burning my computer; my nieces; my cousin Kathy Verso and my daughters-in-law, Kelly and Erin who read the first printed draft and offered such positive response that I persevered in the final push to publish. I particularly wish to thank my male readers, especially my uncle, David Zimmer, whose suggestion to publish the book as a trilogy was the advice that provided the missing piece to the publishing puzzle.

There are many others to thank. Many of these are people I know only slightly or have never met. Thanks go to Allen Abel for his wonderful article in Sports Illustrated (February 20,1995) which gave me Dan Donnelly's arm and Lane Stewart whose photographs for that article haunted my dreams. It was a high point in my research to speak with Irish writer and former editor at the Evening Herald in Dublin, Patrick Myler who was interviewed for the SI article. His article on Dan Donnelly (The Ring, May, 1998) was kindly sent to me by the author himself to help me include old Dan in my novel. Dan's arm can be found in the third book of the trilogy as a bit of comic distraction in the midst of the potato famine.

I have been writing since I was a child. There is one person without whom the dream would have died on the vine. She deserves a special acknowledgement. When I first began to test my wings and seriously put pen to paper, Sr. Mary Matthias SSJ, now known as Sr. Joan Wagner, believed in me when no one else did. She took a dejected Freshman and calmly, sweetly planted the seed of confidence that has finally bloomed in this work. Sr. Joan, I thank you from the bottom of my heart. You taught me to believe in myself and never let go of the dream. Rich lessons indeed.

White dawn that tak'st the heavens with sweet surprise
of amorous artifice,
art thou the bearer of my perfect hour
divine, untrod,
from some forgotten window of Paradise
by mighty winds of God
blown down the world, before my haunted eyes
at length to flower?
by Christopher Brennan, Poems 1913

CUSHING FAMILY TREE

Lord Bentley Cushing b.1768 d. 1820
1787 m.
Lady Eleanor Mcintosh b. 1769 d. 1835

Beverly b. 1788
1806 m.
Jeffrey Wynn

Robert b. 1793
1815 m.
Adelaide Dubois b.1799, d.1820

Madellaine b. 1820, d.1820

WYNN FAMILY TREE

Lord Henry Wynn b. 1735, d.1820
1767 m.
Lady Rose Carver b. 1750, d. 1815

John b. 1768,   Willard b. 1770,   Gerald b. 1781 d.1781,   Jeffrey b. 1784
1806 m.
Beverly Cushing

Margaret b.1808

MEAHRA FAMILY TREE

Seamus Meahra b. 1743 d.1808,
1765 m.
Monica Shea b.1748, d.1795

Sean b. 1767 d. 1808,   Daniel b.1768 d.1809,   Terrence b. 1772 d.1834

Clare b.1774 d.1808,
1792 m.
Thomas Phalen

PHALEN FAMILY TREE

Thomas Phalen b.1772
1792 m.
Clare Maehra

David b. 1794   Paul b. 1796   Thomas b. 1796   Francis b.1808, d.1808
1811m.   1816 m.   1835 m.
Molly Quinn   Anna Dunleavy   Margaret Wynn

Table of Contents

Chapter One

Rose Phalen dumped the filthy wash water into the gutter along the cluttered alley behind Browne's Inn. After a steady rain that started last night during supper, the first of July had dawned warm and steamy. Rose's hair lay thin and stringy like a damp mop across the back of her neck and she missed the cool breeze that always blew across the strand back home. Her gingham dress, so fresh and cheerful last Christmas morning, had faded to a bland brownish gray and clung to her back where a dark streak of perspiration outlined her bony spine and the skirt hung flat and lifeless against her legs.

"I say, give a care, wench! Look what you've done to my boots!"

A middle-aged gentleman in a tidy waistcoat and trousers stood in a puddle of muddy water that had spattered across his fine kid boots leaving dark splotches on the soft creamy leather. He had just handed his horse over to be housed at McRea's stable and was on his way into the pub room of Browne's when Rose heaved the bucket of slop water right in his path.

"Oh, beg pardon M'Lord, I niver saw ye there 'atall. Please I beg ye, let me wipe them fer ye. Ye'll see they'll be good as new in no time 'atall."

1

Rose knelt in the reeking mud filled with decomposing kitchen waste, rat droppings and the remains of a sack of flour that had been slit open by a group of crazed, starving townspeople that morning.

Rose had been setting out tankards and plates for the morning meal when she heard the commotion in the alley. She ran to the rear door and watched in disbelief as a man pulled the driver off his perch and held him down with a knife to his throat. Four women pulled and yanked at the cargo of flour and meal and would have gotten away with all of it had Duffy McGee not intervened and sent them running into the labyrinth of alleys and lanes that wove their way through the sheds and tenements that lined the back of the fine shops of Westport Quay.

They did manage to drag down one sack of flour splitting it on the ground. Amid the billowing white clouds that rose from the broken bag, the women scooped their contraband into tattered sacks and ragged aprons, losing more to the rain-drenched soil than they reaped for themselves. One woman panicked when the sack she brought leaked and the flour she stuffed into it poured out the other end onto her bare feet. She scooped the flour up in fistfuls and stuffed it into her mouth. Coughing and sputtering she choked on the fine powder. Still, she continued to gorge herself on her booty, until her face was covered in flour and her hair was white with dust. Still coughing, she ran to McRea's and drank straight from the horse trough washing the thick mass of white powder down her throat in glutenous gobs that only caused her to gag as she swallowed.

Rose had stood transfixed by the spectacle of the ragged women, like four witches swaying and staggering along their crooked, narrow path, guarding their prize, fighting and scrabbling to keep their share until they could devour it. The driver, released from the clutches of his deranged attacker, was pale and shaken but otherwise unharmed. He went about his delivery as the starving man disappeared behind the thieving women. When the driver later returned with another sack of flour to fill the order the constable took a statement but they all knew his attacker would never be found.

The mess left behind now squished against Rose's knees as she wiped the gentleman's beige kid boots with the hem of her apron. He shooed her away impatiently and proceeded into the back door of the inn beckoning his manservant to come and properly finish the job. Rose looked up at his irritated expression and felt overcome with humiliation. She was almost thirteen years old and here she was a scullery maid at an inn where gentry and common fishermen mingled and made endless demands on her.

"Lass, get me this." and "You, girl, bring me that."

Even Mr. McGee, who had always treated her like a special niece, bringing her and the other children treats and trinkets, barked orders at her and treated her as a servant. Gone were the teasing and funny stories. Gone were the hours of walking the strand and dreaming of a full stomach and a romantic knight taking her away from all this pain and hardship. Her life at the inn was such drudgery, so much very hard work that she had no time for romantic notions or frivolous daydreaming. Up at dawn with Mam and Mary Clare, Rose first prepared a breakfast of thin gruel and tea for Da, Denny and Mr. McGee. Then she and her sister and mother would eat the same watery oatmeal and weak tea before gathering eggs and starting the sausages to popping on the skillet for the guests.

It just about killed her and the others to smell the fine hearty fare they fixed for the paying guests. She carried heaping plates loaded up with crusty toast and griddle cakes, boxty and black pudding while knowing her tasteless gritty porridge would be all she would have to go on until late that evening when the scraps from the guest's dinners would be available. Once in awhile, her mother would manage to siphon off some soup or sauce for them to eat midday with a crust of bread. But the portions were still carefully counted and her mother would rather go hungry than bring down the authorities on Mr. McGee or Da.

Her mother had drilled into them endlessly over the last few months how lucky they were to have a roof over their heads and how kind Mr. McGee had been to take them in. Mr. McGee himself had said more than once that they could eat anything left on the plates and they did have some fine leftovers carefully divided among them.

Three days ago, they served a banquet of fine gentlemen, school chums of Lord Sligo's nephew, Albert Browne. They had come to see the young solicitor off to London where he was joining the firm of Hollister and Cooke. The leavings from their table fed the Phalens and Mr. McGee very well. Meg took scraps of fatty beef and sweetbreads and a pot of gravy, threw in some turnip and squash the men had found too stringy to be bothered with and made a stew from it. She had made a pudding for their guests too that they had never touched, preferring to take the air and head down to the dock and drink porter on the new boat owned by Lord Richard Arbuckle's father, Lord Roland.

The night they feasted on those fine gleanings, Rose had almost believed that this new life in Westport would not be so bad after all. But long after dark when the gentlemen returned to the inn, drunk and demanding a bed lunch or a wench to warm the chilly night or someone to open the pub and draw them another pint, Rose knew that as long as her family was hungry they would never be free. She drew pints and sliced bread and cheese praying that no one would ask for a cold meat plate or a sweet pudding. They had eaten it all and she shivered with fear that they would be discovered.

Mr. McGee and Da had had to quell the ire of two young whelps who insisted that women be brought to their chambers. Mr. McGee stood huge in the doorway as he pointed to the list of house rules that forbade whoring and pimping on the premises. He was fearless when he stood chin to chin with Lord Richard Arbuckle and his cousin Lord Comfrey and suggested that if they needed female companionship they could remove themselves to Marie's or invite some of her girls onto his father's fine new skiff.

Richard merely guffawed at the thought of sharing hired girls with his father and he and his cousin found themselves swaying and catcalling their way down the quay to Marie's for the night. While all this was going on, Rose's Da stood protectively by her side, shielding her and Mam as they pulled pints for the men on the other side of the bar.

The next morning the youths returned in a foul mood from their night out on the town, holding their heads against the morning light. Rose poured them coffee and brought them breakfast, feeling for the first time the hand of a gentleman upon her as Lord Richard squeezed her bottom through her thin workdress. She said nothing to Mam or Da about it and breathed a sigh of relief when the two young men saddled up their horses and rode up to Westport House for the day.

Today she was supposed to be waiting tables again for a group of gentlemen who were coming up from the village of Burriscarra Abbey. She had heard her Da talking to Mr. McGee about it and Rose hadn't seen him as excited about anything in a long time. As she scraped the mud off her knees and tried in vain to rinse the stain from her apron, Rose heard the voice of the gentleman she had spattered calling for his stout. It gagged her to hear her mam, a high-born lady responding with "yes, m'Lord" and "right away, yer Lordship". Since they arrived in Westport, Mam had been very clever in adapting her accent to that of a County Mayo native. Things were different here she said and she could never permit any hint of aristocracy to slip out lest someone discover who she really was.

The young lords from Burriscarra Abbey were at Browne's on a very unusual mission. Despite the fact that the common people of Ireland were dying by the thousands in the street, the youth of the aristocracy still needed their entertainment and have it they would. They had heard that a most spectacular relic was about to pass through Westport and they had gathered to await its arrival.

Young Lord Richard's father was behind the event,

having invested his own money in the preservation of the relic and had personally sponsored the traveling show that had brought it everywhere from Dublin to Donegal. It had been last displayed in Castlebar. The Brothers Ross would move north to Newport. There they would stay working the local circuit through the holiday season after which the showmen would return to their hometown of Sligo until spring.

Today the traveling relic was stopping in Westport and Browne's taproom was filling up fast. It wasn't noon yet and the tables were already filled. The rude young lads returned from visiting Westport House and one of them grabbed her, almost upsetting a pitcher of stout she was carrying to a table full of dock workers. Sailors with money to spend and the occasional tinker and tourist gathered around the outside and down to the freshwater inlet across the road.

Men of every ilk squatted on creepies in the deep shade of ancient weeping willows or sat sunning themselves on the spines of overturned curraghs along the shore. Sawhorses had been set up with long boards for those who would be partaking of meals from Browne's busy kitchen. The cul de sac next to the park-like entrance to Westport House swarmed with men drinking and lying loudly as stories abounded and legends grew longer while the afternoon languished. Every few minutes some restless guest craned his neck toward the Louisburg Road. Everyone wanted to be the first to see the caravan arrive with the promised display.

Rose and Mary Clare carted trays laden with food and stout to keep the men satisfied. The day was still humid and warm but the rain stayed out over the bay and business was brisk. The girls were exhausted carrying trays filled with Bangers and Mash, Beef in Guinness and for those who could afford it, flat, steaming bowls of Browne's signature dish, Dublin Lawyer. At times they found themselves dizzy from the pungent aroma of rich lobster chunks smothered in whiskey cream sauce and piled high in the sliced crimson half shells. Much to their embarrassment, they found themselves dodging the empty, greasy shells tossed at them by the ruder customers as they made their way back to the inn for more.

Mary Clare tried to pick up some of the discarded lobster shells tossed by a swarthy little sailor with one ear missing. When she bent over to reach under the bench that held him and his friends, the man pinched her hard on the back of her thigh. She jerked up, sending the slippery shells flying and began to cry as he and his drunken party all waved their empty lobster shells at her blaming the bright red claws for the nasty pinch. Mary Clare stumbled and dropped her tray as she ran to the protection of Mr. McGee. For the rest of the day, she stayed in the kitchen with Mam while Denny took up the task of waiting tables with Rose.

Around three o'clock Rose was again out behind the pub emptying slop buckets when she heard a loud commotion from inside and Denny calling her to come and see. A huge man, twice the size of Da was barging his way into the throng of people now pressing every corner of Browne's taproom. He had on a thin dirty white shirt that fit his brawny chest like a second skin. The buttons were open to his waist revealing a gleaming, sweat-soaked expanse of hairless bronze that riveted Rose's gaze. Below the shirt was a pair of thick musclebound legs clad in tan leather pants so tight they revealed every ripple of his enormous thighs. His waist was cinched by a thick leather belt that held the shirt taut beneath the pants. High black boots encased a pair of bulging calves and the biggest feet Rose had ever seen.

He bellowed for everyone to stand aside. His mouth was as big as the rest of him, a gaping fob filled with horsy teeth, yellow and chipped from countless encounters with both knuckles and skulls. Thick blond curls framed his broad square face giving him the look of some sort of giant cherubic bully. A bright gold ring dangled from his left ear and little beads of sweat dripped from the curls around his neck. He held his arms like the crucified, standing against the crowd to make a path for the much smaller man behind him.

The man who followed this behemoth was as tidy and

dapper as his protector was fierce. Almost foppish in his burgundy silk morning coat and mauve pants, he swept into Browne's with a flourish and demanded to see the proprietor.

Duffy McGee, wiping his hands on a bar rag, cautiously approached the two. Rose could see his mouth working to keep from laughing and one of his eyebrows was up. She ducked behind the bar where Denny and Francis stood with Da and Mary Clare. Mam quietly watched with the babies from the far end of the bar by the kitchen door

"Sir, I am Mr. McGee, at yer service."

"Very well. We are the Brothers Ross commissioned by Sir Roland Arbuckle himself, t'bring ye the greatest source of pride available in the history of Irish bare knuckle fighting."

The little man stood, arms akimbo, apparently waiting for someone to guess what that was.

Duffy leaned on the bar and spoke right into the pointy face.

"Well, sir, as ye can see, a great many of us have awaited yer arrival. So, if ye'll be getting' on with the show, we'll be getting' on with the watchin'."

The Big Mr. Ross seemed to take offense at Duffy McGee's tone and his huge mitts balled into fists but the Little Mr. Ross simply smacked him on the wrist and he relaxed.

"Well, Mr. McGee, we understand yer keenness t'git on with it but me brother and me know fer certain ye want t'indulge us with a wee drap o'the craither first. 'Tis a hot day astore, 'tis that indeed."

A groan went around the pub. The men had been waiting in the heat for hours and some of the young lords were drunk. They began to protest and Lord Richard Arbuckle took it upon himself to shove his way to the front of the group.

Blocking the way to the bar, he sputtered at Little Mr. Ross

"Now see here, my man, it was my father who brought you here and fed you and lodged your sorry party for the night in Louisburg. We want to see the relic. Now! You can have all the refreshment you deserve after you earn your keep."

Without a word, Big Mr. Ross picked Lord Richard up with one hand and set him unceremoniously on a table, toppling pints and slabs of ham and cheese all over the floor. Seeing a loaf of brown bread bounce off a chair, he reached down with the other hand and still clutching Lord Richard's collar, scooped it up midair and bit the end off with his broken yellow teeth. Gently pressing his brother's massive forearm, Little Mr. Ross persuaded him to release young Richard. Still clutching the loaf of bread, Big Mr. Ross turned to Rose and leaned over, spitting bread crumbs as he spoke.

"Me pint, if ye please, deary. And a nice piece o'that ham, if ye please."

For some reason, Rose curtsied and the place erupted with laughter. Big Mr. Ross turned to the crowd and grinned, the gaps between his broken teeth filled with half-chewed bread. Little Mr. Ross simply sashayed up to the bar and sat on the stool vacated by Lord Richard.

"Whiskey fer me and toast me some o'that bread. Cheese too, thick, no ham." He set about picking crumbs off the bar with his long, delicate white fingers.

The Brothers Ross were just finishing their second drink when another commotion arose outside. This time Lord Roland Arbuckle himself swept into the taproom. Smiling broadly, he greeted the brothers cordially.

"Gentlemen, I see that you have had your repast. I trust you have met my son and that you find this venue to your liking?"

"Certainly, yer Lordship. Now that ye have arrived right on schedule, I might add, we can begin the display. If ye please, we generally prefer t'bring in the great appendage concealed by an appropriate drape and once safely behind the bar, have, if ye will, the grand unveiling."

"The arena is yours, Mr. Ross whenever you are ready."

"Ladies and gentlemen! We the Brothers Ross of the

town of Sligo in that great county of Sligo, are proud to present t'ye, one and all, a spectacle of sich grand proportions and sich amazing history that ye'll not be able t'sleep a wink tonight in yer beds. We are prepared t'demonstrate t'ye, one and all, a piece of Irish pugilistic history of sich greatness and sentiment that ye'll be tempted t'go down on yer knees at the very sight of it. Step back, step back and make room fer the most amazing piece of human flesh t'cross the golden hills and green dales of this proud countryside. And now if ye'll turn yer attention t'me brother, Teddy Ross, he'll be about procurin' this astounding piece of history from his bag."

In the hubbub of the Ross brother's entrance, no one had noticed the long narrow leather sack strapped across Big Mr.Teddy Ross's back. Now, with as much flourish as he could muster, Teddy Ross fit his enormous bulk behind the bar of Browne's taproom. He reached behind him and pulled the leather tube off, bringing it around and laying it on the bar with excrutiating tenderness.

"Ladies and gentlemen...," Little Mr. Ross began.

"Get on with it!" a man yelled from the back of the crowd.

"Stop delaying this, you fools!" shouted another one.

Fortified by the presence of the elder Lord Arbuckle the young dandies began to surge forward and press toward the two brothers. One tried to take the leather pouch away from Teddy Ross and was almost rewarded by a massive fist in the mouth. Meg grabbed Rose and Mary Clare and moved them to the far end of the bar as the young lords began to push and shove Little Mr. Ross.

Suddenly there was a pistol shot as Lord Roland Arbuckle took the situation in hand. No sooner had the bullet lodged in one of the thick blackened rafters of the taproom ceiling than the room fell silent again.

"There will be no gilravage in this establishment. I have brought these gentlemen here to entertain you and bring some relief from the terrible conditions of this community. They have traveled far and have indeed brought you a spectacle of great proportion and curiosity. If you must behave like heathens then you will do so elsewhere. You are young gentlemen. You have never and will not now be governed by shillelagh law. I have assumed responsibility for your well-being and I plan to return you to your mothers whole. Do I make myself clear?"

Turning to the Brothers Ross, Lord Arbuckle nodded.

"Gentlemen, at your leisure."

Taking obvious pleasure in his newly elevated status among the gentry, Little Mr. Ross bowed deeply to Lord Arbuckle.

He raised his hand to Tom for another whiskey and waved the young lords away from the bar.

Only after Tom Phalen handed him his libation did he speak again.

"Now, gentlemen, if ye please, the rules of the program. Ye may file singly t'the bar and see fer yer own selves the great curiosity we have in our bag. Ye may not, if ye please, touch it as ye may contract a witherin' disease."

When they began to scoff at this, Little Mr. Ross swept his rouge-clad arm over his head, sipping his whiskey dramatically and solemnly shaking his head.

"I've seen it happen, lads, don't doubt it fer a minute."

They settled into an anxious silence. Teddy Ross, apparently immune to the withering disease, reached into the long sack. Slowly, with the greatest of care he inched the mummified prize out of the bag. When he had it completely laid out upon the bar, he painstakingly unwound the veil of gauze from around its petrified length.

In a hushed voice usually reserved for the confessional, Little Mr. Ross asked for more light. Tom lit a lantern and set it on the bar. Little Mr. Ross gestured for the first young man to step forward. Suddenly deflated of all pomposity, they began to file forward. Like schoolboys they timidly approached the relic lying lengthwise on the gleaming mahogany bar. Sounds of amazement mixed with disgust filled the room as one by one, both young and old approached.

"Ladies and Gentlemen," intoned the little man in the ruby jacket, "I give ye the arm of the great Dan Donnelly himself, a legend in his own time. This is, as God is me witness, the actual arm that swung the great fist into the jaws of his opponents. This is indeed the petrified flesh of the greatest Irish pugilist there ever was."

"The finger that points forward," and with this Teddy Ross lifted the arm to show the withered black finger pointing directly at young Lord Arbuckle and his friends, "is the proof that the great one found his way to his eternal reward and in his undyin' love for his countrymen points the way there fer the next to arrive."

Lord Richard Arbuckle ducked away from the direction of the skinny black projection bringing derisive laughter from some of the old salts gathered in the doorway.

Rose could hardly pull her eyes away from the arm. It looked so long all stretched out like that with its index finger pointing into eternity. It was the skinniest arm she had ever seen, all black and withered no skin or flesh upon it. The petrified surface was as shiny as wood and, she imagined, as hard. It looked like a licorice stick, tight and sinewed, all bony and black as turf. It seemed the length of two arms and the bone where it had attached to the great fighter's shoulder was flat and porous and not so black as the length of it.

Longing to touch it, Rose could feel her hands itch in her apron pockets. Denny stood transfixed. Mary Clare looked horrified and about to be sick. Mam simply turned away in disgust taking the babies upstairs while Da and Mr. McGee leaned over the bar unflinching from the apparent danger of withering on the spot.

The Brothers Ross preened and pampered their specimen, treating it like a royal baby or the relic of their own mother. They invited any and all to come closer yet shushed and tished if any came too close. Most of the men were entranced by the petrified arm. Some, particularly any who had ever been at war in service to His Majesty the King, shuddered at it and walked away shaking their heads.

While the public filed past, hats held reverently in their hands, Little Mr. Ross kept up a running monologue describing the great Dan Donnelly, his many fights, his burial place, so hard to find. To anyone and everyone, he regaled the amazing story of the great pugilist's last days, crippled by drink, dying penniless at the age of thirty-two.

"My dear friends," purred Little Mr. Ross, warming to his subject, "let me tell ye a true story. This arm was one of two that could reach our hero's knee britches, fastenin' them even as he stood as straight as a nun at vespers. This arm took out the jaw of England's own George Cooper right on Irish soil, right in the fair county of Kildare on a cold day in December, in the year of our Lord, 1815. Oh, what a fight it was! Only twenty-two minutes long, cripplin' the great Cooper, England's pride, in only two crushin' blows t'the jaw."

The little man stooped over, walking first to one end of the crowd and then swinging abruptly to charge at the other end, his deep red coat bobbing over his bent back as he played the fans like a huge, demented, crimson bird.

"And t'prove his greatness, I invite ye t'visit the site someday perhaps in better times, in Donnelly's Hollow. Oh yes, named after the great son of the sod himself. The loyal subjects of this pugilistic royalty have enshrined the very prints of his feet. So much did they revere him they carved out the footprints he made climbin' the hill of the hollow as he walked to its peak t'reflect on the power of his own fist. Ye can see them t'this very day, yes ye can and God strike me dead in this spot if 'tis not the truth I tell."

Dusk settled over the harbor and still they came. Gentlemen from Louisburg and Westport Castle rode in to see the spectacle. Poor McRea could hardly keep up with the volume. Sailors off arriving ships flocked across the gangplanks almost before the boats were tethered. Dirty, half-starved residents of the tenements and alleyways behind the inn clambered down the steep hillside, pouring out of the boolies and hovels along the Louisburg Road.

The little man took a deep breath and continued,

"And more fanciful yet, is the tale of the sweet Miss Kelly. She saw our hero strugglin' against his foe in the ring. Now, Miss Kelly, a lass as fine as any this green land has ever produced, had a keen faith in the restorative power of a certain sweet, for there was indeed, a man on the premises who peddled a candy reputed to have medicinal powers. As the story goes, the dear sister of the great Donnelly's sponsor, desperate to see our hero vindicated in the ring, passed him a chunk of the candy procured at that very moment from a tinker fondly known in those parts as 'The Sugar Cane Man'."

"Lo and behold, as the saints are me witnesses, didn't our boy revive and go on to pummel the evil adversary before her and all present."

"Is it any wonder, me dear friends, that the Prince Regent," leaning into the face of the nearest listener, he cleared his voice and confided with a wink, "'Prinny' to a certain chosen few."

Continuing on the little man exclaimed, "The Prince Regent, himself a devoted follower of the pugilistic arts, put the sword of knighthood straight upon the shoulder of our Dan, the very shoulder upon which this glorious arm hinges even as ye see it before yer own eyes."

A sigh was all that was heard from the hushed and spellbound crowd. Not a chair scraped nor a foot shifted as they listened in rapt attention. The story went on against the squeak of the tap and the chink of the change as pint after pint was poured.

The dark of night descended and the inn ran out of food. When Tom Phalen pulled the last drought of Guinness, Duffy McGee declared the taproom closed. Still they came to file past the display as the Brothers Ross took it out onto the quay. Even the girls from Marie's saw that they were no match for the arm of the great Sir Dan and Miss Marie herself declared a night off until the arm was put back in its sack.

Little Mr. Ross gazed soulfully over his audience and sizing up the wide-eyed girls from Marie's and the few wives and daughters permitted by their men to attend the exhibit, delivered his final salvo.

"Ah, ladies, tis' a tragedy, what happened in the end."

Shaking his head slowly as if it weighed a hundred stone, he passed a hand across his furrowed brow. Standing straight and inhaling deeply, he prepared to deliver the end of Dan Donnelly's tale. With obvious effort he nodded reverently toward his brother Teddy. On cue Teddy Ross lifted the arm into the halo of a streetlamp. Cast in the lamplight, the black, sere limb resembled a tree branch plucked half-charred from a bonfire.

"This arm belonged t'the greatest of 'em all, ladies and gentlemen. Our own Dan Donnelly, never lost a fight, no he did not!"

His voice a solemn whisper, he continued.

"Our Dan, a man among men with strength beyond human comprehension, had his weaknesses. No offense to the fairer sex, ladies, and certainly none toward the hospitality of our fine hosts, but the great Dan Donnelly was brought down not by the fist of a better man, not by the wicked pummelin' sich as he sought to deliver but by the common weakness fer the drink that plagues both scholar and spalpeen. The drink led him to frolic a bit too much with the ladies, which sadly, weakened him and led him astray. His judgment suffered and his businesses failed. Finally, he left us. A poor man, a hero with nothin' left to show fer it, a man of pride and immensity driven t'the brink. And as if it were not enough to die an ignominious pauper, a mere shadow of his former great self…"

Moving in for the kill, he sobbed out the last of his testimonial.

"The dirtiest of scoundrels, night doctors with evil in their eyes, tread upon the sacred ground above him and dug him up! Grave robbers, me friends, grave robbers without the trepidation t'leave the greatest o'them all in peace! Filthy thieves who toppled the lid right off of his coffin and made off into the night with his corpus still wrapped in its shroud."

The crowd gasped at this last bit of drama as the frenzied little man sped from one end of the quay to the other piercing them all with his wild gaze.

"And do we know this t'be the end dear friends? No we do not! For 'tis not the end of the indignities heaped upon one so great. When the doctor received the body of our revered hero, he was aghast. 'Fools!' he cried in outrage. He cast the evildoers from his laboratory and prepared t'return the body to its grave himself. But alas, the temptation was too great! Alone in his laboratory, alone with his sin, he weakened as we all weaken in our hour of reckoning. He circled the body so freshly disturbed from its eternal rest."

Little Mr. Ross paced a small circle before the crowd.

"He pondered his choices."

Little Mr. Ross stroked the thin beard at the tip of his chin.

"And with the speed of a hungry cat he pounced!"

The women squealed and one of Marie's girls fainted at his feet as he pounced toward his brother who handed him a saw.

"He pounced and he took up his weapon!"

Little Mr. Ross raised the saw high in the air, waving it wildly in the lamplight.

"He pounced and he seized his weapon and he severed the famed appendage. He took the pride of Ireland and cut it off to keep for his own evil purposes. And then, he stripped it of its skin."

The women were screaming by now, the men pacing restlessly.

"He tarred it and set it out t'dry until black and shriveled, he added it t' his collection of oddities and freakish remnants from beyond the grave. But the noble followers of the famous fighter would not be silenced. They stormed the laboratory and confiscated the arm of their boyo, dispatching that fiendish doctor to the fires of Hades. Preserved for all generations, it became as you behold it now. T'will never more be Donnelly's arm alone. From now until the end of time t'will be our arm too, the arm of the people of this great land!"

"Dear friends, I give ye Donnelly's arm."

With this he made a sweeping bow, almost slicing the leg of a sailor with the saw. One more time Big Teddy Ross held the arm aloft as the crowd erupted into cheers and wild foot stomping.

As the people hailed the memory of the greatest bare knuckle pugilist Ireland had ever known, the Brothers Ross quickly slipped through Browne's to a waiting cab that would take them by the Louisburg Road out of Westport and off to their next arena. The people began to leave the quay; the sailors and tinkers, tourists and locals gradually drifted off to bed. Marie's reopened and many a sailor never found his way back onboard till morning.

The morning of July 19, 1848 brought another hot, steamy day. Usually Wednesday brought a mid-week lull to business but not this week. Mr. McGee welcomed the delivery of fresh stout and gratefully filled his larder for the landlords due to arrive that night. This was to be a very important meeting during which some of the best minds of the gentry would attempt to grapple with the terrible situation brought on by the prolonged famine. Duffy wanted everything to be perfect and had Meg and the children putting the high shine on every square inch of the inn. Even the little girls had had rags tied to their feet and skated around the bedroom floors dusting every corner.

Rose and Mary Clare fed the young lords their bacon and watched them saddle up their horses for the trip home. Beds were stripped, tables scrubbed and the stinking barrels of brine filled again with pickles. As Meg entered figures into the huge ledger, Rose stirred the linens in the washtub and Mary Clare churned cream into butter. Denny and Francis scoured the inlet for oysters and Tom mended chairs damaged by the callow young men who had carelessly tipped them over. The babies played on the taproom floor and cried when they lost sight of their Mam.

All day they worked, the taproom strung with sheets drying in the warm breeze. By four o'clock, the sheets were down, the beds had been made up, the pint glasses gleamed behind the bar and a savory cauldron of Irish stew simmered on the back of the huge stove. Meg had just pulled the last of the steaming loaves of soda bread out of the brick oven when the little bell at the top of the front door announced the arrival of the first guest.

As for the great arm of Dan Donnelly, it was well on its way to Newport leaving behind the image of its crooked black finger pointing the way through the day's chores, tickling the backsides of the children and spooking the girls from behind every half-closed door. Many who heard the tale took to heart the message of a great man's courage. But most who had stood on the quay of Clew Bay returned to the silent struggle of survival, the great Donnelly consigned to history as they carved out one more day of life in a city divided between the fed and the unfed, the drivers and the driven, those on the inside and the outside of the thick oak doors of the manor houses of Westport, County Mayo, Ireland.

Chapter Two

By evening, the rain had moved in off the ocean and the storm stalled over Clew Bay. Meg stood in the doorway of Browne's Inn having shown the last few guests to their rooms. The breeze was fresh and salty, reminding her of Achill and the morning of Rose's birthday. She was that tired now, leaning into the doorframe. She thought about Maureen and how patient she had been, walking with her back and forth, back and forth across the slate kitchen floor trying to bring a baby neither of them knew would take so many hours to arrive. Hugging herself against the dampness, she thought of all the changes in her life since Maureen had left. Almost ten years had passed. Meg could not believe it.

People had been displaced all over the country, wandering wherever they could find food, working in one townland one day and walking all the way to another county the next. Then, when they died, no one knew who they were or where they were from. No one knew where their family was, where their parents or children might be buried or if they still lived.

The ones who could afford it or were driven beyond staying had already left in droves. Boatloads of Ireland's young had pulled out of Westport, Donegal, Cork and Dublin in the mass exodus of a desperate people. Mothers wailing on quays and piers all over the fair isle sent up a keening that echoed the discovery of the first black tubers.

Her heart ached for Thomas and Patrick but at least she knew where they were. Whole families and single girls like Maureen flocked to Westport and other port cities, trying to book passage on ships that would take them to Liverpool where they could depart this place of death for a brighter horizon. The hopeless ones who had no money for a ticket out of hell just came to see if someone might give them a crust of bread and a kind word before they died.

Meg gazed out at the stream of droplets tumbling in a steady patter off the slate roof and pinging against the blue sign over the door. No one was out. Last night's caravan show of Donnelly's Arm had exhausted the hungry locals who hardly had the energy to go to church. It was a good exhaustion, Meg thought. Today there had been a semblance of cheer among the people as they scrounged for scraps behind the inns and storefronts and lined up at St. Alphonse's Church of Ireland for their daily ration of turnip soup.

Tom watched Meg from behind the bar where he dried pint glasses. Denny sulkily stacked them into a sparkling pyramid and whined that he couldn't visit his new friends in the rain. Tom ignored him, focusing on Meg instead. She was still beautiful, Tom thought. His wife of almost fifteen years, pale and ragged, her thin hair twisted into a plain bun, she still looked radiant to him.

He knew there was no way he could ever repay Duffy for bringing them here. There were locals who would string old Duff up for importing help when so many of them were starving too. But Duffy didn't care. The ones who taunted the loudest would never set foot in Browne's anyway so he knew they wouldn't harm Meg or the children. And even after only a short time eating scraps, Tom's family looked better to him. The children had a spark back in their eyes and he thought their cheeks were already fuller. Duffy had insisted that they drink the plentiful milk he ordered.

Even after a long day of serving and slaving for the gentry, Lovie swept up for Mrs. Carver, the pharmacist's wife who paid her with eggs for her labors. Mrs. Carver kept chickens in a coop behind the apothecary counter, where she could keep a watchful eye on them and paid Rose with a dozen eggs a day. Tom himself walked down to Carvers to escort his daughter home with her prize. These, Meg put to good use, whipping up nourishing puddings and omelets for the children.

Tom had forgotten how good it felt to sink his teeth into a juicy piece of meat and how lovely pan gravy and brown bread tasted on the tongue. The food they ate at the inn was just the leavings of the wealthy but there was so much waste and it was good waste.

There was meat and fat for stews and cold lunches, cheeses and fine crusty bread. Gravy from succulent roasts made a meal in itself mopped up with a few fried eggs and toast. The kinds of food favored by their guests was rich and Meg was in her glory stretching sweet pastries to feed both the guests and the help and making extra portions of porridge at breakfast and pudding at supper. These were the things that were hard to measure and hard to track and Tom was delighted that Browne's was able to provide his family with the healing rations that would see them through the summer. He would not allow himself to project as far as the winter and Duffy had already warned him that once Reek Sunday passed, business could really slow down. God had seen them thus far and God would see them through the next leg of the journey. No point worrying and fretting.

Done with his drying, he set Denny to sweeping behind the bar and down the cellar stairs. He hung the bar rag on a hook and joined Meg at the door. A chill went through him as he leaned against the other side of the doorframe. This was the same place, on the same sort of a night that he had stood debating about taking a curragh to Achill to see his baby born so many years ago.

"So, Darlin', ye thinkin' about the great shriveled

specimen of Donnelly's arm?"

"Heavens no, Tom! That was disgusting and revolting!"

Meg let down her Mayo accent when she was alone with Tom but he shook his head.

"Best not to let anyone hear ye talkin' high-born, Meg Darlin'. The place is crawlin' with aristocracy tonight."

"When is it not?" she asked, lowering her voice.

"Soon no one will be comin'. Duff was talkin' about that this mornin'."

"What will we do, Tom? Will he be able to keep us here once business falls off?"

"Well, he didn't say yes and he didn't say no."

Tom reached across the doorway and pulled Meg into his arms. She felt like a little bird against his chest but he noticed how her face was a bit fuller and he thought her hair was beginning to thicken again now that they were eating better. He kissed her forehead tenderly and sighed as she reached up to touch his cheek.

"This can't go on forever you know," she murmured against his shirt.

"No, it can't but we've not seen the last of it yet. The gentlemen gathering here fer this meetin' o'the minds are the only ones who can change it."

Meg craned her neck to look at Tom's face, receiving a soft kiss on the cheek as her reward.

"I wonder what they'll do?" she sighed.

She shifted around to watch the rain, nestling her back into Tom's chest and pulling his arms around her waist.

"What can they do? Trevalyan thinks the hunger is God's will and him directin' relief! Ye must know the landlords won't risk much t'go up against him. Besides, ye know how they've been chaffin' against the Poor Law ever since it came out in '38. Why wouldn't they be glad fer less tax? Every Irishman that starves t'death, is one less t'support. And that Whig snake, Nassau Senior, spawn o'the divil that he is, would rot the crops himself if he thought it would kill more Irish babies. Why even the Americans are fed up with it."

"Jist last week there was a lad from Boston come back t'see if he could find his mam and da and get 'em t'go back with him. By the time he found them, jist around the corner here in Louisburg, they were so close t'dyin' all he could do was let 'em be. He ended up buryin' 'em with the money fer their fare. He got himself good and drunk and was all full o'blather about Americans sending guns and boatloads o'money t'support the Young Irelanders. Ah, Meg, 'tis not over yet. There's troubles brewin' fer sure. Ye can smell it in the air."

"Tom, don't! That kind of talk frightens me. How can we rebel? We're hardly able to stand up, much less pick up a weapon and fight. There can only be more death and suffering to follow a rebellion! You saw the men who came here. They're well fed, all with horses and side arms. They can smell trouble too. They'd just as soon shoot any one of us in the street as say hello! With Trevalyan and Senior behind them, they've got clear aim and total support. God knows they'd be national heroes if they could put any of our heads on a stake and carry it to the queen! They should all rot in hell."

Tom felt her stiffen in his arms as she vented.

"Now, Meg, yer talkin' like a Catholic ye are. Not a very nice one either."

"I am a Catholic! And I'm nice, too! I just can't see this miscarriage of justice and stand by silently. Sometimes I feel so ashamed to be of their ilk."

She pulled away from him but he held her tight turning her to face him again. His face was dark and serious as he looked deeply into her eyes. It had been so long since she had seen him look at her this way, she felt her eyes fill.

" 'Tis that proud o'ye, I am Meg. Were ye born o'me own clan I couldn't be more proud. Ye niver need t'carry shame with me. I know what ye've given up t'be me wife and bear me babes. There will niver be a day I'm not sure of th'blessin' ye are t'me. Whatever happens t'me ye must know this, Meg. Ye must niver look back and niver give up. Promise me ye'll niver let them win, Meg. I know they are yer people but ye're my people now and our children need ye. God in heaven, Darlin' ye must know how much I need ye."

Kissing her again, this time on the lips, he lingered and savored the feel of her against him. It had been way too long since they had been man and wife together. Feeling her relax against him, he stroked her hair.

Meg clung to Tom and spoke slowly into his chest, her very words threatening to choke her.

"Tom, I couldn't bear it if anything happened to you. You talk as if you know something. I know there is trouble afoot. Duffy moves in a shadow and says so little. Please promise me you won't take chances with our lives. I know I have no right to ask you to keep your head down. These are your people and you must be so aggrieved at their suffering. I will always love you for what you just said about me being your people but the fact remains that I am not. I carry deeply the shame of my kin. Don't you see? If anything happens to you I am nothing. I have no place among the Irish and can't bear to return to the English after what they've done to you."

"Dear, dear Tom, how did we ever come to this? I never imagined us clinging to life like this. I just want to be your wife, to love you and grow old with you, to watch our children grow up and give us grandchildren to dangle on our knees. Oh, Tom, I miss our life, I miss Thomas and Patrick, I miss my kitchen and Maureen and the waves on the strand. Will we ever go back, Tom? Can we ever go back? Please say you'll take me back! Please say you'll be safe and stay alive. I'm so afraid, so very afraid."

Tom stood in silence, his big hands gently making circles over Meg's bony shoulder blades, his chin resting on her hair.

"Tom? Promise me?"

Tom lifted Meg's chin and placed his rough palms on her cheeks. His eyes held hers and she saw in them a sorrow so deep she felt her strength wash to her feet like the ebbing tide. She searched his face for an answer. Her tears flowing freely now, she begged him with her eyes to promise her even as she knew he would never say the words.

Tom tenderly touched her lips with his thumbs and Meg knew he was silencing her pleas. She saw in his face the torment of the damned. This was the face she loved, probing her heart with immeasurable tenderness. Here was the face she could not turn away from filled with pain she could not begin to relieve. She knew he would never, could never, promise.

What was happening to his people was beyond any measure of profit and loss. The travesty of this hunger was so indicting of her people that he would have had every right to put her out, refuse to even look at her. Instead he poured upon her his silent grief, cherishing her even as he cherished his own dying kinsmen. She saw in the furrows around his mouth his profound sadness, not just for the loss of Ireland but for her. There was something so poignantly familiar in the way he beheld her Meg knew she had seen it before.

She searched his eyes and the sorrowful downturn of his full curved lips until like a knife plunging through her breast, she knew. Of course! The searing forgiveness Meg saw in Tom's eyes was the same as the last look Thomas gave her before he died. Meg stood still, her gaze riveted to Tom's face. His sorrow was unbearable to her, his love too raw and pure for her to receive. Meg knew he would fight should he be called to arms but he couldn't bear to say those words to her. She knew he would never promise her a lie, so neither would she hear the words she begged him to say.

Just as Thomas told her with his last silent look that he was leaving her, Meg's beloved friend, her lover, the father of her children was silently warning her that he could be going too. He had even placed his hands on her face the way Thomas had.

"Dear Mother of God, save us."

Meg's prayer came as a deep sigh of resignation. They were nowhere near the end of this. Day after day, ship by sailing ship, like wraiths, Ireland's best and brightest waved from stern and bow, wailing to be saved, fading into the western sun, forever gone. No matter what happened with the potatoes this year or any year, neither Ireland nor her children would ever be able to look back. The cliffs and valleys echoed the keening cry for her lost sons and daughters. The very land was widowed, every rock an orphan strewn across her lifeless breast.

Meg could feel herself shrink inside. Her bones felt like a cage barely containing the running liquor of her soul. She longed to give up, to melt to the floor in defeat, her spirit left to pool in the rain. Never had she felt so small, so shriveled up inside. Panic threatened to seize her and spill out the succor of her soul sifting her bones like dust on the breeze.

Nothing her father had done, nothing Andrew Feeney had said, no pain in her belly, no funeral dirge, had hurt the way Tom's sorrow did. All the tenderness and love contained in his gaze could not conceal his meaning nor could he temper its painful message. Her chest felt empty, her heart so cracked she could not believe she still lived. Here again, stood her past and her future, silently with excruciating clarity, slipping away.

Meg finally looked away from Tom. The rain had slowed and with every breeze little dribbles wended skinny, crooked paths across the blue sign. Like the tears Meg flicked off her cheeks some of them were blown off course by a stray gust. Like her tears, some of them were picked up on the wind and carried off the sign to be dashed somewhere in the dark of night. Like us, she thought, flung far and wide, wasted and ignored.

Finding that thought too much to bear, Meg turned back to Tom. Taking his head in her hands she brought his face down to hers. He took his hands off her neck where they had slipped when she turned her head and wrapped his arms tightly around her, practically lifting her off her feet.

Meg could feel the panic in Tom's embrace. He held her hard, hurting her frail ribs and crushing her against him. She wanted him to crush her. She wanted him to devour her and absorb her into his strength where she would be safe. She threw her arms around his neck and clung to him.

Finding each other's mouth, they kissed again, in hard, frantic silence sealing an unspoken covenant. They drew each other's breath from deep within and shared in that ferocious mingling whatever strength each had to give the other. Neither of them willing to break the seal, they kissed on and on, their lips bruising, their chests aching for breath. Like the descending moruadh, they took each other down into a sea of desperation, clinging to each other for life. Finally, lightheaded and faint with grief, Meg broke the seal.

Tom steadied her and once again gently placed his thumbs on her lips. His face was more relaxed but Meg saw in it a conviction that left her no doubt that if there was fighting, Tom would take up arms for Ireland. There was nothing she could do to stop him. She cringed as he turned and walked away from her. Collapsing in on herself, she watched him through a haze of despair as he called down to Denny to bring up some ham and a circle of cheese. He threw on Duffy's macintosh and turned toward her. She shrunk against the doorpost, afraid of his next words, afraid that she would forever be afraid of his next words.

His thick voice sounded like it came from deep within a well.

"I'll be goin down t'St. Peter's t'see if Fr. Timon has any spare candles. Ye know the crowd last night used even our last stubs strainin' t'see the end of the Ross Brothers' show. Maybe th'good father will lend us some until Duff can buy more. We can hardly expect the guests t'be wanderin' around their rooms in the dark."

A few minutes after Tom closed the kitchen door behind him, three men on horseback trotted by and turned into the alley on their way to McRea's Livery. It looked like some late guests had finally arrived. They would need rooms and a meal. Meg forced her body to conform to the ritual of registering guests. Just having been thrust into oblivion by the careening emotions of the last few moments, Meg could only assume normalcy. Nowhere inside her did she feel even remotely normal.

Meg reached down behind the counter and pulled out the heavy guest book. Just as she straightened up, two of the late arrivals entered the inn. She looked up and with a little scream, let the big guest book slam down on the desk. Looking at her were not one but two faces from her past.

The first one broke into a sly, ugly grin as he recognized Meg.

"Well, well! Look who we have here, Mr. Riordan," he said with a smirk.

Feeling the floor drop out from beneath her for the second time that night, Meg exhaled.

"Mr. Gilchrist. What a surprise."

"Oh, Mrs. Phalen, I wouldn't think so. After all, someone has to represent Lord Jeffrey Wynn's interests at this convocation and he chose me and Mr. Padraig Riordan here to be his delegates. I must attend as representative of my Lord Lucan anyway, so of course, speaking on behalf of my Lord Wynn is no trouble at all. Besides, Mr. Riordan and I have become quite good friends have we not, Padraig?"

Padraig Riordan nodded in agreement though his face looked as if someone were aiming a gun at his head.

Gilchrist continued, his smarmy smile revealing long yellow teeth.

"You do remember Mr. Riordan, do you not? Oh, no of course you don't. He was just a lad when you left your father's home in disgrace. Allow me. Mr. Riordan is the son of your father's financial advisor, Mr. Brian Riordan. You must remember him. But no, he attended your father frequently when he was changing his will but you were locked in your room if I remember the story correctly."

Paddy Riordan gaped at Meg in disbelief. She tried to smile but her mouth had dried up and her face felt like stone. She could tell by his face that Riordan would never have known her had Gilchrist not spoken of her father. The last time he had seen her was, of course, years ago when he came by with his father. It was the day she left for London to stay with her grandmother Cushing, a day from another lifetime.

"Mr. Riordan, of course."

"M'Lady."

His face crimson with embarrassed confusion, the young man nodded politely.

"Oh, heavens, no, Riordan! Not m'lady anymore. Why this is Mrs. Thomas Phalen, wife of a not so prosperous dairyman from Achill Island. Mrs. Phalen appears to have fallen on hard times. How sad. To think that one so privileged has allowed herself to stoop so low."

Riordan's kind face was filled with pity. Gilchrist's smile simply rested on his chin, a thin, contemptuous slit.

"Now, wench, a room for myself and my companion. Now!"

Gilchrist relished his role of guest and intended to keep Meg and her brats running the whole time he was at the inn.

"Where is your husband, Mrs. Phalen? I have business with him. He never reported the last quarter's rents and I am to have the law after him."

Meg opened her mouth and without a moment's hesitation, spoke a colossal lie.

"My husband is dead, Mr. Gilchrist. Another victim of this terrible hunger."

Gilchrist's face registered his disappointment.

"I am indeed sorry to hear that madam. It is the misfortune of the crown that such a blackguard has escaped justice. I shall hasten to report to my Lord Lucan that he will need to engage another agent. Perhaps one who will see justice is done to the lazy louts of Doeega."

Turning to young Riordan, he added, "Our recently departed Mr. Phalen was in the habit of falsifying rent revenues by contributing from his own income the unmet balance of the villagers. You can see how this foolish practice left his widow to starve. While Lord Lucan never seemed to be bothered by this, it was always a concern of mine. If a man would be a fool and a liar, what other treachery would be uncovered upon further investigation?"

Turning and taking the room key from Meg's hand, Gilchrist smiled his jaundiced grin again.

"Mrs. Phalen, you may be assured that we will not let this rest. Your husband is not safe in his grave as long as I am Lord Lucan's undertaker. And I'm sure Mr. Riordan will wish to discuss the matter of a certain stolen horse. Jewel, I believe he was called. Good evening."

Shocked, Mr. Riordan picked up the bags before Gilchrist could command Meg to do so. Without asking, Mr. Gilchrist took the candle from Meg's desk to light their way and Mr. Riordan ascended the stairs to their room leaving her in the dark to contemplate her husband as a horse thief.

She heard Denny come up from the cellar.

"Mam, what are ye' doin' in the dark?" he asked as he thumped the heavy cheese on the kitchen table.

"The last guests needed the candle to get upstairs. Denny, you have to help me."

The panic in her voice brought him to her side.

"Mam, what is it? Yer shakin' all over!"

"Your father is in grave danger," she whispered, peering through the blackness at the dim light upstairs, trying to see if it was safe to talk. As the light disappeared and she heard Gilchrist and Riordan's footfalls through the ceiling at the far end of the bar she knew they had reached their room.

She went to the kitchen, where Denny stood and quickly explained what had happened and pressed him toward the back door.

"Go down to St. Peter's and tell him to stay there until I can come to him. Tell him that Gilchrist thinks he's dead and he must not return here until this group of landlords has left. Hurry back. And don't forget the candles. When you get back I need you to find Mr. McGee and send him to me. Don't tell him anything. Let me do that."

Meg could feel the thrill of adventure shiver through Denny's body as she spoke. He hated all things English and Mr. Gilchrist most of all. Meg worried that he would overplay his hand and expose them all to the law and she warned him to keep his counsel.

"Aye, Mam," he promised but unable to see his eyes, Meg doubted he meant a word of it. At almost thirteen, he barely obeyed her at all. She was counting on his devotion to Tom to protect them.

No sooner had Denny slipped out the back door than the front door opened with a burst of wet air. The rain had started again and blew across the threshold. A large form was silhouetted against a thousand glistening droplets lit from behind by the streetlamp. When the door closed, both Meg and their guest were plunged back into darkness.

"I say, anybody here?"

Meg started at still another ghost from her past.

"Sir? I have no light. Would ye be so kind as t'bring in the storm lantern from outside the doorway?"

"Certainly. My pleasure."

Again the chill dampness swept across the room as Meg re-entered the taproom. She shuddered and grabbed her old shawl from behind the bar.

The guest returned with the lantern and set it on the desk.

Meg rounded the end of the bar, still deep in shadow. She gasped when she saw the face of the gentleman in the light of the lantern.

"Madam, are you there?" the man asked, perplexed that he could hear her but see no one. He raised the lantern to scan the taproom. Seeing Meg at the end of the bar, he gestured toward the book on the desk.

"A room if you please. I sent Mr. McGee word that I was coming."

Meg realized that like Mr. Riordan, he too failed to recognize her. Of course, why would he? He last saw her dressed in silk in the full blush of youth. Now, she hardly had any hair and had become a walking skeleton. How could he ever know her? But what if he looked more closely?

"Aye, sir, forgive me, m'Lord." Meg pulled her shawl over her head and opened the big book. She hoped she didn't look too silly and pretended to shiver in the draft near the door.

She picked up her quill and dipped it in the inkpot. Keeping her eyes cast down, she asked,

"Name, sir?"

Hands trembling, she waited for his reply but he said nothing.

Finally, Meg looked up to see the man staring intently at her.

"What be yer name, sir? She asked again, thickening her Mayo accent.

"Oh, I am terribly sorry, you reminded me of someone. I'm Lord Robert Cushing."

Hearing her uncle's name spoken aloud sent a genuine shiver through Meg and her shawl slipped from her head. He didn't know her, thank the saints but it was only a matter of time before he figured out who she was.

"Are ye with the convocation of County Mayo landlords then, sir?"

"Well, yes and no." Lord Robert said. "I have been advising Lord Sligo but I am actually from Killarney. I would be staying at Westport House but they have influenza in the servants' quarters and advised me to reside here while I'm in Westport."

Surprised that he would confide so much to her, Meg handed him the key to the last available room.

"Ye'll be in #12. Upstairs at th'far end of th'hall. Breakfast is at 7 am m'Lord. We have a shortage of candles at the moment, m'Lord, please take the lantern t'light yer way. Did ye want any refreshment sent up t'ye, sir? Me boyo will be back soon from an errand. I can send up a tray, if ye please."

He looked at her again, a puzzled expression crossing his face.

"No meal, thank you. Just have him bring me a bottle of port with some biscuits and cheese."

Coming around the front of the desk, Meg reached for his bag.

Looking at her skinniness with genuine pity, Lord Cushing picked up his own bag.

"Allow me, lass. You carry the lantern."

Meg led the way up the stairs and down the long corridor. She silently prayed that Gilchrist would not burst from his room and point her out to Lord Robert as the fraud she was. He entered room #12 and again turned to her.

"I must know your name, miss. You bear a striking resemblance to someone I know. Around the eyes"

"Mary, sir. Mrs. Mary Brady."

Meg cringed at her second lie in only a few minutes. She knew Uncle Robert would find out soon enough who she was but she needed to buy time until she could talk to Tom and Duffy.

"Yes. Well, sorry to pry. Good evening then, Mrs. Brady."

"Good night then, sir."

As soon as she reached the taproom, Meg locked the front door and ducked into the alley behind the inn. Grabbing the storm lantern from outside the kitchen door, she pulled her shawl tighter against the pelting rain and splashed through the puddles to St. Peter's Church.

She rounded the corner of the churchyard to see Denny emerge from the sacristy with a box of candles wrapped in oilcloth against the wet. He had run off without a lantern and was picking his way back through the dark yard.

"Denny, did you tell Da?" Meg asked when she caught up to him.

Denny scowled and walked away from her

"Of course I did. I told him what ye said. Why are ye here? Don't ye trust me t'give a simple message?"

"No not at all, that." Meg replied, exasperated with his prickliness.

She explained that she had another message for Tom and he relaxed. Truth be known, she couldn't trust him with the new development about Uncle Robert but he swelled with pride when she told him she needed him to find Mr. McGee and send him to St. Peter's rectory. That would leave him in charge of the inn until the adults returned. This was a very new responsibility for Denny. He couldn't wait to tell Rose to distribute the candles immediately. No argument. He was in charge.

"Now go back and take the new guest his bed lunch and leave one of those candles with him. Then go to bed. We have a huge day tomorrow and we'll be without Da. I'm counting on you to shoulder the load."

She thought of offering him the storm lantern but decided that he would be better able to see in the dark than she would. Watching him disappear into the wet blackness she had a sudden memory of finding Maureen cradling her dead baby in the pouring rain by the banks of the river Clydagh. Would her mind never end being full of her past tonight?

Meg knocked on the rectory door and was welcomed into a circle of light and warmth. Startled, Fr. Timon drew her to the hearth where he and Tom were playing checkers and enjoying a bottle of cheap whiskey. Mrs. Murphy, Fr. Timon's stalwart housekeeper, took Meg's soaked shawl and sat her next to the roaring turf fire. Exhausted she tried to relax and enjoy the fire as Tom and the priest played checkers. But she couldn't. She was trembling inside at her close encounter with her past. The two men were infuriating as they quietly finished their game. How could they be so calm when they were so close to being discovered? Mrs. Murphy poured Meg a cup of hot mint tea and she spilled her story to Tom and Fr. Timon. Tom rose from a creepie where he was sitting and started stoking a pipe. He set the pipe on the mantel and she flew at him.

"Tom! The worst has happened. My Uncle Robert is at the inn! I thought the worst was Gilchrist but now this!"

"Did he speak to ye? Are ye sure?"

"Of course I'm sure! I saw him for only a brief moment but I would know him anywhere. He thought he knew me but I lied when he asked me my name. He said I looked familiar around the eyes. But I told him my name was Mary Brady and he believed me. But it's just a matter of time before he realizes who I am. What will I do? I've told Gilchrist you're dead and Uncle Robert will surely ferret out the truth. Oh, Tom I'm so frightened! What are we going to do?"

"What is there t'do? We've left our home and God alone knows if we'll ever be able t'return. So, Gilchrist can burn it or flatten it and we'll be no worse off. Yer Da' will niver be able t'come after ye no matter who finds ye here. Besides, yer Uncle Robert has always been good t'ye, so no need t'fear him. Ye're me wife and I'll not let anyone dispute that fact. And ye've gone over t'the papists so they can't even throw ye out o'the Irish Church! So, from where I stand, ye're in pretty good shape."

Meg looked up at him and saw mirth behind his sleepy eyelids. The smell of fresh whiskey was hot upon his breath and out of the corner of her eye she could see Fr. Timon shaking with laughter as he poured himself another glass.

"Won't they arrest you?"

"Fer what? I've not broken any law, Meg."

"What about Jewel? You stole Jewel and sold him and my saddle. And you stole my father's horse too! What about Angus?"

"Ah, Meg, Darlin', ye fret about the silliest things. You sold Jewel! I only handled the arrangements. And no one even missed Angus 'afore I had him back in his stall. He nodded to Fr. Timon who poured Tom another shot. So, ye see? The only guilt I carry is the guilt o'drinkin' contraband booze with me confessor. And him in on the sin which ye must know cancels the evil o'the deed."

Now Meg knew he was drunk. She couldn't believe this was the same man who had just left her in the doorway of Browne's Inn. What was he up to? Why was he behaving this way? She looked at his mouth twitching behind his pipe. He was treating this as some sort of female nonsense, like some colossal game.

She looked around to take in the room. The priest lived

in Spartan simplicity. His assistant had recently been transferred to Ennis to take over the little Franciscan church whose pastor had died. His only assistant was old Mrs. Murphy and she looked to be on her last legs.

Suddenly Meg realized what was going on. Tom didn't know what side of the fence Fr. Timon was on. While it was very likely that he shared Tom's feelings about rebellion Tom needed to be very circumspect to protect both himself and the priest. Of course!

Meg was forced to play along.

"I see your point." she lied.

"What can either Gilchrist or Uncle Robert do to us? We're half starved already and have no home but the inn. As long as we could work for Lord Sligo, who can bother us? Certainly the landlords have enough trouble on their hands that one displaced family is nothing to them."

"So, Mr. Phalen, what do we do?"

Meg searched his face for some sort of plan.

"Well, Mrs. Phalen, 'tis my suggestion that ye go back t'the inn, go t'bed and I'll be joinin' ye as soon as I help this holy man o'the cloth get rid o'the evidence left in the bottom o'this bottle."

"But Tom, I told Gilchrist you were dead!"

"So, maybe we'll make a convert out o'him when he sees the miracle our humble priest has done in raisin' me up from the grave."

Fr. Timon let out a snort and collapsed laughing in a wicker hearth chair.

"Well, I suppose you're right but humor me on this, Tom."

Meg saw his shoulders relax as he acknowledged her understanding of the situation.

"Stay here with Fr. Timon tonight and come around the kitchen door early tomorrow. Maybe if you stay in the back or find work in the cellar you can stay out of sight until they start their big meeting. You know I can use your help even if we have to put an apron and mobcap on you for a disguise.

Surely you haven't forgotten that tomorrow we serve tables at seven in the morning for an inn full of lords."

Grinning, Fr. Timon raised his glass.

"Ah, there I've got ye beat. Tomorrow, I only need t'set one table. And, as it happens, 'tis only the one Lord I have t'deal with. And granted, fer all o'that He does provide the meal. But I do have t'do it at six o'clock, and by meself, mind ye. So, ye must admit, I do have ye there, that I do."

Chapter Three

Denny tried to enter the inn by the front door.

"Divil," he cursed, longing to use some of the stronger swear words he heard Andrew Feeney use at Brotherhood meetings but still too self-conscious to say them out loud.

He went around back and slipped into the kitchen. It was pitch black in there but he knew his way around. He was finally getting used to the lay of the land in his new home and finding the box of lucifers hanging next to the stove, he lit one of the long beeswax tapers from his bundle.

He accidentally dropped the lit match on his bare foot, this time yelping out a real swear word that would make old Andrew proud.

"Whew," a voice from the shadows said with a whistle.

"That's a mighty big curse from a wee lad sich as yerself."

Denny's temper, already sparked by his stinging foot, flared.

"Wee lad! I'll thank ye t'remember that when I'm sweatin' like a man fer me supper. In case yer interested me mam's in trouble and wants t'see ye at the rectory."

"And I'll thank ye t'remember who it is yer runnin' yer mouth at. Tis' a fool who bites the hand that feeds him. I'll thank ye t'pay me respect, Boyo."

Duffy's pipe filled with the half-burnt tobacco found in the taproom ashtrays glowed in the corner of the kitchen.

"Com'ere 'til I hit ye, ye spalpeen. What d'ye mean trouble?"

He reached out and cuffed Denny on the ear.

"Take yer hands off me! I'm not yer wee boyo."

Denny shoved Duffy away and backed toward the door. Duffy stood up and made a grab for him but he was gone in a flash into the alley leaving the candle sputtering in the draft.

At the rectory? What kind of trouble could Meg be in that would send her to a priest? Blame! That Denny could get under his skin and now he's left the inn with no one in charge. He thought about running up to the third floor to wake Rose where she slept with the babies but he couldn't risk all that crying with a house full of guests. Duffy grabbed his cap and headed out into the rain.

Denny scooted through the puddles relishing the cool water splashing up over his sore foot. He hated that musty old inn and they treated him like a slave. The work was brutal, lugging and hauling heavy casks up from the cellar, running around this hilly town carrying messages and picking up supplies. He hated being confined to the kitchen, emptying slops and dragging heavy washtubs outside for Mam and Rose. The food was better than at home but there was no freedom. The guests all wanted something or another and they treated him worse than dirt.

The only chore he didn't mind was watching Francis. Francis was a great oyster hunter for a baby and both brothers thrilled to the task of wading in the cool shallows searching for the curly gray shells. Francis was the only one in the world Denny really liked. He and Thomas had been buds, but now that was over. He couldn't think about his dreamy eyed brother. He had shut him up in a tiny spot in his gut and promised himself the day of Thomas's funeral, he would never let anyone take him out. Even the men and boys in the Blackthorn Brotherhood, most who had lost family themselves to this great hunger, could not touch him where Thomas was. Even Mam, when Denny caught her crying in the pantry could not move Denny to go near the little place where Thomas lay dead inside him.

He raced down the quay past Marie's where he could hear someone pounding out awful tunes on the old pianoforte. Down he splashed toward the docks where the Brotherhood met in an old abandoned smokehouse. How he longed to be accepted by the bravest lads in Ireland. He would do anything for them but the only one who paid him any mind was Andrew Feeney. Denny didn't know why Andrew was interested in him. The other brothers had told Denny over and over that at twelve, he was too young, that no good would come from allowing him to be present for their meetings.

One night right after the Phalens had arrived in Westport, one of the lads had offered Denny a smoke. Feeling like a man, Denny had accepted the long white stem of the clay pipe, placing it between his teeth the way he had seen Da. Taking a deep draft of the strong sponc smoke, he immediately started to choke. The older lads laughed and mocked him and to his great shame, Denny found his eyes filling. These brothers were different from the lads on Achill. They were older and much harder. Andrew himself was asked to leave sometimes when the talk turned too serious.

Denny wished he could be like Andrew. He never acted upset when the older men wanted to talk without him. He did everything they said without complaint. The men relied on Andrew and the other young brothers to travel between Westport, Achill, Clare Island and north to Newport. They were much less recognizable and had energy to burn. The boys were so enamored with them and their cause, the older men knew they could trust them. Some of the young brothers were the sons of Brotherhood leaders.

Denny longed for Da to be one of these men. He imagined his father leading a rebellion against the filthy English, charging a castle or taking out a slew of English soldiers. He used to envision his Da beating the guards posted around the fields back home with a slane after turf cutting or slicing their throats with a scythe after harvesting wheat they couldn't even dream of eating. But his Da would never do that. No, his Da was too honorable, too grateful to be married to an English woman. That was his real weakness! His Da could never be a true brother because he had Mam.

Denny tried never to think about that. He hated the fact that his Mam was English. But he couldn't hate her. He hated seeing her cry, and after she took Communion last Christmas at St. Dymphna's, that awful Rev. Nangle dragged them out of the soup line at St. Mary's Church of Ireland. He said Mam was a disgrace to her parents and even Mrs. Trent couldn't calm him down. They all went to bed hungry after that. There was never enough, not even those pancakes anymore. If Mr. McGee hadn't come when he did they all would be dead.

Denny never really thought about his grandparents. Mam never talked about her old home or her mother and father. When he was a wee lad, Da used to tell all kinds of stories about his Gran'da and uncles. He thought of the story Da told about his own Gran'da and his uncles dying for the right to speak out. That was the kind of man Denny wanted to be! That was the kind of man he wished Da was! Like Mr. McGee's cousin Mr. D'Arcy McGee. Did Mr. McGee care that his cousin said he was a coward? That's what D'Arcy said when he got mad about all the "fine English gentlemen" that Mr. McGee put up at the inn.

Denny wanted to tell D'Arcy McGee that Mr. McGee had saved them from dying and if the inn had no Englishmen, they'd be hungry again. Sometimes all this talk about cowards and fine gentlemen confused Denny. He knew the English were bad and the Irish were brave and good but he didn't mind sometimes when an Englishman gave him a penny or tossed him a sweet for carrying his bags.

Sometimes at night, in his bed, he felt tears on his face thinking about the night he told Mam he hated her for being English. He would always remember how hurt she was by that. He wanted to be brave and good like the brothers but his da told him they were trouble and would switch him good if he found out he was sneaking off to the docks at night. He knew he would take that pain with pride but he blushed with shame when he remembered the only time his mam had ever spanked him.

He liked D'Arcy McGee. He wasn't as big as their Mr. McGee but he had almost exactly the same smile. He ruffled Denny's hair the same way and sometimes his voice was the same. He let all the boys call him D'Arcy even the young ones. He said that was what brotherhood was all about.

Sometimes some of the other, older men scowled at D'Arcy McGee for this. They said it bred disrespect but D'Arcy just scoffed at them and called them old-fashioned. They warned him that someday his carefree attitudes would get him in trouble. He even heard Mr. Neary say that if D'Arcy ever got caught by the British the brothers wouldn't know him plain and simple. Mr. Philbin accused him of being a loose cannon and a threat to the larger movement with his big mouth and his hot head.

Denny saw flickering light in the little smokehouse at the back of the old O'Connor Fishery and knew some of the brothers were in there. The rain had finally stopped and what remained of the waning moon was up. The clouds had disappeared as if the rain had washed them all into the sea. He crept around the corner of the smokehouse, keeping in the shadows the way Andrew had taught him. Sliding along the shed wall, sure to keep his head below the windowsill, he squatted. Boyish curiosity quickly overcame Andrew's teaching and Denny stole a look at who was inside.

There were three men, D'Arcy and two men Denny had never seen before. They sat hunched over a map lit by a storm lantern slung from a huge hook once used to smoke whole salmon. An empty whiskey bottle and two glasses sat on the table next to the map. They continued to pour over the map talking in low, tense voices. Denny only caught a word here and there but he knew the men were discussing something important and very secret.

Suddenly one of the strangers stood up and jabbed his finger at the map.

"Here, divil, take ye McGee, we have to come ashore here! The moon will be right and the tide will be right and the men will be right. What is it yer so bloody worried about? We've been talkin' and jawbonin' about this fer months. I say the time is right. We move at the new moon and we do it here!"

He slapped his hand down flat on the map and D'Arcy sprang from his chair, tipping it over.

"No, Morris, not there! There's too great a risk that we'll all be drowned there. My God, man, ye don't trust those of us who know this bay and all her sisters from here t'Newport? We voted not there and that's the all of it! Ye just have t'trust us, man."

"Trust ye? How can I trust ye when yer own flesh is over at Browne's "yes sirrin'" and "no sirrin'" t'beat the band and the very rogues we're up against feedin' his face?"

"Now see here, Morris Leyne, ye leave me cousin outta' this. He's too good fer the likes o'them, I grant, but he's a man o'his word and he promised t'keep his ear t'the ground."

"Then where is the information? Why has he not been sendin' us the information?"

"Maybe he's got nothin' t'tell! He's not had naught but a bunch o'beggars livin' there or a crowd of spoiled boyos lookin' fer a good bitch. Ye know he's good as his word, man. There's not a McGee alive not fer the cause o'freedom."

The third man leaned his chair back and deep shadow swallowed his face.

Drawing deeply on his pipe he asked quietly, "Ye'll not be raisin' yer voices now and bringin' the constable down upon our heads, will ye lads?"

The shadow man asked it as a question but even Denny

recognized it as a command.

The man D'Arcy called Morris opened the door and spat a stream onto the rotten old boards of the pier just missing Denny's feet. They had both lowered their voices now and Denny crouched lower and listened hard.

Morris Leyne paced around the room, finally resting against the window sill right over Denny's head. Denny hunched down further and tried not to breathe too loudly.

He tried and failed to lower his voice and Denny could hear everything he said.

"Well, I don't like this silence. I don't trust this wait and see business. I'm used t'movin' in and takin' an opportunity when it's at hand. Waitin' and watchin' only gives the bastards time to figure out what we're up to. And there's too many of us fer the job. Ye should think about sending some o'the boys t' the States. They're building the movement somethin' fierce over there. We work better with a leaner crew. Not as much risk o'leakin' information."

D"Arcy spoke up.

"Look, the whole Brotherhood meets again Friday. Let's see what develops between now and then. But ye gotta' know they're not gonna' change their minds about the landing. They know the bay and ye jist have t'trust 'em."

"Well, they're fools all. They don't call me Sea Snake fer nothin'. I'm good at this remember? Gun runnin' is what I do. That's why ye called on me in the first place."

The third man spoke again.

"Ye know the guns aren't the all of it, Morris. D'ye fergit the very lessons of Wolfe Tone himself? Ye must realize, man, that the Blackthorn Brotherhood is a small fish in a very large sea here. It's the Young Irelanders'll be leadin' the charge. And they're not likely t'be doin' it here! Ye're all too proud fer yer own good, the lot o'ye."

At this, Morris sprang up from the sill.

"What are ye thinkin', John Mitchell? Good Christ above, Wolfe Tone! That was over fifty years ago! Look at what we've gained doin' it Wolfe's way! First the Peep O'Day Boys and them strippin' us of everything gained by the old Catholic Defenders. Then what? Our grandfathers got what, ten, twelve years of freedom on the land? Our grandmothers walked freely t'church fer awhile and then down comes the hammer again!"

"Wolfe Tone was a diplomat, John. Him and his ilk, Pitt, Fitzwilliam and them. What did they really get us? Lies and half-promises. No, John Mitchell, I'm no baby, sittin' at Wolfe Tone's knee. Give me Daniel O'Connell. Now there's a man t'die fer! Total freedom, take it or leave it. I want none o'Parliament! Divil take them all and their lyin' promises. What good is it t'risk dyin' fer a chance to live half-free?"

John Mitchell had taken Morris's place on the windowsill. He tapped the sponc out of his pipe and Denny felt the hot ash filter down on him. He held his breath as one rather large glowing cinder rested on his knee, relaxing only when it dissolved in the damp night air.

"O'Connell is it? I admire Daniel O'Connell as much as the next man but ye know he won't condone our fightin'. Morris, ye're a great fighter. Not a one of us would argue that. And well d'ye deserve yer moniker, Sea Snake. But ye can niver allow yerself t'grow bigger or better than the cause, lad. Suren', we can burn, shoot, beat and sabotage our way through any part of Irish history but if we don't win the freedom we seek, what good is any of it? D'ye think me mam weaned me t'die in still another failed rebellion like me da? D'ye really want a repeat o'Wexford '98? Keep yer head, man! Ye can say what ye want about Duffy McGee and his houseguests. But ye risk losin' the trust of yer brother D'Arcy here with yer hard words and ye risk the whole plan and the lives o'the rest of us by yer pride. I'm thinkin' it might be yerself should go on to America. Hmm?"

The pier was suddenly awash in light as Morris flung open the shed door, the strong stink of whiskey all over him.

Turning to face the other two, he sputtered in fury.

"Ye may be right John Mitchell! And D'Arcy ye're a fool if ye think I'd not have yer back in any battle! But I'm warnin' ye both and ye can take this t'the others. Think hard on where ye plan t'bring in the guns and think even harder on how ye want t'finish this job. The time is close and if we're not goin' t'fail like they did in Wexford and so many other times, we've got t'have the right information and the right men fer the job. Ye'll find me here on the morrow. And ye'll be that impressed with me self-mastery, that ye will. But mark these words. As much as I respect ye both, I'll have me piece and that's the all of it. We'll bring the matter o'the landing and the final plan to another vote and move on it or I'll be heading north t'Newport t'rally a group who will stand and win."

Denny tried to make himself invisible by hunkering lower on his haunches. He felt his knees weaken and almost wet himself at the thought of being discovered. Fortunately Morris Leyne turned in the other direction and disappeared into a maze of piers and warehouses.

The last thing he heard was the sound of John Mitchell's voice.

"Morris is right, D'Arcy, though I'd be a fool t'let him know I think so. Whatever the brothers decide tomorrow, we have t'send the majority o'yer men to help w'the operation. We' need t'thin the ranks around here, D'Arcy, mark me on this. Git 'em out o'here! The gentry might be asses but they're not fools. We're too many, plain and simple."

With this, John Mitchell snuffed the lantern and the two men emerged from the tiny shed. D'Arcy McGee spoke earnestly as they headed for a waiting curragh but Denny no longer cared what he was saying. Suddenly a warm hearth and the familiar sight of his mam's apron was all he desired.

Denny scooted around the corner of the smokehouse and took off toward the inn using the alley behind the shops. He was half way there before he stopped by a garbage bin and relieved himself. He heard a woman holler through an open window for someone to come back and pay her the rest and realized that he was again behind Marie's. The customer barreled out the back door and almost knocked Denny over as he buttoned his trousers. The man raced up the alley fastening his own trousers as he went. Denny had barely left the shelter of the waste bin when the back door of the whorehouse flew open and knocked him into a crate of old vegetable rinds. Several rats scurried out into the alley from beneath the rinds. When she realized Denny was not the bilking customer, a woman dressed in nothing more than a sheet, bellowed a stream of swear words that would have made even Andrew blush. Denny tore through the dark maze of stinking refuse until he saw the familiar sign for McRea's Livery and knew he was almost home.

He breathed a sigh of relief as he felt the inn's heavy kitchen door close behind him. The pale moon shone through the tiny window and cast a wan light over the pile of candles spilled out onto the table. He realized with a wave of queasiness that he had forgotten about being in charge and prayed to the Virgin that he hadn't been missed.

Mr. Gilchrist tried reading to pass the late evening hours. It was his habit to read or do his calculations late into the night. He was not a man who required many hours of sleep and scornfully dismissed anyone who claimed they did. He seemed to attract people of that particular weakness. Mr. Riordan was just such a man. Mrs. Gilchrist also claimed to need many hours of sleep. She whined that her knees hurt when she didn't get her rest. He knew better. Mrs.Gilchrist would us any excuse to deny him his conjugal rights. He never accepted any of them.

Now he smirked at Jeffrey's sleeping undertaker snoring quietly in his bed. The fool even wore a stocking cap! Claimed the damp night air made his head throb. Weakness all around him! Weak people, weak politics, weakness, weakness weakness! Even his friend Jeffrey was weak. He had once been a handsome model of manly energy and his ribald licentiousness was legendary. Now, he sat like an infant in his own waste, homely as a chicken with sparse white hair sprouting from only one side of his head and chin. Between the sight of his silver-scarred face and the smell of his disgusting discharges, sometimes Gilchrist found even short visits to his lordship sickening. Yet, he had a duty to assist his friend's pursuits, did he not? The man could not be blamed for falling into such a state. He was a victim, pure and simple; a victim of a tragic accident caused by the stealth of his own daughter, abetted by the neglect of his wretched and ungrateful wife. Had the little slut not defied his orders to remain in her room sneaking away with her maid that fateful night, Jeffrey would never have found himself on those treacherous stairs. Then, he was all but abandoned by his twit of a wife.

When Lord Jeffrey Wynn called upon his old card-playing chum Gilchrist to find Lady Meg and her filthy papist husband, what choice did he have? He would have done it for friendship's sake but when Jeffrey offered him such a handsome fee how could he refuse? He was Lord Jeffrey's savior and his service was worth every farthing he collected. He, Robert Gilchrist of the Scottish Gilchrists, was strong; Jeffrey and certainly this sniveling Riordan chap were the weak ones. What would the world be like if it weren't for men like him to carry the load for the others?

He tried to concentrate on his reading but the candle that stupid whore gave him kept sputtering and threatened to go out. It had been just a nub when he got it and now it had almost disappeared entirely. He needed someone to refresh it so he could finish the Parliamentary Papers from February listing the Labour returns from the last week in January.

Those lying Irish pigs! Offering to work in the quarries, almost a thousand of them given work by the good graces of the crown, and across ten counties after over 4,000 total days work only half of them showed up! And they want food for their laziness? He slammed the paper down on the bed. No wonder they struck off 140 of them. They should have gotten rid of more! They deserved to starve.

Where was the help around here? Was there no service in

this place? He would certainly speak to Lord Sligo about the abysmal lack of amenities at this so-called inn. And he was hungry. No one had so much as offered him an apple.

Slipping on his carpet shoes, he padded to the door. The other guests were apparently sleeping except the gent whom he had heard come in after Riordan went to bed. There was a thin sliver of light beneath the door at the end of the hall.

By the time Gilchrist had arrived at the foot of the stairs the little candle had finally sputtered for the last time and gone out.

He called out to see if there was anyone who could bring him another. No answer. Odd. No innkeeper left his premises with a houseful of guests. Another thing to tell his Lord Sligo. He called out again and this time a small voice came from the kitchen. He would have to settle for a child. Preposterous!

"Who's there? Come here at once and show yourself! Are you the one who is supposed to be keeping the guests comfortable?"

Denny cautiously stepped into a shaft of lamplight that snuck through a front window like a long needle across the taproom floor.

"Look at you boy!" Mr. Gilchrist thundered.

"Wet and filthy! Obviously shirking your duty outdoors. Only a stupid tatie-hoker would leave the dry warmth of an inn to avoid fixing a bed lunch for a hungry guest. But then you fit the bill now don't you? Light me a candle and come closer so I can see your face."

Denny scurried to do as he was told and returned, handing the mean looking man the fresh candle.

A thin bony hand jerked him into the light and a pointed chin rough with silver stubble jutted into his face. The man peered closely, first at Denny's hair then at his eyes. The hand released him and he felt a piercing sting as the man slapped his face.

"There's a reminder of who you are, boy. The son of a filthy Irish whoremonger and grandson of a lord! How do you figure that? You have the look of your grandfather about you in your hair and eyes. But there is no question you have the slow blood of the Irish in your veins. Stir your stumps boy and fix me my bed lunch. I mean to wait up until that sleazy lug of an innkeeper comes back from wherever he is. No doubt at Marie's doing a bit of whoremongering himself!"

Denny cut a slab of cheese and toasted a fine heel of bread on the harnen stand. He gasped when he saw how low the fire had gone while he was out spying on the Brotherhood. He stoked the fire and drew a pint of Guinness only to have it thrown in his face and cider demanded instead.

The nasty man laughed at the smelly stout dripping in Denny's eyes.

"Just wait till your 'Lady' mother smells your clothes sour with stale stout. She should take a switch to you for drinking as well as leaving your post."

Denny lugged the heavy jug of cider to the table where the man sat and poured a tall glass.

"Would ye like me t'take this t'yer room, sir?" he asked, quaking at the thought of further punishment.

"Yes, you little monkey. Do you actually think I'd wile away my evening in this drafty taproom socializing with the likes of you? To my room at once and bring me some meat too."

With that he turned on his heel and briskly ascended the stairs. Denny did not know which room the man was in and listened carefully to his carpet shoes slapping rhythmically up the steps and down the hall to the end. He mopped up the spilled Guinness and carved a slab of roast beef from today's dinner. When he was finished he placed a fresh candle on the tray to light his way and carried the awkward tray upstairs.

When he got to the end of the hall, Denny saw light coming from two rooms. Again queasiness threatened his gut. Which room had the man gone into? How was he to know? At a loss, Denny could only guess. He had heard the slippers go all the way to the end of the hall but both rooms were lit.

The tray was becoming heavy. Denny chose the room at the far end tentatively knocking on the door with his elbow trying not to slosh the cider onto the bread. A fine looking gentleman opened the door and smiled as he took the tray from Denny.

"Thank you lad, this is a bit late but quite adequate. I'll leave the tray outside the door for you to pick up later."

The man closed the door and Denny turned to see the other man standing in the other doorway, fuming. He grabbed Denny by the collar and began to hustle him down the stairs.

"You are a greater fool than I thought to pull a stunt like that! How dare you give my bed lunch to someone else and make me wait like a second-class guest. You are not only a fool but a spalpeen if I ever saw one. What you need is a good tanning, I say! And by God, I'm just the man to give it to you!"

He thrust Denny into the shadowy kitchen and grabbed the nearest weapon he could find. His hand rested on a long-handled wooden paddle used to prod loaves of bread into the back depths of the oven. Denny tried to run out the back door but the furious guest was too quick for him.

Seizing him by the collar he swatted at his backside with the bread peel, smacking him hard. Denny knew the crazed man wanted him to cry out but he had taken too many switchings from his Da to give out a single sigh. Down came the paddle again as the man positioned Denny over the end of the table. Denny could hardly keep silent, gritting his teeth at the searing pain from the heavy peel. This was worse than anything Da had ever done! He hardly had any flesh on his behind and this paddle was far heavier than any switch. He had to get away from this crazy man before he killed him.

Denny bucked and kicked as the man continued to struggle him into position. He smacked him a third time. Denny could stand it no longer and cried out only to feel the paddling suddenly stop.

"What have we here my man?"

Denny heard the voice of the kindly man he had just delivered the tray to.

"I come down in search of another glass of cider and what do I find? Sir, if you must beat your son do it in your own home! This is a public house and you have no right to settle your domestic difficulties here. I must beg you to leave the premises immediately and take your boy with you."

Lord Robert began to sweat from his unaccustomed outburst.

The man immediately released Denny and threw the bread peel to the floor with a clatter.

"I beg your pardon, sir. You have the temerity to address me so! I am Mr. Robert Gilchrist of the Scottish Gilchrists. I am here as a guest of the inn on commission as undertaker to Lord Lucan! This young whelp just dishonored me by refusing me the simple request of a bed lunch which he instead fed to you, sir! Now, I do not know who you are sir, but I believe you owe me an apology not only for assuming I sired this wastral but for eating my cheese and drinking my cider!"

Mr. Robert Gilchrist stood sputtering indignantly. He withdrew a clean handkerchief from the sleeve of his velvet robe and dramatically mopped away the spit glistening on his silver chin whiskers.

Denny stood throbbing as he looked from one gentleman to the other. Would they challenge each other to a duel? Good heavens, he had heard of that happening. What if the nice gentleman lost and the nasty one won? How would he explain that to Mam? Oh, he wished Mam were here and Mr. McGee. They would know what to do. He was too a spalpeen and a lazy fool! They would never let him be in charge again! Where was Rose anyway? Where was she when he needed her? Probably sleepin' with all the silly babies on the third floor. Why did he have to take the tray to this mean old man and get a beatin' fer makin' a mistake? Why didn't this sort of thing ever happen to Rose?

"Well," Denny heard the nice gentleman say, clearing his voice. "I see that I made a mistake in identity here. You are not the boy's father. That you have made clear. He delivered your tray to me. That I understand. But that does not explain why I walked into this kitchen to find you in your robe, beating the living daylights out of boy who had the misfortune to be waiting on guests at this late hour! I could have you arrested for disturbing the peace but that would bring scandal to this house. I could apologize for eating a delicious lunch that I had requested upon my arrival two hours ago but that would be silly because I rightfully believed it to be mine. I could make a formal complaint to the innkeeper for harboring a mean-mouthed little scoundrel such as yourself among proper lords such as myself. Oh by the way, I apologize for failing to introduce myself. I am Lord Robert Cushing of the London Cushings, landholders in County Mayo and Killarney. Where was I? Oh, yes, the innkeeper. He's running a business for a close friend of the very man whom you claim to represent. Or I could take that nice wooden bread peel and wallop your bony backside the way you just did this lad's. What will it be, Mr. Robert Gilchrist of the Scottish Gilchrists? I rather like the idea of the walloping but I tired my arm out playing cricket the other day and I rather think I shall not beat you. You're not worth the risk of injury."

Gilchrist just stood, gaping at Lord Cushing, a look of absolute shock across his face. Before he could respond, the kitchen door flew open and Meg and Duffy McGee came in at the same time.

"What is it Denny?" Meg asked when she saw the scene.

The two gentlemen looked askance at the ragged woman and the big handsome innkeeper believing them to be caught in a clandestine tryst.

Despite his youth, Denny knew instinctively that this looked very bad.

"How is Father Timon?" he asked innocently.

"Fine, thank you for asking, Denny," Mr. McGee answered wearily. He owed the boy for this one and added,

"The fever's down and he should be fine by Sunday Mass."

The two gentlemen relaxed. Both appeared relieved that there would be no more excitement that night. The couple was simply out late, ministering to their ailing priest.

"Mr. McGee, I must compliment you on your fine service here at Browne's," Lord Cushing said with a slight bow.

"I enjoyed a most satisfactory bed lunch and came to the kitchen in pursuit of another glass of your fine cider. But please, let the boy bring that to me. I believe Mr. Gilchrist was here first."

With this he bowed again and backed out of the room. Denny stood silently, rubbing his bottom, listening carefully to his lordship's carpet shoes slapping on the floor above, all the way to the end of the hall. Mr. Gilchrist tersely repeated his order and followed immediately, rhythmically rapping his knuckles on the stair rail all the way to the top.

Meg quickly prepared a bed lunch for Mr. Gilchrist and Duffy himself took it to the cranky old man's room. She handed Denny the glass of cider and he too went upstairs. As soon as Denny rounded the stairway, Meg extinguished the lantern and began the long climb to the third floor and her bed.

Despite her fatigue, Meg could not settle down. She slipped between the covers on the bed and drew her knees up. Reaching down she massaged the cramps in her legs. Her legs felt like wood by the end of a day and no amount of rubbing could relieve the tightness behind her knees. She thought, as she often did when she felt the exhaustion of serving people all day, of Maureen.

There had been no word from the States since last spring and Meg owed Maureen a letter. The letters between them had slowed down to one or two a year since the hunger. The days when she and Maureen had been like sisters were a distant memory and passed through her mind now like the misty vapor that gathered around the lamplight outside her window. She shuddered at the effect this terrible hunger had had on very ordinary things. Meg had run out of ink long ago and her last nib snapped when she was writing a frantic note in blackberry juice to Fr. O'Boyle to come and bury Patrick.

Tonight would be a good night to write Maureen. Meg knew there was a supply of both paper and ink kept behind the bar with the ledgers. She climbed out of the bed and slipped her ragged dress over her. This is daft, she thought as she went back down to the kitchen. I have such a day ahead of me tomorrow and I'm wide awake. I'll not sleep a wink before Bea Carver's rooster crows.

Settling in at one end of the massive kitchen table, Meg assembled paper, pen and ink. Now, if she could only capture her thoughts. She opened Maureen's last letter and began to refresh her memory.

Dec. 25, 1846

Dearest Meg, Tom and all the little Phalens,

Happy Christmas from Johnstown!

Julie and Phil and the children just left. We all went to midnight Mass at St. Columba's and Charlie and I had them for a wee Christmas cheer. It's about three o'clock and I can't sleep but Charlie is out like a light. We'll be going over to their place later for Christmas dinner and I'll catch a bit of rest between now and then.

Life has settled down a bit since I last wrote. Charlie has finally let up a little on the drink. Maybe he's getting over losing his mam. He still gets roaring drunk a lot of the time but for some reason, it doesn't seem to be as often. Maybe I'm just getting better at staying out of his way.

Phil and Julie have been wonderful to us ever since Charlie's mam passed away. Phil is with Charlie a lot and has also recruited a couple of the lads on the force to keep an eye on him. Some of the men are as bad as he is but most of them are really decent lads with wives and children of their own. Some years ago, before I came here, one of them murdered his wife and three children before shooting himself. No one wants anything like that again! They have Fr. Cummings from St Columba's as their chaplain and he speaks out quite often about the evils of the drink. Charlie actually seems to like him. At least he listens to him more than he ever did to Fr. Finn.

I still haven't conceived since I wrote you a more than a year ago. Maybe it's not for me to have any babies. I can't believe Mary Ellen would be twelve years old had she lived. Meg, she would be almost a woman!

Charlie still pesters me that way day and night. He can't seem to get enough of me and I can never please him. I've given up trying. It's just the way it is. Our days have become very routine. I take care of the store. I do really enjoy it now and Charlie pays almost no attention to what I do there as long as it turns a profit. It's nice to be able to breathe a bit without him on my shoulder.

He's been promoted to lieutenant which he boasts about endlessly. He busted up a gang of Slavs in the tannery last summer and the department recognized him with a grand dinner and gold watch. After that when Lieutenant O'Rourke retired, he stepped right into the job.

We moved into a nicer house in the fall. We're in a newer development two streets back from the main road. Julie and Phil built there and we bought the land next door. Having them for neighbors is a life saver. I love their children and am godmother to two of the girls, Mary Grace and the new baby, Maeve. Fr. Finn insisted that despite the legendary greatness of the Irish Maeve, a child must be baptized with a saint's name. So, she's Maeve Bridget. So, there you have it.

Charlie continues to be the same jealous fool he's always been and living on Spruce Sreet, away from the crowds on Main, hasn't changed that. He goes after me more for imaginary lovers than any other reason. How stupid he is to think I'd be bothered! He hired a beautiful Polish girl to work with me in the store. I think he hopes she'll draw the attention of the factory workers away from me. He's probably right but between us girls, I think it's the red hair that they like. Or maybe my naturally sassy attitude. And me, the shady side of twenty-five! At least my hair's not graying yet.

I must say, I have developed a bit of a temper myself. Come to think of it, maybe that's why Charlie's sobered up a bit. One night he was stinking drunk and hit me one time too many and I walloped him one with a candlestick I was polishing. He went down like a house of cards and I thought I'd killed him. But the next day there he was at me again. I know he thought his head hurt from the drink because he filed a complaint against Jack Murphy for serving him bad whiskey. I think he's just a little afraid of me now. Somewhere in that wooden head he must remember me crowning him one. Don't worry Meggie, I'm not likely to murder him. I'm still that afraid of him! I'm just learning to duck!

Well, sweet one, I'm off to bed. Charlie's awake and yelling for me. Happy Christmas to me! I hope this finds you all weathering the hunger. Write to me when you can. God bless, and have a blessed New Year.

Affectionately, Maureen

Meg picked up her pen and began to put pen to paper in a beautiful flowing script.

July 20, 1848
Dear Maureen,

I write you in the wee hours of the morning. My sleeplessness works for the benefit of both of us. Where do I start? There is so much to tell. When last I wrote, Martha was only weeks old.

I received your Christmas letter of '46 in the early spring of '47. What a terrible delay in mail since the hunger! But Maureen, so many are dying, I suppose mail is the least of anyone's concerns.

We have not been unscathed by the evil hand of death, dear friend. I am only grateful that you escaped this place of darkness when you did. We lost our cows right after your letter arrived. That's when the real troubles started. That's when we started digging ditches and the children began begging fish on Mundy's Bluff.

I'm sure if you saw any of us, Tom and Duffy included, you would pass us as strangers, we're that thin. Thank God for Duffy, Maureen. He saved our lives.

We're living in Westport now, at Browne's. Since the middle of June, Tom, the children and I are the staff. The family that used to work here left for America and not a day too soon.

I have sad news, dear Maureen. We lost Thomas at Christmas time in '47. He never recovered from the lung fever he got the day of Danny Kinnealy's funeral. For two years he coughed and wheezed until it just wore him out. Then, just weeks ago, I delivered another son, Patrick. He lived but a few days, poor little lad. I have been so weakened by the hunger I knew when I first felt him move that I would have nothing to give him if he lived. Sweet angel was too small to even try feeding at my empty breast. So, two sons gone. We speak little of it. The work here is mighty and we are kept busy day and night. But we're eating and we're not in the workhouse. When I say Duffy saved our lives, I mean it.

What the future holds we have no inkling. The farmers again planted potatoes in the spring and we may have the best crop in history. But we may harvest black rot again too. I can't tell you the terrible air that settles on the whole village when that happens. The sweet green of the potatoes turns spotted and black while beneath the stony soil. We've had had our hopes dashed year after hungry year as we planted and hoed watching our crop of pratie plants flourish in the warm spring sun only to dissolve into thick, stinking muck by the end of summer. I think the worst of it is the suddenness. We're so hungry and the praties are so lush! Maureen I've seen grown men kneeling in green fields begging the fairies to protect the crops only to lay down and weep the next day among leaves spotted with black.

Tonight the inn is filled with landlords and undertakers who will meet for the next two days to discuss the fate of the poor. How nice to sip Turkish coffee and English tea, dine on my homemade pastries and eggs while discussing the fate of the starving masses begging at their fine kitchen doors back home. At least they're talking. I suppose though it would be more merciful if they just lined us all up and shot us. You wouldn't believe the whole families just dropping along the road. And the cities like Westport and Castlebar! Murder and theft the likes of which you never saw. Even beggar children with their throat cut for a loaf of stolen bread. Tom won't let any of ours go more than a few doors away without him or Duffy to protect them. The girls are happy for the protection but it drives Denny wild. I know he scoots out on his own whenever he can.

Let's see what the gentry can come up with to turn this famine around. So far, Trevalyan and his lot have done nothing. God's will, he says. God's will that millions of innocent people starve to death! Maureen, I'm so ashamed of my people. Thank God I go by the name Phalen. I have had to adopt a thick Mayo brogue here. But I fear it will come to naught. My Uncle Robert is one of the men meeting here and I think he's suspicious. He thought he knew me but I lied and told him my name was Mary Brady. Now, I'll have to go to confession.

That's news I almost forgot to tell you! I've become Catholic. The very day you wrote your last letter, I received my First Holy Communion at St. Dymphna's. Fr. O'Boyle, God bless him, can rest in heaven for getting this daughter of the church of Ireland to come over to the Roman church. It was an extraordinary journey to say the least. I so wish I could sit and tell you all about it over tea.

I'm afraid dear Maureen, the days of wading in the shallows off the strand, digging mussels and gathering dulse are over. They are so far from my life here at the inn that they could have been lived by another woman altogether. I wonder if we'll ever go back to our island home. I miss the little window with the lace curtain catching in the sea breeze and the cheery little kitchen so filled with warmth.

Tonight, the smell of the rain off the sea made me feel that if I looked hard enough into the night I would see the thinking rock. I grew to love that wild island, Maureen, just as you did. I loved the sound of the sea and the way the sun crept across the sand in the morning. I miss stargazing on the thinking rock. Remember when you and I would sit out there and plot ways to snare Duffy and get him to marry you? I still think he's your man. But I'm sure it would be wise to keep that from old Charlie.

And then, one day a great rotten thing took hold of the land and betrayed us all. Year after year we struggled but we didn't realize how hopeless it all was until Thomas died. Oh, Maureen, if ever I didn't understand your pain when you lost Mary Ellen, I do now. I was literally mad with grief. The morning I held him in my arms, defying even the law to try and take him from me, I knew how far I had sunk. I knew as the cold of death penetrated my baby's bones and chilled my breast as I held him, how close I was to losing my sanity. But like you, I could not let go! It was as if hanging on to Thomas meant hanging on to life itself.

Maureen, I carried his little body all the way up to the loft! Tom had gone to the byre to see if there was an old blanket we could wrap him in. While he was gone I had braced his little body between myself and the rungs of the ladder, inching and bumping to the top. I was so ashamed that the other children were watching from the hearth. I frightened them so. But finally Fr. O'Boyle was able to talk me down. They wanted to throw Thomas, my sweet lamb, away like so much rubbish in a grave no one would ever be able to find! Thank God Fr. O'Boyle was able to convince the constable to let us bury him at St. Dymphna's.

Poor little Patrick is out by the booley. We didn't even have the priest for him. At least he was baptized. Now he and Mary Ellen and Thomas can play together in heaven. The hardest thing I ever did was leave those babies on Achill and come across the bay. How I grew to love that wild, unfettered island. All my babies born on the windy strand and all I know of married life was left on that shore with my two little laddies.

Do you remember the mornings when we awoke to find the sandpipers and gannets arguing over who owned the beach? And the thinking rock? I remember you sitting on that stone for hours furiously weaving a basket or a chair, fuming over something Duffy did or did not say. Tom and I both spent hours on the thinking rock and imagining our children's future. Oh, Maureen how could we have ever known we'd end up like this? I can't see us ever going back to the island now. Everything we knew has been stripped away.

There is much to like about living here though. Sure, the work at the inn is hard but what work isn't? We're still hungry but we're no longer starving, thanks to Duffy. It feels good to earn our keep and I have to admit that Tom hasn't been as happy in years. The quarters are spare but clean and adequate with comfortable beds and plenty of privacy. The inn was designed to house several servants on the third floor but aside from Duffy we're the only ones living here now. His rooms are in the front of the building and he's given over the entire rest of the top floor to us.

Tiny St. Peter's parish is filled with poor hungry people like us and Fr. Timon is never the preacher that Fr. O'Boyle was but we're content there. Late at night, especially when the inn is quiet, Tom and Duffy and I study the lives of the saints with Fr. Timon. Sometimes, he'll take his little breviary and lead us in the daily office. I love the incantation of the psalms and the beautiful magnificat of the Blessed Virgin. How I ever thought Catholics were going to hell for praying to Mary I'll never know. The words of the Hail Mary are right in St. Luke's gospel!

Well, Maureen, I really must go to sleep. I'll be having to start breakfast soon! As soon as the next mail goes out I'll have this off to you. God bless you dear. Write to me care of Browne's and if by some slim hope this hunger ends and I'm home by then, they'll get it to me.

Give my best to Philip and Julie.

Love, Meg

Chapter Four

Meg put the kettle on the large front burner of the imported Grove's Kitchener stove. Meg had marveled at the size of the stove when they had first arrived at the inn but Duffy had merely shrugged. When a place could house up to twenty-four people and served guests off the street as well, it needed to have a big stove. It had taken Meg a few days to get used to cooking over a stove. Hearth cooking was very different. Over the years she had learned the fine nuances of the turf fire and Maureen had taught her well how to gauge when the brick oven or tin oven was just the right temperature for a batch of bread or a pie. She had only a few days to learn how to use the stove when the huge crowd had gathered for the display of Donnelly's Arm. She still had the little silver burn scars to show her mistakes of that day but somehow they had survived and not one customer had reason to complain.

The kitchen was already heating up and Meg felt sweat beading her upper lip. Dressed lightly, she wore only a skirt and a plain white blouse. Duffy had appealed to Lady Sligo's housekeeper for clothing for his new crew and she had provided two sets of work clothes and aprons for all but the small children. For Gracie, Ellen and Francis, she sent an old nightshirt, some flour sacks and torn bed linens. Meg had spent every spare moment fashioning little shifts and britches from these. None of them had the luxury of undergarments or stockings but at least from the outside, they looked appropriately dressed for their station.

After this meeting there would be one more crowd to feed over the three days of the Reek Sunday festivities. Meg didn't know which made her more nervous, the feeding of highborn lords whose tastes and preferences would be very particular or the masses of peasants who would descend like locusts and eat everything in sight. Thank God Duffy was used to this and was doing the ordering.

She would think about the festival when she needed to. Today Meg had enough on her mind. Once she got through the next three meals and some of the gentlemen left for their homes, she would treat herself to a pot of good strong English tea. By tomorrow night they'd all be gone and they'd have a whole week to prepare for the pilgrims.

Duffy had kept the menu simple, knowing the lords would prefer good, hearty fare over anything fancy. The gentry always seemed to appreciate the basic Irish cooking at the inn. Perhaps they were tired of everything drowning in sauces like they saw on the menus abroad or maybe it was just the way they were used to the dishes prepared by their own Irish cooks. Other than the whiskey cream sauce for the Dublin Lawyer, there was no need for a rich hollandaise or fussy desserts. Gooseberry trifle, hot berry pie and rich bread pudding were Duffy's best sellers year in and year out.

Duffy himself made the whiskey cream sauce. This was a house specialty and

Browne's was known for it as far as Newport. He had ordered the lobsters to be delivered last night and two huge barrels of the fresh crustaceans reposed in the corner of the kitchen. They were now making a terrible racket clawing and prowling around the inside of their final, smelly home, climbing over each other and sliding down the slippery wooden walls. Meg could smell the turf fire behind the inn as Duffy and Denny worried the enormous cauldron over the bricks to start the water boiling for the noon meal.

As soon as she had finished baking barm brack for breakfast, Meg had gone to six o'clock Mass. The whole liturgy took less than thirty minutes and there were only two other women there. Tom knelt at Fr. Timon's side, serving as altar boy. Poor Father Timon would have said Mass if there had been no one present but Tom. Indeed, there were many days when it was just the two of them.

After Mass, she stopped Tom in the vestibule of the church and handed him a few fresh rolls for him and Fr. Timon to share for breakfast. He was not pleased to be consigned to the rectory for the day but was glad for the rolls.

"Now, Meg," he started to protest. But she told him what Duffy had said.

"Tom, he wants you out of sight. Under no circumstances are you to risk being seen. He brought in a lad from the alley to handle the heavy cauldrons in exchange for a platter of leftovers. We'll be fine."

"Well, if Duff thinks 'tis that important, then I'll lay on me neck at Fr. Timon's. But I still don't think Gilchrist can touch me."

"Tom, I'm not a babe in the woods. After last night, I know you know more than you're able to say and Gilchrist is just a smokescreen. And Duffy acts like he thinks I know something. God knows I can't keep my terror hidden from him."

Meg looked hard at Tom, probing his thoughts, not sure how to say what she needed to say.

"Tom, I know we've never really talked about our different backgrounds much over the years. I believe we both have tried very hard to adapt to the other out of love. God knows we've both sacrificed much to have our family on the island. It has never been lost on me how hard it's been for you being Lord Lucan's agent. I know you have done it for me and the children. And it's been hard for me too. I gave up a great deal of life's comforts when I left Clydagh Glyn. But none of it mattered then and I'd do it all over again in a minute."

She paused and took a deep breath.

"I guess what I'm trying to say is that since we've been in Westport, I sense a real yearning in you to get involved more with the locals and in some ways be more Irish. For this, I don't blame you one bit. But Tom, I'm frightened. I am more than frightened. I'm terrified something will happen to you."

"Now Meg," Tom started to protest.

"No Tom, I really believe you're not telling me everything. Duffy has hinted at it ever since we arrived. He says that we've been isolated on an island for so long we have no idea what's been cooking among the local lads. And I listen to the conversations in the taproom. There is talk that a rebellion is very close. No one knows when or where or if its just idle talk but the Blackthorn Brotherhood is involved and Duffy says he can tell just by the number of lads going in and out of Marie's that there is something afoot.

He says he wants you to stay put until he can sort it out. He said to tell you that as soon as he can he'll be down to talk to you and Fr. Timon. Tom, does he mean it or is he hiding you until the Brotherhood is ready for you? You must trust me, Tom. We've never kept things from each other and we can't start now. I can't bear it if you walk out the door one night and never return. You must tell me if this is really about Gilchrist or if you and Duffy are up to something."

Taking Meg by the shoulders, Tom returned her direct gaze.

"Meg, I do trust ye. God, save me, I love ye more than me own life. Ye must understand lass, there's a reason I'm not sayin' what ye want t'hear. I love ye too much t'take the risk. The less ye know the safer 'tis fer ye and fer the children, too. Rest assured, Darlin' that I'll be takin' no unnecessary chances. Duff knows the players much better than I. I trust Duff, Meg, and ye need t'trust him too."

Tom's words chilled Meg's blood and she swallowed hard against the bile rising in her throat.

"Tom, have you been to meetings? Have you seen these

men?"

"No. I can honestly tell ye I've not committed to anything yet, not even an introduction."

"Oh, Tom, then there's still time! We can move on. We can go back to GlynMor Castle and beg my father to take us back! We can go back to Achill and try to make a go of it!"

"Meg! Get ahold o'yerself, girl! Yer talkin' nonsense and I'll not hear it! Ye want me t'trust ye and yer ready to turn me into a cuckold in yer father's house at the first sign of danger? Think o'what yer sayin' lass!"

Suddenly Meg realized how close she was to losing her only line of communication with her husband. She saw how hard his jaw was and how gray his eyes had become. She could not afford to let her fear govern this exchange. To do so would risk Tom's black silence, a prospect more frightening to Meg than hearing the worst kind of news.

"Tom, I'm sorry. Please know you can trust me. I am behaving like a child but it's just my fear talking. Please forgive me. It won't happen again."

Tom relaxed and wrapped his arms around Meg holding her close.

"Ah Meg, we're all that frightened. Don't let us big strappin' lads fool ye 'atall. None of us wants t'bleed a drop except fer freedom. I love ye Meg, and if I thought I couldn't trust ye I'd not know what I'd do. Of course, ye're scared. Ye'd be fool not t'be. But as long as I've been alive, I've been on the outside lookin' in. Duff too. Always walkin' the fine line between Irish and English. Gettin' along by our wits and our charm. But we've been hungry too long t'be playin' th'game any more, Meg. Those who hold the reins on us have tightened th'bit too hard and we've tasted our own blood."

He took her face in his big, rough hands.

"Meg, Darlin', remember the words I said t'ye so many years ago in me da's meadow? I said 'em again in the peach orchard behind Fr. Finnegan's church."

Meg nodded letting two fat tears slip across her cheeks.

"Meg, I meant it then and I mean it now. Comin' with me

is fer the whole of it. We've been t'hell and back already, Darlin'. Fer the sake of our two sons, buried on that island."

Meg's heart broke as Tom's voice caught on the words and she silenced him with her lips. They stood in the vestibule of the tiny church, the only light cast upon them by the flickering red sanctuary candle. He kissed her hard as she clung to him. They stood in the presence of an altar of God, just like the one before which they vowed to be one until death parted them. They clasped each other passionately, as lovers, as the dearest of friends, as soldiers embarking on a frightful quest. Kissing deeply, tenderly, they silently renewed their vows.

There would be no doubting. There would be no worrying about whom to believe. They were in this together and God Himself was their witness.

Meg felt the rush of strength flow through Tom's limbs as she sealed her covenant with him and he tenderly willed that strength to steady her as she spent her fear in his embrace. When they finally pulled back and looked into each other's eyes, it was with a depth neither of them could plumb. The sound of the sacristy door closing jarred them back to the cool darkness of the church.

Tom spoke first.

"Is Fr. Timon involved?"

"Duffy didn't say. Do you think Father trusts you enough to let on?"

"I don't know. He only knows me these few weeks."

"What if you use this time to tell him all about us? Perhaps then he'll feel more comfortable sharing with you if he is. Tom, if anything happens while you're staying with him, you both will need to act as one."

"Ye're right. We'll talk. D'ye think Duff trusts ye? He's told ye quite a bit."

"I think so. If you want me to fill him in on what we just said here, I will. I don't think I'll be able to get down here to see you again today but if there is anything to tell, I'll send Lovie or Mary Clare with a note."

"Come here Meg."

Tom reached for her again and took her in his arms. They both let out a sigh as they felt the warmth of their love pass from one to the other. So much had passed between them just now they could barely bear parting. Now, more than ever they needed to be close to each other. They stood for a few seconds in the deep shadow of the tiny vestibule. Releasing Meg from his embrace, Tom kissed her chastely on the forehead as she reached up and touched his earlobe. This was one of their time-honored ways of saying goodbye and they parted wordlessly.

As Meg went to push open the heavy oak door, Tom softly called after her.

"Go ahead and tell Duff where we stand and Meg Darlin', take extra care t'watch Denny. I gotta' feelin' I just can't shake."

Meg nodded and pushed against the door. The early sun flooded the foyer of the little church. She squinted against its brightness but took no comfort in its warmth. Tom's whispered warning had chilled her again and she shivered as she hastened through the alley to Browne's Inn.

Meg and Rose loaded the trays with platters of sausages and eggs, black and white pudding and steaming fried tomatoes. Duffy and Denny carried the heavy trays into the taproom where the small tables had been lined up end to end making one long breakfast table. There were ten men dining in the taproom. Two had preferred to dine in their rooms. Mr. Gilchrist and Lord Robert Cushing had sent orders down for trays to be brought to them. Duffy sent Denny up with Mr. Gilchrist's dry toast and boiled eggs, buttermilk and morning paper. He followed Denny with the heavier traditional breakfast and pot of coffee for Lord Cushing.

Mr. Gilchrist grunted when he opened the door for Denny but despite Denny's worst fears, he took the tray without complaint. Duffy hadn't even rapped on Lord Cushing's door before Denny was tearing down the hall to the stairs.

"Yes, thank you, right there on the bureau," Lord Robert gestured.

Duffy placed the tray where his lordship had cleared a space, moving a bowl and ewer to the end of the dresser.

"Can I remove that for you sir?"

Duffy went to take the bowl, half-filled with dirty water. Lord Robert shook his head and Duffy looked up to see his face half lathered with clove scented cream.

"No, no I'm not through shaving yet. Just leave it and the maid can get it when she makes up the room. Pour me a cup of coffee and I'll be just fine. I know you have a full house and must be needed downstairs."

"Yes sir. Thank ye sir, anythin' else, just ring th'bell. I'll send young Denny up."

Duffy left his guest to finish his shave and eat his breakfast. As he turned toward the stairway, he saw Mr. Riordan of GlynMor Castle at the door of the room he shared with that awful Gilchrist. Meg had told him about her encounter with the two men and of her lie. He agreed with her that Tom needed to keep out of sight and had made certain she would have the opportunity to tell Tom. Duffy would do anything to protect Tom but as he hurried down the stairs, he shook his head at the extra load that would put on the rest of them in his absence. Checking the taproom setup he went out the front door and around the side alley to check on the progress with the cauldrons.

He entered the kitchen followed by Denny and the hired lad, who called himself Jack and refused to give any other information. They brought a draft full of turf smoke with them that made Meg think of her hearth at home. He instructed the boys to roll the heavy barrels of lobster out to the alley.

"And at no time are ye t'leave them unattended, d'ye hear me? Take the shillelagh and use it if ye have to. Ye'll pay fer any lost ones with yer hide, and that's the truth."

Once the boys had rolled the smelly barrels out to the alley and Duffy had swept out the water they had splashed across the kitchen floor, he started the whiskey cream sauce. Side by side, he and Meg worked at the stove as she filled him in on her early morning conversation with Tom. When she told him what Tom had said about Denny she could feel Duffy stiffen beside her. Instinctively they both turned to look out toward the alley and Meg heard Duffy exhale when he caught sight of Denny's fair hair blowing in the smoky breeze outside the tiny window.

Later that night, when all the dishes had been washed and the pint glasses stacked Denny and the hired lad finished bundling and dragging the trash out to the alley.

Duffy called after them, "Ye'll need the shillelagh agin' lads. All day smellin' those lobsters cookin' ye know half the town is waitin' fer the scraps."

The big clock on the shelf behind the bar chimed eight o'clock. Each toll hammered in Meg's head as she finally sat down at the long kitchen table to have her tea. She had just draped a damp towel over the huge crock where the dough for tomorrow's rolls was rising. It still needed about an hour and she could knead it one more time before popping them into the brick oven.

It was the last thing she had to do before bed and the last thing she wanted to do, tired as she was. But she had forced herself to measure out the flour and yeast right before serving dinner giving the dough time to rise twice before she baked the rolls. At home Meg had baked her bread in the morning but she found that she just didn't have the strength anymore so she moved the task to the cool evening hours wrapping the fresh loaves in cheesecloth to keep them fresh. So far, no one had complained.

Every bone in her body ached and her legs felt like boards. She had spent all morning sitting on the hard bench at the huge table peeling countless pounds of vegetables and cutting lamb into chunks for the evening meal. Meg had no desire to sit again on the bench but there were no comfy straw chairs or even little three-legged creepies in this kitchen. Now, after hours on her feet, truth be known, there wasn't a silk clad chaise or a down filled davenport that would have felt more comfortable to her.

Duffy ran a very efficient kitchen and the long slab of sycamore was used for everything from paring and chopping vegetables to polishing the candlesticks and heavy pewter ware used in the pub. Duffy and Rose had discharged most of the guests and she had sent Mary Clare up to put the little ones to bed.

Uncle Robert had planned to stay one more night and had asked for toasted white rolls and coffee for his morning meal. Now she had started the dough to rising and he had changed his plans.

A messenger had ridden up an hour ago advising Uncle Robert that Lord Sligo's physician had said it was safe for him to come and stay at Westport House. The servants who had taken ill were recovering isolated from the rest of the house and no new cases had developed. When Duffy had delivered the message, Uncle Robert had decided to leave but advised Duffy that he wished to speak with Meg before he checked out.

Once she had a bit of sweet and a good cup of tea, she would start kneading the dough for the fluffy, white breakfast rolls. Now that the dough was already rising, Meg had to go ahead and make the rolls. They would just have to enjoy them themselves come morning. Thus were the spoils of the fickle gentry.

She sat in the kitchen stirring the bronze liquid, waiting for it to cool. Meg knew that her uncle recognized her and she almost welcomed the moment when he would confront her about it. She had hoped he would leave without ever finding out but that was no longer possible. He had watched her and her children very closely as they served the noonday meal. When Mary Clare cleared his plate, Uncle Robert asked her name and she told him truthfully. Meg almost dropped a tray of lobster shells and dirty cutlery when she heard the sweet little voice say,

"Well, sir, I go by the name Mary Clare. Mary Clare Phalen, sir."

Now Meg wondered what he wanted to say to her as she sipped this rarest of luxuries, hot English tea. The steam rose from a tin cup, to be sure, but nonetheless bracing and delicious. She nibbled on a heel of yellowmeal bread slathered with sweet butter. Duffy had a fondness for the maize bread and with the shipments of American corn sent over since the hunger began, he had made it a staple of the inn. It was good, she thought, picking at the crumbs and waiting for Uncle Robert to summon her. As she relished the taste of the sweet bread and tea she marveled at how light her appetite was. She had lain in bed night after night, starving, thinking about the feasts she would eat when the hunger was over but now that she could eat, Meg really had very little desire for food.

It was like heaven going to bed without the gnawing pangs of hunger she had suffered before coming here to Browne's but it took very little to satisfy her appetite. Not so Tom and the children. They ate as if there were no tomorrow and Meg reveled in their appetites. They could never get enough and to be sure, there were only scraps to be had. But they had not gone to bed hungry since Duffy brought them here and the sight of their faces filling out again made Meg's eyes mist over in gratitude. Their bellies had lost that frightening bloated look and Meg thought their hair had begun to grow back. When she combed out the girls' hair in the morning it no longer came out in wads.

When the clock in the taproom struck nine, Meg was just finishing her third cup of tea. She had almost given up on her uncle when he suddenly appeared in the kitchen doorway. Gilchrist and Riordan had just checked out and the evil little man from Newport had vowed to Duffy that he would be reporting the terrible deficiencies of this alleged inn to Lord Lucan. Meg cared little what he said to Lord Lucan about Browne's. She knew as well as Duffy that his lordship had no interest in an inn belonging to a fellow landlord in another city. She suspected he had enough to do without worrying about his nasty little nephew's bed lunch.

Duffy had sent Rose upstairs to strip the bedding in room 11 on her way to bed. She had kissed Meg goodnight and promised to be up and ready for work early in the morning. Duffy ruffled Rose's hair, chuckling when she blushed. They heard the little bell ring at the reception desk and when Duffy shot Meg a glance, she knew it was her uncle checking out. She heard Duffy banging through the front door as he put her uncle's bags out on the stoop. She then heard him call out to McCrea's grandson to bring his lordship's horse around the front. Finally, Meg heard Duff's voice right outside the kitchen window as he oversaw the cleanup outside and hustled Denny and Jack to finish the job before he went down to St. Peter's to get Tom.

There was no sound from the taproom and Meg's heart skipped a beat as she thought for a second that Uncle Robert had forgotten about speaking to her and was just going to leave. She flushed as she felt a wave of both relief and disappointment wash over her.

"Hello, Meg."

Meg's eyes filled at the kindness in her beloved uncle's voice as he stood in the doorway leading into the taproom. She dared not look up and concentrated on a cluster of tea leaves in the bottom of her cup.

Finally, she faced him.

"Hello, Uncle Robert."

"I'm so glad to see you, dear. You have no idea how glad I am to see you. Your mother and I lost track of you right around Christmas."

"Mother? Mother has known where I was? How long?"

Meg was shocked that her mother even knew she was alive.

"Of course, Meg! Your mother has never stopped caring about you. She has had you under the watchful eye of Rev. Nangle since you first arrived on Achill Island. In fact she has donated generously to his mission on the north shore in exchange for steady reports on you over the years."

Meg sat in stunned silence. She had had no idea! When the impact of Uncle Robert's words finally hit her, Meg stood up, furious at the effrontery.

"She set spies upon me? Like a common brigand? How dare she presume to monitor my life in such a sneaky, underhanded manner? Using a man of God to do her dirty work! Does she know about her grandchildren? Does she spy on them too?"

Meg was distraught that the sanctity of their private life had been breached by her mother's stealth for the entire time she had thought herself mistress of her own household. She circled around and around the kitchen table opening and closing her fists inside her apron pockets.

"How could she do this to me? Does she have no decency at all to insinuate herself into my private life and never make herself known?"

"Meg, I, we... well, we thought it was a good thing, the best way..."

"You knew? Uncle Robert, how could you let her do this? You of all people! You know how my father hates my husband! How could you allow my mother to expose our whereabouts to him? He must be waiting like a spider to make his move! All those years! All those years thinking we were far enough away. All those years believing we were safe!"

"Meg! Listen to me! Your mother has never let on to your father a single word about you. She doesn't even live with him anymore. He has disinherited her and she has lived in Killarney with me for more than a decade."

She began to sway and he grabbed her shoulders.

"Here my dear, please let's sit. This is all too shocking, I fear. Here, have another cup of tea and we'll start at the beginning. I just wish Tom Phalen were still alive to hear it."

Meg started at this statement and had a sudden urge to laugh. Here they were dancing around the truth all these years and she was the last liar to speak.

"He's not dead, Uncle Robert. I simply said that to protect him from Mr. Gilchrist."

She sat down so hard she almost tipped the long bench. Uncle Robert took a tin cup from its hook and joined her.

"Look at me Meg."

Meg looked up to see her uncle gazing deeply into her eyes.

"I have always loved you and would never betray you. So I am asking you to listen very carefully to what I am about to say. I can see that you need to hear the whole story from the beginning."

Meg avoided Uncle Robert's eyes as she poured tea into his cup. Finally, she looked up at him. He was so much older than she remembered. His face had grown fuller over the years and his hair had taken on silver streaks around the temple. He had always been a nice-looking man, with kind gray eyes and a broad open face. He favored the Cushings and was much bigger and broader than her own father. She couldn't tell in what way he resembled her mother as her mother was always fairly petite and had the fair coloring of the highland Scots on Meg's grandmother's side of the family.

What she recognized was the kindness of his face. That had never changed despite the tiny wrinkles around his eyes and the thinning of his hair. He was her uncle, much loved and fondly remembered. Now he was about to defend her mother to her after over ten years of silence. Meg would be obliged to reconsider all the thoughts and emotions she had had toward her mother since she last laid eyes on her.

She knew Uncle Robert loved her mother and that he would speak up for her. But Meg had grown older and wiser too and when she had had enough and needed to speak her truth she would stop him and tell him about the beating she had endured and the weeks in confinement. Her mother had been dead to her all those weeks. Whatever her reasons, Lady Beverly had not been there when Meg woke sobbing in the night. She had not been there when Maureen and Mrs. Carrey had first pulled Meg to her feet breaking open the wicked welt across her shoulders. Where was her mother as they lowered her to her bed and the three of them wept at Meg's fresh pain and defeat?

Meg was very angry that the integrity of her world had been breached so furtively. At least the hunger, so devastating in its filthy death mongering, was something she and Tom could face head on. Whether they survived or succumbed they would do it themselves with their own wits and their own mettle. But this new demon threatened to undermine everything Meg had believed about her life since she and Tom arrived on Achill. This knowledge that for all of their lives, all of their coming and going on and off the island, they had been watched, well this was just too much to take.

As she took in all that was both familiar and unfathomable about this man sitting across from her Meg felt her world shift around her. She knew that whatever he had to say, however he said it, she and hers would never be the same. Whole parts of her screamed for him to shut his mouth against the words while other parts sensed that somehow whatever he was about to say would finally bring her some peace.

She took a deep breath and before she could change her mind, she nodded.

"Well, if you must, then begin."

Chapter Five

"Would ye be havin' a wee libation, there, Duff?"

Fr. Timon extended the decanter of port toward Duffy as he entered the priest's tiny parlor.

"No thanks, Father. I'm not much fer wine. I'm strictly a stout man, meself. And Tom? Is he about?"

"Suren' I jist saw him around back. He was about fixin' a fiddle string, I think."

Duffy sank into a faded old velvet couch, its goose down cushions threatening to envelop him.

"It went well, then, Father?"

"Sure, sure, no one was the wiser and ye know ye can trust Mrs. Murphy t'keep her counsel. Wasn't her husband clubbed stupid by the constable and her carin' fer him all those years 'til he died? How about yer end? Any trouble at the inn?"

"Well, yes and no, Father. Gilchrist left thinkin' Tom is dead, which is a good thing, 'tis. But Meg's uncle is the wiser. I left her waitin' fer him t'find her. That promises t'be a talk!"

"Well, maybe some good'll come of it. Ye niver know. Are ye sure ye won't imbibe?"

Duffy knew Fr. Timon was a lonely man and loved his

bottle. He also knew what a friendly man he was and how he hated to drink alone.

"Sure, Father. But only if ye have a bit o'whiskey."

With a pained expression, Fr. Timon poured a shot of the Jameson's the bishop had given him for Christmas. He and Tom had finished the bottle of cheap rye his brother had sent.

"Ye know I love ye like a son, Duff, but I do hate t'waste me good whiskey on a man who prefers stout."

Duffy smiled and extricated himself from the old couch.

"Ye'll just have to learn to take no for an answer."

Duffy lowered his lean frame onto a worn settee that creaked under his weight when he stretched his long legs out before him. There that was better. He'd have to remember not to sit on the couch.

Fr. Timon handed him the whiskey. He looked with fondness at his friend. He had been at St. Peter's for ten years and he had shared many an evening chat with Duffy McGee and counted him among his closest friends.

"Anything from yer cousin Tom, Duff?"

Duffy looked at the priest questioningly.

"Oh, ye mean D'Arcy! We niver called him by his first name. No, he's keepin' things pretty quiet. Last I saw him was Tuesday and he couldn't talk long. But he did say that some lemons would be arrivin' by the end of this week."

"Good, good. We need 'em if we're goin' t'make lemonade by the end o'the month. What about Tom Phalen, Duff? Is he in or out."

"Why d'ye ask, Father?"

"Well, he's been playin' his cards awfully close t'the vest. Last night there was somethin' between him and the missus. I was a bit under the weather so I couldn't quite make it out, ye see, not knowin' 'em so well, as it is. I couldn't tell if he was playin' along about the Gilchrist thing or if that was really the issue. I mean, his wife is English, saints preserve us!"

"I've known Tom Phalen for almost fifteen years and if ye can trust any man, ye can trust him. He probably wasn't sure if ye were involved yerself, Father. How would he know? If he was quiet, it was t'protect ye both."

Duffy filled Fr.Timon in on Tom's history a bit, but reserved any speculation on Tom's position in the Brotherhood. To be sure, he wasn't sure himself.

"I'll be findin' him and we'll talk. Thanks fer the whiskey."

"Ye better thank me fer the best whiskey in Ireland. Maybe ye can poach me a wee drap from yer excess stock?"

"Suren' ye can bring it when ye visit me in the jailhouse."

"Now Duff, ye know I'd niver really ask ye to do thieven'. I'd jist have t'listen t'ye carry on about it in the confessional anyway."

Duffy laughed and put on his cap.

"Are ye plannin' t'come later, then?"

"I haven't decided, Duff. Some o'the lads looked at me a bit funny at the last meetin' and I'm thinkin' they'd rather not have a man o'the cloth hangin' about. Any thoughts?"

"They should know ye, Father. Suren' some of'em aren't from around here but the local lads know ye're in fer the action and available fer 'confessions' anytime they feel they have somethin' they want ye t'hear. They know the value of yer confessional. There's no better place t'pass on the liberatin' words of salvation, so t'speak."

"Well, maybe I'll go. But if I don't, keep me posted, will ye, lad? I see meself playin' more of an unseen role in all this, providin' sanctuary and the like. Best I keep me collar clean and not raise any suspicions. Don't ye think?"

Duffy shrugged. "That I do. But niver think yer not a valued member o'the team. Good night t'ye Father." He turned and called into the pantry, thinking maybe the housekeeper was listening in.

"Peaceful sleep, Mrs. Murphy!"

Seeing no one there, he let himself out the back door to find Tom.

Tom was tuning his fiddle behind the turf pile in Fr. Timon's tiny back yard. Duffy could hear him gently plucking the worn strings as he tried to make the mended string fit in again with the others.

Tom looked up when Duffy came around the tall heap of black bricks.

"Sit?"

"Well, I was hopin' ye'd want t'walk with me."

"Sure. I could use a stretch o'the legs. Ye know I don't do well cooped up. Besides I've done as much as I can t'fix this poor old instrument."

They wandered down toward the quay in silence. Looking out over the bay, Duffy shielded his eyes from the huge redness of the setting sun.

Tall ships lined the harbor, their masts and rigging etched black against the deep red orb. The waves lapped gently beneath the piers and the cool silence of the evening was punctuated by the calls of gulls and gannets heading out to the islands for the night. A gentle breeze carried the pungent smell of wet wood and fresh fish. Trawlers and curraghs bumped against the piers, their swollen ropes groaning eerily.

Hoots of laughter erupted from a card game on the deck of The Marianna and one sailor loudly questioned the legitimacy of another's parentage. One of Marie's girls scurried along the pier, bearing a message to one of the tethered vessels.

After walking some distance in silence, Duffy stopped next to a wooden pile covered in gull droppings and barnacles.

"Meg told me ye talked."

"Aye, she knows."

"She seemed t'take it well."

"Like a soldier, that she did."

"Ah, Tom, yer a lucky man, that ye are."

"Don't I know it, Duff, don't I know it."

Neither of them spoke for a few minutes, each lost in his thoughts. The girl from Marie's was approaching and Duffy turned and casually moved down the pier to the next post.

"Tom, Fr. Timon was askin' if ye were with us or not."

"What did ye tell him?"

"Well, I figured ye need t'tell him yerself. But I did let him know I'd trust ye with me life. And I would, Tom. That I would."

"As fer me, ye know I've already put me life in yer hands, Duff. Meg and the children too. I should have confided in Fr. Timon last night. Meg wanted me to. But the man has a problem with the drink. I just wasn't sure. And what side o'the road does the housekeeper stand on?"

"Ye're right about the drink but his loyalty is sure. Mrs. Murphy? Her husband was clubbed silly fer standin' in the way of a rental agent once when the bastard tried t'take Mrs. Murphy's wedding band as collateral on a catch o'mackerel. Father thinks she can be trusted. I hope he's right."

Duffy rested his elbows on the pile, squinting against the setting sun.

"Tonight's th'meetin'. They want ye there."

"Aye. Late though, isn't it?"

"Eleven o'clock. I heard Mitchell himself is runnin' it. D'Arcy an'he are gettin' t'be pretty thick t'hear me cousin tell it."

Tom shook his head.

"D'Arcy's a bit of a hothead fer John Mitchell, don't ye think? I always thought he was a man more inclined t'stealth."

"D'Arcy thinks he's the second comin' fer sure. I hope Mitchell keeps a tight reinon him fer all our sakes. On a different note altogether, did ye know Meg's Uncle Robert is havin' a heart t'heart with her?

"Now? And me out here takin' the air with the likes o'you?"

"Go back if ye want. Ye probably should be there. I'll see ye later down at the smokehouse, Tom. Pier3. We go in together at ten forty sharp."

Tom left Duffy at the pier and crossed the empty quay to the inn. Pigeons scattered in a silver fan before him, turning back with flaming gold breasts reflecting the brilliant sky behind him. When he reached the blue doorway, he turned to catch the last of the magnificent orange glow. There silhouetted against the western sky stood his best friend, alone as he had always been, gazing out to sea.

Meg looked up to see Tom enter the taproom just moments after Uncle Robert galloped away. She poured herself a cup of cold tea as Tom came into the kitchen.

"Well, my friend, it's been a night to remember."

Meg looked up from her mug and motioned for Tom to sit down.

He straddled the bench across the table from Meg and looked at her seriously.

"Duff told me just now. Had I known I'd have been here."

"It doesn't matter, Tom. He's the same Uncle Robert. He just wants me to be happy and safe."

Meg thought better of telling him about Beverly's spies. Her uncle had explained her mother's reasoning and Meg had accepted her behavior if not her good intentions. Her mother was never a woman to trouble herself with a conscience, despite Uncle Robert's protests to the contrary.

"As you may expect, he wants us to come to Killarney. If not for our sake, for the children. He says he wants to give us back our life."

Tom held his head. He was too weary to explode in fury, which was what this deserved.

"I trust ye told him t'go t'hell."

"Of course not! Tom, he doesn't know what else to do for us. Uncle Robert loves me and has always wanted what is best for me. He has nothing against you or our marriage. He's supported my mother ever since my father's accident and wants to help us any way he can. You know how kind he was about the deed. Maureen owes him her freedom!"

At this Tom did erupt.

"Owes him her freedom? Maureen earned her freedom on her back at the end of yer father's riding crop! He gambled yer inheritance to win that deed. Nobody owes anybody anythin' fer that deed!"

"Tom! There's no need to get so upset! Uncle Robert is only trying to help us!

What will we do when the business at this inn falls off next week? We have nothing! Duffy is planning to leave sooner or later and then what?"

Tom put his head down on the back of his hands, muffling his reply.

"Meg, someone has to run this place even in the off-season. If Duff goes, Sligo will probably be happy to have us stay."

"Why? There are so many of us to feed. You have to know that Duffy has really put himself out on a limb with every mouthful we take."

Tom had had enough. The clock in the taproom struck nine and each chime reverberated in his head with a hard smack. He was not a man given to oaths but the thought of Meg's family interfering with their life after all they had been through galled him.

Springing from the bench he tore at his hair.

"Jumpin' God Meg! I jist can't git me head around what yer sayin'! Yer father almost kills ye, yer mother lets him lock ye away in yer room fer months while he's violatin' yer maid right down the hall and ye barely escape with yer lives. Tell me Meg, where was Uncle Robert then? Ye show up at me Da's house the two o'ye half dead and I'm about takin' ye wherever I can t'make ye safe. We start a life and do jist fine thanks t'me swallowin' me pride like a steamin' horseball and still no Uncle Robert! Where was he when Gilchrist tried t'break me?"

"Where was he when me prize red cow was bleatin' and cryin' across the strand, while we watched everything I worked fer go t'hell? Tell me Meg, where was Uncle Robert when ye were half crazed with hunger and grief, draggin' Thomas up the loft?"

He stormed around the kitchen, arms flailing, his big brogues stomping back and forth across the floor. He saw the table and chairs, hearth and stove in a haze of red fury but he couldn't look at her. He paced and circled and finally collapsed onto the bench again. His back to Meg, Tom continued his rant.

"Don't ye see, Meg? I'm the one takin' care o'ye! I'm the one ye chose all those years ago! It's too late fer Uncle Robert t'suddenly have a change o'heart, t'come around t'be yer savior. Ye want t'go with Uncle Robert? Ye think he'll do better by ye than I have? Well, jist try an'be a Catholic in his ivory tower. Jist try t'raise yer babes the way ye want with yer cold-fish mam meddlin' in yer face every day. Go ahead, Meg, take back yer old life. Take me sons and daughters from me and leave me t'die alone."

He turned and faced his wife.

"And I promise ye this: alone I'll die fer ye'll never see me darken yer Uncle Robert's door fer sure. Ye'll niver have t'worry about that me darlin'. If ye go, ye'll tear me heart right from me chest. Right out o'me chest! But I'll not come after ye, so save yerself the lookin' back."

When he saw Meg's face streaked with tears and filled with pain at his harsh words, he fought the urge to touch her.

Holding her head in her hands, she turned her face away from him and she sobbed out her anguish to the room.

"All I want is to be fed and clothed again, to be free of this mind-numbing, back-breaking work. Day in and day out we scrounge and dig, and beg and pillage! We eat garbage! Scraps that no decent person would want.Just to stay alive!"

Her sobs echoed off the pots and pans lining the whitewashed walls.

"I've lost everything! My home, the dairy, two of my babies. What more is there to lose? Pride? Pride?!"

Now her own anger burst to the surface. She felt the heat flush her cheeks as she balled her fists and pounded on the table. Grabbing the wooden bread board, she threw a fistful of flour down on the scrubbed surface. She tipped the big crockery bowl and turned out the dough. She punched the dough down hard, sending puffs of flour into her face and hair, causing her to cough and sputter.

"You speak of pride while your daughters feel the filthy hands of sailors on them and then are forced to empty the chamber pots filled with their disgusting waste! These are your little girls, Tom Phalen!"

Down slammed the dough onto the board. Still unable to look up at Tom's face, Meg rammed the heels of her hands into the dough, grabbed it with her fingers and slammed it down again. Over and over she worked the dough into a firm ball, pounding out her anger on its innocent expanse.

"How can you even think of your pride when they're reduced to the status of slaves in an effort to survive? And what about me, Tom? Here I am half-starved, hardly over having Patrick and burying him and I'm dragged from my home plopped on a boat so I can work like a stevedore from dawn till dusk feeding this endless horde of hungry men pouring in and out of this inn. I hurt everywhere, my ankles are perpetually swollen, my legs still have sores on them left over from nearly starving to death and my hair still hasn't grown back in some places and maybe never will!"

On and on Meg pounded and flipped the dough until with no strength left in her arms, she collapsed into it, her forearms resting on the smooth white circle.

 Her shoulders heaved as she sobbed out her misery to the silent blob of unbaked bread.

Finally Meg raised her face to see Tom's face riddled with pain.

"I just want to be clean and fed like a normal woman. I don't want much, just a pillow and a counterpane, a few soft things around me and the sight of my children with full rosy cheeks, dressed in clothes that fit them, frolicking and playing as children should. I know we had it once. Now we have a chance to have it again. But no, Tom you have your pride! You have your dignity! You have your Irish name to defend!"

Tom's face went from ashen to crimson.

"So, pride is it? This is about pride? Am I sich an ass as t'think this was about love? About faithfulness and loyalty? This mornin' at the church. Was all that so much pallaver?

How can I trust ye t'stand by me now? How can I believe all ye said standin' in me arms before the altar o'God himself, when yer ready t'sell us all down the river for white bread? Meg, ye can't have it both ways! I'm in fer a penny, in fer a pound here, Meg!"

Tom leaned over the table thumping his thumb against his worn leather vest.

"Look at me! If ye breathe even a hair o'this t'yer uncle, I'm a dead man and Duffy and the brothers with me. Ye'll be cryin' out t'me over the prison wall as they take me t'the gallows and that's th'truth! Will yer Uncle Robert come fer me then? Meg ye must tell me now. Me life depends on it. Have ye betrayed me with yer uncle? Have ye let on, Meg? Do I need t'tell the brothers that they were right t'suspect ye? God above, I'll be lucky if one o'them doesn't get t'me before the English do!"

Meg was on her feet, her face pinched with rage.

"No! Tom! How can you even say that? How can you even think I'd betray you? I meant everything I said this morning and you know it! The very words out of your mouth are a betrayal! I have never given you anything but love and you have absolutely no right or reason to question my loyalty. All I did was listen to Uncle Robert and, truth be told, what he had to offer was better than anything I've had in years! We're dying on the vine here, Tom! Yes, Duffy has kept us going these last few weeks but we're not out of the woods yet and from where I stand we have no future. Go to your meeting. Be a hero! You'll get no objection from me. I made my vows to you Tom and I have no intention of breaking them. But know this: If I ever hear words like the ones that just came out of your mouth, you'll be hard pressed to earn my trust again! Think about that, Tom! We've always been in this together but it's a two way street. If you can't trust me then don't but don't expect me to trust you either."

Tom stood across the table from his wife, rigid as death and just as white. His face searched Meg's, a mask of confusion and pain, beseeching her to convince him this wasn't happening. Finally he shrugged and turned away from her.

"So. I'll be off t'see what Duffy's up to. I'll leave ye t'sort out yer thoughts on the matter."

With that he picked up his cap and went out through the taproom almost knocking Denny over in his haste.

Meg sat motionless at the long table until the sound of dripping brought into focus the amber pool of tea washing across the pale scrubbed sycamore. She had spilled her entire cup of tea and sent the tin cup pinging against the flagstone floor. Stunned into stillness by Tom's outburst and her own furious response, she simply sat and watched the stream of cold tea find its way to the table's edge and dribble down onto the floor.

Meg's tears burned in two steady paths down her cheeks and she made no attempt to stop them. Exhaustion so profound had taken hold of her she could not move. She didn't care if she never left this spot, if they found her sitting in rigor mortis the next morning, the pool of tea at her feet.

She tried to digest Tom's words and found her mind unable to do so. Uncle Robert had been so kind, so caring she thought they would finally be safe. She couldn't believe Tom had been so angry. He basically threatened to dissolve the family if she tried to take her uncle's offer.

Meg dragged the long handled pan onto the table and sat down. Her fingers throbbed as she started tearing balls of dough from the mound in front of her and began making rolls. The repetitious task calmed her. By the time she had finished with the first pan, she had stopped crying and her ragged breaths had quieted. As the clock struck ten, she pulled the last of the rolls out of the oven and began to clean up the mess.

She draped the cheesecloth over the still warm rolls and took a candle from the shelf. Completely empty, Meg took what little strength she had and climbed up to the third floor to go to bed.

Denny watched his father storm out the front door of the inn and hastened to follow him. He knew Da hadn't seen him when he slammed through the taproom and Denny didn't want him to see him now. He ran out the door and stealthily crept along the quay darting from doorway to doorway seeking out any shadowy spot along the way. Denny needed to know where Da was going. He knew there was a meeting tonight at the smokehouse and he wanted badly to be there. If Da was going to be there, he must stand with him. He must show Da how proud he was to be Irish and how being half English meant nothing to him.

Andrew told Denny he wasn't invited; he was too young. Denny knew he wasn't too young to go. He was a man now. Hadn't he heard the plans for the gun drop and actually seen the great John Mitchell only a few feet away? And hadn't he done it all without being seen? Denny knew he was a better fighter than Andrew. After all, hadn't he done all that without Andrew by his side whispering at him every step of the way?

If his da was going to that meeting, he was going too. But he had to be sure Da didn't see him until it was too late to do anything about it. Even if Da flayed him alive for going it would be worth it. This was his chance to make Da proud. He hoped once Da saw him there he'd understand.

Denny was furious at his mam. He had squatted behind the bar the whole time Uncle Robert was in the kitchen and he heard the whole thing. At first he had been afraid when Da had started yelling at Mam. Now he was glad Da had said what he did. His da deserved to be angry. Divil take Uncle Robert and all the English with him! If Mam wanted to go back to her fancy life, then fine. He'd never go back! Let the girls go all prissy and fuss with their hair and lacy dresses. He'd stay with Da. Together they would be freedom fighters for Ireland. Together they would take over the Brotherhood and lead the brothers to victory.

He just had to be at that meeting! He knew Da would be

so proud of him once he saw how brave he was.

Denny hid behind a large pile of barrels and lobster traps. He could see Da and Mr. McGee in the distance, strolling the docks. They weren't together and they acted like they didn't even know the other was there but Denny knew they were waiting for the Brothers to arrive. One by one men approached the abandoned fishery. Denny crouched behind the traps watching intently in the dim light of the few lanterns hung along the docks. The tall ships that were anchored here and there along the bay rocked gently, the inky black water slapping quietly against their hulls.

Sailors settled in for the night marking the quiet with an occasional call or curse. The crew of The Marianna had broken up their card game and one or two drunken revelers weaved their way toward Marie's to spend their winnings or find a pair of soft arms to comfort their loss.

Denny marveled at the way the Brothers found their way to the smokehouse undetected. He had a perfect view along the dock and saw the lantern lit outside the smokehouse without ever seeing anyone approach it. How did someone get inside without him seeing? And how did the brother hang the lantern outside the door without bathing himself in the light of it?

Denny was amazed to see the lantern light now coming from inside the shack. The light outside had shown the Brothers that it was safe to approach. Now that it was inside, they knew that someone was in there waiting for them to safely arrive. Andrew had told Denny about these little signals. The code of conduct for the Brotherhood was full of signs like the placement of a lantern and the order of approach.

At the end of every meeting, each man put his hat in a sack. The scout for that meeting would draw the caps out of the sack one by one. The owner of the last cap to come out was the scout for the next meeting. Then they would go through the names of each one present to review the order of arrival, the direction of approach and the time each one was due to arrive. This pattern stayed the same for every meeting beginning with the scout and rotating from there. Denny had been confused about this and Andrew had explained it.

Andrew told him that for example if Brother B was the scout then all the Brothers starting with C would follow the plan in the order they had learned. The last one to arrive would be A. Then if the next time brother D was scout, the order would start with E and end with C. When C finally arrived, they would do a head count and lock the door. That way any brother who couldn't come was identified. For his part, a brother who was not able to come in the right order or at the right time was forbidden to come at all. Each brother had another brother assigned to him as protector. Later, the missing brother's protector would be responsible for finding out what happened to make the brother miss the meeting.

Denny found it all very confusing but Andrew said that was because he was too young to understand. When he saw a black cloud pass over Denny's face at this, Andrew did confide to Denny that that was the reason why the leaders wanted to keep the group small. It was too dangerous to have too many men working in this secret way. There were too many ways it could get mixed up. It was also too easy to be found out.

Denny understood this and it did make it easier to accept being excluded. Besides, Andrew had clapped him on the shoulder like a real man after he saw how disappointed he had been.

From behind the traps, Denny watched as the system unfolded before his eyes. When the lantern was put out it meant that the first man had arrived as planned. It was a great honor and a great risk to be scout. It was a chance to prove a brother's bravery and trustworthiness. If the scout failed to follow the order absolutely, he put his brothers at grave risk.

Denny knew as he waited that the docks were dotted with brothers either waiting near or approaching a hiding place on the way to the smokehouse. For their protection, the sequence was always the same. The men would see the sign from a distance and the light told the brothers that it would soon be time to approach. There would be a ten-minute wait and then if all was clear, the lantern would be taken in.

Once the lantern was taken in and set in the tiny smokehouse window, they could approach one by one. Each brother had his assigned route, order and time of arrival. The scout was responsible for absolute accuracy and adherence to the orders.

Each man had a pocket watch and at the end of every meeting they were all set exactly for the same time. When the start time for the meeting arrived, the lantern was moved into the center of the room and hung on the big hook suspended from the ceiling. The man who had been scout was now assigned to guard the door against intruders.

If a man arrived after his assigned arrival time he was not to approach the smokehouse. He would be disciplined later for arriving late. If any man was seen approaching the smokehouse after the lantern was taken out of the window, he risked being mistaken for a constable. The light would be doused and the brothers instructed to prepare for armed resistance.

Each brother knew that to disobey the orders set up by the leaders was to risk the life of every member of the Brotherhood. They also knew that they would risk being marked for execution as a traitor to the cause and hunted down in their beds by their very own brothers. No matter what any individual thought about the order of arrival, the importance of the meeting or the fate of the scout, if the light stayed outdoors after the ten minutes, the men had strict orders to disburse and the meeting was called off until the leaders spoke.

When Andrew told Denny these things, one night on the strand back home, Denny had shivered with the seriousness of it all. He knew The Blackthorn brothers were heroes. He also knew that the rules must be obeyed for the sake of the whole movement. His greatest fear was that somehow he would be found at fault for some mistake, causing his beloved brothers to die or be imprisoned. He had lain awake for hours that night, staring into the sweep of the Milky Way as Andrew snored softly next to him on the cool sand. He wished on the North Star that he would be worthy of becoming a brother someday and felt his face flush with shame at the queasiness that thought brought to his stomach.

Denny knew the weakness of his stomach was because of his English blood. Andrew had said that the English were bloody cowards and not one deserved to live. Denny knew that he could never hurt Mam or any of his sisters and he certainly would never want to lose his only other brother. Francis was a great little boyo even if he was still a baby crying for his porridge!

Now, here Denny was, breathlessly waiting for the plan to unfold. He knew he had not been invited to this meeting. He didn't know what Da and Mr. McGee were doing here but he wanted to be with them.

Did not being invited mean the same as being forbidden to attend? Denny wasn't sure. Andrew had never said. Besides, D'Arcy McGee had been so nice to him he was sure that no one would be angry if he showed up. He didn't know where he was in the order, though. Should he just wait until they all arrived and then slip into the smokehouse? Should he just step up behind Da and Mr. McGee when they went in? Maybe he could duck under the windowsill like he did the other night. Denny thought about that but really didn't like that idea. After all, how was he going to prove he could be a real brother by hiding in the shadows like a scared girl?

As Denny watched from his hiding place, the men slipped like eels along the abandoned buildings lining the wharf. One by one they ducked into the smokehouse unseen. Denny knew they were arriving only by the sight of their shadows crossing the narrow sliver of light thrown by the opening of the door. No one could see the entrance to the smokehouse from the water or the quay. Denny had the only clear vantage point and thrilled at the sight as one silhouette after another crossed the little finger of light and was swallowed whole by the shadowy cavern of the little shack.

Two of those figures must have been Da and Mr. McGee but he couldn't tell. Before he knew it, the light was out of the window and only a dancing glimmer showed as the lantern swung from the hook in the center of the room.

With a thud his heart landed in his stomach as he realized that he had missed his opportunity to sneak into the meeting with Da. He knew the door was locked now and he couldn't go in. Now, how was he going to prove his bravery to Da and the brothers? With a sigh he slumped down behind the lobster traps and tried to figure out a way get closer to the window so he could at least listen to the grand plans of Ireland's brave sons and brothers. He was so busy feeling sorry for himself he failed to notice a shadowy figure slipping between the crates and traps and the long crumbling wall of the old fishery. Without warning, a cold, hard hand grabbed his shoulder while another clamped across his mouth.

Meg rounded the bend at the top of the narrow stairs leading to the Phalen's quarters at the top of Browne's Inn. The third floor was narrower than the second and first but there were four comfortable bedrooms. Francis and Denny shared a narrow room tucked under the eaves on the bay side of the inn at the head of the stairs. Rose and Mary Clare were at the back of the inn next to Tom and Meg in another little room that mirrored Francis and Denny's. While the small rooms had only tiny square windows, each larger room had two gables with tall narrow windows overlooking the bay in the front and the sloping hill going up to the Louisburg Road in the rear. Tom and Meg had the large room overlooking the alley behind the inn on the Louisburg Road side. Meg had put Gracie, Ellen and Martha across the hall in the large room overlooking the quay.

Tonight the alley was eerily quiet. Meg was relieved. After

the meeting of all the landlords and her distressing conversation with her uncle, Meg had hoped to spend a little time just catching up with Tom. Their argument was so upsetting to her she wondered how she would settle down. Her body was exhausted but her mind still echoed with the harsh words Tom had spewed at her and she was still shocked at the cruel things that had come out of her own mouth. Her words raced around her head and panic filled her chest when she thought Tom might believe her.

They were not a couple to fight like that and tonight's was the worst argument they had ever had. She could not believe the things they had said to each other. And to think that they had been so close this morning and had pledged their love so sweetly. Why, the Host of Holy Communion had just crossed their tongues but to hear them just now, a stranger would think they hated each other! Shame and remorse washed over her and she wanted nothing more than to take Tom in her arms and beg his forgiveness.

Meg looked out the window as she pulled the shutters closed. They could see the livery stable from their room and often heard McRea bellowing in his thick Scots brogue at the hapless grandsons he employed as stable hands. Tom never ceased to be amused at the antics of the three brothers. If they even knew which end of the horse was the front he would be surprised. They had trouble enough knowing the business end of a broom. Tonight, all was quiet. Even McRea was in for the night.

She began to undress. As she shrugged off her stained skirt and sweat dampened blouse Meg tried in vain to shed the horror of the evening. She noted the cool water in the ewer and blessed Mary Clare's sweet tender heart. There was no doubt she was the one who had made sure her mam had a way to refresh herself before bed. Rose was her workhorse, getting all four little ones to bed every night but Mary Clare was the one who took care of Meg, quietly nurturing her, leaving her bouquets of wildflowers, trimming a candle for her to carry to bed, making sure she had fresh water and towels snatched from the massive linen closet.

Meg sponged her face with the cool water and patted it dry with the thick Turkish towel Mary Clare had left on the commode. Until tonight's episode, she had been pleased that Tom had relaxed somewhat now that his family was eating better and regaining some of their former wellness. The work was very hard but they were used to hard work from working the dairy. The children had had some difficulty adjusting but they were glad enough when they had a plate of colcannon or a slice of fresh baked Spotted Dick and butter in front of them.

Tom was much more in his element bending his back to the task than he ever was overseeing others and he was teaching Denny how to do so many things. She actually thought maybe Denny was softening a bit as she watched him working by his father's side. With a sudden wave of tenderness for her first-born son, Meg thought she'd look in on him before she went to bed. He was very prickly about her doing that but she needed to check on Francis anyway.

As she sponged the fresh water over a small burn on her forearm, Meg let out a sigh. She knew it hurt Tom to see her bowing and yielding to the whims of the gentry, working in the kitchen lifting the heavy pots and kettles, scrubbing and cleaning until her knuckles bled. She had thought it bothered Tom more than it bothered her until her conversation with Uncle Robert. She was so grateful to see her little ones fed. Until he had offered her a way out she would have done anything to keep it that way.

Some of the guests were revolting, preening and sashaying around, delighting in the humble awkwardness of Tom and his family but Meg had convinced herself she didn't care. Tom on the other hand, fumed and burned with shame. It mattered not at all that Uncle Robert would never treat anyone with unkindness or disrespect. Tom couldn't separate him from those who would spit upon her and the children. What seemed to Meg a most reasonable invitation was an insult to Tom's way of thinking. But then, again, hadn't she been angry when Uncle Robert had first suggested it? And Meg had to admit that she still wasn't convinced it was a good idea to move in with her uncle and her mother after all these years.

When they had lived on the strand, they had had very little to do with anyone from Meg's background. This had been a welcome relief for both Meg and Tom. While Maureen had lived with them, Meg had enjoyed a life not unlike the one she had left behind. There were many struggles, to be sure, but she still had a servant and despite the lack of luxuries she had enjoyed at GlynMor, she still had pretty things around her. They had been very comfortable and life had been richer for her than it ever had been in her father's house.

The times when Tom had to go to Newport were difficult reminders of the wide chasm between their old world and their everyday life but more for Tom than Meg. When he returned, Tom's mood was always dark but after a few weeks, the busy routine of their life soothed him and things returned to normal. Life continued in its lovely rhythm until the next trip brought with it fresh humiliation.

Those days were filled with chores, babies and building their business. It seemed they never stopped looking ahead and planning, dreaming and growing. Maureen had been a big part of their life and had done so much work. Not only was she a tremendous help to Meg with the house and the children, but after the first few weeks of dairying, Tom had turned the milking over to Maureen. He knew no self-respecting man would milk his own cows. That was women's work and Maureen was more than willing to do it. He had just needed to prove to himself that he was able to shift from the stable to the byre. Once he mastered the art of milking, he let Maureen deal with the cranky red cow and concentrated on running the farm.

Maureen had taught Meg to milk and eventually convinced Tom that he needed to hire a couple of local girls to take up the work. Life had taken on a sweetness punctuated by the traditional seasonal festivals, visits from

Duffy and the arrival of new babies in their own family and in the village.

Every Sunday they walked over the mountain to church and Meg had grown in her faith. Evenings were spent around the hearth as Tom fiddled and Maureen sang the beautiful lilting melodies of the ancients. Duffy rowed over regularly with his squeezebox and lent his beautiful tenor to harmonize with Maureen's sweet contralto. Occasionally neighbors would happen by and join them for a rousing sing-a-long on the strand. Tom and Meg had never talked about the world they had left behind. Life was good and they were happy. Neither of them wanted to look back.

When Maureen left, things had changed dramatically for Meg. Not only did she have many more babies, she was forced to shoulder much more work. Tom's business was thriving so Meg was able to hire both boys and girls to help with the gardening but everything else fell to her. There were long lonely stretches when Meg wouldn't have a woman to talk to for weeks. Few village women had accepted her and Meg would not force them. Were it not for Peg Sweeney and Mary Feeney she would have lost her mind on the vast windswept strand.

Another woman Meg had relied on for company was sweet old Leona Trent. The minister's wife had taken a shine to Meg right from the start and the day Tom was washed ashore, Mrs. Trent had wanted to completely take her under her wing. This alliance only hurt Meg's chances of growing closer to the other village women and at first she discouraged it. But the reverend's wife brought a refinement to the village that none of the other women questioned the way they questioned Meg. Without Maureen to keep her company, Meg had begun to see Leona Trent at least once a month. Every time she was seen taking tea at the rectory or someone spotted Mrs. Trent's buggy heading out toward Phalen's house, tongues started wagging and the gulf widened between the two worlds. Rev. Trent's death and the hunger put a stop to the visits but the lovely Widow Trent remained a staunch friend even after Meg converted to Tom's faith.

What helped Meg to survive the loneliness of her existence became a scourge for Tom. Wives hissed their gossip to husbands and husbands took the rumors with them to the pub where Tom sought his own friendships. There was always a tension between the life Tom lived as Meg's husband and the life he was trying to hang onto; the life he had lived with his da. Meg didn't want to look back. She was glad to leave the tight unpleasant existence of her parent's house behind. Tom sorely missed his old life. He longed for the world where hard work was rewarded at the end of the day by a tall cool draft at McPhinney's pub with Da and good, simple men who respected him, men just like him.

Coming to the inn had brought those two worlds together again in the most humiliating way. On the island, Tom needed to face the falsehood of their independence only twice a year when the rents were due; here every moment of every day was filled with the glaring truth of their dependency on the rich for their survival. Tonight's outburst made it clear that Tom's pride was deeply hurt by his inability to provide his family with the very least. What had started on the strand the day Gilchrist had taken Tom's cows had ended here in this place where his family lived on the charity of Lord Sligo surreptitiously through Duffy McGee.

When Meg was finished bathing with the lemon verbena soap, also stolen from the linen closet, she scrubbed her clothing and the two little dresses her girls had left for her to launder. She reached up to the rope strung across the room and took down the outfits she had washed the night before. As she hung the damp laundry to dry, Meg thought that Denny's work clothes would really need a bath after cooking lobster all day and scowled that he had failed to leave them for her to wash as he had been told.

Meg went across the hall to the boy's room and gently pushed the door open. There was no chance of waking Francis, he could sleep through a thunderstorm but Denny was a light sleeper. Meg had heard him walking around in the night ever since they had arrived here. She had meant to talk to him about it but their days had been so full she hadn't had the chance.

Even during the day the room was dark but at night Meg could hardly make out the tester bed beneath the sloping ceiling. She thought of returning for her candle but she was so tired she couldn't bear to take one unnecessary step. Francis was stretched out on the near side of the bed. The room was stifling and his face was damp when she kissed him. She groped on the floor for Denny's discarded clothes but couldn't find them.

Finally giving up she left the room without reaching across Francis to his brother's place by the wall. It had been a long time since Denny had allowed her to kiss him goodnight and she knew he would sit up and snap at her if she woke him. The thought of his rejection cast a pall over her heart, already heavy after her argument with Tom.

Exhausted, her feet sore and tender, Meg hobbled across the dark corridor to the room where Rose and Mary Clare slept. This room too was very warm and she felt a pang of remorse that she had not been available to plait the thick masses of curls that lay like blankets across their backs. How many of the small things she had taken for granted when life was free of the threat of starvation! How deep her sorrow was that she didn't even have time for her little ones, forcing Rose to assume tasks beyond her youth and losing the precious moments she had so lovingly enjoyed.

Meg turned to the corridor and crossed over to the front of the house. Her little girls were all sound asleep. Ellen and Gracie snoring softly, entwined like a pair of twins on the thin mattress. Martha slept, as usual curled up in the furthest corner of the bed, fitting her little behind into the juncture of two walls.

Meg knew the wall was probably cool against her back. Martha was a very smart baby and had survival instincts that defied her lack of time on this earth. No matter what the situation, Martha seemed to know just how to make the best of things. Meg marveled at this little grown–up baby.

Of all Meg's children, she worried the least about Martha. This was one to be reckoned with, one who would always take care of herself. There was a strength about her coupled with an indomitable optimism that had Meg shaking her head at Martha most of the time. Neither hunger nor displacement, the loudness of the taproom nor the never-ending bustle around her phased her one bit. She seemed to thrive on chaos. Indeed, Martha always had a smile, loved even the homeliest stranger and played jokes way beyond her years. Meg smiled in the dark just thinking of how her siblings howled with laughter at Martha's antics. Her sunny disposition and big smile had been a bright spot on many a grim day both at home and here at the inn.

Finally, she headed back to the room she shared with Tom, hoping to find him there. The room was empty and her heart was suddenly deeply saddened. Meg always felt terribly burdened whenever she and Tom had a major disagreement. They were such good friends that anger between them caused terrible heartache. How she wished he had been sitting on the bed when she opened the door.

Instead, he had chosen to stay away, probably hoping she would be asleep when he returned. Meg didn't even dare think about the fact that he may be, at this very moment, planning some rebellion with the Blackthorn Brotherhood. She opened the shutters to let in some air and lay down on top of the bed, naked in the dark room. It was so warm she really didn't want to cover herself just yet.

Uninvited, as always, grief overcame her as she lay alone in their room. Her thoughts about GlynMor, her conversation with Uncle Robert, her argument with Tom, her fears about Denny all combined to slam against her chest like a boulder. And as always, whenever she felt overwhelmed by fatigue or hunger or loneliness, her thoughts turned to Thomas.

Thomas was home to her. Even the familiar memories of Achill and their house on the strand were incomplete since Thomas died. For her grief to be complete, she must relive the night she lost Thomas. Not that she needed to envision the indelible image of his face as he looked at her for the last time. She only needed to recall the touch of his hand on her cheek and it all came back. Nothing made her long for her home on the island like memories of Thomas. He was Meg's home. His death was the end of everything fine and the beginning of everything impossible.

With Thomas really was where Meg lived. What she had been doing since they buried him that cold December morning was not living. Since that day when she had almost let the fire die in her hearth, Meg had been nothing more than a palimpsest, like her name erased from a chalkboard, a faint shadow of herself. When grief washed over her as it did this night, Meg welcomed it. It made her realize that she was alive, that she survived somehow, the wreckage of her broken heart. Lying naked on her bed, Meg allowed the gentlest waft of breeze to caress her in her soreness.

She lay perfectly still, feeling no part of her in particular but every part of her as a whole. She hurt inside and out. The aches wrought by hard work and the throbbing of her feet from long hours of standing became for Meg the truth of her existence. Without the sensations of pinching nerves and painfully relaxing muscles, Meg would have had no way to define her sorrow. She was glad for the pain. She needed it. As long as Meg could feel the physical pain of her body she could somehow find a place to deposit the pain of her soul.

It was so odd to her that it was this way. She had never known comfort since Thomas died. Truly, comfort as she remembered it had left her life long before that black day, but the moment she handed his little body over the loft railing into the arms of Fr. O'Boyle, it had left her forever. The pain of starvation had blinded her to her grief. The desperate scrabbling for food and the burden of her pregnancy with Patrick had consumed her. But all she endured trying to stay and keep her family alive had only numbed her to her grief. The grinding pangs of hunger had simply trumped the constant gnawing of her loss.

It wasn't until the one was relieved that the other was able to reclaim its position in her mind and heart. She was no longer hungry. Tired and sore, yes, but that was nothing more than the effect of hard work. The vengeance with which her grief returned once she and her family were plucked from the brink of the abyss astonished Meg. Moreover the intense physicality of her grief was a remarkable puzzle to her. What was it about losing Thomas that invaded her sinews and stretched her entrails inside her belly? What caused a fog to settle on her mind and blot out the next thing she intended to do? Why was she so indecisive, so unable to feel her own skin wrapping her in its safe integrity?

As Meg lay in the darkness, allowing the warm moisture of the summer evening wash over her, she began to sense the separate, individual parts of her body. Her own body had become such a stranger to her over these last several years that she never ceased to be startled to see it. Now she couldn't see it, she could only feel it.

The breeze caressed her like a lover and the dampness chilled her. She felt her breasts tighten and her thighs ripple with gooseflesh. Up and down her arms the tiny blonde hairs stood on end as the shabby lace curtain billowed into the room. No one was there yet Meg felt a thousand sighs of the dead on the sea breeze. Nothing moved but the curtain yet she felt the long slender fingers of the stolen ones probing her flesh, seeking their way home.

Thomas came to her on that breeze. Thomas and Patrick, the wee one she had never known but loved still. They came for her on that breeze, their soundless cries matching her own, caught in the depth of her throat. They wanted their mam. They wanted the milk from her tingling breasts, the warmth of her living arms. For the first time since she sat before her dying fire with Thomas in her arms, she felt her womb ache. Instinctively she cradled her belly. Her arms wrapped tightly around her.

She began to rock herself back and forth, crying, still with no sound. Her face stretched taut around her mouth, as wide open as Lizzie Ballard's, frozen in death. Meg thought her lips would crack with the stretch of it. Still no sound came from her throat. Meg could not cry. She could not find the right sound to relieve the choking grief caught in her throat. There was no sound to release it. She didn't know what sound to make so she made no sound at all. Meg could only rock the babies no longer in her womb. She rocked and rocked trying vainly to soothe their silent cries.

Thunder clapped in the sky somewhere beyond Louisburg and Meg was startled out of her cold, rhythmic comfort. Surprised to feel her cheeks wet with tears, she sat up and wiped her face. Her throat relaxed and she felt bone-deadening heaviness in her limbs. The breeze had turned to wind and the thunder threatened again but no rains came. Like a fine dust, peace settled over her and she slipped her chilly body beneath the covers.

Her thoughts quieted and began to order themselves, returning again to Thomas. Thomas, her sweet lamb, was buried under the mound in St. Dymphna's. Thinking of St. Dymphna's brought the smell of incense and melting beeswax into the room. It was there she had taken her first Holy Communion and sealed the fate of her family forever, leaving the church of her childhood and losing the main source of food they had known since they lost the cows.

Meg had no regrets about leaving the church of Ireland and finally taking up the faith of her husband. Her conversion had taken years and being spurned from the soup line at St. Mary's was a penalty that had made her hesitate to take the final step. But a power greater than hunger had drawn her to the altar at St. Dymphna's on Christmas morning and she had never looked back.

That power was the power of the womb, the power to give life itself. She had known that power the moment Thomas left this world for the next and Patrick had reached out from her to greet his fleeting spirit. It was the power of life, the power of the God who gives it. And didn't God provide them with a much better life than they could have had if she had stayed where she was and they had continued to eat thin turnip soup?

Meg felt her eyelids grow heavy as she succumbed to sleep. She slipped into that deep velvet place between here and gone and she smelled roses on the breeze. Her thoughts turned to home, and her father's gardens.

When she was a child, her bedroom window overlooked her father's rose garden and on cool summer mornings when he was supervising the pruning and feeding of his prize roses she would listen from her window seat as he held up one beautiful blossom after another proclaiming it that year's Rose of Clydagh Glyn.

When her father left the garden, Graber the head gardener, used to wave the cut roses up to her in the window and call out,

"Now, there she is, the real Rose of Clydagh Glyn!"

Lying under the thin coverlet, in the third floor servant quarters of Browne's Inn in Westport, County Mayo, without even a nightgown to call her own, Meg hardly felt like the Rose of Clydagh Glyn. But she dozed off with a weary smile on her face at the thought that somewhere beyond the stars, an old gardener thought she was that lovely a child to behold.

Chapter Six

Beverly looked up from her needlework in astonishment.

"What did you say?"

Robert handed her a glass of sherry and turned to pour himself a strong neat double Jameson's. He had spent a few days at his friend Sligo's and took a slow ride home, knowing Beverly would be gone to the Wexford fair for the week. He was most anxious to tell his sister all about Meg and her family but he had had to wait till she and Reina arrived home on Sunday. She had arrived while he was at church and they now waited to be called to dinner.

"I said I saw Meg and the children and they're dying of hunger."

"Robert! When? How?"

Beverly was on her feet, the needlework tossed onto the chaise behind her. She blinked in the bright afternoon sun pouring through the drawing room windows. Turning away from the windows, she felt the intense warmth on her back. She took a large sip of sherry matching the heat on her back with a deep familiar burning in her throat. Momentarily comforted, she listened to Robert's answer.

"At Browne's. They're living there and working for their keep. But Beverly, I didn't know her! She was paper-thin and some of her hair has fallen out! Her gorgeous curls! The only way I even suspected it was Meg, was by her eyes. They were sunk deep into her face but the same green, clear as ever."

Beverly's warm comfort left her as she gasped at his words.

"Oh Robert! How I would like to get my hands on that filthy stable hand! To let my daughter suffer like that. What about the children? How humiliating to have all those landlords viewing my grandchildren in such straits. Oh, sweet heavens, how will I ever be able to hold my head up?"

"Not to worry. No one knew they were my relations. The children are ragamuffins. The little ones were dressed in little shifts made of some cast-off rags. The older ones were in cast-offs too, livery from George's wife."

"Sligo? Oh, Robert! The shame of it! To think that that man's father once wanted to marry me and now his daughter-in-law is covering the naked children of my daughter. Robert this is too much to bear! How about Rev. Nangle? Did you see him?"

Beverly drained her sherry and went over to the mahogany sideboard that served as a bar.

"No, he wasn't there. Things on the island are terrible by all reports. They have been very hard hit and have lost a huge percentage of their population. Rev. Nangle sent a report that was read at the meeting saying he is completely overwhelmed."

"Did you talk to Meg?"

"Yes. At first she tried to lie her way out of it. I told her I thought I knew her but she gave me a false name. Then one of the girls let the cat out of the bag when I asked her for her name. Mary Clare it was. A sweet little thing. When the rest of the guests had left, I stayed behind and confronted Meg in the kitchen."

Beverly refilled the cut Waterford crystal glass, oblivious to the rainbow that it threw across the front of her pink silk skirt. She sat back down on the chaise and waited for Robert to continue.

"Meg surprised me, Beverly. I had no idea how much she

really enjoyed living on that God forsaken island with Tom Phalen. She's changed a great deal. She seemed to be in no hurry to come home. In fact she was quite angry."

"Angry? About what?"

"Well, she was very vocal about you, actually. She seemed very bitter that you had never shown her real mothering and that you never stood up to Jeffrey on her behalf. I tried to tell her that you were as much a victim of Jeffrey's cruelty as she was but she wouldn't accept it. When I told her that she was mistaken, that you had always cared, had even kept an eye on her through Rev. Nangle, she exploded! Imagine Beverly, at me! When did I ever deserve that?"

"So, she is not only a fool but she's an ungrateful fool. You'd think she would have been pleased to know that I cared about her enough to follow her life. Did you tell her about the donations?"

"Yes, I told her that you had been very generous to Rev. Nangle's mission in exchange for information about her and her family."

"What did she say to that?"

"She accused you of spying on her!"

"Why that bastard has her brainwashed, Robert! He has her convinced that we have nothing better to do than follow them around prying into their private lives! Doesn't she realize that if I wanted to I could have intervened at any time and had her children, my grandchildren, removed from that home? Doesn't she realize that once Tom Phalen failed to provide for them you and I could have simply come and taken them away? Why, we know any number of good homes that would have taken them. How did they end up at Browne's anyway?"

Now it was Robert's turn to refill his glass. Leaning against the sideboard, he swirled the amber whiskey around in the heavy hand-cut tumbler. He watched the rainbow play across the bare parquet floor, dancing here and there, daubing the rich wood with delicate hues of red and yellow, green and blue.

"Apparently they're good friends of the man who manages the inn for Sligo. He brought them over to work there only a few weeks ago. His staff had left and he saw the desperate condition of their lives and stepped in by hiring them on. They really owe the man their lives, Beverly. If they live at all it will be because of the scraps from the plates of their guests. How long they can stay though is up to Sligo. I spoke to him about it before I left but he's feeling the pressure from all the other gentlemen to take a harder line with evictions. As for the inn, business always sloughs off a bit after Reek Sunday and he may have to let them go."

"What will they do? Where will they go then?"

"Well, of course, Beverly, I asked Meg to bring them here."

Suddenly the soft pink silk was awash in deep crimson as Beverly's sherry cascaded down the front of her skirt. The last few drops splashed across the embroidered bodice of her white lawn blouse.

"Robert, look what you've made me do! How you have upset me!"

"Beverly, I do apologize! How stupid of me to carry on so! Please forgive my clumsiness. Your beautiful outfit! One I picked out for you myself! Here, let me get that."

He dipped his handkerchief into a decanter of cold water and began to dab at the hem of the skirt where the worst of the stains was spreading across the silk.

His sister pulled away from him.

"Never mind Robert. I think it's ruined now. Let Reina work on it. Maybe she can salvage it."

Robert rang for the maid and she appeared instantly.

"Reina, you can see Lady Beverly has had an accident and needs your assistance."

"*Oui, Monsieur Robert. Madame?*"

"Oh just get me my pelisse, Reina. Robert, we're not entertaining tonight are we? You have no further surprises for me do you?"

Chagrined by his sister's obvious irritation, Robert shook

his head.

"The ivory satin one, Reina, with the thin peach stripe. That will be fine."

Reina went upstairs to fetch the pelisse leaving her mistress dabbing cold water on her blouse and his lordship pacing back and forth with his drink in his hand. Within minutes, Reina had returned and suddenly having found an urgent need to check on dinner, Robert left the two women alone in the drawing room. Reina helped Beverly out of her damp skirt and blouse and into her pelisse. Beverly said nothing of the exchange between her and her brother. Reina, ever discreet, never asked.

When Robert returned, Beverly again sat on the chaise, a fresh glass of sherry in her hand. After a few moments, she spoke.

"Robert, I didn't hear you say you invited Meg and her brood to move in with us did I?"

"Yes, Beverly, that is exactly what you heard. If you had seen the condition of their bodies, you would have done the same thing. Any Christian would!"

"Not this Christian, Robert. Meg caused absolute havoc in my home. Her behavior almost cost her father his life and me my home. Had you not intervened, I would be ruined because of her. Now you want to have her and all those crying children here? Have you taken leave of your senses?"

"But Beverly!"

"No. Not but Beverly! What about her husband? Am I to welcome him too? Are we to feed him and fatten him up so he can make still more babies on my daughter under this very roof? Robert do you know what you're saying?"

"Beverly, they're family! And they're starving! How can I justify turning them away? I took you in when you needed a place. How can you not do the same for your own daughter?"

"It's not the same at all, Robert! I was in a terrible marriage where I had no choices. Jeffrey had kept me a virtual prisoner for years and would have done so even from his wheeled chair had you not rescued me. Meg chose to go off with an Irish Catholic! A poor peasant with absolutely no ability to care for her and their children. She knew that when she married him. She should have seen this coming. No, Robert, Meg has just what she deserves, no more no less. Please, I beg of you for our sake, for the sake of our family reputation and everything our parents did to establish us in society, do not bring them here! Please don't threaten the peace of our home.They will ruin you, I guarantee it. Just as they almost ruined me!"

Robert sat down on the edge of his favorite, worn leather club chair and took a sip of his whiskey.

"Beverly you know as well as I do that it wasn't always this way. For ten years, Tom Phalen made a very comfortable living and Meg even had a maid until the girl left for the States. We've watched and stood by for almost fifteen years and Meg has never needed us. But now she does! Now they have been ruined by this potato blight through no fault of their own."

"Tell me this, Robert, how does a man who has a successful dairy farm get ruined by a potato bug? If he was so solvent, where is his money now?"

Robert frowned into his empty glass.

"I really can't answer that. Meg said something about a man named Gilchrist ruining them but I couldn't make the connection. He's the undertaker for Lord Lucan's affairs. Lucan wasn't at the meeting. He sent Gilchrist in his stead. What a weasel! That man just oozes evil from every pore. He is Lucan's nephew but I can't imagine why Lucan even has him around. As a matter of fact, I caught the blackguard beating the daylights out of Meg's own son! Now I'm really determined to find out what his connection to Meg is."

"Lucan can't have anything to do with a personal vendetta. That's totally out of character for the man. In fact the last time I saw him, at the landlord's meeting in January, he expressed regret that he would finally have to start evicting. I distinctly remember him saying he hadn't received any rents from southern Achill, particularly Dooega, since the fall of '46. To hear Gilchrist talk, and believe me we heard plenty of Gilchrist at this meeting, Lucan was just now beginning to lose rents and he blamed Tom Phalen. He went so far as to accuse Tom of malfeasance and doctoring the books. I was so sick of hearing the whining of spoiled gentlemen by that time I'm afraid I didn't catch the discrepancy at first. What a fool I was not to pursue the matter! Tom Phalen had a herd of over twenty milk cows. What happened to them?"

"Maybe he had a woman on the side or enjoyed a bit of card playing himself. Maybe he lost the cows to some slick sailor."

"Tom Phalen? On Achill Island? In the middle of a famine? Beverly your imagination is way too active!"

Beverly, sullen and gloomy, slouched against the pillows of the chaise, absently running her finger around and around the empty wineglass, causing a high pitched ring to pierce the air. Without looking up from her lap, she spoke slowly, carefully forming her thoughts.

"Robert, what is this Gilchrist's first name?"

"Why it's the same as mine, Robert. Why do you ask?"

"Well, Jeffrey used to play cards with a Robert Gilchrist. You don't think this Gilchrist may be the same one do you? I mean if Lucan thought Tom Phalen was a good enough businessman to be his rental agent and it seems for years, he was, why didn't Lucan see to it that Tom Phalen and his family were provided for when the hunger hit the island so hard? Doesn't he have a reputation for loyalty to his own?"

"Well, yes, in fact among gentlemen, he does enjoy a reputation for generosity, though he does employ the Crowbar Brigade a bit too often, but he's fair with those who work hard and consistently improve his revenues. If anyone did that it was Tom Phalen. His dairy business was the talk of the island. You know that from Rev. Nangle."

"Even that stuffed shirt Dr. Browne admitted that after Tom's accident he could not believe how well he recovered and prospered. It does seem odd that he would have left him to starve like that. And what happened to the rents after '46? Surely the fishermen were able to harvest something. Why the sudden drop off?"

Beverly yawned. The sherry and the warm afternoon sun were working like a sedative on her.

"Oh, dear Beverly, I am boring you. Look at you; you're almost asleep. I wonder what's keeping our dinner?"

Richard, stealthy as a nun, came and announced dinner.

Beverly rose from the chaise and took Robert's arm.

"No, I'm not bored, Robert. But dinner would be nice. I am hungry."

As Richard eased the heavy, carved Italianate chair under her, Beverly resumed her line of thought.

"So, Robert, you are bound and determined to turn my world upside down by playing the hero with my daughter's family?"

"Well, I don't know if you have anything to worry about, my dear. She refused, after all. And I never even spoke to Tom."

Surprised, Beverly looked up at him.

"No? Where was he? I thought you said they were all at the inn."

"Well, the strangest thing was, Meg told me Tom was in hiding from Gilchrist and she had told him that Tom was dead."

"Dead! Why would she do that?"

Beverly put her soupspoon down with a clink, splashing the light chicken broth on the creamy damask cloth.

"Robert! You don't think that this Gilchrist is actually after Tom Phalen, do you? What if it is the same one Jeffrey plays cards with? Tell, me, what does the man look like?"

Robert described Gilchrist, from his narrow jutting chin to his spindly muscular legs.

Beverly sat very still, her mouth agape.

"Robert, there is no doubt in my mind that the man is one and the same as Jeffrey's nasty little friend. You must look into this for me Robert. This is not just my imagination, now. You simply cannot let Meg and her family come here. Why, this man, if he is after Tom Phalen for whatever reason, will follow him here and I simply could not bear seeing him again. He was vile and repulsive at GlynMor Castle and treated me like a common serving girl. I can't have him snooping around here looking for Tom Phalen. Promise me Robert that you'll think of something else, please!"

Robert looked hard at his sister. He saw real fear in her eyes and her chin trembled with unshed tears.

"Why Beverly, you are truly afraid of this man! What do you know about him?"

"It's not what I know about him, Robert, it's what I know about Jeffrey that makes me sick at the thought of him at Cushing House. If your Gilchrist is the same as my Gilchrist then he'll stop at nothing to ruin me. Can't you see? He's in so thick with Jeffrey that Jeffrey had him spin a web around Meg and Tom. All these years, acting as Lord Lucan's undertaker has given him access to them. What was to stop Jeffrey from reaching his tentacles all the way to Achill Island through his little gambling partner? If Meg wants to be angry at someone for spying she should look at her father, not me!"

Now it was Robert's turn to look shocked.

"Beverly, do you really think so? How could I be so blind? I never made the connection."

"How could you? Did you ever see him with Jeffrey?"

"No, but he was so thick with that Riordan fellow, Jeffrey's own undertaker. He even shared a room with him! And he was so disappointed that Tom Phalen was dead! Of course, he would be. He thought he had no power over him any more. No wonder he was beating their son! But did he know me? I don't think he would have recognized my name but when I identified myself that first night in the kitchen, he had the most peculiar look on his face. And he treated me with extraordinary rudeness at every encounter. Beverly, looking back on that night, I believe he did know who I was. And he did leave with Mr. Riordan. I would put money on the hunch that they are all at GlynMor Castle even as we sit here at this table!"

"But Robert, what do we do?"

Beverly had found her appetite again and motioned Richard to serve her a second spoonful of peas and carrots. A steaming portion of poached salmon in buttery fennel sauce lay on her plate, beckoning her to leave her somber mood behind. There was nothing like the smell of good food to bring Beverly around. There was no crisis or disappointment that a good meal could not sooth.

Well lubricated by her second glass of sherry and further salved by a bowl of silky chicken consommé, and the lovely fish course in front of her, Beverly's agitation slipped away like the setting sun. With a familiar heaviness settling in her feet, she relaxed and savored every mouthful of her delicious meal.

Robert, too, ate heartily, attacking his salmon as if it were still in the water.

In between bites, he formulated a plan, sharing it with Beverly as he went. Finally, as Richard poured thick yellow cream into Robert's demitasse of Turkish coffee, he looked up at his sister with a smile.

"Well, what do you think, Beverly? Is there a trip to GlynMor in my future or not? I believe I owe my brother-in-law a visit. Tomorrow is the last day of July. A good day for travel, I've always thought."

Beverly stirred a second cube of sugar into her own coffee.

"Oh, Robert, I suppose you must go. I do hate to put you through it though. He is such a brute and such a horror to look at since the accident. But if you think it will do any good, go. You'll understand, I hope, why I won't be joining you. This whole business is guaranteed to be frightfully unpleasant and Reina and I both need a break from traveling."

"You know, my dear, I would never expect you to endure such an encounter. Leave Jeffrey and Mr. Robert Gilchrist of the Scottish Gilchrists to me."

Robert pushed himself away from the table, grabbing a

handful of fresh cherries from a silver bowl. With immense satisfaction, he smiled a broad grin.

"Then it's settled. I leave as soon as I can gather any legal ammunition I may need. The sooner the better, for my purposes."

Chapter Seven

Denny Phalen struggled and squirmed against the powerful arms that hauled him through the narrow alley filled with lobster traps and old crates. He was so mad he forgot to be afraid as he tried to bite the hand held tightly over his mouth.

Finally, well away from the smokehouse, the great arms heisted him over the shoulder of a tall strong man. His mouth freed, Denny began to howl and kick. A few girls from Marie's and some sailors from The Marianna laughed at the sight of the man carting the squealing boy toward the Louisburg Road.

Once out of sight, the man plopped Denny onto the ground. Towering over him in the shadow of a streetlamp, the man yanked Denny to his feet and swatted him hard with his hand. Denny, shocked at the sudden pain on his backside fought this humiliation with all his strength but the man came at him in a mad fury. Turning him over his knee and clamping his hand on the back of Denny's neck, he administered a good, long spanking to the boy. When he had finally exhausted his rage, he pulled Denny to his feet by the collar and spoke.

"What in the name of the Virgin were ye doin' on the docks, ye damn fool spalpeen?"

"Da! What are ye doin'? What'd I do? Why are ye hittin'

me?"

"Why indeed? Ye almost gave away the movement ye stupid boyo! The dock was crawlin' with brothers trustin' donkey headed little boys to be in their beds, not stickin' out of a pile o'lobster traps fer every strollin' constable t'see."

"Da, no one saw me! I was in the best hidin' place on the dock. I don't care about yer stupid old meeting, anyway!"

"The divil ye don't! D'ye think Duffy and I haven't seen ye sneakin' around? D'ye think yer mither and I haven't marked the nights when yer not in yer bed? D'ye think lad, that I haven't had Andrew Feeney lookin' out fer ye t'keep ye from harm? Denny, I've been watchin' ye since Dooega! What kind of a father would I be t'let ye put yerself in mortal danger? But this! D'ye know how close ye were t'blowin' the cover of some o'the best of Ireland's sons?"

Denny's anger and humiliation at being spanked like a child quickly turned to fear as he realized the seriousness of his father's words.

Tom knew his anger was fueled not only by the very real danger Denny had put them all in but by the terrible argument he had had with Meg earlier in the evening. He saw the effect of his words and pulled the trembling boy close to his side. Denny, chastened by the rude spanking and deeply afraid of his foolish behavior allowed his da to leave his arm protectively around his shoulders as they walked back to the inn.

"There's nothin' wrong with wantin' t'fight fer Ireland, Boyo. Ye'd be bringin' shame on the name of Phalen if ye didn't. But Ireland will never be served by proud foolish boys who go off half-cocked and play at bein' men. It's all about discipline Denny. If ye can't play by th'rules, ye can't play. Take Andrew. He's a hotheaded young spalpeen if I ever knew one. That's why I put him on yer tail. Yer cut from the same cloth. I knew he would find ye wherever ye went because he'd already been there."

Denny stiffened when he heard that Andrew Feeney had only befriended him so he could spy on him but he said nothing.

The two walked in silence the rest of the way home. Opening the kitchen door they were greeted by the wonderful aroma of the freshly baked rolls Meg had made for breakfast. In the light of the kitchen lantern, Tom turned to Denny.

"Have ye anythin' t'say t'yer father, then, lad?"

Denny suddenly realized how hungry he was.

"Da, can we eat before bed?"

Tom smiled and shook his head. He knew apologies came hard for Denny but hoped his son realized the true seriousness of his mistake. He decided he'd wait until Denny was ready to admit his wrongdoing. Tired as he was, he hoped he wouldn't have to wait too long.

"See what I mean? Yer no man yet! Yer thinkin' of yer stomach when I've just saved yer skin! I should beat yer backside again, ye edjit!"

Denny shrugged and looked down.

"I'm just hungry, is all. I was so excited t'go t'the Brotherhood meetin' I hardly ate any supper."

"Let's see what we can find."

Tom lifted the linen towel that Meg had placed over the warm rolls. He took several of the little brown orbs and set them on the table. There was a bowl of cheese curds and a wedge of hard cheese beneath a china cover in the center of the table. Another china dish held a slab of butter. Tom and Denny slathered the butter on the still warm rolls and devoured them. Licking melted butter from his fingers, Tom went into the taproom and drew two Guinnesses while Denny popped cheese curds into his mouth.

"Here ye go lad. Ye've learned a man's lesson tonight. I think it's time ye fell asleep with a man's brew in yer gut."

Denny ate and drank his fill, screwing up his face at the bitter stout. Once he was satisfied, he let out a resounding belch.

Tom raised an eyebrow and matched Denny's belch with one of his own.

Denny started giggling as the stout went to his head.

Within minutes the giggling turned to tears and he flung himself into Tom's arms.

"Da, tis' that sorry I am I almost got the brothers killed! I'll niver sneak out again, I promise. I just want t'be a hero and I want t'be Irish and not English and I thought Andrew was my friend and I just wanted ye t'be proud o'me!"

Tom smiled to himself as he watched the Guinness take effect. Stroking Denny's tawny hair he spoke softly.

"Denny, Denny, me own boyo. D'ye think I'm not proud o'ye? D'ye think I don't see ye doin' the work of a man with the body of a boy? D'ye think I'm not noticin' ye as ye watch out fer yer sisters when this place is full of drunks and gropin' sailors? Of course I'm proud o'ye! Yer me own boyo! Suren' there have been times like tonight when I've had no choice but t'lay a whelpin' on ye, yer that stubborn, ye are. But I niver met a lad with more guts and determination than ye've got. No sir! But ye need t'grow up first. Ye need t'learn t'curb yer temper and use yer brain. Think things through."

"Da, why were ye outside th'meetin' with Mr. McGee if ye weren't plannin' on goin' in?"

"Well that was a man's decision, lad. It was me intention t'go in with Duff. While I was waitin' there on the dock I had a bit o'time t'think on some things. There's a passage in the Bible that says that there's a time fer livin' and a time fer dyin', a time time fer war and a time fer peace. Now understand me well, lad, I'd die fer Ireland in a minute if I were a single man. But I have all of ye t'think of now don't I? What would happen t'Mam and the wee ones if I were t'die or be jailed in some hellhole prison ship? I know what it's like t'grow up without me mam and me memories of her all filled with smoke and screamin'."

"If me da had gone the way of me uncles I'd have been alone with no one t'care fer me. Then maybe I'd have been a true brother and found me path in the ways of war. But then I niver would have met yer mam and none of ye would be me sons or daughters. I know ye don't like bein' half English but if yer mam had married some other man, an Englishman maybe, ye'd be all English. Now aren't ye glad I came along t'give ye some o'me blood in yer veins? Sometimes an experience like me watchin' me house burned t'the ground makes a man into a warrior. Fer me it was the opposite. I've been a man of peace since I saw all that as a lad. Sure, I get as fired up as any Irish patriot but when all is said and done, I want no more than me hearth and me wife and me children around me."

"But Da, yer a brave son of Ireland! Ye need t'stand fer her freedom! How can ye back away when they're makin' us starve? Ye see the same thing I do!"

"There are things ye simply can't understand Denny. When I said 'twas a man's decision not to go into the meetin' I meant it. Ye haven't had the years t'know how a man has t'think on his feet. Yer passions have t'be winnowed and yer direction honed. Someday ye may be a great fighter but ye're just a boyo now with a belly full o'hurt and a head full o'questions. Give yerself time t'grow up. Find a battle worth fightin' and only fight fer a winnin' cause."

"No, Da! I don't want t'live under anybody! I want t'be as good as the next lad and as rich as anybody else! I want t'be free and niver be forced t'plow and harvest crops that get taken away while I starve fer the leavins'. I'm goin' Da. Someday I'm goin' t'live where I can be free."

Tom felt a cold shiver run through him and the fear of losing his firstborn son to the empty rhetoric and high ideals of the Blackthorn Brotherhood gripped his bowels.

"Denny, when ye grow into yer man's body and take a wife or take the collar ye can decide where ye'll be livin' and what ye'll die fer. And I'm that sure ye'll choose well. But now ye're a boyo. Yer job is to learn and learn some more. This hunger has been a monstrous thing but ye're survivin'. What are ye learnin' from that? If ye're payin' attention, ye're learnin' the value of teamwork, of friendship and loyalty, of the love between a man and a woman. Ye watched yer mam survive the loss of two sons in a year and still get up every mornin' and care fer the ones left behind. Ye need t'pay attention, lad. Then when ye've learned how t'live ye can go out on yer own and take up yer life."

"But Da, I am a man! I know what t'do!"

Tom could see that the stout was working on Denny and he knew he needed to bring this conversation to an end before his son ended up in a crying jag.

"Denny, think about it. Think about what ye saw from yer perch tonight. The men, every one of'em filled with the righteous rage yer carryin' yet not a one movin' so much as a hair without thinkin' o'how 'twould affect the others. Every one of 'em intelligent, resourceful and true patriots and not a one would go against the orders of the leaders and change th'plan. That kind of discipline takes years of experience, years of learnin' t'be a team."

"Ye weren't invited tonight. But ye took it upon yerself t'disobey the wisdom o'the men and go anyway. I was afraid ye'd try t'come. Especially after yer mither and I had words. Then I saw ye movin' in the shadows by th'crates and I knew just what ye were up to. I had t'stop ye before ye ruined everything."

"Ye see, lad, Duff and I could see what ye couldn't. There were two constables headin' fer the docks not a hundred yards behind ye and their lanterns threw light right on ye. It was the angels themselves that kept the men from seein' ye hidin' there. Andrew was supposed t'be watchin' ye but we saw him on the pier with his back t'ye. Duff signaled Andrew and they met between those two and where ye were hidin'."

"They started a bit of a donnybrook t'distract the constables and I hauled ye kickin' and screamin' right past 'em. T'them it was just a couple o'boyos mixin' it up and a man draggin' his son away from one o'Marie's naughty girls. So, Duff and I weren't meant t'be in there. Andrew was busy sulkin' instead o'watchin' ye and I hope Duff throttled him good. You two muttonheads almost queered the whole plan and got yer brothers thrown in jail. The whole thing was over in a few seconds. As far as I know the lads in the smokehouse were niver the wiser."

"So, ye see what I'm tryin' t'tell ye? Wait a bit, lad. Someday ye may be a great fighter but I honestly hope ye niver have t'see battle. It's peace I'm wishin' fer ye, Denny. Peace."

Denny was beginning to nod off. Tom hugged him and sent him off to bed. He rinsed the two glasses and was just about to snatch another roll from the tray when the front door opened and Duffy ducked in. He held a bloody rag to his nose and there was a cut over his left eye.

Tom felt every bone in his body ache as he turned toward his friend.

"Looks like young Feeney packs a good punch."

"I wish this was from that young hothead. Truth is, me nose is probably broken from a wallop o'the shillelagh. Christ on the cross I'm in pain! And what's worse is our great hero is now a guest o'the queen in the Westport jail!"

"No! Duff what went wrong?"

"Well, it seems young Andrew has been wanted fer some petty theft and a few other small time crimes. The constables were all too happy t'have him in their custody. I was fool enough t'think they were tryin' t'get him t'lead them t'the boys so I tried to interfere with the arrest. I got me nose in where it didn't belong and here ye are, lookin' at it! I'm that lucky I'm not in the cell right next to him."

Tom went over and poked around Duffy's nose, deciding it wasn't broken.

"Ow! Take yer hands off me man! I'm no horse, ye omethon, and ye niver mastered the art of fine medicine, fer sure. I'll thank ye t'leave me poor nose alone."

Duffy looked at Tom over the wadded rag.

"Did ye get Denny all right?"

Tom nodded.

"Got him, walloped his behind and I hope, talked some sense into him. He'll not likely be much help t'ye in the mornin', though. He had his first Guinness tonight. The poor lad was shakin' like a leaf."

"I'm just glad he's fine and the brothers aren't all on their way t'the gallows. I saw Morris Leyne and that McManus lad walkin' t' Gillie's so I guess the meetin's over. I just wish they'd be done with Westport and move on. Are ye sorry we didn't go in?"

"No, not really. Meg has been so worried that I would get thick with them but honestly Duff, seein' me son so close t'bein' caught by the law was enough fer me. Me rebel days are over. Me da and I used t'be more involved but even in those days, we only pulled off a bit o'gun runnin'. I'm just not cut out fer that life. This hunger takin' Thomas and little Patrick and almost killin' Meg. It's enough fer one man to deal with."

Tom dried the two glasses and set them on top of the pyramid behind the bar.

"What about you?"

"No. I have plans, Tom. I want t'go t'the States but not with a price on me head. Me cousin D'arcy is enough trouble fer one family, God only knows. They may have me labeled a rebel just by relation! That constable wasn't from here, probably brought in fer Reek Sunday. But he knew me. He whacked me face with his stick and called me by name when he did it. Can't hide it. We McGee's all look alike."

The clock in the taproom struck one. Tom headed for the stairs.

"Ye're sure yer goin' t'be all right?"

Duffy nodded.

"She's stopped bleeding. I'll just stay up a little to make sure it doesn't start again."

Tom turned toward his friend.

"Goodnight then. Thanks fer comin' between me family and disaster once again."

Duffy waited until Tom was all the way upstairs and quietly slipped out the kitchen door. He quickly crossed the alley. He heard the gentle snorting of a horse as he passed McCrea's Livery. Coming around the corner of the stable he saw the lantern in the window of St. Peter's rectory. Good.

He had hoped Fr. Timon would still be awake.

He went around to the kitchen and knocked softly on the door. The priest shuffled across the floor in his felt house shoes and looked cautiously out the kitchen window. Seeing Duffy there, he opened the door.

"Lad what happened t'ye? Ye're a sight! And look at yer nose!"

"Father, d'ye have a minute?"

"Suren' I was that worried after ye when I saw ye weren't at the smokehouse."

"Thank th'saints ye were there! I need t'hear what was said."

Father Timon looked over his spectacles at Duffy.

"And I need t'know what kept ye away."

Duffy told Fr. Timon the story of his absence.

The priest seemed very relieved when Duffy was through.

"Saints be praised, Duff! How close we all came t'the gallows! Oh, how foolish young boyos can be!"

"Can ye tell me then what was said at th'meetin' Father?"

"Well, the decision has been made t'carry out the rebellion further inland. The leaders have already gone. I admit, I'm a bit disappointed meself. Ye look t'the leaders of a group like this t'be a bit larger than life but they squabble like schoolboys fer every bit o'glory."

The priest shook his big head and poured a glass of whiskey. Sipping it slowly, he continued.

"Mitchell at first, seemed cool-headed enough. Then yer cousin Tom got a bit mouthy and Terry McManus threatened t'box his ears. If it weren't fer the presence of yers truly, representin' the cloth, don't ye know, they'd have had a rebellion right there in the smokehouse. Th'locals are all safe in their beds now but I know there are hurt feelins' all around.

Mitchell took yer cousin, Pat Donahue, Charlie Duffy, Tom Meagher, and Richard O'Gorman with him to Wexford. They plan t' join up with the other lads from Young Ireland. Morris Leyne is takin' Mike Ireland and Terry McManus with him t' just north of Newport where the drop off will be. Then they all hope t'meet in Wexford by the end o'the week t'be done with it. We wondered where you and Tom were and Mitchell in particular was concerned about that young Feeney. But they'll get word soon enough."

Duffy stood up. He was tired and wanted to see if he could catch up to Morris and Terry before they left Gillie's. He wanted them to know for sure he had been with them till the end and that he and Tom had saved their hides. Andrew he didn't care about but he was damned if his cousin and the others would ever think ill of him or Tom. His big worry about Andrew Feeney was his mouth. Duffy just hoped Andrew wasn't too stupid to realize that he'd implicate himself if he said anything.

"Well Father, I have one more stop t'make afore I can go t'bed. Thank ye fer yer help. I'll see ye tomorrow. If ye hear anything let me know."

He slipped out the kitchen door and made straight for Gillie's. Entering by the back door, he saw the two men deep in conversation at the bar. Gillie's was so dark and smoky, Duffy almost choked as he banged his knee into a barstool. His nose hurt and his eyes were beginning to swell. The place was empty even for a Thursday night. No one had even a penny for a pint anymore.

Morris Leyne turned when he heard the commotion.

"Where the hell were ye tonight?"

He took a hard look at Duffy's face.

"Jaysus! What happened t'ye?"

Duffy quietly explained to the two men what had happened and they offered to buy him a pint. Sipping the thick head of his first stout of the evening, Duffy listened to the men report on the meeting.

Morris Leyne drained his pint and threw a few coins on the bar.

"Well Duff, I'm that sorry we niver had a chance t'take up arms together. Tis that grateful we are fer yer takin' a clubbin' t'protect us tonight. Watch out fer the Feeney lad. He's a hothead fer sure. They'll niver make a brother out o'him. He's got his own battles t'fight. As fer Tom Phalen's boyo, we sort of adopted him but poor lad is just too young. Hopefully he'll niver have t'taste the smoke o'battle."

Terry McManus turned toward the door urging Morris with a shove. Looking back at Duffy he added,

"If we do our jobs maybe he niver will at that."

Duffy nodded and wiped a bit of foam off his lip. The three men parted, two onto the quay and one through the kitchen door to the alley and home.

Tom sat in a hard chair by the open bedroom window. The words he had said to his son were cruising around his head making him too restless to sleep. The night was humid and windy and a heavy cloud cover blocked the light of the moon. He knew Meg slept soundly by the rhythmic sound of her breathing.

Dear God, he loved her! How could she ever have said the things she said tonight? Where had she been these all these years that she hadn't seen how he had hated what it took for him to provide her with the life she had enjoyed. Had the hunger gotten into her head and made her forget the bitter gall he tasted every time he thought of his life as Lord Lucan's rental agent? Or was it his fault? Maybe he hadn't complained enough about it to make her realize how it pained him every waking hour. He shook his head and reached for his rosary but he found it impossible to pray. He loosely held the rough, carved Lord's Prayer bead spinning it around and around between his thumb and forefinger.

What was he going to do? He gagged at the thought of taking anyone's charity, especially Meg's family. Yes, Uncle Robert had never been anything but kind to them but Tom had worked so hard to make a life for Meg and their children. He had compromised so much, swallowed so much pride! She knew that! She had to know how it pained him to be the lackey of the aristocracy.

Lord Lucan's agent! Where did that get them? Ruined at the hands of a smarmy, sniveling spider like Gilchrist. He should have gone to Lord Lucan himself. He should have demanded his property, honestly paid for, rightfully his. Instead he compromised everything he believed in to secure a life that at least resembled the one Meg left behind.

His da always said the road to hell was paved with good intentions. Well, didn't he know that now! All of his good intentions had landed them here. And this was hell. All of his humiliation: the borrowed suit, the dairy farming that he had never enjoyed, heads turned away in the pub, the spit from the filthy mouth of Maggie Ballard on Meg's cheek.

He and Meg both had endured so much. For what? For a lace curtain in her window? For a feather bed and Christmas pudding? Those were the things she wanted. She had said so in round pear shaped tones tonight. She had made it known to him that if he couldn't provide her with the fine things she wanted then she would find someone who would! Uncle Robert! Who would have thought he'd be cuckolded by her own uncle?

Bitterness rested heavily in Tom's chest as he spun the little bead around in his hand. The tiny links in the rosary chain threatened to snap and he set it down. That would be just about right. Break your rosary Tom. That would fix everything. Resting his elbows on his knees, he ran his fingers through his hair.

"Dear God," he prayed, exhaustion forcing his eyes closed.

"What should I do? Show me what t'do. Heavenly Father, ye told Joseph what t'do and he did it. I thought ye were guidin' me heart all along. Now I'm not so sure. Help me! I can't find me way and I can't ever again say the things or hear Meg say the things we said tonight. She's all I have, all I want. Show me what t'do!"

Tom sat up and looked into the pitch dark of the bedroom, his eyes blurring with unshed tears. The wind whipped the curtain around and he dried his eyes with the hem of it. Tom hated crying. He had had few tears over the years and most of them on the journeys home from Newport. He hadn't even cried when Thomas died. That loss had been so devastating he had had no tears powerful enough to make a difference. Besides, Meg had cried enough tears for both of them.

Suddenly the clouds parted and moonlight flooded the room. Tom saw Meg outlined on the bed. The sight of her naked and sound asleep made him catch his breath. She looked as beautiful to him as she did in the moonlight at St. Anselm's the night they had escaped from Clydagh Glyn.

Curled up on her side like a little child, she lay in total peace, her face illumined by the moon. He sat for several minutes just gazing at her face. All the care and weariness of Meg's waking hours had disappeared leaving her lovely and serene. Close enough to reach out and touch her face, Tom noted the outline of her brow and how her long blond lashes lay like soft feathers fanned out across the delicate curve of her cheek.

Meg's lips were slightly pursed as if she were thinking or about to speak in a dream. It had been so long since he had really kissed her. He recalled the long ardent kisses they had shared once in a peach orchard many years ago. That seemed like another couple living in another life. How sad to be barely living! How tragic to be with someone so dear to you and not be able to find the time or the energy or the privacy to share the kisses of youth.

Tom's heart ached with regret. How could they have said the things they did? Meg's words had scalded him and he was tender where she'd burned him. He knew he had hurt her too and wondered that she slept so peacefully while he sat in the dark unable to find his rest.

She slept with one arm tucked across her chest beneath her breasts, pushing them fully into the light. How he loved those breasts. Soft and smooth to the touch, sweet with Meg's own scent. How many times had he burrowed into the deep cleft between those ivory mounds or taken one of the pink nipples into his mouth? He smiled sadly in the shadows.

Meg's torso revealed the lean signs of the hunger but her little belly still showed a bit of roundness from bearing children. His children. He gazed upon the soft, creamy skin over the place where he had planted the seed of so much life and where Meg had housed their beautiful sons and daughters, cherished beneath her heart.

His eyes traveled across her tiny waist and rounded hip, like marble gleaming in the soft light. He longed to run his hand over the exquisite curves knowing exactly how they would feel beneath his fingers. One thigh crossed over the other, hiding her private places in deep shadow. His eyes followed the long slender expanse of her leg to where the bones of her ankle gently sloped down to her foot. Her toes were tucked under the sheet but he didn't need to see them. Like every other part of her, he knew them by heart.

His eyes returned to linger long upon Meg's breasts. His mind carried him all the way back to the first time he saw them, pure and virginal, a sight that had rendered him completely helpless. Dear God, he had been nervous that day in his father's house. Every dream of having Meg had realized itself the moment he lay her down on his crude, smelly bed. He felt himself flush with embarrassment all these years later, alone in the dark.

How ashamed he had been afterward that he had no fine linens or sweet straw to offer her. He remembered taking her for the first time as if it were yesterday. Every tiny button of her chemise had been like a gate opening to him. Every bit of lace that had shielded her purity from the hands of other men had yielded to his fingers. He knew now that what they had done was wrong.

He was always grateful to God for allowing them to come to each other as man and wife and to replace the lust of their early union with the fullness of married love. Thank God for Fr. Finnegan, who could have condemned them both for their sin and yet chose to bless their union with mercy and seal them with the grace of a sacrament. How different it could have been had he refused to marry them or crushed Tom's heart beneath harsh judgment when it had been so ripe for repentance.

He remembered how willing Meg always was, how sweetly she surrendered to him as he stripped the layers away, how her excitement had always thrilled him. He would never have her clothed. That would be so cold, so insulting. No, he could only take her the way he did that first time, deliberately, gently, carefully folding her riding habit and setting it on the creepie next to the hearth. He could only have carried her barefoot into his bedroom, laying her down and kneeling next to the bed. Like a pilgrim worshipping a goddess he had gently unfastened her underclothes.

He smiled to himself at the memory of her corset. What a challenge that had proven to be the first time! She had giggled as he had struggled with the ribbons and tapes that imprisoned her. But he would not let her help him. He still believed that it was his duty to allow his lover the dignity of being undressed. After all, everything about a woman was enshrouded in mystery and he reserved the right to discover Meg's secrets for himself.

If a woman was to strip herself naked before a man, standing in the light waiting to be seized, how was that different from being dumped on a couch with her skirts thrown over her head and not a word of tenderness spoken? The very parts of a woman that a man took for himself were so hidden, so protected that they must be probed and parted gently. How else could it be?

Women were so unlike men that way. Men were right out there and there you have it. No mystery about a man! What God gave him was there for a woman to see, plain and simple. It was the man's job to properly display himself and coax her to open herself to receive him. No, Tom never liked the men who cared little for a woman's pride, who would wound her with their selfishness. He seethed at the boasting of fools as their pints loosened their tongues and filled the pub with their tales of conquest.

Perhaps that's why Meg was so attractive to him from the start. She was filled with charm and grace. Her dignity was so fine he could never have besmirched it. And to prove it here he was, looking on his own wife naked in the moonlight.

He could easily climb on her and overpower her as she slept. It would be his right and her duty to receive his lustful urges. But he would never do that to Meg. What would he gain by hurting her that way? Power? Control? Dignity? Hardly! All he would gain by forcing his wife to satisfy his needs would be a resentful wife and a cold hurtful wall between them. Not to mention the self-loathing that would follow him to his grave.

In Tom's mind, to force from a woman her purity and hurt her when she was most vulnerable was a crime worthy of hanging. He had been taught that from a lad and watching poor Maureen suffer through her terrible ordeal had firmed his resolve that his sons would know how to properly treat a woman.

Well, enough dreaming of the past. Tom was so tired he barely crawled into the bed. With the moon still shedding its pale light on Meg's form, he slipped in next to her. The pain of their heated conversation still throbbed in his head and as much as he had wanted to caress Meg's flesh as he reminisced about the past, he didn't touch her. The moon once again went deep in the clouds and the room was plunged into darkness.

A black curtain fell across Tom's sweet memories and the rudeness of the present descended over him again. He didn't need to wake her for his own pleasure. There was already a cold hurtful wall between them that chilled his desire. A wall made of words and tears. Somehow they would reconcile. This he knew. For now he would have to settle for a few hours of sleep. Tomorrow would come crashing in the window soon enough.

Chapter Eight

Late Friday afternoon, Meg was in the larder sorting and counting the dozens of eggs and bricks of butter nestled in between huge wheels of cheese and thick smoked hams. The shipment had just arrived in anticipation of the Reek Sunday pilgrims and Denny had just loaded everything onto the rough-hewn wooden shelves that lined the delightfully cool room in the basement of the inn. The stone walls of the larder were a foot thick and when the inn was built, the masons had wisely placed it in the center of the cellar where it never received the heat of the sun.

As Meg pulled the huge door closed behind her she heard a commotion from upstairs. Tom was bellowing and she heard a terrible thumping sound. In an instant Meg was up the stairs and through the kitchen door. She came upon the scene of a scuffle that was obviously just finished. One look at Duffy's angry red face and Tom's equally purple cheeks made her think they had been mixing it up themselves. The bruises and swelling across Duffy's nose made him look even more like a pugilist.

Duffy paced furiously back and forth.

"Of all the stupid daft, pea-brained things, Tom! Yer soon t'be bringin' the constable down on us that ye are! What are ye thinkin' man? Is it the gallows yer so hell bent on climbin'?"

"I'll not be havin' some filthy omethon placin' his diseased hands on me own daughter and I'm that ashamed of ye thinkin' I'd jist let a thing like that go by, Duff! Ye know me better than that!"

The night before, Meg ahd fallen asleep before Tom came in and they had still not reconciled after their blow-up. His mood all day had been black.

"Well, I do know fer sure yer timin' could be improved. I'm jist that glad it was a Frenchy and none o'them Lymies in the Queen's navy ye decided t'deck. Holy St. Patrick's breastplate, Tom! It's only seconds they were gone before ye started dishin' out blows!"

Usually Duffy could diffuse a touchy situation but even he could not soothe Tom in his foul mood. When a drunken sailor took Mary Clare on his lap and began to slide his hand up her little leg, Tom had literally vaulted the bar and grabbed the child from the man. Then, never hesitating for a moment, he belted the sailor in the jaw and threw him bodily out onto the cobblestones.

Fortunately, the man was so drunk he hadn't known who hit him. The constable found him rubbing his jaw and bellowing a stream of French epithets at the front door of Browne's. The constable understood the insult if not the meaning of his shouted accusations threatened him with his shillelagh. Eventually the sailor returned to his ship still waving his arms and making vulgar gesticulations.

Duffy had been furious with Tom though he had understood why he did what he did. He knew that if the man had been a lord or a magistrate, Tom could be on his way to the gallows for his effort. Meg had never seen Duffy so angry and Tom was deeply affected by the hard words his friend had for him. But Duffy was right. Tom would have to be more vigilant in protecting his children and less volatile when he found them in danger. They were living the life of the poor urban serving class and were lucky to be alive. If the law went after him, there was nothing Duffy could do for him.

If Duffy's warning weren't enough to convince him, Tom learned that very evening how little the gentry valued the lives of the underclass. Even though Reek Sunday was still three days off, a few pilgrims had begun to drift in for the festivities that led up to the actual Mass. Along with them had come the early vendors and hucksters. There was a ragged family of tinkers who set up their goods on the quay in front of the inn. They had been driven from the front of the stores and restaurants further down by the river because they were an ugly lot, half-starved and foul-smelling. The woman had almost no hair and two of the children had running sores on their legs from days of walking through brambles and prickly hedge roses. The toothless father was so skinny he held his trousers up by two pieces of twine tied through holes cut in the waist and stretched over his shoulders and across his back.

Duffy walked outside planning to send them around to the back alley but Meg felt so sorry for the poor family she persuaded him to let them stay where they were. She and Duffy were about to go back into the inn when a stray dog wandered down the quay snarling and snapping at imaginary adversaries. The peddlers did not see the mangy creature nor did they hear it growling as they banged their pots and pans and poured out their trinkets into baskets and tin basins. The youngest of the children, a girl of around two, wandered toward the dog. The dog, rabid and mad, lunged at her.

A wealthy old man was just disembarking from a phaeton to enter Carver's Apothecary when the little girl screamed and buried herself in his sweeping cloak. The dog turned his attention on the man and went to bite his leg. At the same time, the driver of the coach pulled his pistol and shot the dog, saving both the child and the man.

The frightened baby clung to the gentleman and screamed in terror. The startled man, fully aware of how close he had come to being bitten by the rabid dog, grabbed the little girl and pulled her roughly to stand before him.

Disregarding her terror, he pushed her face to within inches of the dead animal. He shook her and forced her to come face to face with the bared foam-covered teeth and glazed eyes.

"See what you have done you wretched brat! Look upon the face of the mad dog. You with your oozing sores and detestable odor drew this cur to you. How dare you direct his attention to me by taking refuge in my cloak? Look closely at the muzzle of the beast that almost took my leg off! What insolence! What bold depravity! Look closely at those eyes, those canine teeth, that foamy lip! I hope that countenance of madness wakes you in your sleep, filthy child of Satan! Go from me now and never soil my path again!"

With that he flung the little girl onto the cobblestones where she lay shivering and shaking until he stepped over the dog and went on about his errand, kicking her aside with the pointed toe of his boot. With a shriek, her mother scooped the poor child up and cradled her against her shriveled breast. Before she could calm the screaming baby or her other children who were now all crying, the constable began shoving her toward the wagon. The family was then told to move behind the buildings or have the law after them. Realizing that a large crowd had gathered during the spectacle, the tinker agreed to move the wagon and cash in on the misfortune of his daughter. Business was business, after all and with this crowd the whole family could eat tonight.

Meg had been very upset. Two gentlemen had come into the taproom shaking their heads and laughing over the episode. One of them insisted that the tinker had brought the dog himself to create a scene and attract customers. The other man thought he was full of blather and told him so. They went back and forth making such a mockery of the tinker and his family that Meg was sickened by their callous and foul remarks.

No one noticed Denny but he had watched the whole scene from the doorway and retreated into the shadows at the end of the bar where he stood in rigid fury. He stayed there in silence clenching and unclenching his fists until Tom called him to take someone's horse round to McRea's.

Meg's heart ached for the woman who had almost lost her baby and for the child who would certainly wake screaming in the night haunted by the ferocious image of the mad dog. What made people so heartless, Meg could never imagine. That man probably had children and grandchildren himself. Is that the way he treated them? His nastiness reminded her of her father. How would her father treat his grandchildren if he met them?

She doubted he ever would but there was always the possibility. Over the last few years, especially since they lost Thomas, Meg's thoughts had turned to Clydagh Glyn and her home in the green valley. It always surprised her when she felt a pang of longing to go back to GlynMor Castle but since her conversation with Uncle Robert, she had not been able to rid herself of the images of the gardens, the stables and bridle paths. She longed to feel the wind in her hair again as she took a fine horse from a trot to a full gallop across the meadows. She hadn't ridden in so many years she had probably forgotten how but she longed to smell the warmth of horseflesh and feel those powerful muscles gliding beneath her as she flew across the green hills of Clydagh Glyn.

Then she would see her father's face as he raised his crop against her. She heard him hollering for Maureen and felt the creeping fear of her last trip down the upstairs corridor of her old home. Why would she ever want to return to the place that had brought her so much pain? How could she miss the wickedness of her father and the indifference of her mother?

This, itself, was a source of pain for Meg. That she would even desire in the least to return to that place made her wince. What was wrong with her? For so many years, she hadn't even thought about Clydagh Glyn or GlynMor Castle and now she couldn't stop thinking of it. It seemed that Uncle Robert had opened a door for Meg and she had an irresistible urge to go through it. She knew if her family went to Cushing House, they would live in luxury and comfort for the rest of their lives. But Meg also knew that doing that would kill the only man she ever loved and she knew just as certainly that she could never do it.

As angry as she had been the night before, all Meg wanted now was to hold him and know that everything was all right between them. The day had been horrible and this nastiness on the quay had topped it off. The tension left over from their argument the night before fueled Meg and Tom to finish their many chores in record time. They hadn't spoken at all and had gone out of their way to avoid each other.

She was relieved that the children had been sent to bed early and had missed the awful spectacle in the street. Every day the number of pilgrims would double and by Saturday there wouldn't be a spot of grass or roadway not littered with campers and their belongings. The constabulary had called in recruits to beef up the force and Marie had shuttered her windows and taken her girls on the road. This was not the kind of crowd to bring her any business and they were off to the nearest fair to peddle the treasures under their petticoats.

Adults and children alike had been working like animals to get ready for the crowds. Every room in the inn was booked by wealthy easterners due to arrive over the next few days. They even had two bishops staying at St. Peter's. Poor Fr. Timon was apoplectic and driving Mrs. Murphy insane.

Tom and Meg ascended the stairs to their room in silence. Tom sat shirtless in the window trying to catch a breeze on the warm night air and read the newspaper. His pipe smoke drifted over Meg as she washed out the laundry and hung it on the makeshift clothesline. Tom's pants from yesterday were still damp because Meg hadn't been able to wash them until that morning. The heavy corduroys crowded the fresh wash and Meg hoped the flimsy line would hold it all.

Tom never looked up from the paper even when she undressed and rinsed out her own things. Meg slipped beneath the thin bed sheet and turned her naked back to her husband. She wanted to reconcile but wouldn't be the first to speak. After all he was the one who started the fight last night.

Finally he crossed the room to his side of the bed and extinguished the candle. Meg heard his trousers hit the floor and the bed creaked as he eased himself down on the mattress.

They both lay there in silence, neither willing to yield to the other. Meg felt her temper rising and tried to keep calm. What was he waiting for? He must know the argument last night was his fault. He had said such terrible things! Sure, she had spewed back her own venom but he had started it. It was his apology to make.

Tom lay with his back rigid in the pitch dark and made every effort to keep his distance from his wife. Meg could tell he was struggling to put space between them. The bed was not big and they usually slept in each other's arms or like spoons. Tonight Tom was hanging onto the edge of the bed to avoid touching her. If it weren't so sad it would have been funny.

Just as Meg thought they would have to fall asleep angry, Tom let out a yelp and began to wrestle with an invisible foe. In an instant, Meg too was flailing and struggling to free herself. They were being attacked by a cold, damp enemy that enshrouded them and threatened to smother them. Kicking and hollering, they tried in vain to throw off their attacker. All they succeeded in doing was to become more entangled in his clingy, wet web.

The commotion brought Duffy roaring up the stairs. He had been retiring to his own room when he heard the yelling and scuffling and thought the worst. Barging into their room with his candle sputtering, he stopped in his tracks. There were his two friends, wide-eyed and naked except for several pieces of damp laundry draped over and wrapped around their limbs. Duffy could see that the clothesline had given way under the heavy, wet clothes and landed on Tom and Meg. The candlelight revealed Tom wearing on his head a little white dress making him look like a giant baby in a bonnet.

Meg was wrapped in a pair of Tom's trousers and his work shirt had wound itself around her neck and covered half of her face leaving her gaping one-eyed into the light. Tom's torso was wound in Meg's skirt and he had one hand in the sleeve of one of Rose's blouses.

The sight of them in such straits brought a howl of laughter to his throat. The day had been so tense Duffy had really had had just about enough of their feud. Now, seeing them all tangled in wet laundry, shocked at his appearance in their doorway was more than he could take. Bowing formally, he backed out of the room and without a word descended to his own quarters, his laughter leaving a trail behind him.

Meg and Tom were left in the darkness to sort out the mess. Tom extricated himself from Meg's heavy, wet skirt and lit the candle on the table next to the bed. Unaware of the lacy little garment on his head, he started to laugh at the sight of Meg with his shirt around her neck. She, in turn, began to giggle at Tom's stubbly chin protruding from the little dress.

Tom, realizing he had the dress on his head yanked it off but it was too late. All of the tension of the last twenty-four hours dissipated, as Meg laughed so hard she began to gasp. Tom looked at the little dress and shaking with laughter himself, tried to put it on Meg's head. She tried to wrest it away from him and he pulled it away dangling it just out of her reach. Meg decided to pull Tom's pants on and dress herself in his shirt. Tom then took Meg's skirt and began to prance around in it with the little dress again on his head.

The sight of his hairy chest above her work skirt and the dainty dress outlining his stubbly face was too much for Meg. She rolled around on the bed in Tom's damp clothes, coughing and sputtering with laughter. Tom continued to mince around the room until he too doubled over and collapsed on the bed.

Meg reached up and tugged the dress off Tom's head. He then grabbed his shirt and in one motion pulled it off Meg, leaving her naked from the waist up. At the sight of her breasts, the memory of the night before flooded through him.

He stopped his laughter and she saw the look of desire flit across his face. She could not remember when she had last seen that look. It was gone in a second but Meg knew she could put it back on Tom's face. She knelt over him, her anger gone, her fatigue and achy muscles replaced by feverish desire of her own. Tom seized her by the shoulders and pulled her down on top of him. Together, they frantically tore the other's clothes from their bodies, flinging them into a damp heap on the floor.

Grabbing and grasping at each other, they tumbled around like wanton children. They hadn't come together like this in so long they felt like it was the first time. Their hurt and anger had been so deep over the last day that they were raw and desperate for love. As if to take back their hurtful words, they devoured each other's mouths. They kissed deeply and recklessly and probed and grabbed each other with abandon.

Tom flipped Meg over and descended upon her, kissing her hard. Meg responded like a she-wolf clawing his shoulders and thrusting herself into his lean, hard body. Meg's wild eyes and grasping hands drove Tom into a frenzy. He could not take his eyes off of her and the sight of her pleasure at his hands made him mad to have her. Their passion rising to fever pitch, they tumbled around, locked in a ferocious embrace, their mouths drawing the very breath from their lungs.

Tom was like a man starved, a prisoner given a stay of execution. Had Meg been capable of rational thought, she would have been shocked at her own behavior. There were no words between them. Like the storms off the ocean they overtook each other, wild and lusty, filled with powerful currents long buried by the struggles of life. They rode each other like two gulls bobbing on the huge breakers that crashed across the bay on the tail of a hurricane.

Groaning like the wind, they came together seizing each other, until their groansturned to cries. Meg was like a woman possessed her lips like fire on Tom's skin. He took her slender body in his hands like she weighed nothing, sliding her beneath him. She wrapped her legs around him and rolled him on his back sitting astride him, her head thrown back in pure pleasure.

The candle sputtered as a moist breeze gusted across the bed. Suddenly plunged into darkness again, Meg and Tom felt a chill that only increased their mad passion. Thunder rolled across the sky as the storm that had failed to dampen Westport the night brfore finally arrived. The curtains in the three long windows flapped in ghostly half-light as lightening flashed and a hard rain began to pelt the tin roof of the smithy shop in the alley.

The chilly night air gave them gooseflesh and Meg shivered involuntarily. Tom took this as an invitation to warm her with his hot demanding mouth and he pulled her down. Again she found herself sliding beneath him as he burned her with hot kisses. Up and down the length of her body she felt his lips searing her chilly flesh. Inside and out she felt the rush of his warmth as the dark room turned eerie, pierced with the flashing light of the storm.

On and on the thunder rolled. On and on Tom ran his hands and his lips over her soft skin, manipulating her flesh and thrilling at her rising passion. Finally she could bear no more and tried to push his hands away but he took her hand in his own and held it with loving firmness. He wasn't finished with her yet. Not until he drove her completely mad and heard the desperate sound of her whispered surrender, would he pull his mouth away and slip himself into her.

Finally, with a clap of thunder crashing and rumbling right over their heads, he knew she was ready. Sliding his hands beneath her he raised her up to meet his body in the primal act of consummation. Feeling Meg's legs clinging around his waist Tom felt his own passion rise beyond his control. He could see nothing in the pitch dark of the room but he slipped effortlessly into Meg's waiting body. She cried out as he brought her again to fevered climax.

Meg tried to hold tightly to his shoulders but her arms

were limp. She lay spent and contented beneath him and he bent to kiss her lips. Meg kissed him with hot tenderness, her lips like scalding little pillows against his own. Tom felt a rush of love pass through him more powerful than the storm that crashed and blew outside. He felt his body rising on the crest of a yearning so great it hurt his chest. He groaned aloud as he poured himself into his wife and she with all her love received him. Together they gripped each other in a single movement until neither could tell where one ended and the other began. The thunder rolled off into the distance and the storm moved on.

One more feeble wink of lightning flashed across their bed just long enough to light their faces for a second before they parted. What they saw in that tiny flash of light confirmed what they had just known in the dark. Nothing would ever come between them. They belonged to each other in a way that was older than life and stronger than death. For an instant, heaven chose to light their faces revealing each beloved feature to the other. What had been sealed between their bodies in the dark was now imprinted on their minds forever.

Tom slowly pulled himself from Meg's embrace, gently unwinding her legs from across his back and setting them down on the bed. Tenderly he touched her breast one more time with his lips and caressed her cheek in the dark. Meg ran the back of her hand across Tom's rough beard and outlined his brow with her finger. Silently they separated and slipped beneath the sheets. They entwined their fingers and closed their eyes. In less than moments, they were asleep.

Sunday morning, Meg and Tom roused their children early and headed to six o'clock Mass at St. Peter's. Only the locals were in attendance as many of the pilgrims had already begun the ascent to the top of Croagh Patrick for their own Mass. Meg bent to untangle Gracie's rosary as the bells announced the arrival of the priest on the altar. When she looked up she was shocked to see the face of a dear friend, thinner and older but unmistakably the same kind face of the priest who married her and Tom.

She looked at Tom who was grinning in recognition of this cherished friend. They stood proudly and waited for Fr. Finnigan to recognize them. It wasn't until he ascended the pulpit and began to give his homily that a look of pure delight crossed the priest's face and caused him to falter in his remarks.

After Mass, he invited them to stay for breakfast with him and Fr. Timon and the two bishops. He knew Mrs. Murphy had outdone herself given the general scarcity of food. He, himself, had not expected to eat as well as he had. It was a great stroke of luck to be housed with two bishops. Somehow even the poorest parish could afford to feed a bishop or two.

It was very hard to decline the offer but they had to feed an inn filled with hungry pilgrims. Fr. Finnegan was so taken with Francis and the little girls that he asked if they could stay and perhaps Mrs. Murphy could give them a little something in the kitchen. Francis and Mrs. Murphy had become fast friends and Meg was so thrilled to see Fr. Finnegan after all this time that she consented. Off they went to enjoy a treat from Mrs. Murphy and maybe even get to meet the bishops from Castlebar and Cashel. Fr. Finnegan promised to visit them all at the inn after the pilgrims left and things had quieted down.

Still in the afterglow of Friday night's lovemaking, Meg and Tom hustled through their work. The children worked like Trojans and late Sunday night when the exhausted crowd had begun to thin, they collapsed into bed. Meg and Tom were very proud of their children as they tucked them into their beds. Denny, who had worked harder than Tom had ever seen him, was asleep in seconds. Rose too, fell asleep before they even finished their prayers. When they went to bed Tom reached for Meg with renewed affection. Neither of them had spoken about their passionate reconciliation and neither of them mentioned it now. They were content to revel in the memory of their free, unfettered expression of love.

Tom rolled over and took his sleepy wife into his arms. She smelled faintly of the lemon verbena soap she had just used to wash their work clothes as he had securely fastened the clothesline and helped her hang them. There would be no more collapsing of wet laundry onto the bed.

He kissed the back of Meg's neck and she reached up and gently touched his earlobe. Within one sigh they were both asleep.

Fr. Finnegan was as good as his word. By Wednesday the inn was empty and he had stopped for a long afternoon while he waited for a family from his parish to pick him up. They had come for the pilgrimage and stayed to visit relatives in Louisburg. He expected them shortly after dinner and was thrilled to have time for a long visit when Tom and Meg were actually free.

All through the hot afternoon they sat along the inlet cooling their feet in the water as the children waded and played in the shade of the willow trees. The water of the Carrowbeg River where it flowed out to join the ocean was clear and green and the rushing of the breeze through the long sweeping branches soothed them almost to sleep. They had all earned an afternoon of rest and the cool of the ocean breeze was like heaven on their hot, tired faces.

The oysters that made Browne's so famous were in abundance despite the hundreds used for the meals of wealthy pilgrims. Meg had surreptitiously steamed a whole kettle of them and Fr. Finnegan was ceremoniously popping them into his mouth. Ellen had taken a shine to the kindly priest and giggled every time he slid one of the sweet gray creatures off its shell into the little crock of drawn butter. Then she watched him as he dramatically leaned over the crock and never losing a drop scooped the dripping delicacy from the butter to his waiting mouth. The more she giggled, the more exaggerated his movements became until finally, he lost one on the ground and the whole scene erupted into a hilarious scramble for the slimy oyster which had slid under Ellen's creepie. If any of them felt guilty for having poached a few oysters and sneaking them down their throats while others went hungry, they didn't for long. They all knew they would feel the pinched belly of hunger soon enough.

Tom and Meg told Fr. John all about their life on Achill, about their farm, their good years and their struggles. He asked about Maureen and they told him all about the deed and her life in America. Meg left out the unhappiness of being married to Charlie O'Malley. It was enough for the kind priest to know that she was alive and prospering. With tears, they related Thomas's death and the plunge into hardship caused by the hunger. Fr. John's eyes misted over too as he told of losing 'the little mother' to the fever that took so many the winter of '46. He had nearly succumbed himself to the same fever which left him with a very weak heart. Otherwise, he had weathered the famine fairly well.

After his mother died, he had been transferred from the lovely parish where he had married Tom and Meg so many years ago to a large church in Castlebar. St. Brendan's was where the parishioners were traders and shopkeepers, law clerks and bookkeepers. There were several priests on staff and as an assistant, his workload was far less than at St. Mary's. There were even a few wealthy parishioners who were part of what the locals called the ascendancy.

These were the descendants of some of the mixed Catholic and Protestant families who were raised Catholic and were now bringing their own children to their church. These members of the parish, whose land and wealth spanned generations, were the mainstays of the diocese. Were it not for these few families, some of whom boasted ten or more children, all prosperous heads of families themselves, the death toll from the hunger would have been even greater. They had given generously for relief of their fellow parishioners. They were particularly solicitous of their clergy, an admission that brought a blush to Fr. Finnegan's cheeks.

"Aye, they've truly saved our lives," he said of these generous providers.

"Me doctor told me after the fever, me heart was no good. 'Twas bad t'start with, like me da. God took him when I was just a lad. That's the reason the bishop transferred me t'the bigger church. Now I'm one among many and the job is far and away easier on me. God be praised, if it weren't fer bein' at St. Brendan's, I'd ha' niver survived the first year o' the hunger!"

Meg gasped when she heard of Fr. John's ill health.

"Fr. John we have wonderful physicians here in Westport. Please let one of them take a look at you. Maybe Dr. Browne can help you."

'Thanks, Meg but I'm in no pain, just weak is all. And suren' haven't I shown them all I'm not after departin' anytime soon? I'm not ready fer heaven and if it's all the same t'God I'd be skippin' purgatory. As I see it, I have a bit o'work t'do here before I'm in shape t'negotiate eternity with St. Peter."

Tom slid Mary Clare on his knee and wrapped his arms around her waist.

"This one is going to be our nun, Father," he boasted as Mary Clare grinned and burrowed shyly into her father's chest.

"Is that so, Mary Clare? And a fine vocation it is, indeed! How is it ye've decided so young?"

Mary Clare blushed to the roots of her hair. Suddenly tongue-tied, she could only smile at the priest's question.

Francis leaned forward and propped his elbows on Fr. Finnegan's knees. Assuming a man-to-man posture he confided to the priest.

"She's that holy Favver, that she is. Always prayin', that one."

His curls bobbing, he nodded in Mary Clare's direction.

This brought another round of laughter from the adults.

"Out o'the mouths o'babes, indeed!" Fr. Finnegan exclaimed.

Francis, having garnered far more attention with his adult imitation than he had expected, began to play the ham.

Mary Clare, by now embarrassed almost to tears, wriggled off her father's lap and escaped into the inn. With a playful swat to the bottom for being fresh, Francis was sent to wade in the shallows. Undeterred, he splashed raucously, eliciting screams of protest from his sisters.

The little family sat with their friend until late afternoon when Duffy came out to join them. He had been busy with his ledgers and sums after the last few weeks of business. Meg noted a look of gravity on his handsome face but when he greeted Fr. Finnegan there was nothing unusual in his voice.

"Father, I'm Duffy McGee and I believe ye have news o'me family up yer way."

"Pleased t'meet ye Mr. McGee. Aye, I saw yer twin brother Connor not long ago. He brought his youngest to make her First Holy Communion. He lost his wife and his oldest son t'the hunger, I'm afraid. Suren' I hope I'm not the one t'give ye that bit o'bad news."

"No, I knew about Mary. Terry's Brigid told me that when she wrote about Terry and their little lads. So many gone. I niver even knew Terry's boyos and only met Mary on Connor's wedding day."

"Well, Connor and Mary weren't starvin'. He was smithy fer three townlands. Mary was quite the healer with her herbs and talismans. She and the boy had taken t'nursin' th'sick in the village and they both died o'milk fever on the same day. A turrible loss. Mary had delivered the child o'the woman with the fever and young Martin was about prayin' over her. The next day they were all gone; the mam, the wee babe and Connor's own two. That Mary was a saint right from heaven and Martin was about t'start seminary in the fall. Turrible loss. The good news is that Connor took in Brigid and her five and right after the First Communion I married them."

"Connor married Brigid? And took on Terry's children? What a man me brother has grown t'be! How many are they then, Father, now that the families are blended?"

"Let me think. Fourteen now, counting Terry's mother-in-law who was livin' with 'em. She's not long fer this world, though. A very frail lady, she is. Connor said t'tell ye he's after takin' the whole family to America as soon as she passes on and he can unload the blacksmith shop. He's all fer joinin' Gerry Shea in Montana. Lots of Irish in th'mines. Copper it is out there."

Meg was suddenly awash with melancholy when she saw the look of longing cross Duffy's face.

"Gerry went to America? I didn't hear."

Fr. Finnegan looked from Meg to Tom trying to decide if he had said too much. When neither of them spoke, he went on.

"Well, Duffy, th'way I heard it, he was asked by Lord Sligo t'go on his behalf. It seems His Lordship bought a prospectin' spot and they wanted t'go and now he and Katie are startin' over."

Duffy mulled this over, his face a dark mask of pain. Tom and Meg could hardly meet his eyes.

"Did ye know about this then, Tom?"

Duffy looked out over the bay when he asked the question of his friend.

"Now, Duff ye know I had no idea 'atall! D'ye think I'd not have told ye? The only time I saw him in the taproom the man niver even said goodbye."

Still not facing them, he asked, "Meg?"

"No, Duffy, I haven't spoken to either of them since we left Westport House for Achill Island 13 years ago."

Duffy looked at Fr. Finnegan, his face less congested now that Tom and Meg had spoken.

"Well, then Father, 'tis that grateful I am t'ye fer bringin' me up t'date."

Before he could say any more, Fr. Finnegan's friends, the Mahadys, rounded the last curve of the steep slope leading down from the Louisburg Road. Several noisy children jockeyed for position next to where they thought the priest would sit. There were three sacks of rags in the back of a bright green low-back cart drawn by one dappled gray horse. The children balanced on these cushions while their parents rode up front on a plank bench painted yellow to match the two wide wooden wheels and the scalloped trim around the door in back. The cart's wheels crunched to a halt across the crushed shells that formed the rough pavement around Browne's front door.

Fr. Finnegan picked up his shabby carpetbag and handed it to a large freckled boy of about thirteen. Hugging each of the Phalen children one by one, he made the sign of the cross on their foreheads. When he came to Tom and Meg he put one hand on each of them and blessed them as a couple. Much to everyone's surprise, the kind priest intuitively blessed Duffy for a safe trip across the ocean. Tom and Meg smiled, remembering how much the mind reader their old friend was.

Just as he was about to get in the cart, Mary Clare came running out of the inn.

"You forgot me!" she cried.

"Niver! I knew you were comin'!"

He took her face in his slender hands and lifted her chin.

"May th'Lord bless ye and keep ye.
May He let His face t'shine upon ye
and have mercy on ye.
May He show His countenance unto ye
and bring ye His peace."

He looked into her eyes and saw tears welling up.

"Mary Clare, darlin' child o'God, ye have the look about ye. I'll be waitin' fer ye t'join the blessed sisters. Be sure t'let me know when yer ready so I can offer me Masses fer ye."

"Thank you Father."

Mary Clare threw her arms around Fr. John's waist and hugged him hard. Then, embarrassed at her display of pious affection, she bolted across the narrow road to hide again in the inn.

Now it was Fr. Finnegan's turn to feel emotional. Unable to say anymore, he silently climbed into the cart and allowed the little Mahadys to swarm over his lap.

His thick glasses hid the tears that welled up as he took in one of his finest achievements as a priest. He remembered clearly the night he heard Tom Phalen's confession and through a blur he watched the little group grow smaller and smaller until the cart rounded the top of the hill and turned to the east and home.

Chapter Nine

Lord Robert Cushing peered into the long hall mirror adjusting his kidskin vest and smoothing his thinning hair. He scowled at his flushed face and wiped the back of his neck with a linen handkerchief. The day was warm and humid, the kind of weather Robert found most uncomfortable. He had just arrived at GlynMor castle and stood waiting in the massive foyer either to be shown into the drawing room or hustled out the door. Stiller, the old cod, had gone to announce him. He wondered what was taking him so long. He looked around at the dingy wall coverings and worn carpets and shook his head in disgust. This gorgeous old house had been closed up for so long he found it hard to breathe. The heady scent of roses and the faint odor of urine permeated the great hall and the musty pall of disuse weighed heavily in the air. Robert longed to throw open the windows and allow the breeze off the moor to clear the air.

He had left before dawn, riding hard on one of his favorite racers across the green hills of Killarney north to the valley nestled along the banks of Derryhick Lough where the clear crystalline waters of Lough Cullin ended their tumultuous journey eddying lazily along the banks of an anonymous creek running along what used to be his family's property.

Chester, his sleek red chestnut had recently won a nice purse in a steeplechase held just south of Cashel. After the race, he had had several offers for the four-year-old horse but he wasn't interested in selling. Chester was the grandson of the great racer Glencoe. Glencoe had brought a fortune to his owner, breeding at Tattersall's Dawley Wall farm near Uxbridge the year before he was shipped to the United States.

Chester's sire, Pavillion, was the son of Glencoe's filly Perfect Pearl and Lucky Day, a beautiful bay stallion of Beverly's. Beverly had just sold Pavillion to an American gent who had inherited an old estate in the Liffey Valley and needed stud horses to start a stable. He had seen Pavillion at Ballinisloe last fall and had finally agreed to match Beverly's price for the pretty Chestnut. Lucky Day had died last month leaving Beverly in the market for a new horse. She still had her favorite, Bay Rum, who always brought a big price for stud service. He was simply a beautiful animal, stronger than any of Beverly's other stallions and wonderfully even-tempered. After she sold Pavillion, Beverly had begun the search for a new racer. She and Robert had gone to fairs and races across the country and she had set her sights on one or two but had made no decision yet. Robert knew once she saw her horse, his sister would know.

Robert loved all his horses but he was particularly fond of Chester and had himself walked the colt around to the stable behind the manor. After inspecting the condition of the stable and yard, he felt confident enough to leave his prize possession in the hands of the head man, Peter. He walked around to the front entrance, realizing how warm he was in his serge frock coat and Irish chamois breeches. He had ridden in relative comfort most of the morning but by ten o'clock it had turned quite warm. He felt his starched linen shirt wilting beneath his coat.

He cared little about impressing Jeffrey with his fashion sense but he hated being unkempt. Being less than impeccable made him feel less in control of a conversation and today he had to be in control. Robert knew he was dealing with some of the worst snakes in Ireland, the kind St. Patrick wasn't able to drive out. He wanted to have all his thoughts in order before he confronted Jeffrey.

He hadn't been in Jeffrey's presence since he had removed his sister from the bastard's clutches. Now he was about to face him again on behalf of his niece and her family but what was he going to say? He had thought hard about it on the ride north. He had stayed at Fellowes and Chadwick Inn in Castelbar the night before where a wedding celebration had left him with a terrible night's sleep. He intended to inform Jeffrey that he was on to his collaboration with Robert Gilchrist to destroy Meg and her family. He wasn't sure what difference this would make to Jeffrey but he was prepared to threaten him with the law if he resisted calling off that filthy dog. Robert thought he probably should have gone to Lucan first but he wanted to see for himself just how this scheme worked. If he couldn't make any headway with Jeffrey, he could snoop around a bit among the servants. There were always a few willing to talk.

Stiller entered the foyer from the kitchen and limped over to where Robert was standing. Robert noted the stooped shoulders and halting gait and marveled at the age of the man. He had to be eighty years old! He actually felt sorry for the old butler. What a miserable lifeless existence he must have in this place.

"Sir, my Lord is not here. He has taken the air. I don't expect him to return before supper."

"Taken the air? How does he accomplish that, Stiller? I thought he was confined to his rooms."

"Very simple, sir. George wheels him about the premises. When he wants to inspect the far reaches of his holdings, he has George drive him in the landeau. I believe if you wish to find him, you will have to look in the southwest orchard. Cherries, sir. Cook has informed me that they took a midday meal with them."

Robert knew this setback presented him with a great

opportunity. He scanned Stiller's face for any suspicion but all he found was boredom and fatigue in the old man's expression.

"Thank you, Stiller. May I trouble you for a midday meal myself? I'd be more than content eating right in the kitchen. I realize you haven't entertained in the first floor rooms in many years but I must say I am quite hungry."

Stiller stood stiffly, the effort obviously causing significant discomfort.

"Well, sir that would be highly irregular. I'm not sure my Lord would approve."

Robert was already on his way to the kitchen.

"Oh, I'm sure he would not," he called over his shoulder. "But this was my home before it was his and hospitality was a hallmark of my parents' reputation. I'll show myself to the kitchen."

"As you wish, sir."

Robert shot another look at the butler and smiled. The poor devil looked like a man on his way to the gallows. Chuckling to himself, Robert anticipated the fireworks display once Jeffrey discovered his fortress had been breached.

Several servants were taking their meal when Robert sauntered unannounced into he cool brick kitchen. They scrambled like ants when they saw him. Many of them had no idea who he was. One very old, wrinkled man stood quietly at his place, trying and failing to stop a grin of recognition from spreading across his face.

Robert extended his hand.

"Ben! As I live and breathe, you're looking well."

"Lord Cushing, sir! I thought niver t'see ye agin. 'Tis yer eyes are deceivin' ye that in my ninth decade I look good. But I thank ye fer thinkin' so, sir."

Looking around, Robert saw three young scullery maids, all strangers, staring agape at the presence of a strange gent in their private domain. Cook clapped her hands and they silently disappeared into the yard lugging baskets of linens and bedding to wash and hang. With their master in his dire condition, every day was washday and the piles of foul smelling underclothes and sheets never ended.

He turned to the cook, Mrs. Carrey's niece, Sharon, now supervisor of the kitchen and laundry. Despite the years that had passed since he had been at GlynMor, he recognized her unusual cornflower blue eyes.

"Sharon, is it? I wonder if you might fix me a lunch. I would enjoy a visit with my old friend, Ben. Perhaps one of the girls could bring it out to the stable along with a nice glass of ale."

He turned to the old groom.

"Would you enjoy some company, Ben?"

"That I would, and no denyin', sir. Tis a long time since ye've been t'the stables here and I saw yer beautiful animal and wondered whose it was. Now I'm that glad I prodded Peter t'take special care brushin' his lovely red coat."

Their voices faded as they left Sharon to prepare a tray. When the maids returned to drag the huge washtubs outside, Sharon ordered them to keep their ears open and report to her anything they heard. This was an extraordinary visit and things were sure to heat up once his Lordship returned.

In the little shed where Tom had sat plotting Meg's rescue so many years ago, Lord Robert Cushing drained his ale and bit into an early plum. Putting his feet up on an old worn saddle, he contemplated the grizzled old man before him.

"I have recently seen Lady Meg and some of the Phalen children. It is on their behalf that I've come to GlynMor. I have reason to believe that a Mr. Gilchrist of Newport has ill intentions toward her and her family. My concern is great enough to have prompted me to come here and find out more about him. So, Ben, tell me. What do you know of this Gilchrist fellow who comes around?"

Ben's head jerked up in sudden interest at the mention of the Phalens.

"Sir, if ye please, can I ask after Tom Phalen? Is he well? Do they have a big family?"

"I didn't see Tom but as far as I know he's alive and as well as can be expected given the depth of starvation I saw in Meg and the children. They have seven children living and two deceased. They are living at the moment in Westport and slowly recovering from near death. I daresay the whole spectacle shocked me to my very roots. I am compelled to do whatever I must to bring them home and make them well. And ridding them of Robert Gilchrist is the first step."

Ben shifted uncomfortably in his rickety old chair.

"Me bones hurt all the time now. I wonder sometimes why I'm still in the land of the living. But lookin' at ye sittin' here m'Lord, makes me wonder if this is why I'm still around. Sure I'll tell ye all I know about Gilchrist. It's that disgusted we all are with his panderin' t'his lordship and his nasty evil ways with the lot of us. If he has anythin' t'do with harmin' a hair on Tom and Lady Meg's head, I'll see him hanged. Beggin' yer pardon sir."

Lighting a pipe, he continued.

"As ye can see, none of us is starvin' here at Glynmor. We're that fortunate, that we are. But if Mr. Robert Gilchrist had his way, we'd all be dead. 'Tis our good fortune that Lord Wynn's undertaker is Mr. Riordan. He's that nice a fellow, he is."

Lord Robert leaned forward and tried to nudge the old groom a bit. This could be a very long process at the rate they were going.

"You must make haste to tell me all, Ben. Once Lord Jeffrey returns there will be hell to pay and I'll most likely be expelled from the property. Just about Mr. Gilchrist please, if you know anything."

Ben began describing a most unpleasant man, one who had insinuated himself into Lord Wynn's household early on. Years ago, before Lady Wynn left, he was just an occasional poker partner of his lordship but after a few years he seemed to have more sway over his lordship than Mr. Riordan or even Mr. Guttman, his lordship's solicitor.

He spoke of the sinister tête-a-têtes he had heard about

158

from George, of the money that had passed hands on a regular basis, of Mr. Gilchrist's loud arguments with Mr. Riordan. Ben himself had had no direct contact with Mr. Gilchrist but the servants who had were deeply afraid of him. If they thought Lord Cushing could help rid GlynMor of his influence they would surely talk to him.

"George would want t'be talkin' t'ye, sir, and Riordan. Any o'the girls too. Gilchrist tried some ugly things with'em but they're all from one family and Cook has their brothers workin' here too. When Mr. Gilchrist found out they live at home, he backed right off."

Ben smiled to himself.

"He'd niver go after Cook again either, sir. The only time he tried and that was when her ladyship was still here, and Cook was still a housemaid, she told him she was full of pestilence and disease and her latest beau had just been waked. Now, ye saw fer yerself that she's the picture o'health but Mr. Gilchrist lost interest mighty quick."

"George will talk? That surprises me, Ben. He's always been so loyal to Jeffrey."

Ben shook his head.

"Sir, so much has changed since those days. Poor George has had the life of a nursemaid t'the divil for longer than ten years. His lordship is the same tyrant from his wheeled chair as he was from his saddle. We all stay, sir, because we have nowhere else t'go. Lord Wynn cares little what we eat or wear or where we sleep or who we are."

"As long as his needs are met and his money holds out, we mind our own business, eat his food and bide our time till he dies. I know that sounds bad and maybe I'm an old fool t'be sayin' it t'ye but ye asked me and I'm tellin' ye. He niver asks about me. Peter has covered me work since I had a brain seizure that left me with this withered arm. The staff here is the finest around. They've taken good care o'me, that they have. And not a word t'Himself that I'm shirkin' me duties. I suppose he thinks I'm dead by now."

"The others work just as hard as they would anywhere.

Ye can see fer yerself the grounds and the house are kept well and all. The horses are groomed and Peter takes them out regularly fer exercise. We know nothing but hard work, sir. And we're not fools t'watch our neighbors fallin' t'the Crowbar Brigade and get caught complainin' about our lot. All in all it's a good life we have here. Knowin' ye're here t'help Lady Meg, I'm not afraid t'be tellin' ye the truth but George is th'man who knows the ins and outs of it all."

Lord Robert nodded.

"I will need a place to hide. Stiller knows I'm here and I've asked to see Jeffrey. Had I known he was out for the day I would not have made my presence known. What do you suggest I do to throw Stiller off my scent? I want to learn as much as I can before I see Lord Jeffrey."

"Simple, sir. Ye just leave and make a big fanfare out of it. Then Stiller will have nothin' t'tell. George can meet ye wherever ye go. He and Stiller have very little t'do with each other anymore. Go on down t'the old Phalen place. No one will know ye're there. I'll send George down after he sees his lordship t'bed. That'll be early tonight fer sure. He's not long fer this world either, I'm told. But again, George can tell ye better than I."

Robert rose and kicked some loose straw off the tip of his black Wellington boot.

"Thank you Ben. I'll go now and see what Sharon or Peter can tell me. He glanced at his pocket watch. In about an hour, let Stiller know I'm leaving. I'll have Peter bring my horse around the front so we can make my departure official."

"Ye're most welcome sir. Don't worry about a thing. And sir, when ye see Lady Meg again, let her know I was after askin' fer her. And young Tom too."

The old man shook his head, as a little smile creased his sagging face.

"Seven babies. Nine t'start with. Tom Phalen, now there's a man fer ye."

Robert Cushing sat on an old bench outside the kitchen door of Tom Phalen's old house. The early evening breeze whistled through the crumbling stone walls of the pigsty and a flock of mourning doves cooed in the rafters of the old loft. Some of the thatch had caved in and he could hear mice scurrying around under the rotten old straw.

George should be here soon, he thought, as he lit an expensive Turkish cigar. He was devilishly tired and ached from sitting on the hard sycamore bench. He thought of his favorite worn leather club chair and sighed. It would be good to get home. This was probably a fool's errand anyhow. Jeffrey would probably not be willing to see him and if he did, what made him think that bastard would do anything to help his daughter after years of plotting against her?

He had taken his supper at McPhinney's, a sorry old pub a short stretch of the legs from this decrepit cottage. There was no one else in the pub and it looked like there had been very few customers in a very long time. The owner was long dead and the young whelp behind the bar had shot him a hostile glance when he entered.

He decided to stay, thinking he might find out some information. There was no real dinner being served but the youth had killed a few rabbits that afternoon and had them stewing with fresh onions, carrots and a few parsnips. He looked like he could use the whole pot, he was that thin. But this was still a working pub and despite the lack of trade, seemed to be surviving. He ate his stew, a greasy, gamy concoction and mopped up the broth with a heel of dry brown bread. Robert had been hungry enough to eat a large bowlful and be glad of it, washing it down with a pint of local brew. The ale was a bit flat and certainly not the rich stout he was used to. Now, as his stomach churned in noisy protest, he cursed himself for not having Sharon fix him a meal to take with him.

Robert hadn't learned much from the lad after all. Old Tom Phalen had never returned to his homestead, not many of the regulars came around anymore, he'd lost his da to the hunger in '46. But the boy seemed reluctant to reveal much about the folks in the big house. He denied even knowing George or Peter and hadn't seen Ben in months. Robert had left as soon as he finished his meal. No use trying to get anything more out of that scowling grouch.

Just as the sun was starting to color the western sky, Robert heard the crunching of footsteps. George came around the corner of the pigsty and into view. Robert was surprised to see how little the man had changed. Other than the thatch of white hair that had replaced the brown Robert remembered, Jeffrey's man looked much the same as he had for years. He still wore the same trim livery and his lean face was clean-shaven. His form was slender and fit and his face unwrinkled despite his advancing age. Robert believed him to be about sixty but he looked forty at most.

"Good evening M'Lord. Ben said you wanted to see me sir."

George stood before him, a quizzical expression on his face. Robert stood and walked over to the servant, his hand outstretched. George shook it with a smooth, strong grip.

"Yes. Good to see you, George, you look well."

George nodded.

"Thank you sir, I am, sir."

"I'll come right to the point, George. I've been to the manor today and I've spoken to some of the servants. I am enquiring after a man named Robert Gilchrist. It is imperative that I learn anything there is to know. I suspect he has been somehow responsible for the dramatic downturn in the life of your former mistress, my niece, Lady Meg Wynn."

He cleared his voice.

"Now Mrs. Thomas Phalen, of course. What can you tell me? I ask you to be frank, please. It would be in your own best interests to be completely honest with me. There is no point trying to protect the man."

George had been pondering his miserable existence as Lord Jeffrey's man for many years, especially so in the last several months. Today he had had enough, dragging his master all over his farm, listening to him whine about this thing and that, feeding him lunch, helping him relieve himself and cleaning him up when he was through. The man was impossible to please and caring for him was like trying to satisfy a giant two-year old child. George was exhausted. Robert's timing could not have been better.

But George was no fool. He knew that if Lord Wynn ever believed George had betrayed him, even after years of loyal service, he would be banished from his fine quarters and left with no references for another position. At his age, George was simply biding his time until his employer died and he could move on to another master in another fine house. He had already had offers from more than one of his lordship's friends over the years.

He had no family in Clydagh Glyn and had thought one offer particularly enticing. Lord Jasper, the Earl of Bennington, had encouraged George to live on the island of Malta administering his summer home. Lord Jasper knew Jeffrey was dying and was waiting for George to be legitimately free. George had as much as accepted the offer. The warm Mediterranean sun would do wonders for his achy knees. But there was still the matter of finishing his term with Lord Jeffrey. George was indeed a very loyal servant and it was simply not in his nature to abandon his employer of over thirty years, especially in such unhealthy condition.

"Sir, I have my future to think of and as first servant I hesitate to speak of any of the private doings of my master. Surely you must understand this."

Robert nodded emphatically.

"Of course, George. I would expect nothing less from any servant, Jeffrey's or mine. But this is a very serious matter. This Gilchrist has designs on Lord Jeffrey's family that do not exclude murder by starvation. I have seen Lady Meg and her children. Trust me when I say they are barely hanging onto life. After serious thought I have decided that I must, in all moral conscience, try to find out if he has a role to play in the demise of Tom Phalen's very prosperous dairy farm and the death of two of his sons from the hunger."

George looked stricken at Lord Robert's words. The staff of GlynMor Castle had been so insulated from the hunger. There was a generous budget available to them for both necessities and luxuries. They had hardly been affected by what had been going on right beyond the boundaries of Lord Jeffrey's holdings. Had their master not been an invalid, unable and uninterested in any life beyond his room, they would probably have suffered more. He would have been about evicting and ruining people to keep his coffers full.

But since his accident, Lord Jeffrey Wynn had lost all interest in the outside world and had concentrated his energies on seeking whatever pleasure there still was to be had. Making the lives of his close servants and associates miserable, once his favorite pastime, had long ago been replaced by playing cards and drinking way too much whiskey. Not to mention the laudenum. Had George realized how dependent his master really was on him for the potent drug, he would have been amazed. George, for his part, procured the medicine regularly and when his lordship requested it he obediently brought it to him.

"Sir, I had no idea!"

"Neither had I, nor for that matter had Lady Meg's mother. We had been following their life ever since they left but with the hunger so bad on Achill, our sources had not been in contact with us for some time. I need to establish a case against this Gilchrist and present it to Jeffrey. If he refuses to acknowledge his complicity, nay, his orchestration of this diabolical treachery, I will take it to the law."

"George, I do not want you or any of the other servants implicated if this becomes a case of public legal scrutiny. It is my desire to handle this at all costs within the confines of the family. I have no desire to bring down scandal upon this house or anyone who carries my father's name."

"The first thing I need from you is a complete report on the state of Jeffrey's health. Then we can see if Mr. Gilchrist exerts undue influence on him. I am far more interested in pursuing Mr.Gilchrist than Jeffrey. I see no benefit in dragging a half-man through the streets in a wheeled chair to answer for his sins. Even if Jeffrey is paying Gilchrist to do his dirty work, Gilchrist is the one who is guilty."

George stood dumbstruck. His knees throbbed, his back ached and his body felt like thirty stone of sand.

Robert saw the impact of his words and gestured for George to sit down on the low bench. He was too agitated to sit and paced back and forth puffing on his cigar.

George had never sat in the presence of a gentleman while the gentleman stood.

"But sir, you…"

Robert waved him impatiently toward the seat. Good heavens, servants were a hard lot to deal with.

"Think nothing of it, George. I have no desire to sit and you look like you could fall over. Sit. Please."

George took his seat and looked hard at Lord Robert. Here was a man he had not even seen in over ten years. A man whose last visit caused a terrible row resulting in weeks of misery for George. He had no less authority over him than his own master yet he hardly knew him. George was not often put in such a delicate and potentially dangerous position and he wasn't quite sure what to do. As he watched this gentleman watch him, he realized he had no choice but to obey his request. Well, he thought, in for a penny, in for a pound.

"Sir, there isn't much to tell about m'Lord. He is mortally ill, has been for some time. Truly, I am no physician but I am astounded that he wakes up every morning and carries on. Every time I walk into his room I expect to find him gone. He is completely helpless. Can barely feed himself and in the last few months, chokes on anything but soft things. He tries to get drunk but lately the whiskey causes him to cough. He hasn't enjoyed cards in the last few months either so there have been no visitors. Today, when he demanded to travel around the farm it took me and the three young O'Brien lads to get him downstairs. If he asks again, I've decided I will refuse. I was so afraid we'd kill him trying to carry him back upstairs. If the laudanum doesn't do him in, certainly another day like today will do it."

Robert interrupted him.

"George, how much of a threat can he be if he's such an invalid? And why is he taking laudanum? Is he in that much pain?"

George shook his head.

"He's really no threat at all. The threat is more a memory of his volatile old self. He was a bit of a myth among the staff and at least with the girls, there was good reason to fear him. As for the drug, no he doesn't feel much of anything now. I'm sure when he started it years ago it was for the terrible pain in his face from the burns. The scars pulled something fierce and he always felt the burning even after they healed. The laudanum was the only thing that made it possible for him to talk and eat. But it wasn't long before he needed it just to get through the day. The last few months it makes him sleep. When he's awake he's cranky and miserable and begging for more of the drug."

Robert was shocked at the expression on George's face as he listened to his report. The man looked as if he were going to cry.

George shrugged.

"It's been a bit rough, sir. There's no denying, it's been a bit rough."

Robert nodded soberly.

"George, Jeffrey has been a fool for as long as I have known him. I see now that his one great achievement has been to win your loyalty. You may disagree but the man never deserved you and you have every reason to be proud of yourself for staying with him all these years."

"Thank you, sir. Very kind of you, sir."

"Well, it's true. Any man would be lucky to have you in

his employ. Now, about Gilchrist. What can you tell me?"

"Well sir, that's a story."

George proceeded to tell Robert a long tale of manipulation and subterfuge that had been going on ever since Tom Phalen had taken Lady Meg away from Clydagh Glyn.

Gilchrist was a relatively new poker partner of Lord Jeffrey's when all that happened. He was, in fact, at the game Lord Jeffrey had played the night of his accident. At the time, he was the office manager for a large law firm that handled the affairs of Lord Lucan and several other landlords in the county, including Lord Wynn. Mr. Guttman had been one of the partners in the firm until he suffered a fall that made it too difficult to navigate the building that housed the practice.

Shortly after he recovered from his accident, Mr. Guttman left the firm, but Lord Wynn kept him as his soliciter. Mr. Guttman had also been one of Lord Jeffrey's poker partners, had in fact, introduced Gilchrist to his lordship, but stopped attending the games shortly after his accident. However, his lordship still played poker with Mr. Gilchrist. When Gilchrist left the firm to take the position as Lord Lucan's undertaker he made regular trips to Clydagh Glyn on Lord Lucan's behalf. These trips always included a visit to Lord Wynn and a nice, long evening of cards. George had been Lord Jeffrey's hands and eyes during these games.

"Then you were privy to all of their conversations."

"Every word, sir."

Lord Robert sat down next to the other man. Together they watched the sky turn shades of pink and gray. Lord Robert pursed his lips around little rings of cigar smoke that floated into the dusk.

"Go on, George. Tell me everything."

"Well, sir, one night they started talking about women and Mr.Gilchrist had had a great deal to drink and was speaking in quite unflattering terms about Mrs. Gilchrist. It seems she was with child again and not willingly fulfilling her duties. My Lord had also been drinking heavily and began to rant about Lady Beverly and how she had failed him as a wife for years. Gilchrist made some snide remark about letting her get away with cuckolding him and my Lord became livid with Mr. Gilchrist. Had he been able to move, I'm sure he would have had his hands on the man's neck."

"They argued for a while, as drunks are wont to do and began comparing notes on their various exploits. In the course of the argument, Mr. Gilchrist remembered a serving girl at the club where they had played cards the night of the accident. It seems one of the men had tried to win a bit of skirt from her as part of the kitty. Then they tried to remember all the lads that were there that night."

"Suddenly Gilchrist mentioned a deed that Lord Wynn had won off an American gent. This got them going about the accident and the deed and how it disappeared. When Gilchrist saw how agitated the conversation made his lordship he shut his mouth and left. But I know he saw an opportunity to make money."

"The next time they played, he brought a contract. He would track down the deed or have Tom Phalen in jail for stealing it. All he wanted were his expenses and a yearly allowance. I can't remember how much it was but it was a great deal of money. Lord Jeffrey was so smitten with the idea of ruining Tom Phalen that he signed it. Or I should say I signed it in his name."

George put his head in his hands in despair.

"Dear God in heaven, I have murder on my head! I signed the contract! I signed Lady Meg and Tom Phalen's death warrant!"

"Not at all, George! Not a bit of it! You merely acted on behalf of your master allowing Gilchrist to retrieve his rightful property. Mr. Gilchrist is the one who has the blood of Meg's children on his hands."

"What do we do now, M'Lord? He's never found the deed and Lady Meg's family is in ruins."

Robert wondered about the whereabouts of the deed now but said nothing. He shifted the subject away from the deed.

"What were Jeffrey's feelings about Lady Meg after all the dust settled?"

"Well, he was very angry. He blamed her for all his troubles and more so, Tom Phalen. He's calmed down over the years though. I thought he had just lost interest like he had with the house staff but I think now it was the laudanum. He gets very maudlin sometimes, sir. Sometimes he even has tears. I know it's the laudanum but as he has declined, he's given to long rants about his childhood and Lady Meg and even Lady Beverly. I can't say how much of it is real and how much is just the drug but some days he goes on for hours."

"For example?"

"Well sir, about his mother. Did you know that she had a tryst with an Irishman much the way Lady Meg did? A laborer and no better?"

"What? Go on with you, man! It never happened!"

"As God is my witness, he said it himself!"

George took a deep breath and plunged into his story.

"According to Lord Wynn, he actually witnessed his mum in the man's arms when he was a boy of about ten. They were in her bed and the boy thought the man was hurting her. He tried to save her but the man walloped him one, never even climbing off his mum. He tried again and the man kicked him away. His mum spoke up and before the brute slapped her into silence he heard her say the words that changed his life forever. He told me sir, that his mum cried out words he would never, could never, forget."

George stopped and inhaled deeply.

"Sir, my Lord Jeffrey heard his mum say to the man, 'How can you treat your own son that way?' As God is my witness that's what he told me."

Robert sat in stunned silence. His head felt like it was spinning off his neck but somewhere deep in his soul he knew that George spoke the truth. This revelation made so much sense of his brother-in-law's behavior. Hearing George's words was like placing the final piece in a jigsaw puzzle. No wonder Jeffrey hated the Irish with maniacal passion. No wonder he was compelled to hurt every woman he knew. Poor Beverly! She had married a man so wounded he spent his whole life striking out at everyone he could reach. Jeffrey is just a tortured boy in a man's body who can only assuage his pain by torturing others. God save them all! What to do now?

He rose to his feet and crushed the remnant of his cigar beneath his heel. Without facing George, he finally spoke. He heard the words as from a distance and was surprised at the sound of his own voice.

"When was Gilchrist last here, George?"

"About a week ago, sir. He collected Mr. Riordan and they went off to Westport for a meeting."

"Really? Do you know the nature of his business?'

George looked sick and swallowed hard.

"Well, sir, he only stayed a brief time. He told my Lord Wynn that the Phalen's were no longer living in the house on Achill and he needed more money to track them down. He suspected they had moved back to the mainland but figured they couldn't have gone too far because they had only just left Achill."

"He asked m'Lord if he had any further instructions for him and Lord Wynn said that they could all go to hell for all he cared. He was having a very bad day and wanted nothing to do with Mr. Gilchrist, sir. He's usually more interested in Lady Meg."

"Gilchrist went on as though Lord Wynn had never spoken. He asked about the deed and the horse Jewel. For some reason Mr. Gilchrist seemed to think Tom Phalen stole that horse from m'Lord but Jewel was a gift years ago from Lady Meg's suitor, Mr. Parker. Lord Wynn told him he didn't care about the horse but demanded to know why Gilchrist hadn't found this deed after all these years. Mr. Gilchrist was very put out."

Robert's ears perked up at this. He strongly suspected the deed was the one Meg had mentioned in his conversation at

Browne's Inn the other night. She had said she had given it to
Maureen Dougherty and the former maid had used it to set
up a life in the United States. Again, he decided to keep his
counsel and probe a bit further.

"Do you know what property the deed was for?"

"Well sir, I never saw the deed but I believe it's for
property somewhere in the States."

Robert listened carefully to what George was saying.

"And Gilchrist?"

"He's made much of his ability to prove Tom Phalen
stole it and has it in his possession to this day. All I know is
Mr. Gilchrist has taken a great deal of m'Lord's money over
the years promising to get it back. If you want to know the
truth, Lord Wynn could probably have bought the land
outright for all the money that jackel has bilked! I know! I
wrote the drafts for him. In fact, I wrote a large draft just last
week. Five hundred pounds! Lord Wynn ordered me to write
it before Mr. Gilchrist left."

"Five hundred pounds! For what?"

"Well, Mr. Gilchrist claimed that while he was in
Westport he would go to Achill once and for all and root out
the guilty parties. He was very upset that Lord Wynn no
longer cared about the horse. Of course, his fee went down
so he had to make a big to do about the deed then."

"Poor Lord Wynn. He's really just a helpless old man and
this creeping, slithering snake is taking his money and doing
nothing for him. Most people think Lord Wynn is simply an
evil snake himself but that's all gone now. If you see him
you'll know what I mean. He soils himself, his eyes are almost
sightless and he drools constantly from the droopy side of his
mouth. He can't weigh more than a few stone and he's grown
to look like a bird!"

Suddenly George became very agitated and stood up
from the bench.

"Sir, my Lord Wynn had been a sad, broken man since
the day I met him. He's never recovered from his wife's
rejection of his affections all those years ago and despite his

cruel treatment of Lady Meg, never wanted her to die of hunger under any circumstances. It's Tom Phalen he hates for bedding her and disgracing her name and his. And all that's really about his mother."

Robert stiffened at hearing such intimate information about his sister. He had never known why Beverly hated Jeffrey. He still didn't understand but this information gave him some idea of why Jeffrey hated her. He had always wondered what happened between them. He remembered them as being very much in love on their wedding day. Until this conversation, Robert would have been content to remain ignorant. He would never have entertained the thought of trying to find out.

George took out a clean white handkerchief and blew his nose loudly. The sun was slipping below the stand of yews that used to be Lady Meg's favorite riding trail.

"Sir, I've told you things I was trusted to keep to myself. I feel like a regular bugger if you must know the truth. As I said, Lord Wynn has been very good to me and I really have been a loyal friend to him. I must ask for your word as a gentleman that what I've told you will be used only to help him die in peace. I know he would like the chance to see Lady Meg before he dies. He was terrible to her and most of his tears are about that. The business about his mother must never go further, m'Lord. I would never forgive myself if he ever found out I told anyone."

"Thank you George. You have my word, without question. This hasn't been easy for you. For now, I believe it would be best to just keep this entire conversation between us. Given what you've said about Jeffrey's current state of health, I see no harm in my staying at GlynMor, at least for tonight. Just show me the best place to sleep where I will cause the least trouble for the staff. You and I know they have nothing to fear from my sister's husband but I'm not ready to reassure them of that quite yet. What you have told me is most alarming and I have to digest it before I can decide my next step. Please be assured that I will handle this matter with the utmost discretion. Now, what about Riordan? Where is he?"

"In Dublin, sir. His wife's mother passed on. He just left this morning and I expect will be gone several days. She has quite a few holdings and there is much to be settled as his wife is the only heir."

"Good. And Guttman? How often does he come around?"

"Only when summoned, sir. And I do the summoning at m'Lord's behest."

"Excellent. We need to handle this business privately. And you must notify me immediately if Mr. Gilchrist returns. It is imperative that I know."

"Yes, sir. I will send a messenger on horseback to your home if you wish."

"Of course, George. That would be fine. But I intend to stay here a bit and see if Mr. Gilchrist might not show up here in the next few days. I have a feeling he may be back sooner than you think."

George looked questioningly at Lord Robert.
"Sir?"

Lord Robert decided not to share the fact that he had just spent almost two days with Mr. Gilchrist in Westport.

"Let's just call it a hunch, shall we George? Well, I say, this has been a bit of an ordeal for us both. What say we retire to our chambers to spend the rest of the evening relaxing?"

"Yes sir, thank you sir. A very good idea indeed, sir."

Robert Cushing stood staring out the open bedroom window into the night, a soft breeze ruffling his hair, the smoke from a half-spent cheroot curling around his head. He had not been to sleep and it was almost two. It was certainly not wedding festivities that kept him awake this time. Rather, he had tossed and turned in Beverly's massive, white, enameled bed unable to settle down. He was so tired, he wondered at his sleeplessness. What troubled his thoughts? Was it knowing Jeffrey slept on the same floor albeit in the adjacent wing of the huge old castle? Did he sense the restless evil of a house where so much pain had been inflicted? How could he not find rest in the home of his childhood? Surely the memories of his parents' love and the happy days he spent here should trump anything that happened to someone else.

Maybe it was just the room, so feminine and unfamiliar. When he was a boy, he slept in the room that eventually became Meg's. Pouring himself a glass of sherry, he thought about those carefree days when the only thing he needed was a fine horse and three good meals during the day and the comfy feel of a sweet feather bed at night. As long as he and Beverly were able to sweet-talk their dear father and stay out of the way of Nurse Patterson, life was golden. Their mother could be a formidable woman but she was kind to her servants and while not as permissive as her husband, allowed him to spoil Robert and Beverly as he wished.

Sipping the sherry, made on his own estate, he thought of their summers in Scotland at his mother's childhood home. For the life of him, he couldn't remember the name of the town near the farm she grew up on. He was really getting old if he was forgetting things like that. They had been back to the farm every summer he was at home and occasionally as an adult. Adelaide had loved the farm. She said it reminded her of the one her own grandparents had in Normandy.

Adelaide. So many years gone and he still grieved her. Not so often as in the beginning but still with the same burning lump in the center of his chest. And Madeleine. Their little girl. What would she have been like had she lived? She'd be almost forty years old now! How could that be? He felt the familiar sting pierce the back of his eyes as he fought off the tears that had always accompanied the thought of Adelaide. How he had worshipped her. She was so beautiful, so soft and kind.

Suddenly he felt his heart skip a beat. He always remembered that his beloved wife was beautiful but he realized with a start that he had forgotten just what she looked like. He remembered her scent, the feel of her hair in his hands and the way she looked after making love. But he had lost the clear image of her face, the way her eyes sat in her head and the shape of her nose. How could he not remember the shape of her mouth and the soft curve of her neck? Had he entered his dotage that he'd forget the most important face he'd ever laid eyes on?

Adelaide! What kind of love is it that forgets? Yes, it had been many years since he placed his last kiss on her lips but he wanted never to forget!

He set the glass down and began to pace anxiously back and forth across the rich oriental carpet with its busy pattern of tiger lilies entwined with strands of pale green ivy. He fleetingly wondered if ivy of that color really existed but returned immediately to his quest. He just had to conjure up the image of his dead wife's face. He would not sleep until he did.

Back and forth he paced, unable to see her in his mind's eye. Frantic, he rubbed his sleepy eyes and tried to peer into the pitch dark. Did he actually hope to see her out there? He could barely make out the form of the stables and the ancient trees behind it. The moon was new and low in the sky. No, he wouldn't see Adelaide out there. She had always been a little afraid of the night. She would not be out there.

This is ridiculous Robert thought, sitting down on the bed, running his hands through his hair. He was just exhausted that's all. He couldn't expect to see anything, tired as he was. He had a miniature of her at home but had stopped taking it in his waistcoat pocket years ago. If only he had it with him now. Then he could put to rest these useless recriminations and get some sleep.

He climbed back into the bed and drew the counterpane across his legs. No sooner had his head hit the pillow did he spring up again. There is a picture of Adelaide here! There must be. He had given a nice little portrait to his mother when he and Adelaide publicly announced their betrothal. His mother had been so thrilled with the match that Adelaide had had it done especially for her. Could it still be here? Beverly used to put it out in the library but would Jeffrey have tossed it away? Of course not! What a fool he was! Jeffrey couldn't even go downstairs without help.

Robert threw on his robe and grabbed a candle from the bed table. He lit it with the tip of the little cigar and headed down the corridor to the front stairs. In the dim moonlight the cascade of marble was barely visible but Robert knew the feel of these steps beneath his feet like a pair of old house shoes.

Once he was in the library, he lit more candles and stood in the center of the room. Turning this way and that he took in every table top, every shelf and the huge ebony mantel with the pillars of black marble carved to look like Nubian princes. It wasn't there. He remembered the oval gilt frame lined with burgundy velvet matting that so beautifully framed her face. Where was it? He was convinced that it was in this room. He would not rest until he found it.

He began to search the bookshelves, shoving rows of books from one end to the other. He found an old portrait of his parents painted when they first moved to Clydagh Glyn and set it out to take back to his house. He found books he had left here as a young man when he went to university. He found a small box of medals and military honors his father had earned as a sailor in Her Majesty's navy during the war with the colonies.

Robert was beginning to think he'd never find the portrait. If it was in plain sight there was no way he would have missed it. He had placed his hand on every shelf of the library and moved hundreds of books in his search. He heard the mantel clock chime four. Good Heavens! It was almost dawn and here he was like a madman chasing a ghost around the library of a home he was not supposed to be in! Well, devil take the hindmost, he had to find Adelaide. Besides, who was going to question him if they found him? Most of the books in this library belonged to him or his father. Jeffrey had never enjoyed them except as a backdrop.

Robert looked again in an old roll top desk of his father's. Most of the items on the desktop were Jeffrey's. Ledgers and old documents were bundled at one end of the smooth mahogany surface. This had clearly been Jeffrey's desk. There was no sign that Beverly had ever used it. Jeffrey had been a very tidy bookkeeper, in his day, Robert thought as he thumbed through the papers.

There were receipts from the original planting of the rose garden back in 1808 and every bush added to it over the years. Odd that there were receipts for bushes purchased as recently as the current year. He could tell that Jeffrey hadn't put them there. He had initialed every receipt until the year of his accident. The others were merely clipped together in a separate pile.

There was a paid invoice from several new suits of clothes. Robert shuddered at the discovery of an old newspaper from June 1, 1835. Holding the yellowed sheaf, he realized it was probably the last one his brother-in-law had ever bought.

Next he explored the drawers on the left side of the desk. They held an assortment of old papers and documents belonging to his father. He was surprised Jeffrey had never gotten rid of them. He picked up a bible and opened it to the first page. In his mother's hand he read the details of his parent's wedding. Fingering through the fine, silky pages, he felt a bulky envelope slide out of the back of the book and land on his lap.

"What is this?" he asked himself, startled to hear his voice echo in the cavernous room.

The envelope had been sealed with the Cushing crest but had been opened. The *old* wax was dry and crumbled when Robert touched it. Inside was a letter in his father's hand. Recognizing the bold, broad strokes, Robert remembered his father's words about a man's character being reflected in the strength of his signature.

Careful not to tear the delicate old paper, he unfolded the

letter.

30 *March, 1810*

My dearest Eleanor,

It is with mixed feelings that I respond to your letter of 21 February. It is a source of great concern that I am not able to be there with you during this time of such great sorrow. Lettie was a wonderful dog and the gentlest of companions in my absence. I admit she loved you far better than me but my eyes misted over when I read of her accident. I know how keenly you must feel her loss.

I do have good news that will, perhaps, lift your spirits. I was able to consult with some very fine doctors of veterinary medicine here in Yorkshire and have received some sound advice on the breeding difficulties we've been having with Impetuous Fancy. There were two fellows who thought she may be too old but more than a few thought we should be able to get her to respond to a new tonic preparation. One lad, Dr. Batton was kind enough to give me a sample of his concoction. I am anxious to try it on her and see if we can't bring her around.

Speaking of bringing around, I'm delighted to hear that Beverly and Jeffrey are planning a visit next month. I will be home within a fortnight and my hands are itching to tickle that beautiful granddaughter of ours! I must say that she is the best thing to come out of that marriage. I know we have spoken of this sadness many times since they returned from their wedding trip but it still remains a mystery to me how we could have been so wrong about that match. They seemed so well suited and he came from such good people! You know the Wynns longer than I and we've both said that there were never two more upstanding people. Though I have to admit that Lady Wynn is a bit flirtatious for my taste. Give me an old fashioned Scots girl any time! Cool on the surface with a warm fire burning deep inside. That's my Ellie. I offer no complaints about our match, my dear. Made in heaven!

Getting back to Beverly, she seems to be fond enough of little Margaret though she is never the mother you were. And Meg! What kind of a name is Meg? For such a wee bairn as she is I suppose Margaret is bit of a handle but Meg is so blunt or something. Not my favorite. As you know, I would have preferred Anna after my mother or Eleanor after you. But I still think she's the prettiest little lass around.

Again, Beverly could be warmer toward her but perhaps she is just so unhappy in her marriage she can't find joy even in her daughter. Above all, my love, I am aggrieved that Beverly's situation brings tears to your pretty gray eyes. Would that it were not so.

Try not to fret over Lettie, my dear. I know how you loved her and how tormented you are by her untimely death. I beg of you, do not blame yourself. Nothing you could have done would have stopped that runaway horse no matter what the devil who owns it said. You had every right to bring Lettie to the fair and he should have been more careful with his animal. Why, sad as it is that we lost Lettie, it could have been someone's child! God blast it though, I wish I had been there to get the blackguard's name! But I was here, so far away. For that I am deeply sorry.

I will be home sooner than you can say your name

backward. I may even bring you a new pup. There is a litter of beautiful Wheaton terriers here at Dr. Batton's little clinic. If you could find it in that great dear heart of yours a place for a new pet I know you'd love one of them. Beautiful dogs!

Take heart, my dearest.
Ever Yours,
Bents

Robert smiled at his father's moniker. Bents. Only his mother got away with calling him that. Even his own brothers had to call him Bentley.

He leafed through the remaining papers. There were a few love letters from his mother to his father when he was at war and some records of acquisition for two townlands his father bought when he first moved to Clydagh Glyn. There were baptismal records for both him and Beverly, and the record of his parent's marriage. The papers were in fairly good condition but of no real value save for sentiment. To Robert's dismay the drawer did not hold the oval framed portrait of his wife.

Sitting in his father's wheeled office chair, he listened to the leather seat creak beneath his weight. The sound was so reminiscent of days spent playing under the huge desk while his father wrote letters and reviewed his holdings, that he stopped and just listened. Fatigue now threatened to overpower him as he sat moving in the chair, savoring the sounds that brought his father back into the room. He felt his presence so powerfully that he was afraid to turn around lest his father's ghost would be standing there behind him.

He had just about given up finding the portrait when his right hand brushed a slight indentation in the mahogany veneer next to the ink well. When Robert pressed his forefinger against the near edge of the indentation, a rectangle about the size of a small platter opened up. He lifted the piece of desktop out and looked inside. There were no drawers on this side of the desk and he realized now that the hole created by the missing piece revealed a deep storage space completely hidden by the false front panel of the desk.

Robert brought his candle close to the rim of the opening. There wasn't much in the space but he caught a glint near the bottom that looked like the latch on a small box. Reaching down into the depths of the space he drew out a little leather chest. Of course it was locked and no amount of fishing around produced a key.

He finally set the candle in its holder down at the bottom of the secret space and trying not to set the whole piece on fire, maneuvered it around until he had seen all four walls and corners. Sure enough, as he withdrew the candle he spotted a string dangling along the back wall of the little space. Quickly Robert pulled out the candle and reached back in. The string was hung from a nail and Robert could feel a key at the end of it. He tugged at it and it came away without a fight.

Leaning back in the chair, he sat staring at the mysterious box and it's key. He had no idea what he would find in the little trunk and he almost hesitated to find out. His eyes burned in his head and his muscles throbbed with fatigue. Slowly he picked up the key and inserted it into the lock. One half-turn to the left and the little box popped open revealing a sheaf of papers and more military medals. Some dusty old rose petals and shriveled orange blossoms were wrapped in a lace hanky and set across another smaller, white bible. It was Beverly's! These things were mementos of his sister's wedding. He was suddenly overcome by a profound sadness. Knowing how pleased his parents had felt about Beverly's marriage to Jeffrey somehow made it more tragic. His heart was heavy as he realized the burden of sorrow both he and Beverly had placed upon the two people he had loved the most. How terribly sad to have arranged two marriages for your children and have them both end so miserably.

In the bottom of the chest was a soft, blue silk envelope tied with a dainty pink ribbon.

He untied the ribbon. A small book and several pieces of

jewelry slid out. There were two necklaces, one of diamonds the other of deep blue sapphires. In the bottom of the envelope were two pairs of matching earbobs and a long slender rope of pearls. Robert was fairly certain that these were not his mother's. She had had many beautiful necklaces and brooches but Beverly had anything of value that had been among her things when she died and she had given Meg her ivory brooch.

Meg! He now knew where Lord Sligo's wife had gotten the ivory brooch he'd bought Beverly for Christmas. No wonder Beverly recognized it. It had been their mother's! His eyes stung as he connected their genteel past with Meg's need to sell such a cherished part of it to feed her starving children. The tragic irony of it hit him like a shot to the chest.

Slowly he recovered his composure and began to carefully examine the pieces. He judged them to be very valuable. The one necklace was literally encrusted with diamonds. They were cleverly nestled into five tight rows. Beginning at the innermost row, tiny round stones gave way to increasingly larger ones until in the fifth row tear-drop cut diamonds as big as his thumb nail fanned out along the edge of the necklace. The woman who wore these would have to have had a long slender neck and perfect shoulders to accommodate the depth of the many rows. The diamonds were fastened to fine silver netting with a drape as soft as any fabric. The earbobs were designed with large round diamonds at the lobe from which dangled three smaller tear-drop diamonds.

Robert gasped when he saw the intricate metalwork on the sapphire necklace. He was impressed at the little bit of tarnishing on the piece. The chain that held the cluster of jewels was made from several carved squares linked together. Each square held a beautiful silver flower surrounded by delicate filigree. This whole piece had an oriental look to it, the flowers being water lilies, poppies, lotus blossoms and calla lilies.

Hanging from this exquisite chain was the largest

sapphire Robert had ever seen. The color was an extraordinary deep blue. Several square cut aquamarines surrounded the center stone. When Robert held the necklace to the light, this had the effect of changing the sapphire's color from deep blue to almost green. The earbobs were designed the opposite way with the aquamarine in the center encircled by small sapphires.

These jewels were simply astounding. The pearl rope, made from dozens of perfect pearls, was long enough to be wound around a woman's neck several times. Gently replacing the pieces in the pouch, Robert again wondered who had once owned them.

He picked up the little book and opened it. A lock of straight sandy baby hair slipped into his hand. There was a faded inscription in the front of the book.

To Rose, for all your private thoughts, with love, Mother.

Rose. Robert was certain that was Jeffrey's mother's name. The strands of baby hair might have been Jeffrey's. He turned the first page and a single rose petal fell on his lap.

4 December, 1779
Dear Diary,

How I wish my first entry wasn't so troubled. I am so conflicted, these words burn from my quill. My husband is never here. His Majesty's service keeps him from me for such cruel stretches. Months, years have gone by and I am without him. How can he be so long from me and still I hear nothing? Is he even alive? Mother and Father are so kind, keeping me and the children in such comfort. But my only true comfort will be to see the face of my friend and lover once again in my window. Dear, dear Henry, will I ever see you again? Will I ever feel your lips on mine or your arms around me again? Our youngest is nearly seven and you have yet to see him. Christmas approaches and again I will fall on my knees and beg for your return.

18 December, 1779

Dear Diary

Sorry news. A Major Billings has just left. He has been serving with His Majesty's Army in the colonies and has news of my Henry. He took ill with smallpox two years ago and though he survived, is quite disfigured. He has been in the custody of one of the native tribes around New Amsterdam. He told Major Billings he cannot return to me because he is too homely and is afraid of frightening me and our children.

Does he not see that I am captive to his fate? With him I am forced to love and couple with a man horrible to behold and without him I am left to live a solitary life of cold bed and lonely limbs. Never again will I enjoy the warm embrace of the marriage bed. Never again will I be able to solicit the good advice of my friend or the strong hand of the one I love. Oh, what morbid future! What deadly pallor on the face of my days! How am I ever to enjoy one moment of my life?

I have no one with whom to share the seconds as they tick by! And yet I do! He is here on this earth but alas, I cannot *have him! He is here but across the vast water and I can have no other. Though many walk about the avenue, handsome and tall, hats tipped in polite manner, I dare not respond. I am married yet I am not. Oh, sweet horror! What is to become of me?*

I have said goodbye to Maj. Billings. He returns to the regiment he shares with Henry. I have given him a letter to Henry begging him to come home no matter his visage.

Robert skipped ahead to the center of the little book to a passage marked by a ribbon.

26 June, 1780
Dear Diary,

Henry has been home now for three weeks and has yet to approach our bed. I long for his arms around me but he knows I loathe the wreckage of his face. I cannot help myself. The children don't seem to mind as much and neither do I in normal discourse or casual company but the thought of resuming marital relations is appalling to me. Poor Henry knows this without my saying so. Were his lips to touch me I'm afraid I would faint dead away so horrid are the scars that surround them. He is pathetic. Not ever the man who kissed me with such hard passion on our wedding night.

Robert put the little book down. He felt very sorry for Lord Henry Wynn and hesitated to read on. He knew from George's story what was coming. Picking the book up again he knew he must read some more. He was compelled to verify George's sad tale.

17 July, 1780
Dear Diary,

Tonight I find myself so very happy. Maj. Billings and his new bride held a reception for the returning battalion and Henry and I were invited. My shyness around Henry was swiftly diminished when I saw how beloved he was by his troops. His beard has grown in full and red, covering the worst of the scars around his mouth. Despite his disfigured face and scarred hands, he looked tall and dignified in his beautiful red coat and plumed hat. He looked so good, the solicitor, Mr. Ginghold offered him a position clerking in his law office. He was like a man reborn! I was very proud of him and when he came to me tonight, he discreetly darkened the room for my sake. I suffered his advances quite willingly and even enjoyed our reunion. Perhaps we will recreate our happy home.

4 December 1780
Dear Diary,

Henry's lung condition has worsened. He says he bears

scars internally from the smallpox. Whatever it is, he is very weak. My exhaustion puts me at risk of losing the child I carry. Caring for Henry and the other children has made me very weak too. I haven't slept a full night since All Hallows Eve. May God have mercy on us all.

25 December, 1780

Dear Diary,

Happy Christmas! Henry was able to sit up for the whole day. How he enjoyed the children and they him. Maj. Billings and his wife joined us for the day. She is grieving her mother. How blessed I am to still have Henry, so many have succumbed to this lung fever.

3 January 1781

Dear Diary,

Welcome to the world our little Gerald. A fine little man. Henry is so proud. I too, am proud and very tired. Maj. Billings stopped by for a congratulatory toast. He recommended his blacksmith to come and look at Bert's hoof. There's not a shoe made that doesn't bother him and he's our best carriage horse.

16 April, 1783

Dear Diary,

So long I have been silent! One whole year now, since we lost Gerald. He was always such a weak little thing, like a kitten. I thank God we had him for so many months. My heart feels shriveled. The other boys are away at school and I creep around the house in silence. The servants will not look at me. This anniversary has been like a pall hanging over Henry and me. It's been a year and I am still as hollow as an old tree. Henry has had a relapse of his old lung condition. Could it be the dreaded consumption? He claims so, but I think not. Sometimes I fear he enjoys poor health a bit too much. If not for Mr. Quinn, our life would be a desperate void. My heart begins to beat again when he comes by though he has stretched out the work in the kitchen as long as he can. I cannot bear to have him gone from me so I have commissioned him to make new andirons for all our fireplaces now that he's installed Cook's new stove. I plan to keep him coming around by asking him to make her new pots as well. His presence is all that takes my mind off of my dead baby.

20 June, 1783
Dear Diary,

Henry hired Mr. Quinn today as his personal blacksmith. The money from his father's estate has set us up very comfortably and his inheritance of so much land will make our sons wealthy. We are so relieved. Henry's father for so many years threatened to leave everything to Harold. Now Harold has shamed the family and been banished to the colonies. Henry has it all now. We are rich. When I heard that Mr. Quinn was moving his smithy onto our land I could not believe it! I can't keep my eyes from admiring his arms and thighs. The man is so strong and so powerful I can hardly sit in his presence and find myself pacing around the kitchen. Cook doesn't quite know what to make of it. I know this amuses Mr. Quinn and today when she went to market, he started imitating her. We got to laughing and couldn't stop. Before I knew what happened I was in his arms and his kiss was on my lips. Oh how I've dreamt of kisses like that one! Poor Henry does not visit my bed too often these days. I miss married love but he claims the exertion gives him pain in his chest. I can't imagine a pain with enough gall to enter Mr. Quinn's huge chest!

Now that Mr. Quinn is officially one of the staff I will call him Christian. He must still refer to me as M'am. Henry seems to care little what I do these days so I suspect he doesn't mind.

10 May, 1784
Dear Diary,

Christian and I have committed a serious indiscretion. We have been meeting in secret since the New Year. I have missed my courses and have told Christian that I suspect I am with child by him. He denies it is his but I know it is. I so badly want it to be his, it must be his! I am overjoyed to be carrying Christian's baby and I know he will be happy when he recovers from the shock. He has never married, though he has said many times that were I unmarried he'd snatch me up in a moment's time.

Henry has been amorous as well over these last weeks. What is it about spring? Tonight, just to please my husband and assuage my terrible guilt, I have invited Henry to come to me in our bed. He did not question me on it and actually seems pleased by the idea. I know he adores me and I am the very worst of women wantonly betraying my vows with Christian. I must be successful at arousing my husband's passion tonight. He must never suspect I carry Christian's child. I could not bear his pain.

12 May, 1784
Dear Diary,

All is well. My Henry enjoyed our time together the other night. Now when I bear him a son or daughter some months from now he will surely not suspect my sin. Meanwhile, Christian and I cannot resist each other and sin still at every opportunity. Never have I imagined such a man in my bed! We meet in his little apartment behind the smithy. The boys are away at school and Henry is tending the books at Ginghold's despite his inheritance. He likes it, he says. On the maids' day off Christian and I meet here in my own room.

Robert could not believe anyone would confess in writing the things Jeffrey's mother had written. He wondered if

Henry ever knew. He lived to be a fairly old man and never did develop consumption from what Robert remembered. There was never any indication that he felt anything but love for Rose. Robert remembered her funeral. Adelaide and he were just returned from their wedding trip. Henry had nothing but wonderful things to say about Rose. Robert remembered now how silent Jeffrey had been. Now he had to read a few more entries and he was going to bed. He could hardly focus on the neat script.

9 October, 1784

Dear Diary,

Christian is breaking my heart. I have grown large with this baby and he no longer desires me. He has taken up with the Williams' parlor maid, a young widow with four children. I weep endlessly at his hardness of heart and have no one to confide in but you, my silent friend. Thanks be to God, Henry thinks it is merely my condition that distresses me. Christian has been almost cruel in his dismissal of me. He is going to Dover to visit his brother and does not know when he will return. Henry has engaged another blacksmith to take his place. I am in terrible, dismal straits.

30 November, 1784

Dear Diary,

Delivered of a healthy boy. Henry named him Jeffrey after a favorite uncle. I don't care what we call him. He looks so like the other children, Henry will never imagine he does not belong to him. The boy has given him the best health I've seen in him in a year. No word from Christian. My heart is shattered.

Robert leafed through page after page trying to see when Christian Quinn reappears. The little book was designed to hold five years of entries but Rose wrote sporadically, sometimes only recording one or two entries a year after her lover left her. Flipping to the last year, he noticed that the regular entries resumed.

5 March, 1793

Found this diary in my trunk. I have much to report. Christian returned last year. Believe it or not, Henry was again in need of a blacksmith having been forced to dismiss Christian's replacement when he injured a horse while shoeing him. So, Christian is back living in the apartment behind the smithy. I shamelessly fell into his bed without a moment's hesitation. He, however, is not the same. He has hardened in his years away. He left Dover under a cloud after some fight in a public house. Our union is much more passionate now with somewhat of a hard edge to it. I can't define it but I find him more thrilling than ever. He has not met Jeffrey yet as he is away at school.

6 May, 1793
Dear Diary,

Jeffrey is home! The house has come alive with boy things and noisy enthusiasm. Henry is so very glad to see Jeffrey and he is just as glad to be home. The older boys are living abroad and my heart aches with missing them. They and their wives come by for holidays but months pass between visits. Both Henry and I have found Jeffrey to be the one joy we still have. Christian has yet to meet him. Perhaps tonight we can arrange it.

9 July, 1794
Dear Diary,

A terrible thing has happened. Christian and I were in my bed this afternoon and Jeffrey walked in. He was supposed to be visiting Willard and Suzanne until Saturday but their youngest came down with a rash and fever. Suzanne sent Jeffrey home early. Today is Miss Wren's day off and when he realized she wasn't here, he came looking for me. Christian was cruel to him and without thinking, I blurted out that he was his son. Jeffrey of course, has known nothing of this. Ever! He has never had an inkling that Christian is anything more than the family's blacksmith.

Christian has never acknowledged Jeffrey saying that he looks too much like Henry to be his own son. We've argued about it for months but I have yet to convince him. How can it not be so? I know I was able to conceive with Henry even after his illness. Poor Gerald was proof of that. But in my heart I know Jeffrey must be Christian's son. Why else would I have such an overwhelming desire to have it so? I couldn't have conceived such a lovely boy from Henry's tired old seed. My body lies so stiff under Henry and is driven to such heights by Christian's powerful virility. Jeffrey simply must be the result of Christian's fine arousal!

I had hoped that getting to know Jeffrey would lead to some relationship but Christian has only ever shown Jeffrey meanness and indifference. Now I have left my angel crying in his room. He is crushed by things he doesn't understand. I fear I have marred him for life and if Henry ever finds out Jeffrey is not his son he will die of a broken heart.

What have I done? Christian was so enraged he slapped me many times before he finally finished with me and left my bed. Even the pain of my much-deserved punishment could not banish the thrill of my lover's rough hands upon me. He has such power over my weak flesh. I can only beg for his supreme dominance to satisfy my endless need. But, oh what a grievous mistake I have made! What will I do? My world is shattered. If Christian leaves me again I will be lost. As it is, I must live my secret to the extreme to keep Jeffrey quiet and Henry unaware.

Robert finally could read no more. He had found the words he had been looking for and it was time he left before he was discovered. The early light was beginning to peek around the heavy library drapes. He took the diary and the jewelry and slipped it all back into the satin envelope. As he folded the flap, his thumb ran lightly over some loose stitching along the edge of the silk lining. Thinking the piece had simply been mended, he failed to notice the concealed pocket that had been cut into the silk lining and awkwardly closed with embroidery thread. Taking all his treasures with him, Robert went back to his sister's bedroom.

Once there, he washed his face with the cool water in the ewer. He was so disturbed by what he had just read that he forgot his disappointment at not finding the portrait of Adelaide.

His stomach was churning still from the greasy meal he had eaten for supper and he needed something to calm it. Perhaps Beverly had something in her vanity. She had always had a healthy appetite and had often spoken of taking a bromide solution after a large meal.

He found a box of bromide powders in her top drawer. This was just the ticket to bring him relief. He mixed the medicine in a wine glass with a bit of water and tossed it down.

Returning the box to the drawer, he saw the oval frame lying face down on a pile of hankies. There she was. His Adelaide. He turned the portrait over and the memory of his beloved wife flooded his heart. Taking the portrait to the bedside, Robert climbed into bed and once again pulled up the counterpane. He fell asleep with the little painting in his hand before he could even stand it up on the bed table.

Chapter Ten

Robert Gilchrist shifted uncomfortably in the corner of the seat of a hansom cab. He shared the cab with a shriveled dowager whose body odor was ill disguised by a great quantity of sweet talcum powder. She nodded sleepily across from him, her bulging reticule bumping against her black silk skirt with rhythmic rustling thuds.

He was annoyed that he needed the cab in the first place but when he returned home after the landlord's meeting he found his family gone and both of their buggies with them. Graves, his miserable butler, had reminded him that they all left for Tipperary to visit Mrs. Gilchrist's sister for the remainder of the warm summer months.

He had been particularly furious that he could not exercise his conjugal rights after the long, boring meeting and the monotonous journey back from Westport. Having found only Graves, his ancient butler, and his equally ancient wife at home, and feeling very sorry for himself, he had gone in search of a maid or goose girl to amuse him.

After picking his way through the bland cold supper left on the sideboard, he had walked down to Miss Lily's and satisfied himself with one of her girls. He had paid Miss Lily an extra tuppence to arrange for a cab to pick him up in front of his home at six the next morning. He had ended up walking home in a downpour that continued even until he stood at his door.

When he arrived home from Miss Lily's he found a message from Lord Lucan instructing him that his presence was requested at a birthday party and foxhunt for Lady Lucan. Lady Lucan was his Aunt Beatrice, the sister of Robert Gilchrist's mother. He cursed as he handed his acceptance to Graves.

The hunt lasted three days. He had had to go to Castlebar where his uncle had a home nearby. He thought he would have to wait until he could politely beg his leave before he could head on to GlynMor. Fortunately, the rainy weather had completely spoiled the hunt and he had been able to leave after the first day.

Now, as the carriage bounced along the ruts formed along the muddy road, he keenly felt every bump. That old boil that reared its ugly head every time he overextended himself pained him with every bump along the way. Moreover, he knew that when that nasty thing pocked his left buttock, he would soon develop the deep chest cold that left him feverish and fretful for days. He regretted leaving home without so much as a mustard plaster for his chest. Perhaps once he arrived at Jeffrey's, George or Stiller might fix something for him.

Robert Gilchrist had had just about enough of this assignment. His encounter at Browne's with Lord Cushing had left a bad taste in his mouth. Besides, now that Tom Phalen had succumbed to the hunger, what good was pursuing Lady Meg? He never thought Jeffrey was as interested in punishing his daughter as he was in bringing Phalen to justice. He intended to tell Jeffrey he was finished with this effort and collect his final payment. Surely there were plenty of fools out there with the money to pay a man like himself to carry out their personal vendettas for them.

Tracking Tom Phalen for Jeffrey had been lucrative enough but the real pleasure had been in ruining the stupid omethon. That had never been Jeffrey's idea. No, Mr. Gilchrist of Dublin St. Newport had taken that upon himself and had taken great pleasure in accomplishing his goal. But now he was bored with it all. He intended to leave GlynMor Castle at the end of this day and never look back. On to bigger and better things.

He looked at his fine Swiss watch and saw that it was almost one. The cab made a sharp turn and he pulled back the curtain to see rain dripping from the yew trees that lined the long drive into GlynMor. His head throbbed and his eyes felt heavy as the carriage pulled up to the massive oak door. Thank God he was finally here. He needed a drink badly and his chest hurt when he took a deep breath.

The old woman across from him awoke with a snort. She was going on to Puntoon to see her daughter. He would be well rid of her sweet stink.

Pulling his carpetbag off the seat Gilchrist threw it at the driver and descended from the cab. He turned to the woman, who looked at him as if she had never seen him before.

"Madam, I wish you safe travel."

She merely snorted again and he closed the door. He ascended the stairs and pulled the bell cord. Looking around in the gray light, he noted that Jeffrey's climbing roses were extraordinary this year and the ivy topiaries on either side of the door were beautiful and full. He marveled that a man who couldn't even wipe his own chin still commanded enough respect that his staff worked as diligently as if he wielded his stick over them every day. He had no idea that they lived well on his friend's money and kept up the place as if it were their own home.

Once inside, he was shown to the drawing room where he poured himself a whiskey and stretched himself out on one of Beverly's fine brocade couches. Stiller had gone to announce him but he was in no hurry to see Jeffrey and when the old man returned to tell him his lordship was napping, he settled in for a little nap of his own.

He was aroused by the sound of voices outside the

drawing room door.

"He arrived not longer than an hour ago, George. I showed him into the drawing room."

"Thank you Stiller. I will attend to Mr. Gilchrist. His Lordship is having a difficult day after his excursion yesterday. I'm not sure he will even see Mr. Gilchrist."

Robert Gilchrist sat up and closed his eyes against the pounding in his temples. Not see him! After he rode all this way in that filthy cab with that insufferable woman that imbecile had better see him! He turned to see George enter the room with a tray of cold meat, cheese and fresh bread. A steaming pot of Turkish coffee spread its rich aroma around the room.

"Mr. Gilchrist. Welcome again to GlynMor Castle. I thought you might enjoy some refreshment after your trip."

"You thought? Let me remind you that you're not paid to think!"

George fumed at the rudeness of this man. Having just spent the last several hours at the futile task of making his master comfortable and cleaning his environs, he had just been summoned to Lord Robert's rooms. He had had Sharon make him and Lord Robert a lunch and was on his way back to his own room when Stiller had stopped him.

"Yes sir, as you wish sir. I will announce you to Lord Wynn immediately."

Taking the tray he backed out of the drawing room leaving Gilchrist gaping at the disappearing food. Instead of announcing the scoundrel, he went directly to Lady Beverly's chambers to find Lord Robert. Let Mr. Gilchrist find his own lunch.

"Come in, please."

Lord Robert was still in his silk robe and house slippers when George crossed the room and placed the tray on a lacquered Chinese trunk in front of the cold fireplace. His lordship sat dejectedly in one of the pale green silk fireside chairs and leafed through some papers. A soft wool lap robe was thrown across his knees.

George noted how damp it was in the room and immediately began to build a fire. Once he had the turf bricks going and warmth began to fill the hearth, he stood and began cutting cheese and slicing bread for Lord Robert. Pouring him a cup of the thick black coffee, George contemplated how to tell his lordship of Mr. Gilchrist's arrival.

"Do you think Jeffrey can see me today? I have some things I need to discuss with him."

George proffered a pitcher of heavy cream. Robert nodded and George added it and two cubes of sugar to his cup. He was surprised that Lord Cushing had changed his mind about making his presence known and raised an eyebrow at how quickly his lordship guzzled his coffee.

"Sir, I'm sure you can approach Lord Wynn but I can't guarantee he will receive you. He is not having a good day and was barely civil during his morning ablutions and exercises. He fell asleep as soon as I dressed him. I'm sure you can only try. I must tell you though, sir. You are not the only one seeking audience with his lordship. Mr. Gilchrist sits at this moment in the drawing room awaiting a summons to his lordship's chambers."

"Does he now? I wonder what brings him here. George, I need to think this over. Perhaps you can slice me some of that cold beef and pour me another cup of coffee. Please help yourself as well. I'm not sure now that I should make myself known to Mr. Gilchrist or Jeffrey just yet. You're sure no one knows I'm here?"

"No sir. Sharon thought this tray was for me and Stiller saw me take it into the drawing room for Mr. Gilchrist. No one is the wiser, sir, at least not until Mr. Gilchrist orders a tray of his own."

Lord Robert smiled wryly.

"Yes, Mr. Gilchrist and I have a history of getting each other's food. It has been a rather unpleasant ordeal. But that is not my immediate concern. We need to think of the best strategy for getting Tom and Meg Phalen and their children into safe quarters. I know from his own mouth that Lord Sligo plans to close Browne's for the off season to save money. If that happens they will have nowhere to go."

He slowly sipped his second cup of coffee and stretched his long legs toward the warmth of the fire. George chewed his bread and meat quietly, waiting for Lord Robert to speak again, marveling that he was actually eating in the presence of a lord.

He wanted nothing to do with any plans. It was enough for him to have all these strangers in the house and deal with his master's temper. He had slept badly last night worried that there would be hell to pay when his lordship found out Lord Robert was prowling about. Now Gilchrist was thrown into the mix. George just wished they would all go away so he could decide whether he wanted to go north to visit a friend who lived near Lough Cullin tomorrow or simply spend his afternoon off loafing about and catching up on his reading.

As Lord Robert Cushing and George discussed their next move, Robert Gilchrist stood fuming in the drawing room. He scowled as he watched that pompous, old ass Stiller stir sugar into his tea.

"Will there be anything else sir?"

"Yes you old fool! I demand to see Lord Jeffrey within the hour. And don't give me any of your blather about him being asleep. I will see him and that's final."

"Yes, sir. As you wish sir."

The elderly butler backed through the doorway and gently closed the tall ornately carved doors behind him. Gilchrist hollered at the silent mahogany sentries and waved his fist.

"You better do as I wish! I am Mr. Robert Gilchrist of the Scottish Gilchrists. You measly man-servant! How dare you keep me waiting like an unworthy suitor?"

He erupted in a fit of coughing and gulped the amber tea, scalding his tongue in his haste.

"Devil! Look what you've made me do! Well if you won't show me to your master's rooms I will simply show myself!"

Gilchrist paced around, gnawing on a bit of dried fruit and gingerly sipping his tea. He needed to rehearse what he intended to say to Jeffrey. If only he didn't feel so miserable. He had hoped to be in absolute control of the discussion and now he could hardly concentrate. Another paroxysm of coughing caught him as he poured himself a second cup of tea. He choked on a howl as the amber brew slopped down the front of his neat gray herringbone trousers spreading a stain across his fine gray kid boot.

He was mopping his boot with a linen napkin when the mahogany doors opened again. This time one of the maids entered. She was a little bit of a thing, ugly as a pig with a red splotchy complexion and a bush of red hair topped by a little lace cap that had tipped to one side. She had not known anyone was in the drawing room and squealed her surprise as she shoved a bucket of steaming suds through the doors.

"Oh, sir! Excuse me sir, I was sent t'clean the floors. I had no idea ye were in here sir!"

"Well, here I am you idiot! Take that mess out of here and fetch me someone who knows how to treat a gentleman. I want to see Lord Wynn and cannot seem to get the attention of anyone in this household!"

"Yes, sir! Right away, sir. I'll fetch Mr. Stiller, sir."

"Not that old baboon! I want George! Fetch me George or don't bother coming back!"

"Yes sir, as you wish, sir. I'll get Mr. George right away."

The frightened girl ran from the room leaving her soapy solution behind.

After waiting a few moments, Gilchrist decided to find George himself. He stormed out of the drawing room and headed for the huge double stairway that swooped like a giant bird into the main foyer. He began the long ascent to the second storey. Confound it he was weak! This was an outrage! Robert Gilchrist was never weak!

He stopped half way up the wide marble sweep of stairs to catch his breath. Whatever infection had a grip on his lungs it was presenting at a very inconvenient time. As he stood on the stairs waiting for the strength to return to his legs, Gilchrist again heard voices outside the drawing room doors. This time they were discussing him.

"But M'am, I know he was in here. Suren' I just left him. He was wantin' t'see his lordship and was that fed up with the waitin'."

'Well, he's not here now, is he Molly O'Brien? Get in there then and get the floor washed before he returns. Did he say which lordship he was after seein'? Himself or the brother-in-law?"

"No, M'am. I don't know anythin' about no brother-in-law."

"Yes ye do. The tall handsome one who came bargin' into me kitchen yesterday as free as ye please. He's gone though. No sooner did he light upon the place, help himself t'lunch and he was gone agin'. Made no sense t'me atall, I tell ye."

"M'am who's brother was that?"

"Lady Wynn's brother. Ye niver knew her. She lives with him now. She and Himself upstairs had a fallin' out a long time ago. Ye weren't even born, I'll wager. Their daughter, Lady Meg, ran off with the head groom, Tom Phalen. Caused a big brouhaha and she's niver been back. His lordship beat her so hard we all thought she'd die but she made it and got out from under him fer good! I was only yer age when it happened but I'm the one who got her out! Not just her but her maid too. Singlehanded, I did it. A girl no older than ye are standin' here in this hall. Can ye believe that? No one was the wiser and I'd do it agin, no question. We all thought the world of her ye know. Lady Meg is a grand woman, that she is."

"And the stableman? Did he love her?" Molly asked, her eyes dreamy with the romance of it all.

"Like the sun loves the sky, he did. And a handsome couple they made! He was as brawny and big as a tree and she all curls and long lashes. I was so glad t'hear Lord Cushing yesterday tellin' George that they were survivin' this turrible hunger. They lost some children but the two of'em are still alive somewhere in County Mayo. Lord Cushing talked about bringin' em home with him. Fancy that! A stable hand livin' like a lord!"

"Saints above! Can ye imagine?"

"No, but I can imagine yer suds getting' cold. Ye better git in there now and finish that floor. And don't be dumpin' the water til ye do the back corridor, mind ye."

"Yes, M'am."

Gilchrist stood in rigid silence, stunned by what he had just heard. Tom Phalen is alive! Lord Robert has been here and gone! Now didn't that just change everything. He climbed to the landing and found a chair beneath some paintings of Chinese warlords and cowering maidens. He leaned back against the silk covered wall and tried not to start coughing again. Looking across the corridor he saw that there was a series of these paintings along both walls. He liked these works and fancied having them in his own chambers. Jeffrey never enjoyed them anymore. Maybe he would take his final payment in the form of artwork.

Now that he knew Tom Phalen was still alive he was more determined than ever to see him hanged for theft. He figured he'd never make the charge of horse thief stick. Theft of the deed was a much stronger case. He needed to arouse in Jeffrey enough anger to give him the freedom to pursue the deed. If he could just get one more payment out of him he would be satisfied. That and the artwork, of course.

Mr. Gilchrist was tiring of this assignment anyway. He had actually felt relief at the news that Tom Phalen was dead. Now he had to follow through till the end with his plan to ruin him. Jeffrey had been no help in recent years. Even in the beginning he had been lukewarm about destroying Tom Phalen. Too afraid it would bring his daughter to ruin too.

Jeffrey hated Tom Phalen. Of that he had no doubt. The daughter was another story. Despite the strength he had shown in the past, wielding his rightful authority over that girl, Jeffrey had a weakness for her that Gilchrist found very distasteful. Whenever they discussed it, even when Jeffrey was in his cups, he could only go so far when Jeffrey would stop him. He had even thrown him out of his room once. Just for calling her the whore that she was!

He had accepted that he would never be able to penetrate the shield that descended when the talk turned to Meg. As long as the money kept coming for his efforts to humiliate Tom Phalen, he would stop short of harming Jeffrey's precious daughter. But no one could have predicted the opportunity he would have to ruin Tom when the potato crops failed year after year.

Robert Gilchrist simply could not resist the chance to sink Tom completely. He knew he had to act quickly and he had. Stealing his cattle and destroying his dairy was a stroke of genius if he must say so. Disguised as a tragic consequence of the hunger, absolutely no one was the wiser and the sneaky undertaker had made a tidy profit on the sale of the cows.

Lord Lucan, that sentimental old woman, was so overwrought about his lifelstyle and properties that his nephew could barely abide him. He had never even questioned the failure of the rents after the season of '46 failed. That was the last time he had collected the full rent from Doeega and his report had been accepted by Lord Lucan without question. So far he had hesitated to employ the Crowbar Brigade to evict the lazy beach squatters on the island.

None of this troubled Robert Gilchrist. He was after all, family. The deep affection between his mother and his uncle all but guaranteed free reign over Lucan's holdings. He had run roughshod over the whole lot of them and no one had suspected. The thought brought a thin smile to his lips. Weak! Why were they all so weak? So many fools and so few Gilchrists to save them! Well, if they wouldn't be saved at least he would be rich as he watched them all sink into the bog.

Now he sat in the upper corridor of GlynMor castle not far from Jeffrey's suite. What should he do next? He could barge into Jeffrey's room and stand his ground but he thought that would only get him thrown out again. He could simply admit himself as a visitor on an errand of mercy but even in a laudanum stupor Jeffrey would never believe it. From what he surmised of Jeffrey's current health he could hardly suggest a rousing game of poker.

What he really wanted to do was return home and crawl into his bed. His head ached mightily and his chest felt like he had swallowed hot coals. He had suffered terrible chills on the long carriage ride but he now felt hot and dry. Even his hair hurt where it sprang from his head. Robert Gilchrist was not a man who suffered ill health. He rarely caught colds like weaker, less prudent men who played rugged sports in damp weather. He never hurt, never stumbled, never needed an elixir or a tonic to carry on. Except when this plaguing ague took hold of him, he was simply well.

As he sat listening to his raspy breaths and dying to strip off his warm wool jacket he cursed the damned fool that gave him this foul ailment. If he could ever know who it was he would see him in the workhouse. Probably that sniveling brat of Tom Phalen's. Couldn't take just punishment like a man, crying and wiping snots everywhere! He probably was to blame, serving food to innocent wayfarers spreading his contamination everywhere. He hoped a just God would smite him where he stood in his filthy rags in the taproom of Browne's Inn.

Suddenly Robert Gilchrist had a plan. Head back to Westport and catch Tom Phalen right there at the inn. Forget Jeffrey! He would have Phalen arrested for stealing the deed and bring him to Castelbar for justice. No one would defy him! He was the undertaker for a lord and had just been at the landlords' meeting. People had seen him. People would know him. No one knew Tom Phalen and it wouldn't matter if they did. He, Robert Gilchrist of Dublin Street, Newport, was the voice of authority in this case. Why even if the constables in Westport were foolish enough to question him he could easily buy their cooperation.

Weren't they all desperate for a good meal? And wasn't he just the man to buy it for them? Just put that thieving piece of Irish garbage in jail and the money was theirs. He, Robert Gilchrist would take care of the rest. Why, they'd be out of Westport on the next coach and no one would even miss Tom Phalen. Once he had Phalen securely apprehended, he would return and demand his full pay and the artwork he had so admired. Jeffrey might even feel well enough to attend some of the trial. Didn't he travel about his estate in his wheeled chair? His man George would enjoy a bit of a holiday in the city.

Gilchrist decided not to stop in and see Jeffrey. He ambled down the broad stairway and summoned Stiller to get him a carriage. Once the boy brought it around from the stable, he climbed aboard and ordered the boy to take him into Clydagh Glyn. From there he would have to hire another of those confounded uncomfortable taxis to get him to Westport. Meanwhile, he'd enjoy a nice meal and some good strong whiskey. He might even stop at Brooke's and buy some camphor liniment. He knew just where to find the right girl to massage it into his ravaged chest.

Chapter Eleven

D uffy sat on an upturned curragh. The day was coming to a close and the sky was already streaked with pink. Ellen climbed on his lap and he stroked her hair absently. Meg wondered what was on his mind. Surely he couldn't believe that they would keep anything from him about Gerry and Katie Shea! He had been quiet and taciturn the whole week since Fr. Finnegan had said they were gone to America. Meg knew Duffy wanted to go too. She wished he could find Maureen and take her as his wife. The only obstacle to that dream was one Charlie O'Malley. Meg shrugged to herself. That was all in the past. After Maureen left, Duffy had assumed his role of perpetual bachelor boy and never mentioned their last walk on the beach. His need for family seemed to be met by playing the fond uncle to their children.

He turned to Tom, his expression unreadable.

"Fr. Timon wants t'see us both, Tom."

Tom's head shot up and he sprang to his feet.

"Well, then let's be goin'."

Meg knew this somehow had to do with the Blackthorn Brotherhood. They had heard rumors that there had been a full-blown rebellion somewhere near Tipperary right after the meeting here in Westport. She suddenly felt cold and hugged Martha to her, taking warmth from the baby's body. Martha wanted to play in the water and tried to wriggle away. Ellen started to pout and whimper when Duffy put her down.

By the time Duffy and Tom had turned to walk over to the rectory, both little girls were howling and Meg gathered them up to go back inside. It was time to get dried off and start supper. Francis and Gracie protested behind her as she corralled everyone through the taproom and into the kitchen. Meg threw together a stew of leftovers and fried up several slices of stale bread in bacon grease.

Her heart was troubled and she was short with her little troupe. Business had been very slow the last week and Meg had been very frugal with the scraps left from the big push the week before. They seemed to sense the tension in the big kitchen and went out of their way to test her patience. Finally, she waved her wooden spoon in their direction and dragged one of the wooden benches across the room along the wall. Lining them up on the bench, facing the wall, she directed them to be silent.

"This is the naughty bench and you have been naughty so you must sit here until I tell you to get up. If one of you speaks, you will feel the sting of this spoon against your backside, do you hear me?"

They nodded solemnly at their mother who so rarely threatened them with punishment.

"Good. Now, turn to the wall. You are being very naughty and I am very upset with you. If I see one of you so much as turn your head, none of you will have supper tonight. Think about it. Denny would be happy to eat yours for you."

They all turned obediently toward the whitewashed wall. Francis sat straight as a ramrod while Gracie concentrated on her folded hands. Ellen sat defiantly with her head high and her jaw set. Martha repeatedly slid off the bench, every time being dragged silently back into position by Francis who was as hungry as Denny any day.

Meg continued to stir and fry as the children sat quietly. Just when the girls began to wiggle and Martha refused to allow Francis to touch her again, Mary Clare came into the kitchen offering a reprieve for both mother and children.

"Mary Clare, please take the children upstairs and ready them for bed. And ask Rose to come down. And see if you can find Denny. I need them to help me with dinner. Once the babies are ready, you can bring them down to eat."

Mary Clare hustled her four younger siblings up the stairs as they raced and clambered to be first. Just as she rounded the stairway behind them, Denny slammed through the front door.

"Mam, where's Da?"

Meg turned at the breathless urgency in her son's voice.

"Why? What's wrong, Denny?"

"I just saw a cab pass and I swear I saw that awful Mr. Gilchrist."

Meg felt her face flush and her heart began to beat so hard she thought it would come through the thin material of her blouse.

"Where?"

"Up on the Louisburg Road. The driver dropped someone off at a house. They were unloading the woman's trunk when I saw his ugly face in the window."

Meg tried to think. How much time did they have if he was planning to come to Browne's? Why was he here? How could she warn Tom and Duffy?

"Were there any others around? Any other passengers? Did he see you?"

"A few but I don't know if they were all going to that house or not. No, he didn't see me. I was behind a bush the whole time."

Rose appeared at the foot of the stairs.

"Mam, can't Denny set the table jist this once? I'm that close t'finishin' Miss Austen's book, Pride and Prejudice. I found it and can't...What's wrong, Mam?"

Meg told Rose what Denny had seen.

"Go to Fr. Timon's and let Da and Mr. McGee know what's happened. When you return, be careful to see if Mr. Gilchrist is here. If you see a cab outside or hear his voice, go back to Fr. Timon's. Do not come into the inn, Rose! We need someone who can run messages between us and your Da. Can you do this?"

Denny looked like he would rupture.

"Suren' I can do this, Mam! Ye know I'm a big, strong lad!"

Meg shook her head.

"Mam! How can ye let a stupid girl do the job of a man? Let me go! I'm the one t'warn the other men!"

"No, Denny. I need you here. There is no other man here to protect me and the children if need be. I also need you to tell me everything you know about the men in the brotherhood if there are any still in Westport. They could be in grave danger and walk into a trap if Gilchrist is about setting one."

Denny fumed at Meg's words. No way would he betray the whereabouts of his brothers to this English woman even if she was his mam.

"I'll not! Ye'll jist turn 'em in t'save yerself!"

He regretted the words as soon as they were out of his mouth, not because of the horrified, pained expression on his mother's face but because they brought a resounding slap from his sister that stung his cheek like fire and snapped his head back forcing him to stumble against a chair.

"Ye spalpeen! How dare ye speak t'Mam like that? Ye' haven't enough brains t'fill a bird's skull! If Da could hear ye he'd tan ye good! Ye can count on me tellin' him the danger Mam is in because she has sich as yerself fer her protector!"

"Rose, just go! We haven't time for this! Denny won't let anything happen to me or the little ones. I trust him."

Meg's eyes bored into Denny's as she spoke the words, hoping his anger would falter and he would act out of loyalty to his siblings if not her.

Denny stood rubbing his face, his bravado deflated by his

211

sister's scorn. Rose left by the kitchen door. Meg turned away from her son and put the stew on the back of the stove and pulled the last of the fried bread from the pan. No sense in setting the place on fire.

"Denny," she said without looking at him, "If we are to survive this terrible ordeal we must do so as a family. Whatever you think of me, you must set it aside for the sake of your father and your brother and sisters."

Trying desperately to keep the tears out of her voice, Meg continued.

"I don't know why Gilchrist has come back but your father and Mr. McGee are in danger. We can be sure of that. If there are any other brothers around, they will be too. You must believe that I would never do anything to bring harm to your father! You must know how much I love him and all of you children! Rose is the best one to be messenger. She will draw less attention to herself because no one will suspect a girl of being involved with the brotherhood. You, on the other hand can go places she can't, like Marie's for example."

Denny's head shot up and his face flushed crimson at the mention of Marie's. What could his mother be thinking? He never even imagined his mam even knew about Marie's much less suggest that he'd go there!

"Now, listen to me carefully. There's a good chance Mr. Gilchrist won't be here for some minutes. I'm sure he's planning to employ the constable's assistance. He may be there now. I want you to go to Marie's and tell them to prepare to hide your father and Mr. McGee in one of her secret rooms."

Meg turned to her son and saw the look of shock on his young face. Poor boy! She had to force herself to keep from enfolding him in a big protective hug. No matter what hurtful things he said to her, he was still her baby and she longed to make his world safe and trouble free.

"Denny, dear, I know all about Marie's. She's a bad woman but she's loyal to the cause and I'm sending you to tell her because that's what Da told me to do if there was trouble.

Well, there's trouble now and I need you to just do as I say. Your da and Mr. McGee will need a place to run to. They can't stay at Fr. Timon's. It's too risky. Tell Marie to have one of her girl's go out and find any brotherhood sympathizers and hide them as well or have them get out of Westport. Go now and hurry back as fast as you can. I meant what I said about you protecting us."

Meg put her hands on Denny's shoulders, suddenly recognizing that he was as tall as she. She looked her son square in the face.

"We're counting on you."

His green eyes reflected both courage and fear but he said nothing. Meg held his gaze until he dropped his lids. Without saying a word, he threw his arms around her and hugged her hard. He left her standing in the kitchen shocked beyond tears, her wooden spoon still in her hand.

Within minutes, Rose was back from the rectory.

"Da and Mr. McGee said t'get over t'Marie's and let her know. Let her know what, Mam?"

"It's better if you don't know, Rose. I've just sent Denny over there. Did he say anything else?"

"Jist that they'd be waitin' t'hear when they should go there and once they were gone fer ye t'close the inn and all of us t'come t'the rectory. Mam, Da should niver go t'Marie's! She's a bad woman, ye said so yerself!"

"Never mind about Marie. The rectory? How would we be safe there?"

"Fr. Timon said they would get us out o' Westport altogether."

Meg's heart sank. She appreciated Fr. Timon's offer but the rectory would be the first place Gilchrist would look. Besides, how could she ever leave Tom here and go into hiding? Where? Why? Where could they possibly go to get away from the long arm of Gilchrist's posse? He was bent on seeing Tom hanged for a horse thief and if he ever got wind that Tom was still alive he'd turn over every rock in the county to find him!

Meg still believed this was a personal vendetta and she was determined to face it head-on. Her conversation with Uncle Robert had stiffened her backbone and she was feeling every bit Gilchrist's superior. If Mr. Gilchrist wanted a confrontation, he could have it with her. She would let Fr. Timon take the children as soon as Tom and Duffy were safe but she would stay here and face Gilchrist. She would have Denny with her. She would be fine.

"Darling, I want you to go back to Fr. Timon's and this is what I want you to tell your da."

Meg put her arm around her first-born and together they sat on the naughty bench while she told Rose her plan.

Denny at first went straight to the front door of Marie's but hesitated to go in. The saloon was crowded with sailors. Loud raucous music poured from the open front door, punctuated by the bragging of men and the laughter of women. A girl not much older than he sashayed up to him and winked suggestively.

"First time, Sweetface?"

Denny could feel his face redden and his heart began to race. The girl was a round-faced redhead whose peasant style blouse revealed a pair of high uncorseted breasts with the promise of more peeking through the paper-thin fabric. She blocked his path with her leg, lifting her skirt and petticoats to reveal a skinny thigh that she proceeded to rub gently back and forth against his crotch. Shocked at both her boldness and his body's immediate response, Denny bolted from the doorway and never looked back until he was at the water's edge.

How was he ever going to get into Marie's to tell her about Da? He didn't even know which woman to talk to! He had just turned to make another attempt when he saw a cab pull up to the front door and Mr. Gilchrist step out. Before the driver even had his bag on the ground, Mr. Gilchrist had his arm around the girl with the skinny thigh and was fondling her bosom. Together they went inside to be swallowed up by the smoke and the din of the taproom.

Now what was he going to do? He was supposed to be setting up a safe hiding place for Da and Mr. McGee! Now Mr. Gilchrist was there in the very place they wanted to hide! One of the girls came out with a sailor and headed for the Marianna. She looked nice. Maybe she could help him.

He approached her but she was obviously engaged in the same kind of thing he had just experienced. The sailor lifted her skirt and pinched her hard. She let out a little scream and smacked him. The sailor lifted her skirt again and tried to grab her from the front. The girl started laughing and threw him off. Together they kept up this little game of cat and mouse until they were right in front of Denny. He gulped hard and called out to them but no sound came out of his mouth. They passed him and he tried again, this time to their backs. They simply ignored him. Finally he chased them and caught up with them at the pier. Tugging on the sailor's sleeve, he finally got their attention.

The sailor cuffed him and shoved him back toward the quay.

"Allez! Allez!"

"Ye' go on now, Boyo, ye heard the man, Go!"

Denny was desperate and blocked their path.

"Ye have t'help me! I need t'see Marie!"

"Ye need t'see Marie, is it? And what makes ye think she'll be seein' the likes o'you, ye edgit boyo? Ye' gotta' wait in line like everybody else and I'll tell ye right off, Marie ain't liftin' her skirts fer yer skinny self!"

The sailor didn't understand a word of this. All he saw was a foolish boy arguing with a girl he was paying to service him. He took his pistol out and pointed it threateningly at Denny. Denny looked with panic from the barrel of the gun to the sailor to the girl and wanted to cry. He didn't know what to do!

The girl seemed to sense that he wasn't looking for

someone to entertain him. He was so young and so frightened. Denny saw her expression soften as she put her hand out for the sailor to wait. He lowered the pistol and kneaded the girl's buttocks possessively with his free hand.

"What d'ye want Marie fer, lad? Come on, make it quick! I'm bein' paid by the trick not by the hour!"

"Me da! She needs t'hide me da in her secret room. It's the plan and Mr. McGee too! The English are after me da and the brothers!"

The girl looked at the sailor's questioning face and back at the entrance to Marie's. She knew Marie had been hiding members of the Blackthorn Brotherhood for weeks in her attic but she had told her girls that they had all finally left. She knew she should let this boyo see her, especially if there was news Marie should know about the Brotherhood. Marie's whole house could be in danger if she were caught off guard.

She also knew that Marie would whip her good if she failed to satisfy a customer and this sailor was growing very impatient. If only she could speak his language but she knew not one word of French. The spoken word was never a problem in her line of work. The girls and their customers had a very simple way of communicating that had been used since the beginning of time.

The girl thought a moment but the sailor began to pull her toward the ship. She flashed a promising smile at her customer and blew him a kiss. He pinched her again and shoved her toward the pier. She called to Denny over her shoulder.

"Go t'th' kitchen door and ask fer Porky Billy. He's the cook. Tell him Peggy sent ye. If he doesn't box yer ears he might listen t'what ye have t'say."

Before Denny could reply, she was on board the Marianna and out of sight.

Still shaking from having a pistol in his face, Denny ran around the far end of the row of shops along the quay. Once he rounded the end of the mall, it seemed to take forever for him to navigate the alley, crowded with piles of garbage and barrels and crates. A few homeless wretches reached out to him, begging for anything he might have to eat.

At the sight of the square of light coming from Marie's kitchen, he quickened his step. Coming to the door, he stood for a moment to catch his breath. The top of the door was open to let in some air while the bottom was kept closed against the rodents racing up and down the alley. He could understand why the cook did this. He had seen at least one dead man in the alley and knew the rats that ran across his feet were probably on their way to feast upon the poor sod's flesh.

Denny stood for a second trying to acclimate himself to the layout of the kitchen. The room was tiny with a hearth along the left wall. The cook was a huge hairy individual in a filthy white uniform. He sat thumbing through a newspaper filled with drawings of naked women. Denny knew that the man was not reading. He needed no education to enjoy this paper. Andrew had shown Denny one just like it when they had still been on Achill.

Denny cleared his voice. The man looked up from his paper and slowly picked up a meat cleaver. Holding the huge knife in the air, he smiled a toothless grin.

"What can I do fer ye, lad? Same as I did fer the last bloody fool who bothered me fer free food? Ye'll find him at the bottom o'th'bay. Not hungry anymore, I'm proud t'report."

Denny was shaking and almost wet himself. How many times would he be faced with a deadly weapon before he got his message to Marie? He wanted nothing more than to be back in the kitchen at Browne's eating bacon fried toast. He gulped hard but despite his fear and inexperience, he was very glad Mam had sent him and not Rose for this job. God only knew what these people would have done to her. Thinking of Mam and Rose brought to mind the look in his mother's eyes and her last words to him echoed in his mind. They were counting on him. Da and Mr. McGee were counting on him. He couldn't let them down.

"Excuse me Mr. Porky Billy, sir, but it's not food I'm after. I have a message fer Marie. Peggy sent me t'ye. It's about some o'the brothers."

The huge man set down his girlie paper and walked over to the door. His torso completely filled the opening, blocking most of the light from the kitchen. He lazily swung his meat cleaver by a leather thong back and forth in the shaded alley as he leaned across the half-door. Denny involuntarily backed away from the blade as it glinted in the tiny strips of light on either side of the cook's massive arms.

"The brothers, is it? And what would a wee lad like yerself have t'say about the brothers? And how is it ye know me name when I niver seen ye 'afore?"

Denny bristled at being called a wee lad but he was so frightened by the toothless man with the rancid breath that he simply answered him.

"Sir, the message is from me da, Tom Phalen and Mr. Duffy McGee. They need t'hide out in Miss Marie's secret room."

The expression on the cook's face changed and he took Denny by the collar.

"Stay here ye' spalpeen. Don't even move or I'll hunt ye down like a dog."

In an instant he was gone into the taproom.

Denny waited for what seemed like hours watching the rats run around while two or three of the starving people tried to catch one of them. He thought he would retch right over the kitchen door if he actually saw them catch one.

He felt a tap on his shoulder at the same time he saw the cook return to the tiny kitchen. He turned around to see a woman about his mam's age standing with a small whip in her hand. Slowly, rhythmically, she tapped her palm with it as she stood glaring at him.

"Well, if ye have somethin' t'say, Boyo, say it. I don't need the likes o'ye t'be wastin' me time. What's this about th'brotherhood?"

Denny for the third time felt his heart leap to his throat

as he stood eye level to the nasty little whip as over and over it smacked gently against the woman's palm. How was he to know this was really Marie? She had very big hands and gold rings with huge stones on every finger. Her face was covered in heavy powder and she reeked of very bad perfume. He had to believe this was Marie. He had no choice.

"M'am, I uh, well, Peggy told me t'ask the cook t'tell ye I was needin' t'see ye. Me da and Mr. McGee are at Fr. Timon's and me mam said I needed t'git ye t'hide 'em in yer secret room. Mr. Gilchrist is after me da and it could be just about the horse but he could get t'him fer bein' involved in the brotherhood even if he didn't exactly go t'the meetin' last week. He planned t'go and Mr. McGee too."

Denny paused for breath and the woman leaned into his face. Denny was almost overcome by the strong smell of heavy cologne combined with liquor and cheroots.

"Yer da. Is he a customer?"

"Uh, no m'am not exactly though suren' he's niver said a word aginst ye."

"Then why should I hide him? What has he ever done fer me?"

It never occurred to Denny that Marie might refuse him. He stood gaping at her with his mouth open until she smacked him lightly on the thigh with the whip.

He thought he was in for it now. First the pistol, then the cleaver, now a whip. One of them was sure to get him. Suddenly a brilliant idea occurred to him.

"M'am, me da has done ye a great service and so has Mr. McGee. They brought the Brothers Ross t'Westport and ye had a good night fer sure after all the men saw the great Donnelly's arm, that ye did."

The big madam threw back her head and guffawed. Heads turned and the cook looked up from his girlie pictures. Marie never laughed. And here this lad had made her bray like a donkey.

"Ye're right about that Boyo! Ye're right about that. Good fer you, ye gave me a good stitch now, that ye did. All right then, yer da and Mr. McGee did do me a favor that night. They ran out o'stout and sent their thirsty customers my way. We did indeed have a very good night that night, didn't we Porky?"

The giant was leaning in the doorway again and nodded his great head up and down in agreement.

"That we did Miss Marie, not an egg or a piece o' cheese left t'tell of."

"So, here's what ye tell yer da. Come on down t'Marie's. I suppose a churcher like him won't be lookin' fer a girl, now would he? Maybe the big blond one would like somethin' t'warm his bed though?"

Seeing the distress on Denny's face, she laughed again. Tucking her whip deep into her huge cleavage, she placed her plump, dimpled arm around Denny's shoulder.

"Now lad, get moving. Yer da and Mr. McGee'll be safe with me. The sooner the better, eh?"

"M'am? Me mam said the brothers are in danger too, if there be any left here. She told me t'warn ye."

Marie shook her head at this and looked around as if someone might be listening.

"Ye'll not be getting' a word from me about the whereabouts of any of our fine fightin' men, Boyo. But thanks fer the warnin'."

"And M'am? There's one more thing."

Denny shrunk from Marie's touch as a cloud passed over her face erasing her former amusement.

"What?"

"I saw Mr. Gilchrist go into yer tap room jist now. He's the one who's after me da."

Marie's face turned thoughtful and she pulled out her whip and started tapping her palm again.

"I see. Well, ye need t'leave that t'me. I can keep Mr. Gilchrist busy. Jist git yer da over here and leave the rest t'Marie. Now, git before I warm yer britches! And tell 'em t'use the back door."

Denny was gone in a flash. Before Marie was able to find

out who had Gilchrist in her room, he was safely in the kitchen of Browne's Inn.

Meg stood up from the table when her son bolted through the kitchen door. She had fed the other children and kissed them goodnight before Mary Clare took them back upstairs to put them to bed. Rose had returned and was just finishing her meager meal. Meg placed a bowlful of stew in front of him and dipped two thick slices of fried bread into it.

"Now, what are we to do, Denny?"

"Marie says t'have Da and Mr. McGee come by the back way. She'll hide 'em. She wouldn't say about the others."

He wolfed down the stew and bread in seconds and washed it all down with a cold glass of cider.

"Rose, go now and tell them everything Denny has said. Have them go round the back to the kitchen door. Here. I packed them some food and cider in case Marie isn't about to feed them."

Seeing that there was no more stew or bread, Denny took another glass of cider as Meg began to wash the dishes with trembling hands. Just as she was hanging up the damp towel and putting on the kettle for tea, the front door of Browne's Inn opened. Meg and Denny exchanged glances as she went toward the taproom silently praying that this was just another random guest, a stranger here to stay the night.

Meg recognized the voice before she even saw the visitor's face. This was no stranger. Meg started at the sight of the familiar face as their first guest of the evening waited to be registered and assigned a room.

Rose went at once to the rectory. Passing McRea's Livery, she almost collided with a frail old lady who was giving instructions for renting a cab in the morning.

"Excuse me M'am, terribly sorry!"

She never slowed down to see the woman's look of surprise.

Arriving at the rectory, Rose passed the message on to Tom and Duffy.

"Da, what is this all about? Mam's all quiet and serious and now ye're goin' t'Marie's! Marie's, Da! Ye said yerself ye'd tan any of us if ye ever found out we'd ever been there! Da, ye can't go there! Who are ye hidin' from?"

"Come here, Lovie."

Tom took his daughter on his knee and stroked one plait of dark hair with his thick, square fingers.

"Ye know all about trust now, don't ye? Ye've heard it from the pulpit every Sunday since ye were a wee lass and ye see it every day as Mr. McGee feeds us and keeps us safe at the inn."

He gazed seriously into her deep blue eyes.

"Well, it's time t'put that trust t'work. Ye don't know what's happenin'. I know that's hard fer ye. But now ye have t'go on blind trust. Mr. McGee and I are in a bit o'bother right now and we need t'hide out from Mr. Gilchrist. He means us grave harm, Rose. That's all ye need t'know. We simply need t'hide out fer a bit until he goes away."

"But Da, have ye done wrong? Are ye goin' t'jail? What if he catches ye?"

Rose was biting back tears and had Tom's other hand tightly in her own.

"Can't we jist run away? Can't we jist get a buggy from McRea's and leave?"

"Dear, Lovie. My firebrand! Ye're always ready t'stand and fight and now ye're ready t'run."

He saw her face fall at his words and the tears finally came.

"Not that I blame ye, darlin'. It's a natural thing and not a bad idea atall. It's jist that men like Mr. Gilchrist have a way o'findin' folks no matter where they go. Fer now, we're better off hidin' out until he goes away or we can find a truly safe place t'go."

At this Rose buried her face in her father's chest and cried.

"Oh, Da! How will we know what happens t'ye? What will we do?"

Tom took her chin in his hand and accepted a clean hanky from Fr. Timon. Gently wiping her face he continued.

"Now, Lovie. Ye're the messenger, remember? Mr. McGee and I need ye t'be brave and smart and keep the lines of communication open. Between yer smarts and Denny bein' a boyo, we'll know everything we need t'know and be safe and well hidden in Miss Marie's secret room. But we need ye t'be brave and smart, Rose. No tears. That'll give us away fer sure."

Rose sniffed and set her jaw.

"I'm never goin' t'leave ye Da. If yer hidin' then I'm hidin' too. No matter what, I'm not leavin' Westport as long as yer hidin' at Marie's. I'm the messenger!"

Tom looked hard into Rose's eyes.

"Now listen t'me, Rose Phalen. Ye're full of brave words and 'tis that glad I am t'be hearin' em. But this is no time fer stubborn lasses t'be bullheaded and foolish. If yer goin' t'be a help to us, ye need t'be obedient. Denny'll tell ye how the whole thing works and the consequences o'strikin' out on yer own. Ye have t'promise me ye'll do everything Fr. Timon and yer Mam say, even if ye think ye have a better idea! There are things ye can't know and decisions that aren't yers t'make. D'ye hear me now, Lovie?"

Tom's heart ached as he watched Rose's shoulders slump. He hated to take the stuffing out of her but he couldn't afford another episode like the one he had had with Denny.

"Rose? Can I count on ye?"

Slowly she raised her head and looked directly at him. He saw in her eyes a clear intelligence that reassured him of her ability to be trusted.

"Aye, Da. Ye can count on me. And Denny too. I'll see t'that."

He took his firstborn in his arms and wrapped her in a long embrace. He could feel the strength of his love firming her resolve and stiffening her spine. When he released her,

Tom's own eyes were stinging as he realized fully that he may never see this beloved child again.

Picking up the parcel of food and jug of cider, he turned to his friend.

"Ready Duff?"

They left by the kitchen door. Rose stood looking after them, her head tingling where Mr. McGee had rubbed his hand across her hair.

Chapter Twelve

Marie DeVianney waited impatiently in her office for Porky Billy to report to her. She hated situations like this and despite having faced down worse, had never gotten used to it. Here she was providing a simple service to men of every walk of life, every political persuasion, every class and nationality and she kept finding herself playing Morgan le Fey to protect men who weren't even paying customers.

She was getting too old for this. All she wanted was to keep her house running, her girls fed and off the street and save enough to keep herself out of the workhouse. This endless hunger had impacted her business so badly that she herself had been forced to earn her keep. Were it not for her ability to entice the officers of the many ships that moored in Westport's docks, she would have had to let her girls go and close her doors three years ago.

She knew she was well past her prime and she was used to having a few young ones in her stable that appealed to the older men and brought her big money. But since this famine, she hadn't been able to find any young girls with any meat on their bones. She could hardly invite her customers to wrack themselves against protruding hipbones and try to cup flat lifeless breasts, now could she? Thank God she had sold the Dublin house before the hunger started. The money from that sale was half gone but she was a frugal woman. If she budgeted well and could convince the ship captains that her special techniques were worth their gold, they'd get through.

No, Marie DeVianney wasn't worried about starving. Her concern was not about losing her girls. Between her little whip and the three meals a day she fed them, she had her stable under control. The girls weren't going anywhere. Marie was worried about being closed down.

Sure, there were enough gentlemen in her clientele who would be ruined if she exposed them as customers and she was not above blackmail. It was this unrest with the Blackthorn Brotherhood in town and this nasty little Gilchrist snooping all over the place that made her nervous. She thought it would settle down after the last of them left a fortnight ago but now here she was hiding two more. And one of them a well-known local with ties to Lord Sligo! No, Marie didn't like this new development one bit.

The curtain that separated Marie's office from the corridor swung open and Porky Billy came in. Marie knew no one would hear their exchange. Her office was a secluded cubby no bigger than a closet, way in the back of her house, far from the ears of girls and customers alike. It opened into a short hallway that led directly to the tiny smoky kitchen by a flight of rickety stairs. Marie never entertained there. It was hot, smelly and generally very uncomfortable. Only she and Porky Billy were even aware of its presence at the top of the stairs.

The big woman in the red and purple striped caftan sat up straight in her chair and blinked at the ugly ape-like features of the cook. There was no warmth in the bloodshot blue eyes rimmed with black kohl and fringed with stiff, heavily dressed lashes but the man returned her cold gaze with one of pure devotion. Her baggy cheeks fell into ripples that shook as she popped her head up in anticipation of his words, the deep pink rouge on her cheekbones highlighting the contrast between her real face and the thick plastering of white powder that failed to conceal her advancing age. Her heavily pomaded blonde hair never even moved when she raised her head.

"Well?"

Porky Billy smiled his foolish, toothless grin. He loved Marie like a schoolboy and would do anything to win a few moments in her ample arms. Twenty years her junior, he had been with her since he was thirteen and she had found him starving in a Dublin gutter. She had taken him in and put him to work as a special feature for certain of her customers. In her own way, she loved him too. He had made her very rich with the arty set in those early years.

When he grew too old to be desirable and had shown a certain level of skill in the kitchen, Marie kept him on as cook. It was clear that he would never leave her unless she drove him away and she had no reason to do that. He was as loyal as a hound and just about as ugly. Marie knew that he would be at her beck and call as long as she let him have a poke every now and then and that was small price to pay for the best lamb stew this side of the Liffey River.

He stood before her, smiling, full of pride at being her accomplice in the running of an underground movement for Ireland's brave lads. He loved no one but Marie and sweet mother Ireland and if he could help one he was happy. If he could please both, he was ecstatic.

"They're up there. It's bloody hot in there but no one'll find 'em. The others left some clothes and a pair of old boots. D'ye want me t'get 'em? Maybe ye can get a price fer 'em."

"No. I don't need their stinkin' boots. Maybe one o'these new ones can use 'em. What about Gilchrist?"

"He's with Gabrielle. He brought some stuff fer a chest cold and he wants her t'nurse him. Slather him up good, she says."

"Well, that snake is goin' t'pay fer her time! He better not think he's keepin' her fer himself while payin' customers are waitin'. Anybody down there?"

"Jist a couple o'sailors from the Marianna. Nobody else is in port. She sails in the afternoon tomorrow and it's a couple o'days till the Smithbourne and the Sweet Jane are due to dock. The Cobalt left this afternoon fer Australia so we won't see those boyos fer along time."

"Where's Peggy?"

"Still on the Marianna. She left an hour ago with one o'the Frenchy ones. D'ye want me t'git her?"

"No, I need ye here. She'll be all right. Last time she went aboard she turned a half dozen tricks. Brought me some good rum too. Leave her there. Who does that leave? Pearlie has the clap and Denise is at her time o'the month. Are Bunny and Philomena busy?"

"They're tryin' t'git somethin' out o'the two sailors in the taproom."

"Well, we may not make a lot tonight. Depends on Peggy. That Gilchrist better not try anything, though. Gabrielle is young and stupid. Make sure he knows ye're watchin' him. It would be better fer our secret guests if he stayed longer but he has t'pay. I don't care who he is!"

Porky Billy stood dumbly across from Marie's desk, making no move to leave.

"Ye can go now, Porky."

"Sure, Miss Marie. I was jist wonderin' seein' as how it's a bit slow tonight. D'ye think we could, ye know…"

Marie gave him a veiled look.

"Not t'night, love. I've too much on me mind fer that tonight. Jist keep a close eye on things fer me. And set that Gilchrist straight."

Disappointed, the cook turned to leave.

"Sure, Miss Marie, ye know I'll be doin' that."

"And Porky? Once they're all gone, if we can git 'em all outta here alive, ther'll be plenty o'time fer mama love."

He shot her a glance of gleeful anticipation and left her alone.

Robert Gilchrist lay on his back against two heavy gray pillows. The soggy old mattress creaked as he turned and gazed with contempt at the naked girl fumbling with her thin blouse next to the bed. Good Lord, the stupid thing can't even dress herself! Well, what did he care as long as she knew how to undress. In fact, as long as he was still naked himself, he wanted her undressed while she applied the soothing ointment to his chest.

"No. Leave it off. In fact take the skirt off too. I want you to massage these healing oils into my chest. I've taken cold and as long as you're here you can do that for me."

"But sir, ye've had yer pleasure and Miss Marie…"

"Damn Miss Marie! Do as I say or I'll have Miss Marie whip you while I watch. Now off with the skirt and on your knees on the bed! And untie that hair. I want it down around your face. If you're going to be a whore I want you to look like one, not some damn schoolgirl."

The girl hastily complied, tripping over the top of her skirt as she dropped it to the floor and landed, sprawling across the bed. She awkwardly got to her knees and took the bottle of balm from her customer. He watched her every move as she massaged the ointment into his narrow, wrinkled chest. The powerful aroma of camphor and mint wafted into her nostrils as she worked the greasy fluid into his skin.

Gabrielle could feel his eyes ogling her breasts as they jiggled back and forth with the effort of her work. She knew he would not be able to keep his hands off her and waited for the pain of his pinch.

"The ribs, too. I have pain in my whole chest."

She tried to reach across him and apply the ointment to his ribs but he caught her hand.

"Straddle me, you stupid whore. That's the only way to do it. Here, let me help you."

He grabbed Gabrielle roughly between her legs and swung her around until she sat astride him. With a sneer he pulled her thick hair in every direction until it framed her face in a huge cloud of matted red curls. Running his hands down her spine, he pinched her hard on the buttock and spoke again.

"What's keeping you? I said massage the oil into my ribs, you brat! How am I ever to feel better if you dawdle like that?"

Gabrielle winced at the pain from his pinch but made no sound. She had found that the stronger she reacted to a customer's torment, the more they enjoyed hurting her.

She slathered unguent on her hands, enjoying the hot, tingling sensation of the camphor and the contrasting coolness of the mint. What a remarkable feeling! As she worked the strange salve into Mr. Gilchrist's ribcage, she could feel the cold heat penetrate her hands and fingers.

Just as she suspected, Gabrielle soon felt Mr. Gilchrist's narrow fingers kneading her breasts and pinching her nipples. As she endured his attentions, she continued to rub his ribs, up and down, up and down. This motion caused the natural swaying of her hips to arouse him beneath her. If he managed to do what she knew he planned to do, she would have to collect another fee from him. Miss Marie was ferocious about that and Gabrielle was not interested in feeling the little whip across her backside.

"Sir, if ye want more service, ye're goin' t'have t' put the money on the table first."

'Damn you, brat! You'll get your money! Just finish the job!"

Gabrielle was about to cry. If she got caught on top of a customer without the money being placed on the table first, she would be in deep trouble. She set the jar of ointment on Mr. Gilchrist's belly and tried to ease off the bed but he grabbed her wrists. She wriggled her legs to the side until she had one foot on the floor. Miss Marie had taught all her girls how to get away from a greedy customer and this was not the first time Gabrielle had used this maneuver.

Just as she managed to get her other foot on the floor, her arms painfully twisted in Mr. Gilchrist's grip, the door was flung open and Porky Billy barged in.

"Let 'er go! Yer not t'be takin' more than ye paid fer. Now put the money on the table or git out."

"How dare you, you filthy ape? I'll have you flogged!"

Gilchrist let go of Gabrielle's wrists and she jumped clear of the bed. The fact of his naked arousal in the presence of this freakish, toothless omethon hit him with such force that he sat up with a start. Looking down at himself he realized too late that the vessel of camphor and mint unguent had popped off his belly and was now poised upside down over his proud manhood. Before he could grab it, the heavy jar landed upon him, smothering his most sensitive parts as the remaining ointment oozed out of the jar to coat everything in its path.

Horror registered on Mr. Gilchrist's face as he felt the indescribable sensations of camphor and mint ointment penetrate his privates. He desperately tried to scoop the thick ooze from between his legs only succeeding in spreading it still further across both front and back. With his entire crotch on fire he began dancing and writhing around the room shrieking in pain.

Judging by the look on his face and the sounds coming from his mouth, Porky and Gabrielle both imagined that the cold draft caused by his cavorting only increased the effect of the unguent against his unfortunate skin. Soon his cries were punctuated with spasms of coughing that doubled him over, further exposing his burning privates to the air. With a faint smile on his face, Porky closed the door behind them and Gabrielle fastened the last button on her blouse with no problem at all.

Tom and Duffy looked at each other, alarmed at the sounds coming from the room below. Who was being tortured and why in this place?

"Duff, I thought Rose said all the brothers were gone from here? D'ye think someone might still be here? Man alive, someone is payin' fer somethin' down there!"

"Aye, ye can barely stand the sound. Like an animal bein' flayed. I can't imagine who it is, though. Morris and Terry left while I was still standin' there. I'm sure they were off t'find the others. But why here anyway? If they wanted t'flog a man they'd do it in public. Or at least in th'station house yard. I can't tell ye' what we're hearin' but I sure wish it would stop!"

"I can't stand it fer the man! It is a man, I think. A girl would be higher don't ye think, Duff?"

Duffy looked at Tom with astonishment.

"Jaysus save us, I can't believe we're sittin' here in the attic of a whorehouse tryin' t'decide if we're hearin' the death throes of a man or a woman! What kind of a world are we livin' in?"

"Duff, listen! He's chokin' now. My God they're pourin' boilin' water down his throat until he chokes t'death!"

"Tom, fer the love o'God, man! Git ahold o'yerself! Whatever they're doin t'the poor sod, we'll be next if ye make so much noise. There's nothin' we can do fer him. Nothin' atall!"

Tom slumped against the crumbling wattle and mud wall. Marie's was an old building with a thatched roof in serious need of repair. He could hear the mice scurrying through the thatch and could smell the damp stench of rotting reeds.

He would have made a great contribution to the brotherhood. How did they do it? What decent man could listen for hours to the sounds of another man's torture? Whatever the poor lad downstairs did, he was sure getting his now.

He and Duffy had promised that big lad with the thick jaws they'd be quiet. He hoped he hadn't made a liar out of himself and been heard down below. Well, time would tell. The filthy cook had told them Marie would probably want to see them before she turned in for the night. But Marie didn't turn in for the night until daylight so they might as well try and get some rest. If only that screaming and coughing would stop!

No sooner had the coughing started did they hear the voice of a woman loud and hard with anger. They clearly heard her tell the wounded man to dress himself and get out of her place immediately or she would have the constable after him. When he wasn't coughing Tom distinctly heard the man pleading for mercy and time to recover from his ordeal. The woman simply threatened to take a whip to his skinny backside. This was followed by more pleading and promises to be gone as soon as he was dressed.

A great deal of crashing and thudding followed amid threats to put him out on the street as naked as the day he was born. Duffy hastily wiped a clean spot on the dirty pane of the tiny window behind his head. He strained to get a glimpse at the source of all the screaming. All he saw was a skinny old man bent to the task of putting his underwear on in the middle of Westport quay as his trousers and jacket were thrown out after him onto the cobblestones.

Tom tried to see past Duffy's shoulder but neither of them could see his face. They watched as he finished dressing himself and waddled painfully down the quay to find more suitable lodgings without seeing who the poor victim was.

Again, Tom and Duffy found themselves staring at each other wondering what manner of place this was and what kind of people held their lives in their hands.

When Meg had crept into the taproom she had expected the worst. Had their guest been a man she would have assumed in the twilight that it was Mr. Gilchrist. Instead, she beheld a woman in her sights, one who was a welcome sight to her eyes.

Moments later, Rose returned from Fr. Timon's and Meg had shooed her upstairs to help Mary Clare settle the babies in bed. She had made tea and popped a few sweet buns in the oven and set the table for two. Meg was greatly distracted by the upsetting developments but she looked forward to some time in the kitchen with an old friend.

Their guest was sitting primly on the naughty bench waiting for Meg, when Denny flew in the kitchen door and Meg hustled him upstairs where he could tell her his story. He barely noticed the woman on the bench and at first, tried to resist Meg but he quickly collected himself and with a poignant sense of maturity spilled his news.

When he was through, Meg stood numbly at the top of the stairs. She felt her life shift yet again in a direction over which she had no control. Down she went to properly greet their guest, her face frozen in a welcoming smile.

"Mrs. Trent, I can't believe it's you! What a wonderful surprise."

"No, dear, I am the one who is wonderfully surprised. I was so worried about you and your family when you just disappeared from the island. No one knew where you went or if you were simply swept out to sea! Rev. Nangle was greatly distressed. He had promised your mother never to lose sight of you for her."

Meg pulled the buns out of the oven and sprinkled cinnamon and cane sugar on the tops. She somehow felt that she was stealing from the inn indulging herself and her friend. Then again, Mrs. Trent was a paying guest and must not be denied.

Pouring the strong, steaming tea and passing the butter to her friend, Meg could not stop smiling. Here she was, playing tea party in a borrowed kitchen while Tom and Duffy sweat like dock workers in that stifling attic over at Marie's. Denny sat in the taproom sulking as he half-listened to the women chattering in the kitchen. He was disgusted at how easily his mam slipped into her aristocratic role as though nothing was wrong and she hadn't just been shaking with fear that the bell would announce Mr. Gilchrist and not Mrs. Trent.

What he didn't realize was that Meg was playing her role to the hilt to throw her old friend off the scent of their crisis. The fewer people that knew where Tom and Duffy were and the less fuss made about their situation the better. Mrs. Trent was, after all, a loyal British subject and Meg's husband was hiding from the law.

Meg felt the tea soothing her insides and decided she might as well enjoy this. There was no knowing what tomorrow might bring. And it had been so long since she had had a woman to talk to. She could not believe her good fortune.

The two women talked and talked each in a great hurry to tell the other all the news since the Phalen's had left Achill. Yes, their house still stood undisturbed. No, Peg Sweeney had not left to join her husband on the mainland. Yes, sad to say, Fr. O'Boyle was dead as were almost all the Creahans and Maryellen Feeney. Peg had taken over the store and post office though there was no food and very little mail.

Mrs. Trent's face lit up as she told Meg about Peg.

"Oh, I'm so glad I remembered! You received the only mail we've had in months! I had planned on mailing it back to the sender from the post office here."

She pulled a letter out of her reticule and handed it to Meg. It was from Maureen! Oh, how sweet to have word from Maureen. She thought of the letter she had posted just a while ago and imagined it still sitting in the hull of the Marianna waiting to be taken to the States. Now she would have another one to answer!

"Oh, thank you Mrs. Trent! How kind of you to bring it along. I can't wait to read it."

Meg slipped the letter into her apron pocket.

"You must read it now. I am terribly fatigued after the long journey and should really be heading up to bed. I have so enjoyed our visit. In the morning I plan to leave for Castlebar. I'm trying to break up my trip to Ballaghey where I have family. My missionary days are over but I hope to be of some service to the rector and his wife at St.Andrew's. It's where I met the reverend, God rest his sweet soul. It's where we were married."

The older woman struggled to her feet and Meg called Denny to help her with her bags. He came at once and politely guided Mrs. Trent to the steps bringing her humble carpetbag and hatbox behind her. Once Meg heard them at the top of the stairs, she pulled out the letter from Maureen.

Tearing it open she returned to the kitchen where the tea was still hot and the light from the setting sun was still fairly bright. Sitting in the window to catch the lowering light Meg began to read:

May 10, 1848
Dearest Meg and family,
This letter must be short though there is much to tell. I have finally had a child! In fact, I've had two! Little Colin Charles O'Malley and Mary Margaret O'Malley were born in robust health on April 30, 1848 at 3:00 am. All is well though I had to be abed for months while I waited for them to come. The doctor would have none of me minding the store or even cooking meals. Poor Charlie had to accept it. Doctor's orders! We had a widow from the parish help us for room and board. Weighed on the meat scale in the store Colin came to 5 pounds even and Mary was just a bit heavier. They are beautiful and both of us are thrilled beyond measure.

Twins! After losing so many! God has been so good to us! I am doing fine and Phil and Julie have been wonderful. They are godparents finally! After Charlie and I have been for them more than once. I am so sorry Charlie's mam wasn't alive to hold them just once.

My other news is not as good. Charlie had a scuffle with a big Swede down at the paper mill and took quite a beating just two days after the twins were born. He has recovered but has a bit of trouble with balance as his injuries were around the head, especially the ears. Between that and the drink I think he's not long for the force. They have him working the desk but he's very unhappy with that. Hopefully this will pass and he can go back to his command. He was over the moon about the babies and now he won't even look at them. Says he has trouble focusing.

I know you know how happy I am to finally be a mother. My heart is ready to burst! I would walk through fire for them, Meg. All the tears over all the lost ones are dried as I sit and rock Colin in my arms then pick up Mary and do the same. How I wish you could kiss their downy blond fuzz and feel their little hands curl around your finger. I promise I will tell them all about their 'Auntie' Meg and 'Uncle' Tom. Give everyone a big hug for me. I have to go, Colin's looking to be fed.

All our love,

Maureen and Babies (and of course Charlie)

Meg sat for a few minutes just absorbing the wonderful news about Maureen's new babies. A son and a daughter! How proud she and Charlie must be. She folded the letter and put it back in her apron pocket. She'd read it again later when she went upstairs. Now she had to close up the taproom and lock the doors. It had been a long day and a lot of upset from Denny's sighting of Mr. Gilchrist, first on the Louisburg Road and again at Marie's.

She breathed a sigh of relief that the face at the door had been that of her dear friend and not his ugly, snarling puss. Maybe he planned to stay at Marie's for the night. After the ruckus she could use a quiet evening and an early bedtime. If only she could be sure that Tom was safe. She would just have to trust God and Miss Marie for that.

Meg had just reached over the registration desk for the key to lock up when the front door burst open and another guest practically fell into the taproom forcing Meg to jump up onto the first stair.

"Mr. Gilchrist! What happened to you?"

Meg couldn't believe she even cared enough to ask but the sight in the doorway startled the question out of her.

"As if you care! I need a room and I need a doctor immediately!"

Meg just stared at the man. He was barely dressed, his outfit hastily thrown on, his clothes a wrinkled mess. He stood in his stockings, his fine gray suede boots in his hand. She looked at his hair awry and his face scarlet with the effort of walking from Marie's. He stood with his legs apart and moved gingerly from one foot to the other as he scowled at her from the doorway.

Meg had seen him in a state before but never had she seen him dressed with anything less than impeccable taste. Now, here he was looking like he had tumbled right out of bed, reeking of camphor and the faint fragrance of mint.

"Well, Mr. Gilchrist I can rent you a room but I have no doctor here. In fact I know from Mr. McGee that Dr. Browne and his assistant have both been called to Westport House. They have had influenza and now both the Marquis and one of the children are ill."

'Well, then maybe you can tell me where your thieving husband is, my dear Mrs. Phalen."

He stooped uncomfortably and slipped on his boots as if it were the most natural thing to do in the doorway of an inn. Then he deliberately tied his cravat in the tall mirror at the foot of the stairs. Satisfied that he looked somewhat normal, he turned to Meg, a smirk curling his thin lips.

"Don't lie to me again. I know he isn't dead as you so cunningly told me the last time I was here. I've come with one purpose, my dear little lady of the manor. I intend to put your whoring husband in jail where he can rot until the crown sees fit to hang him."

Meg was shocked at how his words emboldened rather than frightened her. Her visit with Uncle Robert had truly straightened her backbone. She looked at him with contempt.

"Who do you think you are Robert Gilchrist? You are nothing more than a sniveling, little lackey waddling into a bar in your stocking feet. You stink of camphor, your nose is running and you need a shave. I should have you thrown out of here. Instead you threaten me. What is it you want to hang my husband for? Marrying above his station? Succeeding at building a life for his family? You know nothing about my husband. You seem to believe he is still alive. I can't help what you believe but I know the truth. Dead or alive he'll always be ten times the man you'll ever be."

Gilchrist looked like he would rupture. Even his hair stood straight up on his head. A look of confusion passed across his face but quickly changed to rage as he realized that this trip and all his agony could have been for naught. Maybe Tom Phalen really was dead! He decided to call Meg's bluff. He pulled himself up to his full height and approached the stairs, cornering Meg against the wall.

"You little bitch! You know as well as I do that he's alive. And he's a thief who will be hanged, I assure you. I had originally thought he was a horse thief but your father, whose home I have just left, informed me that the horse, Jewel, was a gift to you from a young man and therefore not stolen from his stable the night you ran away in disgrace. However, you may not be aware that I know also that a certain deed was in your father's possession that night and he had it in the pocket of a jacket that was stolen from his room by you or that whore of his. Well, your great man of a husband is responsible for the whereabouts of that deed and until he produces it, he is guilty of grand larceny in the theft of your father's property."

He relished the shock that had replaced the self-assurance on Meg's face.

"I can see from your face that your husband is indeed alive. Were he not, you would care little for my bit of news and it is very clear to me that you care a great deal. Now, tell me where he is or by God I will have you and all your bastards in the workhouse by tomorrow morning."

Gilchrist had Meg up against the wall and was pressing himself into her body. The stench of camphor was almost overpowering and Meg could feel his bony chest crushing against her bosom. His face was so close to hers she could almost taste his foul breath and his silver stubble threatened to scratch her cheek. For a brief second she thought he would kiss her and the ridiculousness of that image made her smile involuntarily. Within seconds she was laughing in spite of herself.

"How dare you laugh, you insolent whore? Look at you! Ugly as Satan, your fine hair all falling out and your bony ass showing through your rags. Where is the beautiful Lady Meg that stole the heart of the Irish pig stable boy? Look at you now, your hands worn to the bone with scrubbing, your apron stained from cleaning chamber pots and spittoons! Where is the fine lace and silk, the corset to lift your sagging, useless bosom? You laugh at me? You would be so bold, so foolish, so downright stupid as to laugh at me? You are nothing Miss High and Mighty! You are less than the whores at Marie's. At least they make a little money for their effort. There's not man alive that would pay for your sorry carcass."

Meg stopped laughing as soon as she had started. As Gilchrist's vitriol registered in her mind she felt her temper rising. The passionate love she and Tom had made the other night left no doubt in her mind that she was desirable to the only man that mattered. Gilchrist's words, meant to hurt and disarm her only fueled Meg's own fury.

She shoved him away from her and tried to get past him. He pinned her to the wall and she struggled against him. She was no match for him and he knew it. Even with his tender parts still smarting from the ointment, he was far stronger than she was.

Just as she felt herself sinking to the floor, Denny bounded down the stairs followed by Rose and Mrs. Trent, brandishing her longest hatpin. They had heard the shouting and the scuffling and had come to help. Gilchrist never knew what hit him as Denny leapt from the middle stair and tackled him to the floor. At the same time, Meg, freed from his grip drew back her hand and rammed the full force of her palm into his chin.

Down he went like a house of cards. But he was not to be taken out that easily. He swung around and grabbed Denny by the ankle pulling him down on the floor. With his other hand he began to pound the boy's face into the floor. Meg went wild and began to kick Gilchrist in the ribs, in the buttocks anywhere she could put her foot. Mrs. Trent joined the fray wielding her hatpin like a dagger. It was Mr. Gilchrist's good fortune that she never found the right opportunity to plant it firmly in his backside. But Meg's bare foot and Mrs. Trent's pin were not very effective weapons. What finally brought old Gilchrist down was his cold. The exertion of the scuffle started paroxysms of coughing which threatened to cease his breathing.

Denny stood back from him in disbelief. Meg leaned over him in shock, praying that he wouldn't die and they'd all be hanged for murder. Rose scooted down the stairs and around the crumpled man as he gasped and choked on the floor. She brought him a glass of water. In his panic he grabbed it from her and guzzled it. Gradually the coughing stopped and Mr. Gilchrist slowly rose to his feet. Without a word he straightened his cravat, gingerly touched his chin and wiped both blood and spittle from his mouth. Then he was gone.

Mrs. Trent sat down hard on the step, her hatpin still in her hand. No one said anything. Meg straightened her dress and hair and tried to thank Denny but he was too shocked to hear it. Rose took the empty glass to the kitchen and set it on the counter. When the front door opened again, everyone was in about the same position as they had been in when Gilchrist left.

He pointed at Meg.

"That one. And the boy. They tried to rob me and do murder upon me. I will see them hanged."

Rose shouted.

"Run Denny, run!"

Gilchrist shouted at the constable to get him but he was already gone.

He looked at Meg's stricken face and smiled the same evil grin that he used the day he announced that Tom's cattle were being taken.

"Don't worry Mrs. Phalen. We'll catch up with him.

You'll get to watch him hang on your way to the gallows."

Gilchrist looked at Rose trembling behind the bar.

"And don't you worry little girl. We'll be hangin' yer papa too and his friend the innkeeper as an accomplice. When we're through with them you can always get a job at Marie's. She needs young blood and I'm not sure you'd like the workhouse very much. Yes, I think I'll recommend you for Marie's."

The constable placed the cold hard handcuffs around Meg's wrists and shoved her toward the door. As she felt the door close behind her, she could hear Rose wailing behind it.

For the second time, Denny Phalen found himself at Marie's kitchen door. Porky Billy was even less enthused about his appearance than he was the first time.

"Please Mr. Porky, sir, I need t'see me da and Mr. McGee! It's an emergency! I need t'see them. Me Mam's going t'be hanged and they're after me too!"

"Boyo, what palaver are ye flingin' at me now?"

He came over to the half-door and leaned out into the dark alley. One look at Denny's face told him this was no cock and bull story.

"What are ye sayin'" Boyo? Ye're not about puttin' Miss Marie in harms way are ye?"

"No, no sir, Mr. Porky, sir. I jist need t'talk t'me da about this. Please, Mr. Porky let me see me da."

Try as he might to be brave, Denny was about to cry.

"Sir, I niver meant any harm, believe me! It's jist that when Mr. Gilchrist was hurtin' me mam I couldn't help it!"

Now he really had the cook's attention.

"What did ye do Boyo? Ye niver killed 'im did ye? Tell me ye're not bein' hunted fer murder!"

"No, he's not dead, fer sure. Didn't I jist see him standin' at Browne's havin' me mam arrested by the constable and her, the sweetest mam in the world?"

Now Denny was crying and the big cook dragged him into the kitchen to keep anyone from hearing him. Porky Billy closed the top half of the door and the temperature of the kitchen immediately soared.

"Wait here and don't move. And stop that snivelin'. Marie don't like tears. Somebody cryin' always gets more reason t'cry from her, if ye git me."

He climbed the stairs as fast as his legs could maneuver his big body and disappeared into the dark of the upstairs corridor. Denny sat on a creepie next to the chair where Porky Billy had been lounging when he found him peeking at the girlie pictures. While he waited for the cook to return, he reached down and began to flip through the tattered pages. Denny was fascinated by what he saw on those pages. There were pretty girls no older than Rose posing in front of shops and carousels, in curraghs and on balconies. All of them undressed!

He heard footsteps and hastily replaced the newspaper on the table next to Porky Billy's chair. This time Marie entered the kitchen from the stairway that Porky Billy had just gone up. Denny could see by the way she tapped her little whip on the palm of her hand that she was very upset.

She looked at him steadily. Her voice was very low and very cold.

"What d'ye have t'tell me?"

Denny gulped and told her what had happened.

"And I am supposed t'do somethin' about this? I, who have niver seen a nickel of yer father's money on me table? I want him out of here!"

This last she said right into Denny's face, the cheroot smell stronger than ever.

He was desperately trying not to cry. He didn't want Marie to give him any more reason for tears.

Marie looked at him again. Denny wanted to squirm under her fierce gaze but something told him to stand straight and hold still. She went over and opened the top of the kitchen door. It was stifling in the kitchen and Marie's powder was beginning to cake. To her surprise there was a girl about to knock on the door. She let out a little shriek when the door suddenly opened from the inside revealing the big face of Miss Marie herself.

"Oh, Divil take ye! Who are you hangin' around me door? Don't I have enough trouble fer one night without the likes o'you scarin' me half t'death?"

Denny heard a little voice respond.

"I'm Rose. Rose Phalen. I need t'see me da."

"Yer da is it? How many das are there in here? It seems we have a whole congregation o'das! Hmmm. Let me look at ye. What's t'keep me from puttin'ye t'work fer me trouble? Yer da is it and what makes ye think I know where yer da is, or even who yer da is? Git away from here before I throw ye into a room and let the sailors decide who yer da is!"

"No, please, I need t'see him. I know he's here. I'm the one who sent him here."

Catching sight of Denny in the kitchen, Rose gasped. Marie realized that the whole alley would be at the door in a minute and she opened the kitchen door and dragged Rose in. Once again the top of the door was closed against the homeless population of the garbage piles.

Now Marie was beside herself. She swung around and faced the two of them her voice hissing with anger.

"Ye come here. Ye disrupt me business. Ye bring yer da t'me attic t'hide and I do it fer ye. Not fer yer da but fer Ireland, mind ye. Fer the good of Ireland! He's a brother, ye say. He's in danger ye say. His friend too, ye say. Now ye're back tellin' me ye need t'see him. Yer mam is in jail ye say. It's Gilchrist yer runnin' from ye say."

"Now first of all, why should I believe ye? Second of all, why should I help ye? Ye're nobody t'me. Yer no kin or friend t'me! Yer jist a pimple on the ass o'time fer all I care! Give me one good reason why I shouldn't turn the whole lot o'ye over t'the law!"

Denny and Rose looked blankly at the madam looming larger than life in the tiny kitchen. Finally Rose stepped forward.

Swallowing hard she began, "Miss Marie, I understand why ye don't want t'trust us. Our da and mam are on th'wrong side o'the law but they've niver broken even a little law. Mr. Gilchrist almost killed Mam. That's why Denny hurt him. Now they're after Denny too."

Rose paused, remembering what Mr. Gilchrist said. Looking directly into Miss Marie's eyes she spoke very fast.

"Mr. Gilchrist said ye can use a young girl. I'm thirteen but I'm kinda' skinny since the hunger and I could pass fer younger. Ye might like Mary Clare more, she's much prettier but she's goin' t'be a nun. I promise ye. Git me da safely out o'here and help us git Mam out o'jail and I'll come here and work fer ye. I even know a little French from Mr. Mulcahy's hedge school. I promise I won't be any trouble, I won't eat much and I'll work hard. I'm very good in the kitchen and I can carry heavy trays jist in case ye didn't want me fer, ye know, kissin' sailors. I kissed Mam's looking glass once so I know how it's done."

Marie stood staring at Rose Phalen in disbelief. Denny looked at his sister in a red haze and felt the room spinning. He sat again on the creepie and put his head between his knees. He imagined Rose posing for the dirty newspaper on Mr. Porky's chair. More than ever he wanted to cry.

Rose simply stood looking directly into Marie's kohl rimmed eyes, her face an open book as honest and sincere as if she were showing her favorite lamb at the fair. Never had Marie had such an offer. The big madam was simply speechless. This child had just offered herself in exchange for her father! What kind of man must he be to have such a daughter?

Slowly Marie recovered her voice.

"Well, lass, I think we can work somethin' out without ye actually comin' t'work here. I'm thinkin' yer da wouldn't really want ye t'do that, even fer him. Ye jist leave the sailor kissin' t'me an me girls."

Rose stood between Marie and Denny, biting her lip. She

was sorry she came. This woman wasn't helping them. She didn't even think Rose could help with kissing the sailors. Well, the least she could do was hide Denny in her secret room with Da and Mr. McGee.

She cleared her voice and started to speak again.

"M'am, I'm sorry ye can't use me help with the kissin' and I probably can be of more use t'me mam watchin' the children but Denny still needs a place t' hide. D'ye think ye'd have space fer one more in yer secret room?"

Marie smacked her whip hard on the arm of Porky Billy's chair.

"Shut yer pretty pink mouth before I have t'smack ye! D'ye not see me thinkin'?"

Beads of perspiration began to form on Marie's upper lip and the powder on her forehead had caked to the point of cracking. Her eyes were like two penciled slits beneath her thin painted brows. She paced back and forth to and from the door and tapped her whip against the skirt of her colorful caftan, soft slapping sounds punctuating her steps.

Finally she looked up. Her gaze went right past the children to the stairwell behind them where Porky Billy was gesturing to her.

"Yes, Porky?"

"M'am, the lads in the attic, er, secret room are askin' about all the commotion goin' on in the room below, earlier. They seem t'think we was torturin' one o'the brothers. What d'ye want me t'tell 'em? Besides, they drank all their cider and they're lookin' t'pee."

Denny and Rose looked from one to the other as Marie's face went from powdery white to crimson. They tried to imagine what was going to become of them now.

"Jaysus, Mary and Joseph and all the saints in heaven! Get 'em a piss pot fer cryin' out loud! Here take Junior here t' the secret room along with it. He needs t' see his da and hide out so he can do both and even piss in a china pot if he pleases. As fer you, Lady Jane, git! Git out while yer shoes are still good! Ye have a bit o' doin' yerself t'find a place fer yerself and yer young ones before they come and haul the lot o'ye t'the workhouse! And if ye dare bring 'em here I swear I'll sell ye all t'slavers!"

Rose looked at Denny, her eyes filled with tears.

"Git! I said! I'll not be havin' the law comin' around here closin' me down. I gotta' eat too ye know."

Denny ran toward Rose and hugged her hard. After one more long look at each other, Rose turned and ran out the door into the alley. Porky Billy picked up an old chipped chamber pot with a mismatched lid and handed it to Denny.

"Here. Ye might as well earn yer keep."

With a little shove, he followed Denny up the stairs into the black hole of the upstairs corridor.

Chapter Thirteen

Leona Trent had never been out of her bedroom uncorseted in all her adult life. She also had never imagined herself, at her age, sprinting across the back alley behind Browne's Inn. She could hardly believe she now stood in the kitchen of a Roman Catholic rectory in her nightdress and pelisse. Thank God she had chosen the heavy corduroy one. Perhaps the priest would never guess that underneath she wore only a thin cotton gown.

As if to acknowledge the awkwardness of this odd encounter, Fr. Timon immediately sent for his housekeeper who was placing piles of freshly folded altar linens on shelves in the upstairs closet. Mrs. Murphy always knew what to do when odd things happened and this was exceedingly odd.

Mrs. Murphy stood stock still in the cellar doorway staring incredulously at the bareheaded little woman in her nightclothes waving a hatpin at Fr. Timon.

"And then he just left, Father, he and the constable just took her and left! And he promised he'd see the children in a workhouse by morning. Those poor babies! What are we to do?"

Fr. Timon looked at Mrs. Murphy, his face ashen.

"Mrs. Murphy, we have a situation here and it will take a miracle to make it right. This is the Widow Trent, Caroline did you say?"

"Leona, Father."

"Yes, yes, forgive me."

He blushed at his mistake and went on.

"Her husband was Canon Trent at the vicarage in Doeega. Mrs. Trent perhaps you can tell it best."

The beleaguered priest sat down heavily on a wooden bench and held his head in his hands as Mrs. Trent relayed her message to Mrs. Murphy.

When she was through, Mrs. Murphy looked at Fr. Timon and saw that he was totally overwhelmed by this development. She was still grappling with the trembling presence of an elderly half-dressed Protestant woman in her pastor's kitchen at ten o'clock in the evening. It was clear that neither of the others was able to make a decision about what to do. Well, there was no going back now. It wouldn't be the first time she had had to take charge.

"Where are the children now?"

"The boy ran off somewhere. Rose went to warn her father. And I felt it best to leave the little ones asleep, for now. I hope I did right!"

At the mention of Rose warning her father, Fr. Timon's head shot up.

"But he's at Marie's! Are ye tellin' me the little girl went off t'the local whorehouse alone?"

Poor Mrs. Trent looked like she was going to faint. She grabbed the edge of the table to steady herself.

"Well, I don't know. I had just checked into the inn when all this happened and have no idea where Tom Phalen is! How could I have stopped her even if I had known? Oh my heavens, that poor little girl! After her mother was taken away, she just told me she was going to find her da and bolted out the door."

Mrs. Murphy took over like a general in a losing battle.

"We need to find her and get the other children in a safe place before this man has them taken away. Mrs. Trent, you go back to the inn and get the children. Bundle them up and bring them over here. Fr. Timon you must go and find Rose.

I will fix a place for the children in the guest room. We can hide them there until we can get them out of Westport."

Fr. Timon's jaw hung slack at the suggestion that he find Rose. What if she was inside the whorehouse? What if Marie wouldn't let her go? What if someone saw him going in there?

"Mrs. Murphy, don't ye think…?"

Mrs. Murphy was ready for this.

"No Father. I can't be the one to go down to Marie's. It would be even more of a spectacle if I were to show up there than yerself! At least ye can say ye were lookin' fer sinners t'forgive! We need t'think o'the children and we need to be quick about it."

Mrs. Trent was already out the door moving as fast as her old legs could carry her through the alley to the inn. Fr. Timon reached for the closest source of comfort he could find before he left. Finding the altar cruets freshly filled for tomorrow's early Mass, he grabbed the unconsecrated wine and pulled out the stopper with a pop. Drinking it straight from the little bottle he took small comfort from the familiar heat on his tongue. It wasn't good. It wasn't even whiskey but it would have to do.

He put on his beretta and headed for the door. He turned to appeal to Mrs. Murphy one more time but she was already in the parlor pulling blankets and pillows out of a chest.

Fr. Timon closed the gate to his yard and turned toward Marie's. He picked up his pace as best he could, jogging through the clutter of people and refuse. Just as he rounded the far side of two huge trash bins behind Gillie's Bar, he spotted her. Relief flooded his chest as he realized she was safely out of that filthy place and he would not have to go in there and get her.

"Rose, Rose, come t'me child," he called.

She ran into his waiting arms and dissolved in tears.

"There, there, my brave little one. Come along with me now. Mrs. Murphy will know what t'do. There it is, darlin' ye jist need a cuppa and somethin' t'eat and ye'll be jist fine, ye'll see."

On and on the priest rambled kindly. Rose took comfort in the string of words though she wanted neither tea nor food. By the time they reached the rectory, she had pulled away from him and was on her way to the inn to see to her siblings. He watched her go until she was past McRea's and out of sight and went into his house in search of something more substantial than altar wine to calm his frayed nerves.

Mrs. Murphy had indeed put the kettle on and was scrambling the last of the bishop's eggs for the children. A plate of buttered bread sat on the table. When Fr. Timon came into the kitchen without Rose, she let out a gasp.

He raised his hand to shush her.

"I found her. She's fine. She's helping the widow with the others."

"What about the boy?"

Fr. Timon shook his head.

"I niver saw the boy but Denny Phalen has spent many a night on the docks. He can take care of himself."

Fr. Timon went in search of libation regretting the prodigal use of the last of the good food left over from the bishop's visit. Well, they had survived on stringy vegetables before and would be fine with them again.

The back door opened and Rose herded a sleepy Francis and Mary Clare into the bright kitchen where they stood rubbing their eyes in the lamplight. Gracie and Ellen followed with Mrs. Trent bringing up the rear. Rose carried Martha who, true to her reputation, had slept soundly through the whole ordeal.

Fr. Timon watched as Mrs. Murphy tenderly fussed and soothed the children with milky tea and scrambled eggs. Amazed to be in the rectory kitchen at night Francis thought it all great fun and wiggled comfortably in his chair. Gracie rested her head on her arm and picked at her eggs. Ellen, finding her thumb, lay down on a bench and fell back to sleep.

Rose placed Martha in one of the overstuffed chairs in the parlor and sat down next to Mary Clare at the table. When she smelled the buttery eggs and the steamy familiar scent of tea, she realized how hungry she was after all the excitement. Mary Clare turned to her, her eyes serious and wary.

"Where's Mam, Rose?"

Rose looked up at the adults for guidance.

Again, Mrs. Murphy took the helm.

"Mary Clare, once you finish your bed lunch and we get the babies settled, we'll have a nice chat about everything."

Mary Clare pushed her eggs around her plate, her big eyes filled with fear. She scraped the soft yellow eggs onto Francis's plate and slid off the bench. Without a word she went into the parlor where she nestled into the chair with Martha, holding the baby tightly in her arms.

Rose took the sleeping baby from Mary Clare without a struggle and she and Mrs. Murphy settled the little children in the big bed where only a few days ago, a bishop had slept. When she came back downstairs, Rose found her sister sitting in the parlor, staring into the dark.

"She's dead, isn't she Lovie?"

Mary Clare was the only one she let use her da's pet name for her. The younger girl spoke again in a tiny voice.

"Mam's dead."

"Peaches! Don't ye be sayin' that! Musha! The little people!"

Rose ran to her little sister and gathered her into her arms. Mary Clare was stiff and her hands were like ice on Rose's forearms but Rose held on tight. No fairies were going to get them or their mam.

"Mam's dead and we're all goin' to die too. Mam and Da are gone and we'll all die in the workhouse, Rose. Where is Da, Rose?"

She turned her wide vacant eyes on her sister then looked right past her into the kitchen.

"There she is, come to take us away. I've dreamt of her, ye know. I could niver see her face in me dream but it was always the same. Mam and Da dead, and the vicar's wife come t'git us and put us in the workhouse."

The younger girl suddenly sat bolt upright in the chair.

"They'll niver make a protestant outta' me, Lovie! I'm fer the convent and that's the all of it. I'll die first before I'll let them take me. But it is all me own fault, that it is."

Rose pulled back and looked into her sister's eyes. Peaches was really frightening her with all this talk. Had she already been taken by the fairies? Was this a changling girl in Mary Clare's body who said these strange things?

"Mary Clare, what's all yer fault?"

"The lady comin' fer us. I heard that man who calls himself Uncle Robert talkin' t'Mam. He was tryin' t'make her give us up, Lovie. He was tryin' tmake her let him take us t'his place. He said he could give us a better life but she wouldn't do it. He found out who we are when I told him me name. So, ye see, it is me own fault and none other. If I hadn't told him me name he'd niver have known who we were and niver bothered Mam about us atall. But I didn't know, Lovie, I didn't know. I jist told him. 'Mary Clare Phalen, sir.' And that was it. Next thing I knew he was tryin' t'take us home!"

"Peaches, I saw Uncle Robert too. He is Mam's real uncle, her mam's brother. Mam told me he is really a very nice man. And the lady in the kitchen is only the Widow Trent. She lived on Achill with us, remember? She's nice too. She'd niver hurt us. She's always been kind to us. She used t'give us food when Mam was still protestant."

"Well, it doesn't matter now, does it? Mam and Da are gone. Where's Mr. McGee? Is he dead too? Where's Denny? Did they already get him? Lovie, where's Denny?"

Mary Clare became very agitated when she realized Denny was missing too. She began to struggle with Rose and fought to get out of the chair.

"Peaches, ye can't go out there and be blatherin' all about people bein' dead and bad dreams and the like. They'll think ye're daft and then they will take ye away! Da is hidin' with Mr. McGee and Denny is with them. Mam is, well, Mam is, O God save us all, Mam's in jail fer hittin' Mr. Gilchrist! That's why Denny's hidin' with Da. He jumped on Mr. Gilchrist and now he's runnin' from the law."

Mary Clare stopped struggling and looked carefully at Rose.

"So, no one's dead?"

"No, ye edgit. No one's dead."

Mary Clare collapsed into her sister's arms and let out a deep sigh.

"Thank God."

She then sat up straight and looked right at Rose.

"What about the lady then? What about that Uncle Robert?"

"Well, we need t'work out a plan. Da must have known there'd be trouble. When I talked t'him tonight, he said we must be brave and smart. But above all, he said we must be obedient. He looked right at me when he said it Peaches, so I know he meant it. We need t'stick together but we can't really help ourselves. We need t'be smart and let the grown-ups help us."

"Ye talked t'Da? Where is he?"

"He was here with Fr, Timon when I saw him but he's hidin' in a safe place now. I can't tell ye where. I promised."

"Well, if that's what Da said then fine. If ye say it I believe it. But I'm tellin'ye this, Rose Phalen. I may only be ten years old but nobody's makin' a protestant outta' me."

"Don't worry, Peaches. 'Tis that sure I am they wouldn't have ye!"

Fr. Timon came in and asked the girls to come into the kitchen.

Rose took Mary Clare's hand and together they slowly went from the dark parlor into the lit kitchen. It was time to find out what was about to happen to them.

Meg stood shivering in the damp cell deep beneath the streets of Westport. She tried in vain to make sense out of the hours since she stood in the kitchen of Browne's Inn and turned stale bread in a pannie full of sizzling bacon grease. Everything had happened so fast. Tom gone into hiding. Mrs. Trent showing up at the door. Denny running away. And now here she was like a common criminal in a dungeon where rats ran freely and filthy black water dribbled down the walls from the gutter above. How had it all happened?

The shock of being assaulted by Robert Gilchrist and Denny's heroic attempt to rescue her had left her weak in the knees. But being arrested! That had practically stopped her heart. Her temples still pounded with the sound of Rose's voice crying after her.

There was a narrow cot against the wall. She looked at the filthy mattress that covered the length of it and bile crept up the back of her throat. Every bone in her body hurt but she could not bring herself to lie down on the flimsy gray thing. Thank God she was alone and not forced to share this tiny cubicle with anyone else. There were no other prisoners upstairs in the station house when the constable's deputy brought her in. If there were any down here, it was too dark to see them.

Gilchrist had been brutal, exaggerating the event at the inn so badly she hardly recognized his rambling account of what had happened. He had lied so profoundly she had tried to speak up earning a hard slap from the constable for her efforts.

Gilchrist had said that not only she but Denny as well had attacked him with weapons and set upon him with murder as their intent. He ranted on and on about how he had tried endlessly to deal fairly with them for years as Lord Lucan's nephew and undertaker and how they had chased him off the island more than once brandishing scythes and pitchforks all the way to the shore.

Even the constable, as eager as he was to honor a man of such high standing in Lord Lucan's household had finally had enough and wrapped up the report with promises of a quick and early extradition to Castelbar in the morning. He had no idea why Mr. Gilchrist wanted this prisoner to be tried in

Castlebar and he wasn't even sure it was legal to send her there but he assured the man he would see her on her way in the morning as he closed and latched the door behind him.

After Mr. Gilchrist left, the constable simply nodded at his deputy and he thrust Meg roughly toward a long winding stone stairway where he shoved and prodded her down into the bowels of hell. She had not been allowed one word in her own defense. When she heard the clink of the cell door and the turn of the key, she thought she'd die. When the deputy slammed the door at the top of the stairs she was plunged into darkness relieved only by the thin light of a streetlamp filtering through the tiny barred window near the top of the wall. The howl of the banshee echoed in her mind and soon she swore the souls of all the dead swirled around her. This somehow comforted her and she tried to focus on the gentle spirit of Thomas and the sweet baby soul of Patrick.

She felt again the sensation of being in someone else's skin the same as the last night she spent at GlynMor Castle. The floor was damp and cold against her bare feet and she began to feel imaginary creeping things on her ankles and legs. Terrified, she sat down on the cot, pulling her feet up under her and backing as far as she could into the corner. There she stayed wide-eyed and sleepless until the first rays of dawn lightened the room. She looked around and saw that if there had been anything there, it was gone now.

Tom and Duffy tried to rest in the stifling attic but sleep eluded them. They had talked and talked about what they should do and still had not come up with a workable plan. They would have to split up and they would need the help of Marie and her girls for it to work. Before they could set anything in motion, they needed to know they would have the support of the madam of the house.

Tom needed to get off the mainland. He knew that Gilchrist wouldn't rest until he found him and thought the last place he'd look would be back on Achill. He wouldn't go near Doeega. He could head for the hills and hole up in one of the boolies in the high pastures. The wheat harvest was almost done but he could hire on as a hand and blend in with a group of strangers. Since the hunger, there were roving bands of men all over the place. As long as he didn't have to go far from Meg and the children he cared little where he laid his head.

He turned to his friend in the dark.

"I'm sich an ass, Duff. God should strike me dead fer an imbecile."

"Why? Now what did ye do?"

"Well, Meg could have gone with her Uncle Robert t'Killarney and I made sich a stink about it. Ye know we had a terrible row about it all sorts o'hollerin' and all. "Suren 'twas shameful. But we made up and all."

"I know about the makin' up. The night of the laundry."

Tom could hear the smile in Duffy's voice.

"I'm bein' serious, man! I'll not be havin' any comments about the laundry. 'Tis not about the laundry. 'Tis about me bein' an ass and not makin' sure Meg was away and safe! I mean, shite man! I niver even said a proper goodbye t'her! When am I gonna' see her again? What will she do? 'Tis the workhouse fer women and children. Ye know that man!"

Duffy could say nothing to comfort his friend. He pitied Tom while at the same time he was tremendously relieved that he was not saddled with a family. He was going to try and get on board the Marianna and work his way across to the States. He did have some money on him. He had just done the books and had the week's takings in his pocket when he went over to Fr. Timon's. That he wanted to keep for bribing Marie and in case he needed something once he got to America. All he knew was he had to get out of Ireland.

The rebellion had failed. That was what Fr. Timon had wanted to tell them. The lads had tried. For six days they fought the British all the way from Wexford to Kilkenny and on to Tipperary. All of the leaders had been caught. Every man, including his cousin D'Arcy was in Her Majesty's custody and all expected to be hanged. Duffy had to go and the Marianna set sail tomorrow morning. It was his last chance and he was going to be on that ship.

"Tom, ye know Meg'll be all right. She'll find Uncle Robert and he'll protect her and the children. Ye have t'look out fer yerself, man! Yer no good to'em dead, now are ye? We jist have t'convince Marie that she needs t' help us t'protect her own wrinkled hide. Ye know that's all she cares about."

Before Tom could answer, the door opened and Denny flew into the darkness.

"Da! Are ye here Da?"

"Denny! Whatever are ye doin' here, lad? Denny! 'Tis that good t'see ye, Boyo!"

"Keep it down, the lot o'ye or they whole house'll be pokin' their noses where they don't belong."

Duffy sat up and peered at the massive form outlined by the faint light of the hall beyond. The attic that held the secret room was one half of Marie's third floor. The other half housed seldom-used rooms that were reserved for Marie's private customers.

"Say, can we get a candle in here? I know ye're anxious t'git rid of us as soon as ye can. If we could see we could plan better and be gone sooner."

Porky Billy grunted and left the room. He returned to the dark attic with a candle holder and three short half-burned stubs.

Duffy struck a lucifer and lit the tallest of the crusty stubs. The room was suddenly awash in soft light that revealed Tom's stunned face.

"Denny, why are ye here? Where's yer mither?"

Denny was about to answer when Porky Billy spoke up.

"I'll be leavin' ye t'yer grand reunion. Jist keep it quiet or ye'll be out on yer arses in no time. Miss Marie'll be up t'talk t'ye before long. I suggest ye have yer plan worked out. She's not havin' what ye'd call a good night and she's a bit twitchy."

Once the cook left, Tom took Denny by the shoulders

and asked him again why he was there. Denny tried to be brave but safe in the attic with his da, he broke down. Tearfully he told the two men everything that had happened, even the part about Rose coming to Marie's.

Duffy let out along low whistle and Tom put his head in his hands and groaned.

Denny looked from one to the other for any sign that he had done well. Finding none, he found a spot over in the far corner of the attic and sat down on the floor facing the wall. He was no brother. He was just a stupid old boy who brought trouble wherever he went. Everything he had done, everything he had risked, the pistol, the big meat cleaver, even the whip meant nothing. Da wasn't proud of him and Mr. McGee hadn't even looked at him.

He turned and looked at them over his shoulder. Mr.McGee lay on his back looking at the rafters and Da was still holding his head. Why didn't somebody say something?

Finally Tom spoke but it wasn't what Denny hoped to hear.

"Where are the other children now, Denny?" "I don't know, Da. After Rose left here, Mr. Porky Billy brought me right up."

"Oh, God, Duff what can I do? I need t'see t'me family. I need t'get out o'here. Me babies are gonna' die in the Westport Workhouse! I can't be hidin' out in this attic like a coward! Where is Marie? I need her t'help me now!"

Duffy propped himself up on one elbow and looked at his friend sadly.

"Tom, ye know I love ye like a brother. If I could help ye again I'd do it, believe me. But I'd be no help t'ye now. My name is linked with the rebellion and me cousin is in jail and I gotta' go. The sooner ye're shed o'me the safer ye'll be. I'm fer askin' Marie t'git me on board the Marianna before dawn and at three tomorrow afternoon I'll be on me way t'the States."

His voice caught and he swallowed hard.

"Ye have me prayers and me love and I'd give ye me

money too if I didn't need it t'bribe me way across the ocean. In return fer that I'd be leavin' a better man if I knew I had the same from you."

Again, Tom groaned.

"Oh, God, Duff, ye know ye have it! If it weren't fer yer friendship we'd have starved and niver been sich a burden t'ye."

Duffy started to protest but Tom waved him away.

"Not that ye ever acted like we were a burden, no. But I'm no fool, man. I know what risks ye've taken ever since ye brought us over here. And look at us now! Fat as Christmas geese we are! And we have ye t'thank and no one else. But this, Duff, this is beyond me. What the hell am I goin' t'do?"

Denny sat watching the two friends. He felt bad fer his da and Mr. McGee. He still wished they would say something good about him but they were too busy saying goodbye and trying to figure out what Da was going to do. They hadn't said anything about him. What was going to happen to him?

"Da."

Tom looked at Denny and patted the floor next to him. Denny eagerly came over and sat next to his da.

"Denny, 'tis that glad I am t'see ye. Ye've done noble tonight, lad. I see ye learned a great truth that night on the docks and 'tis that proud I am fer all ye've done fer me and Mr. Mcgee. But now we have t'make some serious, hard decisions. I want t'take ye with me but I'm not sure jist how t'hide ye. Yer runnin' from the law now and Gilchrist is out fer yer blood. We need t'stick together but he can't know where ye are."

Denny didn't know whether to swell wqith pride or sag with relief at his father's words. He took a deep breath and spoke.

"Da, I want t'go with Mr. McGee. I want t'go on the Marianna to America. I can work my way over jist like he is. I'm not afraid. Please let me go!"

"Ah, Boyo, ye know that would jist kill yer mam. I could niver face her, lad! What would I say t'her?"

Duffy spoke slowly and deliberately.

"Ye could tell her he's with me and I'd care fer him like a son. Ye can tell her not t'worry, I'd see him in church every Sunday and in school with the nuns. Ye can tell her that he's got a price on his head and if he stays in Ireland as long as Gilchrist is huntin' him down, he'll live a hard life, runnin' with the Brotherhood and shootin' his way out of every corner. Tom…God this is hard t'say! Ye can tell her these things if ye ever git t'speak t'her again. As it is that may niver happen, man and ye have t'face that possibility."

'What're ye sayin, Duff? Is it that weak I am t'be givin' up without a fight? She may be the half-starved wife of a useless washed up dairy farmer but she's still the daughter of an earl! At the least she'll git her day in court and I plan t'help her any way I can."

Tom was suddenly struck with an idea.

"If I could only git a horse, I could go after her Uncle Robert. He's the one t'help her. I could have him back here in three days. He's only in Killarney! It'll take 'em that long jist t'get a magistrate. He'll have her out o'jail without a trial, I know he will!"

Duffy reached into his pocket.

"Well, I know Marie keeps a horse at McRea's. Maybe she would let ye borrow it. Let me see how much I have here from the till. It was all the takins' from Reek Sunday. There was actually a bit o'dough in there."

Duffy counted out the money in his pocket. He had fifty pounds and one gold crown that a gentleman had tossed to Mary Clare as he was checking out. Most of what he had was loose change from pints and breakfasts and the occasional tip. But it was no small amount and he was grateful to God that he had planned to take it up to his room for safekeeping.

Tom was shocked at the amount. If Duffy could spare him some of it he would be able to manage quite well.

"What d'ye need fer yer fare?"

"I was plannin' on workin' off a third class ticket. But I could cover Denny's fare."

"No, Mr. McGee, I can work off my fare too!"

Denny was afraid if Mr. McGee had to pay his way he'd change his mind and refuse to take him.

"Let me see. I have a flyer I picked up at the apothecary last week."

AT WESTPORT
FOR NEW YORK
To sail on or about 31st. July
The Marianna
Beautiful first class berths
All Copper clad and fastened
595 Tons

George Vestal, Commander

This swift lovely clipper is now unloading her cargo of silks and spices from the West Indies and will be returning to that tropical paradise with stops at New York and Baltimore on the way. Enjoy the finest lodging and accoutrements available in our first class.

Please apply directly to Captain Vestal or
At the office of

John Reid Jun., & Co.

Ship agents, Westport Quay
Westport, 20th. July, 1848

"It doesn't say what the fare is but I'm sure I can cover it for Denny. God knows he's worked hard enough he should get something from the till."

Tom looked long at his son. He knew Denny wanted badly to go to America. He'd always been a restless soul, never satisfied with life in one place. The trouble he'd caused over the years had probably been the result of being cooped up in a little village on a remote island. What had satisfied the others had probably felt like a prison to Denny.

Then there was the English/Irish issue. How he struggled with that! Maybe a fresh start in a land that had no royalty, where everyone had the same opportunities to work hard and do well would be just what Denny needed to grow into a man.

But what about Meg? What about the two sons she had already lost? Could she bear to lose another one? What would it do to Francis? He adored his brother. And Denny was so young! My God, he was just twelve years old! Tom sighed. The same age he was when he lost Mam. How hard his life was after that. But at least he had Da. And until this hunger, he and Meg had had a good life together. Maybe there was a little girl somewhere in New York or on the American prairie who was waiting for his son to come over and marry her. His eyes burned with tears at the thought of all he would miss in his son's new life if he let him go.

Tom knew Duffy would be a wonderful surrogate da for Denny. There was really no one else he would trust him to. Uncle Robert would be good to him but Denny would fight like a tiger every step of the way. No way would he spend a willing night under that English roof. Tom knew Denny would run away as soon and as far as he could.

America. A whole ocean between them. They'd never see each other again. Tom knew Denny wouldn't write. He knew Meg would grieve him till the day she died. Dear God in heaven, what was he to do?

The door opened again, interrupting his thoughts. Marie entered the room, filling it with the heady scent of lilacs. Instead of her silly little whip, she had a fan in her hand this time and waved it feverishly against the heat.

"It's gettin' late, lads. Ye need t'tell me yer plans fer leavin'."

Duffy spoke first.

"I have a bit 'o money. I'd like t'buy passage but I'm willin' to hire on t'the Marianna when she sails tomorrow. If ye have any influence with th'captain, I'd be obliged t'ye. Me cousin in th'brotherhood has been arrested and I don't know if they're lookin' fer me here yet or not. I doubt I should be strollin' down th'dock fer all th'world t'see."

She turned to Tom.

"What about you?"

"Ye probably know me wife's been jailed on trumped up charges. Attempted murder. I need t'get t'Killarney where she has family that can help her. I'll need a horse, some money and rations."

"And th'boy?"

A pregnant silence filled every empty nook and corner of the little room.

"Th'boy, Mr. Phalen. What are we t'do with yer boyo?"

Tom tried to speak but no words came out. He could not bring himself to form the syllables that would take his son away from him. Beads of sweat popped out of his hairline and descended in little rivulets down his face. Denny held his breath, waiting for his father to decide his future. Duffy sat cross-legged and looked down at his folded hands as if he was praying.

Finally, Tom grabbed Denny in a vice-like embrace that threatened to crush him.

His voice breaking, he croaked like an animal in pain.

"The boy'll be gittin' on th'Marianna with Duff."

Chapter Fourteen

Meg heard the thud of the big door being opened at the top of the stairs. The sun was shining in a narrow band across the cell and Meg realized she had actually fallen asleep. The bailiff's keys jingled as he clumped down the steps and she ran to the door hoping he was going to let her out. To her surprise there was a man stretched out on the cot in the cell across from her. She had had no idea there was anyone else there with her. When the guard stopped across from her cell, she called out to him.

"Sir, if I may have a word with you."

He had his back to her and was rapping on the bars of the other cell with a shillelagh.

"Shut up, bitch. It's not yer turn t'talk," he said without turning around.

In a sing-song voice, he called out to the man, "Come and git yer fine breakfast, Boyo. This is yer last day as a guest o' the queen. Ye're not welcome here anymore. It seems the sailor ye robbed has flown the coop and yer free t'go as soon as the magistrate says the word. This is indeed yer lucky day, Boyo. Lucky fer you that the fool was too drunk t'remember ye and the Cobalt's gone t'sea. Suren' yer a lucky man, indeed. I fixed ye a wee bit o'gruel. Added a bit o'fine cane sugar by way o'thankin' ye fer entertainin' me and the lads durin' yer stay with us."

Meg thought she would retch at the implication of the bailiff's words. She had heard of women being molested in prison but they were mostly street-walkers. She had never heard of a lady going to prison. Of course, the men in prison would be captive victims to the assaults of the guards. Her heart ached for the poor man.

"Go t'hell, ye bastard! And take yer bloody gruel with ye."

Meg started at the sound of the prisoner's voice. She knew that voice! The guard opened his cell door and despite his brave words, the man pulled himself as far as he could into the corner of the cot, cringing as the guard approached.

He didn't touch him. Instead he threw the gruel at his head, covering him with the slimy, gray slop.

"Well Mr. Feeney, we'll miss ye, we will. But no need t'worry. Our fun and games aren't over. There's a lady on the premises."

The fat, snarling guard turned to Meg.

'Ye wanted a word with me did ye? Well, ye'll git a word and plenty more, girlie. Once this crap bag is out o'here, me an the lads'll be down fer a nice long visit. If we like ye, maybe ye'll git some gruel fer breakfast in the mornin' too."

Meg stood trembling with fear and rage. The bailiff laughed and shook his bald head as he climbed the stairs.

Meg barely recognized Andrew Feeney, he was so thin and ragged. She looked at the young man who had terrorized her in her own yard as he picked the glutenous mess out of his thinning hair. Her stomach threatened to revolt when she saw him actually shoving it into his mouth. When he scooped it up off his mattress and filthy trousers and licked it off his fingers, she had to turn away. Ashamed, she realized how well Duffy had taken care of her and her family. Not long ago, she had been so hungry she would have done the same.

When he got up and began to pace around the cell, she walked again to the bars. She could see that every step caused him pain.

"Hello, Andrew."

His head shot up at her recognition.

"Jaysus. It's her ladyship! What the hell are ye doin' in here? Shouldn't ye be takin' yer breakfast in some morning room somewhere?"

He peered through the bars trying to get a good look at her.

"God save us, ye look like death. If I didn't know ye I'd swear ye were one of us. Looks like famine is the great equalizer, M'Lady. Our guts are all th'same. No food and all of us lose our hair."

He patted the sticky strands on his head.

"Tell me, what is a great lady like yerself doin' behind bars. Last I saw ye, ye had a nice house, about a dozen fine brats and a husband who wasn't home a lot. Could it be that ye took up a professional lady's life? No, that wouldn't work with sich a crowd in the house. But then again, ye might have sold yer brats t' white slavers. But that'd be hard to explain t'the gentry. Hardly th'kind of thing ladies discuss over tea."

Meg was exasperated with his banter.

"Andrew, stop it! I'm in here because a man lied and charged me with attempted murder! My husband is in hiding as a suspected member of the Blackthorn Brotherhood and my eldest son is out there somewhere being hunted down for the same alleged crime of which I'm accused. I have no idea where my other children are. Now, whether you care for me or not, we are kin and maybe you can help me. You are getting out of here today and I am not. You have skills that you learned from the brothers. Help me! Or for God's sake at least help find Denny!"

At the mention of the Brotherhood and Denny, Andrew flushed. He had let them all down badly. When the guards had used him he had screamed like a girl. His whole body was filled with pain and he had wrapped himself in a cloak of self-loathing. Could he possibly see an opportunity to do some good here? He looked at Meg seriously.

"I should be gettin' out by noon. I heard th'guards say that th'magistrate was due here around ten. I can scout around I guess, but I have t'keep me nose clean or I'll be dinin' with ye again, tomorrow."

"I need you to get a message to my husband. He is in hiding at Marie's along with another man. I can't reveal his name. I need you to see if you can find anything out about him and tell me. Also, you must get him the message that I'm here."

"I need to know where my children are. They were at Browne's when I was arrested. Sleeping, poor lambs. I need especially to know how my eldest daughter, Rose is doing. She was so upset when they took me away. There is an older woman named Mrs. Trent who will help you. You can trust her, she knows everything and she was a witness to last night's events. You can trust Fr. Timon, too. He knows everything I've told you. Can you remember all that?"

"Rememberin' all that is not th'hardest thing I'll be doin' today. I'm half-starved and can hardly walk. I'll do what ye ask though. I know now that rape and humiliation ain't jist fer English gentlemen and Irish lasses. The divil comes in all shapes and sizes. Even Irish jailors know th'routine."

He sat down gingerly on his cot and looked up at Meg.

"Mark th'time I get out. Give me an hour t'gather yer information. Then be ready t'listen at yer little window up there. I'll be able t'tell ye what I can but it'll have t'be quick. Not a lot o'questions. Th'window is near an alley and th'bailiff comes in and out on th'other side o'th'building. There are a lot of people lyin' about so it won't look too strange, me layin' there talkin' t'meself."

There was no time to say any more. Meg and Andrew could only look on sympathetically as the bailiff dragged a man with a bloodied head into the cell next to Andrew and heaved him on the cot. The only sound after the door slammed shut was whimpering interrupted by the sound of bile splashing on the concrete floor.

"There. 'Tis that convincin' ye are t'be the envy o'me whole stable. God, yer a pretty one!"

Denny squirmed with both discomfort and humiliation as Marie DeVianney adjusted the curly blonde wig on his head. Were the situation not so sad, Tom would have enjoyed a smile at his son's expense. As it was, he hated this little charade as much as Denny did. It put the finishing touches on his son's departure from him forever.

"Now, lad, tell me th'plan again. I want t'be sure ye have it right."

Denny turned to Marie, his chin jutting out in defiance and repeated her instructions back to her.

"I'm pretendin' t'be one o'yer girls. Mr. McGee is pretendin' t'be one o'the sailors from th'Marianna. He's takin' me t'the ship fer a fling 'afore he sails. Peggy is over there now, greasin' th'skids with some o'her sailor customers. She'll lead th'way t'git us onboard. Mr. McGee an'me'll hide out wherever Peggy's sailor puts us. Once we're out of th'harbor, Mr. McGee'll try t'git two passages in exchange fer us workin'. If he can't, he'll buy two passages. Once we're set, I can stop bein' a girl."

He scowled at Marie. He couldn't bring himself to look at Tom.

"Then ye'll work like a dog fer th'captain until ye get t'New York Harbor. I don't know where Duffy McGee thinks he's goin' t'find any passage on that little scow. It ain't like no coffin ship ye know. And ye can count yer blessings fer that. But mind me words. Ye may be hidin' all the way to America. Captain Vestal may be friend o'mine but stowin' away is still a crime. Yer not gonna' be wantin' t'be found!"

Tom spoke up at this.

"Enough, woman! Isn't it enough that a lad o'twelve is leavin' home forever without even sayin' goodbye t'his mam? D'ye have t'scare th'livin' daylights outta' him too?"

"Well, Mr. Phalen, I jist want him t'know th'risk. It'll make him more careful and possibly save his life."

Duffy put his hand on Tom's shoulder and looked at

Denny seriously.

"Don't worry, Boyo. We'll be fine. 'Twill be a grand adventure! Sailin' the high seas, seein' all kinds o'sea monsters an' smellin' th'salty air. I've wanted t'do this all me life and now I have a mate t'do it with."

Tom shot Duffy a grateful look. Let him fill Denny's head with fantasies. The child was so frightened he could hardly breathe.

Porky Billy came into the little room with a small canvas sack and handed it to Marie.

"Jist so ye don't think I'm completely heartless, I had Billy fix some food."

She passed it to Denny.

"This is fer ye t'share with Mr. McGee. And make it last! Ye'll not be likely t'git much from those Frenchy sailors no matter how much they liked Peggy's petticoats."

Denny took the parcel. He shuddered as he remembered the pistol barrel so close to his face. He hoped all the French sailors weren't as mean as that one.

Marie and Porky left them alone to wait for Peggy's return. They had a few hours before Denny and Duffy had to leave. Along with the parcel of food for the trip, Porky Billy had brought them some bread and cheese and a jug of cold cider to wash it own.

Together the three fugitives ate in silence. Denny had pulled the wig off and sat looking desolate in his dress and rouge colored cheeks. Marie had even dressed his eyes with kohl and painted his lips.

Tom looked sorrowfully at Denny. Here he was, trying desperately to memorize the features of his son and his son was made up like a trollop. He couldn't get over how much Denny looked like Meg in the curly blonde wig. He had spent so much time being irritated with his son he hadn't ever noticed what a handsome lad he was. Now all he had before him was a caricature of a street-walker in an ill-fitting flounced dress. He could feel his big heart breaking in his chest. How would he ever tell Meg?

Marie had arranged for her horse to be brought around as soon as Duffy and Denny were safely at sea. She was a sorry old nag but strong enough. Tom would head straight to Killarney where he planned to recruit Lord Robert to dispense with Gilchrist and bring this nonsense to a quick end. Until the fateful moment when Denny and Duffy had to leave, the three would make the most of their time in the attic.

Andrew Feeney was a free man. He tried to shake off the stink of his cell and stooped to rinse the gooey dried oatmeal from his hair. He had broken into the kitchen of Browne's Inn and was pumping water over himself at the big sink. No one was around but he knew he only had a few minutes before someone might come into the taproom and discover him there.

He wondered where Meg's children were. His next stop should be Fr. Timon's. The woman Meg had spoken of was nowhere to be found here. Maybe she was over there. Smoothing his wet hair, he looked around for something to eat. He spied the cellar door and grabbed a storm lantern, lighting it with a lucifer.

Looking for a larder, he crept down into the dark. He gasped when he saw the provisions for the inn. He had been very disappointed when he had tried to rob the till and found it empty. But here was a treasure trove of goodies. He wondered where the innkeeper was. It wasn't like Duffy McGee to leave all this food unguarded with all the hungry people around outside but there was no one around today. Last night the fuss of Meg's arrest had been enough to scatter the vagrants ahead of the constable and his posse. He stuffed himself with cold meat and cheese and guzzled a quart of milk, savoring the cream that coated his upper lip.

He looked around at the barrels of salted kippers and pickled herring. Lifting the lid of one huge crock, he was almost overcome by the aroma of pickling spices as two huge chunks of beef floated in brine waiting to be boiled up with cabbage and carrots. When he passed Reid's Shipping Agency he had overheard two gentlemen discussing their three P.M. departure time on the Marianna. He knew he had to be on that boat and had no intention of leaving this food behind.

Back upstairs, he filled a sack with cheese and a dried fish, a huge sausage and several rolls and loaves of barm brack. A second, smaller sack held two jugs of cider and two bottles of whiskey. Finally, he wrapped a sharp knife in a rag and slipped it into his pocket. Shouldering his heavy load he headed out into the early afternoon.

He found a place to hide his booty behind the turf pile in the rectory yard where no one would find it. Looking like any beggar, he rapped on the priest's kitchen door. Mrs. Murphy scolded him to go away from the window. He hissed that he had information about Meg Phalen that brought Fr. Timon running.

Once inside, he told them everything he could about Meg and they told him what they knew.

Mrs. Trent and Fr. Timon had approached the bailiff around dawn in an attempt to see Meg but had been rebuffed by the cruel jailer. He did tell them that Meg's accuser wanted her brought to Castlebar for trial and intended to have her removed as soon as he had her children placed in the workhouse.

They knew then that they had to get the children out of Westport and with the help of McRea and his eldest grandson, Mrs. Trent piled the Phalen children into the cab she had hired for herself. By the time Fr. Timon rang the bell for six o'clock Mass that morning they were all on their way to Castlebar to try and find refuge with Fr. Finnegan at St. Brendan's.

When Andrew asked about Tom and Denny, Fr. Timon flushed from his collar to the roots of his bristly red hair. While Rose and Mrs. Trent woke and dressed the children, he had gone to Marie's to ask after their father and brother. It was the least he could do for Rose who had been so brave about it all.

He had spoken to the big bully in the kitchen and had been told the plan for Denny and Duffy to escape and for Tom to go for help. He definitely felt that, had he not been wearing his collar, he would have learned nothing. Sadly, Mr. McRea had had to send the little family on their way before he returned so Rose never did find out what was happening to her da or her brother. When Fr. Timon arrived at the livery, Mr. Gilchrist was just storming away from the place, cursing and fuming that he'd see the lot of them in the workhouse.

A trembling boy of about fifteen explained to Fr. Timon that Mr. Gilchrist had wanted the early cab and had threatened to burn down the stable when he found out it had already left. The regular coach wasn't due to arrive in Westport until one o'clock and wasn't scheduled to leave again until two. Mr. Gilchrist would just have to wait.

Andrew thanked Fr. Timon and picked up his bundles on his way out. Mrs. Murphy had given him a few slices of buttered bread and a small flask of cold tea. He promised he would try to pass this through the little window to Meg.

Well, now he knew why the inn had been deserted. He thought of all the food in the cellar. How he wished he could have carried more. Maybe he could go back for another bundle. Now that he knew that the man hiding with Tom Phalen was D'Arcy McGee's cousin, he knew out of respect for the Brotherhood, he should try and steal as much from that swine Sligo as he could. He could certainly use some good whiskey to bribe the sailors into hiding him on the Marianna.

Using his sacks of treasures as his pillows, Andrew pretended to sleep along the back wall of the Westport jail. Facing the wall he almost gagged at the stench of stale urine left by many a passing man and dog.

"Psst. Meg Phalen can ye hear me?"

Meg started at the sound of his voice.

"Yes, I can. Is it you Andrew?"

"Aye. Who else?"

"Were you able to learn anything?"

First Andrew slipped the food and tea through the tiny window. Then he told her everything he knew. He answered all of her questions but when she asked him about Denny, he hesitated to tell her the plan.

Thinking the worst, Meg began to cry for her lost son and begged Andrew to tell her how he was killed.

Andrew rushed to reassure her that he was still alive but then bluntly informed her that he was leaving Ireland with Duffy McGee on the next ship out. Hearing her gasp and the thud of her body as she hit the floor, he thought she had fainted.

But the sobs that tore from her chest and threatened to give him away let him know she was still conscious. He hadn't heard that wrenching sound since his own mam left him at his Aunt Mary's and went away to die in a cesspool of a hostel where people suffering from consumption were quarantined. He remembered how her hoarse cries seemed to rise from her very roots and his own eyes filled as he heard his sister weeping for her lost son.

"Meg he'll be fine. He's with Duffy and I'll watch out fer him too. Ain't we in the Brotherhood together? Ain't we blood kin? Ain't I taught him all he knows about survivin'?"

Meg didn't know whether to thank him or curse him. Her brother Andrew was the last person she ever had expected to have a heart but she heard real concern in his whispered voice. She never had a chance to do either as the constable and the bailiff came clanking through the door and descended the stairs before she could answer him. At the sound of their shouts, he grabbed his bags and tore off to Marie's. He hoped Marie would pass his booty on to Duffy or store it until he could return for more. The Marianna was due to set sail in about two hours and he wanted to get whatever he could from the inn. The bells in the clock tower of Westport Town Hall were chiming the hour just as the horses pulling the one o'clock coach went thundering past him on its way to McCrea's.

Mr. Gilchrist paced impatiently back and forth inside McRea's Livery, looking at his watch every few minutes. He heard the bells from the town hall ring one o'clock and the coach was not here. He went out to the alley in a snit and headed around the bend on the far side of Browne's where he was almost run down by four galloping Clydesdale horses pulling a huge black buggy through the passageway to McRea's.

He turned on his heel and chased after it, cursing and waving a brass handled walking stick. Not watching where he was going, he stepped his left foot into a big steaming horse turd. Frantically trying to miss the fresh droppings, he hopped and danced to the right but he was too late and with a splat his foot landed smack in the center of it, smearing the sides of his gray suede boot to the ankle.

The horses pulled the coach to a sudden stop at the spot where they knew they would be fed. These huge animals had been running this route between Castlebar and Westport since they were colts and the promise of a good rubdown and plenty of feed brought them careening around this bend every other day at one o'clock. Neither of them even saw the man they almost trampled. Mr. Gilchrist meant nothing to them. Their eyes were on their oat bag as he grabbed a stick and tried to peel their excrement off of his foot.

With a heavy heart, McRea sent his grandson to the jail to have the bailiff bring the prisoner around. The old Scotsman had admired the poor lady from Achill and now this little bastard would have her hanged and her children orphans. What had she done to him? He was all hollering about attempted murder. Well, five minutes with him in a courtroom and not a jury in Ireland would convict her.

Andrew Feeney stood in the upstairs window of Browne's Inn and surveyed the alley below. He knew this was the room Meg and Tom had slept in. He could tell by the laundry line with their clothes hanging on it. It was eerily quiet inside the big building with no guests and no workers bustling about. Someone had put a closed sign in the front window and the big blue door was locked. He had let himself in through the kitchen door this time having left it unlocked when he carted his sacks of loot out earlier. He still had some time before he needed to sneak aboard the Marianna. Porky Billy had taken his other sacks and after helping himself to one bottle of whiskey as payment for the favor, told him he'd protect it until Andrew came back for it. He wondered if he would ever see the stuff again.

The big black coach was almost ready to leave. The Clydesdales had been taken to McRea's for a well-deserved rest. Two beautiful black stallions and two matching greys were harnessed and pawed the pebbled dirt impatiently. The coachman and driver were slowly making their way up the alley from Gillie's where they had been forced to have lunch when they saw that the inn was closed. The only passengers were Mr. Gilchrist who paced around and kept looking at his watch and Meg who had just been dragged from the jail and thrown unceremoniously into the buggy, weeping and pleading for her children. The bailiff made much of securing a pair of heavy leg irons to her before he threw her into the coach and slammed the door on her.

Andrew could feel a trickle of sweat crawl down the center of his back as he stood in the hot bedroom and watched his half-sister, the Lady Meg Wynn, reduced to such a state. He tasted bile as he recalled his vicious attack on her so many years ago.

Now he knew she was no different than his own mam for all her fancy titles. If you were poor you were powerless, you had no rights and you were always guilty even if you were as innocent as Christ. He couldn't wait to taste the freedom of the sea and start his new life in a land that declared all men created equal and had no king or queen. He couldn't believe that in a few short weeks he would be standing on America's shore where any man, rich or poor, could rise to great heights and make a life for himself.

He would make Mam proud. He would vindicate her miserable life and early death by getting richer and living better than any of the so-called gentlemen who had made her their plaything and kicked him aside like a dog. He was pulled from his thoughts by the sound of the driver's whip singing above the heads of the horses as he gave them the signal to go. Within seconds the buggy rounded the corner and headed up the hill to the Louisburg Road. As he watched his sister being taken away to be hanged, he actually felt a lump in his throat.

Once the coast was clear, Andrew took a heavy burlap sack filled with whiskey and another sausage and headed for Marie's. He wanted to be sure he had all his gleanings before setting off for the pier.

Tom sat facing the tiny window, his arm around his son. Denny leaned into Tom's side as he used to when he was a wee lad and they would sit on the thinking rock together watching the frothy tide roll in. Denny had had his tears and was calm and patient as they listened to the big bells in the town hall toll two o'clock. Any minute now, that apeman and that farce of a woman would be back to take Duff and Denny away. How he could relinquish both his best friend and his first-born son to that unlikely pair of saviors he didn't know. After all they had been through just trying to survive, that it all should come to this was the most painful reality of all.

Denny's mascara had run in black streaks down his rouged cheeks as he cried like a baby for his mam. He had listed all his sisters in a litany of woe starting with his favorite, Rose. Tom smiled at the stammered apology Denny had offered for, of all things, letting Billy Feeney throw goose turds at her and Mary Clare back in their hedge-school days. What Tom wouldn't give for those problems now. When poor Denny got to Francis he buried his head in Tom's side and cried inconsolably. Tom knew he cried not only for his favorite oystering partner and little buddy but for Thomas and maybe even Patrick, the brother he never had the chance to know.

Duffy lay stretched out on the floor trying to catch a much-needed nap. He knew it might be weeks before he could stretch out to his full length again much less sleep while he did it. He covered his face with his cap as two flies pestered him, buzzing around his head.

The day was warm and sunny, a beautiful day for the Marianna to leave port. Tom could hear the call of gulls mixed with the hollering of the Marianna's crew as they prepared the ship for the journey west.

The attic was hot and Tom could smell the dust as he and Denny sat watching the tiny motes floating in a sunbeam. He didn't care what the weather was like outside. Inside Tom's heart, a storm had raged since yesterday, as he fought the urge to run to Meg's rescue. He hadn't felt this helpless since he had been shoved out the front door of her father's house almost fifteen years ago. The only thing that kept him from bolting out the door was the fact that Marie had wisely locked them in the little room. She had obviously been hiding desperate men for years.

The sound of a key in that lock stirred Duffy and brought Tom to his feet. Marie and Porky Billy entered and stood in the center of the room.

Marie took one look at Denny and swore. Tom felt the muscles in his face twitch and Denny looked like he would start crying all over again. Did that woman not have any heart at all? She went to the door and bellowed for Peggy. When the girl came running, she ordered her to bring some of her make-up and a wet cloth.

Porky Billy handed Duffy a bulging canvas sack.

"One o'yer brothers, the skinny one who landed in jail

the other night says he thought Lord Sligo owed ye some back pay so he took the liberty o'collectin' fer ye. He says he'll see ye aboard and he has more where that came from."

Duffy looked in the bag and found it filled with cheese, kippers and sausage. He smiled when he recognized the brand for which Browne's was famous. Andrew wasn't as useless as he had thought.

Marie refreshed Denny's face and refitted the wig to his head. The room suddenly became very small. Tom knew it was time. He had had his chance to be with his little boy and now he had to let him go. Best to make it quick. He couldn't bear to have his son clinging to him and begging to stay.

He turned to Denny and took his hand like a man. He shook it and pulled his son into a tough manly embrace, clapping him hard on the back. Denny stood stiffly and spoke his goodbyes in a clipped deep voice that Tom hadn't heard before. One corner of Tom's mouth turned up at Denny's attempt to sound grown up.

Tom then turned to Duffy.

They said nothing to each other but stood each with his hands on the other's shoulders. There were no words to express all the things they wanted to say. Again Tom was reminded of another departure. He and Ben had shared the same kind of silent communication the night he took Meg away from Clydagh Glyn.

Before he knew it, Tom was left in the attic with Porky Billy. He could hear Marie's voice growing fainter as she descended the stairs issuing orders to Peggy and warnings to Duffy and Denny that she'd be after them herself if any harm came to one of her best girls. Now all he could do was wait until Marie gave Porky the sign that it was safe for Tom to come down and take off for Killarney.

Chapter Fifteen

Beverly caressed the long ebony nose of her new colt. She had been awake all night waiting for this latest horse to be born. The delivery had been difficult and Robert's mare, Galway Girl, lay resting on a bed of fresh straw. Galway Girl was young and this was her first foal, sired by Bay Rum. Beverly had been so excited that she would have one more issue from Bay Rum. He was getting old and she hadn't been sure he would mate again but he certainly did her proud with this sleek little fellow.

She and Robert had decided to name this foal Priceless whether it was a colt or a filly. Galway Girl was such a beautiful black Arabian and Bay Rum so strong and powerful an animal that both she and Robert anticipated great things from their offspring. This horse would be priceless as the next great racer of his generation. She took his face in her hands and kissed the silky nose affectionately.

Beverly had another horse almost ready to foal. Gilded Lily, the beautiful white mare Robert had bought her for Christmas, was due any day now. Beverly had mated her with Sunday Morning, the son of Dublin Belle. Robert had given him his whimsical name the day he was born when he saw his light gray dappled coat and shimmering silvery, blonde mane. Sunday Morning and Gilded Lily were both such exceptionally beautiful horses, she couldn't wait to see what their foal would look like.

Meanwhile, she had this little one to add to her beloved collection. Priceless looked up at her soulfully with deep brown eyes fringed with black lashes and nuzzled his nose into her hand. Beverly felt a pang that Robert hadn't been here for the arrival of this much-anticipated new baby.

"Thank you Charles. You did a wonderful job. I will be sure and mention that to Lord Cushing."

"Yes, M'Lady. Thank ye kindly, M'Lady."

Feeling rumblings in her stomach, Beverly realized that it was already late morning and she hadn't eaten since supper last night. Ambling stiffly through the stable door, she couldn't decide what she wanted more, a long, hot soak or a good hearty breakfast. She was getting too old for all night vigils. She opted for the soak. Reina could bring her a tray and she could nibble in her tub. Then later she would have Cook fix her a nice fricasseed chicken. She'd had a taste for that dish for some time now.

Late in the afternoon Beverly rested in her favorite wicker chaise on the cool stone patio overlooking Robert's formal gardens and the splendid fountain he had imported from Italy. The burbling of the water as it gushed high above the statuary at the fountain's center was refreshing. It was almost as hot today as it had been in Milan the day they saw it in that huge artisan's bazaar. Now, she languished, lazily gazing out over row upon row of gorgeous roses and topiaries of ivy interspersed with whimsical statues of nymphs and cherubs, woodland animals and children playing.

When was he coming home? She had heard nothing from him since he left for GlynMor Castle. But then again, it was only a few days. She wouldn't know anything about his visit with Jeffrey until he returned. She only hoped that Jeffrey wasn't giving her brother too much difficulty.

Beverly sighed. How different her life was since she had left her husband. The thought that she might still live in that cold, drafty castle made her shudder. He was so nasty and so sneaky that his horrible disposition crept into every corner of the building. She had had nowhere to run from his temper and his evil, manly urges. Night after night she had endured the smells and sounds of his drinking and smoking, carousing and debauchery. Year after lonely year she had only her bedroom suite and her balcony to call her own, fearing even those sanctuaries would be breached by his knock at the door or his sinister laugh in the stable yard.

Thank God Robert had rescued her. She knew she would have to return when Jeffrey died. Beverly wasn't even sure the property would revert to her after his death. By law it was Jeffrey's and he would never leave it to her now. She was sure he would have changed his will to exclude her and Meg.

She wondered who would get GlynMor. It was a very nice piece of property and had great potential for farming, grazing or dividing into smaller plots and renting to the locals. She hoped it would never be divided. It had been her childhood home and her parents had loved it. When her father had given it to her and Jeffrey for their wedding, she had cried in his arms with gratitude. To think of the unhappiness that had marred her dear Papa's generous gift! She knew she only hated GlynMor because Jeffrey was there.

Beverly shuddered again and closed her eyes against the sun. Enough thinking about unhappiness and Jeffrey's will. It was after four and the rich aroma of biscuits wafted from the kitchen to combine with the savory smell of chicken stewing. Her dinner was almost ready, she could tell. Her light lunch had left her hours ago and her mouth watered as she anticipated her supper.

Richard had just called Beverly to the table when she heard the pounding of hooves in the gravel yard. Who would be approaching the servant's entrance at this hour? And riding at such a hard gallop? She hadn't heard of any new suitors among the maids and certainly no working class suitor would have access to a horse. Her dinner trumped her curiosity as she decided to let Richard deal with the visitor.

Beverly allowed the footman to slip her chair under her and smiled to herself as the cook's niece, Moira, ladled steaming turtle soup into her bowl. She preferred company to dine with but she had sent Reina into the village to buy her some chocolates and she was late returning. Instead of enjoying company, she would read the new book Robert had bought her for her birthday. Spooning the steaming soup with one hand, Beverly opened the slim volume with the other.

She was very fond of the popular lady's romances circulating among the London literary crowd. Her brother was such a dear to supply her with these little treasures. They were impossible to get in Ireland. Full of racy language and illicit romantic liaisons, they were banned from all of the bookstores. One could only buy them from a store that stocked a second, secret line of more sophisticated authors.

Ever since she was a young, unmarried woman, Robert had always respected her right to explore all sorts of writing as she wished. She used to tease him about his double standard. He would never read anything undignified himself nor would he ever have purchased anything indiscreet for Adelaide. When they were young, Beverly would secretly pass on her little volumes of romances to her sister-in-law who would devour them as lustily as Beverly did.

She turned the frontispiece and savored the title, *The Colonel's Daughter* by Colin Nevreath. Beverly loved Nevreath's books. Cover to cover they were naughty, filled with buxom women and daring adventurers. She basked in the hot, tropical settings of his stories and daring exploits of his beauties. Always drawn irresistibly to muscular pirates or slick, hard gambling men, defying convention and stern restrictive parents, the heroine would always choose the demon lover over the steadfast planter or preacher chosen by her father for her to wed.

Beverly never saw the parallel to her own husband as she immersed herself in the fantasy of loving a violent, demanding man whose sexual urges could not be tamed. Instead, she reveled in the power the heroine had over her man. In the end, she always chose the rakish hero, not because she desired cruelty but because he satisfied her own lust in a way no other man could. As she turned the page and lifted the thin onion-skin sheath, Beverly tingled with anticipation as she gazed upon the lithograph of a swarthy man in buckskin, bending a dark haired native beauty backward over his arm as her sarong slipped from her plump bosom exposing her flesh temptingly to his lips.

Moira had just cleared Beverly's soup bowl when a loud commotion from the kitchen forced her to look up. She slipped the thin volume surreptitiously into her skirt pocket as a vision from her past burst through the door into the dining room, shrugging off the restraining grips of Richard and Moira's brother Harry.

"M'Lady, ye have t'help me! Where is yer brother, Lord Robert?"

Tom Phalen continued trying to wrest himself free of Harry's strong arms as Beverly looked up in astonishment at her former groom.

Beverly was so shocked to see Tom Phalen she simply stared at the man. Having just shifted her eyes from the illustration of a great bear of a man hot, sweaty and filled with passion, she now beheld the man in her own dining room! It wasn't until he broke free of Harry's youthful grip and almost hurtled himself onto her lap that she realized who it really was.

"Mr. Phalen! Remember yourself! How dare you come in here filthy and disgusting demanding anything of me? I should have the constable arrest you for trespassing! Look at how you have injured my footman!"

Beverly gestured at Harry, struggling to his feet after Tom threw him off like so much baggage and sent him skidding across the polished floor into the heavy carved leg of the sideboard. Harry rubbed the back of his head where he had hit it on the corner of one of the crests that decorated the cabinet doors.

Tom ignored her imperious commands. He towered over her chair and threatened to sweat on her blue silk blouse. His unshaved face, much thinner than she remembered, was lean and handsome and his blue eyes glinted like steel beneath his dark brows. His hair was thinner and tinged with gray but the damp curls around his temples and the nape of his neck were as attractive as ever. He reeked of sweat, both his own and his horse's. Beneath his filthy shirt, his chest heaved with angry passion and Beverly found herself strangely excited even as she tried to shrink away from him.

"You're mad! Get away from me! Richard! Harry! Take him out of here! He's mad I tell you! He needs to be locked up!"

The two men again seized Tom but the old man and the youth were no match for him. His strength was fueled by fear and rage giving him the strength of ten men.

"They've got Meg! They're goin' t'hang her! Ye hafta' believe me and ye have t'help me! They're goin' t'hang yer daughter!"

At this Beverly finally took notice of his words.

"What?"

"I said they're goin' t'hang yer daughter. Me wife, the mother o'me children!"

Beverly put one hand to her throat and waved the butler and footman away with the other. Reluctantly, they released Tom. He fell, exhausted, into the chair closest to Beverly. She started to protest but the crazed look in his eyes told her not to test him any further. Moira stood nearby holding a tureen filled with steaming fricasseed chicken and a basket of hot biscuits sat within inches of Beverly's plate. She reached for one and broke it on her plate without taking her eyes off Tom's face. She looked with curiosity at this specter from her former life and tried to shake off the effect of his steamy presence.

Beverly wanted to eat her supper. She wanted to read her little story. She wanted Reina to return with her chocolates. She did not want to look at this hulking intruder sitting at her table uninvited, spewing nonsense about her daughter. She did not want his presence to excite her. Those feelings were fine for late night reading safe in her bed. She did not welcome them at supper. She felt foolish for having brought her naughty little book into the dining room. Oddly, Beverly felt somehow responsible for bringing to life the man in the lithograph. She must banish this effect from her mind. She must begin her meal. That would set things to order.

She raised her left hand and Moira came forward. As the maid spooned thick bubbling chicken broth over the biscuit, Beverly picked up her fork. The girl scooped tender pieces of chicken and vegetables onto Beverly's plate and turned to set the tureen on the sideboard.

Lady Beverly turned her attention to her meal. She could feel fury emanating from Tom's body as she quietly cut the chicken and raised her fork to her lips. She knew he must be hungry after riding all the way from wherever he had been. Well, he could eat in the kitchen with the servants when she was finished.

As she reached for the basket to take another biscuit, she felt the smooth hardness of his hand on her wrist. He gripped her hard and she knew she would not be able to pull away.

Tom's voice was deadly quiet.

"Did ye not understand, M'Lady, what I said?"

Beverly tried to pull away, her own fury mounting. The fork still in her hand, she struck out at him. He pulled his hand away in time to avoid being stabbed, sending the biscuit tumbling to the floor just as the two servants grabbed him from behind. Beverly again waved them away. She knew she had to hear what he had to say and she would only prolong it by resisting. He leaned over and picked up the biscuit, breaking it in half.

"Ye won't mind me eatin' this now that it's not fir fer a lady's consumption. I'll be havin' a lick o'butter on it, thank you."

He picked up the silver knife from the butter dish and helped himself.

Beverly was astonished at his effrontery. She realized that the years away from GlynMor and his success as a businessman had changed Tom Phalen. He was no longer subservient and Beverly found herself a little afraid of him.

Better she should go along with this charade and get him out of here.

"Moira, set a bowl for Mr. Phalen. And bring us both a glass of cider."

She turned toward Tom.

"Tell me everything. From the beginning."

Tom washed his biscuit down with cider and dove into the chicken dinner. As the astonished servants looked on he spilled out a story so bizarre they looked from one to the other in amazement. Only the serious look on their mistress's face made them believe its truth.

Fr. Finnegan shook his head; trying to make sense out of the terrific tale he had just been told. Miss Gerrity, the elderly cook for the rectory, sucked air through the space between her two front teeth. Fr. Finnegan hated the sound of that miserable habit and had committed himself to tolerate it as a penance. Listening to the skinny old spinster doing it now though, was almost more than the saintly priest could bear.

He took off his thick spectacles and wiped them on a clean napkin. What could he say to this sad, frightened little woman sipping peppermint tea in his kitchen? He cleared his throat.

Avoiding the stares of the children peering through the window, he spoke.

"Mrs. Trent, what ye've done was absolutely th'correct thing t'do. Of course we will do our best t'find places fer th'children. Ye understand, of course, that Castlebar is as hard hit by this awful hunger as anywhere in th'county. There aren't even enough coffins t'bury th'dead and, God save us, no one strong enough left t'cart them away if there were coffins. I don't see how we can keep them out of th'workhouse but nothing is impossible with God. Me pastor is a good man but there have been so many every day at th'door."

He mopped his brow. His chest had felt heavy since his return from Westport and he had known that familiar shortness of breath when he lay down at night. It seemed as if everything made him a little sweaty. He could feel Cook's watchful eye upon him. She sucked her teeth rhythmically and never took her eyes off the back of his head.

"Mrs. Trent, is there anyone ye know who could take them? I hate to see them split up but I know of no one who can take them all. Perhaps th'sisters at St. Monica's could take the older girls but th'little ones and the baby? I'm at a loss! Is she even weaned?"

Mrs. Trent blushed at the question. She didn't dwell on such personal matters and here was a priest who should be ignorant of that sort of thing asking her such a question.

"Well, I don't know, Father. We'd have to ask Rose. The baby looks to be around two years old."

Miss Gerrity cleared her voice loudly.

"If ye don't mind me interruptin' Father. Me niece can help with th'babe if she's still nursin'. She has a new one herself and plenty o'milk."

Mrs. Trent gasped, prompting Father Finnegan to turn around in his chair and frown at Miss Gerrity.

"Thank you Miss Gerrity. That will be all."

The spinster huffed at the tone of dismissal in the priest's voice. Turning on her heel she went sucking away into the parlor.

"We do have a fairly well off parishioner who actually has an inn and restaurant in Louisburg. He just opened a pub here in Castlebar and may be able to house them there with some help. Perhaps the older girls should stay with the little ones. They must have someone to mind them and then they could stay together. Let me have a word with Mr. Fellowes. Let me see if he can help."

Rising from her chair, Leona Trent felt hopeful for the first time since she had arrived at the rectory.

"I will pray for all of you. I wish I could stay and assist you further but I must be on the late afternoon coach to make my connection in Newcastle. There aren't many coaches that go all the way to Ballaghey. The next one would be at least a week and I simply cannot afford to board somewhere until then."

"Not 'atall, Mrs. Trent! 'Tis that grateful we all are fer everythin' ye've done. D'ye by chance have an address where I can reach ye once everythin' settles down? I'm sure ye'll be wantin' t'know how it all turns out in the end."

"Yes, I do. I'll be with my sister, Elsbeth Peabody. You can send mail care of her in Ballaghey, County Mayo."

"Well, then, I guess you must be goin'. Did ye want t'bid farewell t'the children?"

"No, Father, if you don't mind, I think it would be easier for them if I just slipped out the front door. Miss Gerrity said she sent for a cab to take me to the station to pick up the coach. I can see that it's here."

Mrs. Trent picked up her shabby carpetbag and Father Finnegan helped her with her hatbox and a small sack of fruit Miss Gerrity had packed for her journey.

After the widow was gone, Miss Gerrity resumed her cooking and tooth sucking while Fr. Finnegan dealt with the children. Msgr. Gerrity, brother to the cook, was due back from a meeting at the chancery shortly before dinner. Fr. Finnegan wanted to be the one to break the news to his pastor himself so he had to act fast to find somewhere for them to go until he could talk to the Monsignor.

He gathered them all to him, giving each one a biscuit from the platter in the pantry. He knew they had not eaten since the day before and the little ones had been crying. He looked with pity at their expectant faces, smudged with tears and the dust from their long ride. He had only water to offer them to drink and he led them to the pump behind the turf pile.

When she saw the pump, Rose decided to wash her grimy siblings and before Fr. Finnegan could protest, she had all but Mary Clare stripped naked in his yard. Under the spigot they went while their sisters ran their hands up and down their skinny limbs sloshing the cool water over them and rubbing them clean. They ruffled each child's hair under the pump rinsing the dust from their curls.

Before he knew it they were refreshed and sparkling. Rose took their shirts and dried them off, dressing them in the damp rags. They would be dry in minutes in the afternoon sun. Rose stood proudly at attention.

"Now, Father, whoever takes us will know that we are clean and without things crawling about on us."

Fr. Finnegan smiled. "

Well, let's try Sr. Catherine at St. Monica's. Now that you're all clean, ye might as well follow me."

Mary Clare scooted to the front and slipped her hand into Fr. Finnegan's smooth palm. Looking up at him, she smiled.

"Fr. Finnegan, please may I stay at St. Monica's? I mean forever? Can I be a sister? Ye said yerself I had th'look about me."

"That I did but I can't make that decision fer yer parents Mary Clare. That's up t'yer mam and da."

He looked down at her with a sidelong glance.

"I'm sure ye know that now, don't ye lass?"

Her deep blue eyes filled with tears.

"Yes, Father."

Silently she slipped her little hand out of his and rejoined her sister. The priest felt his heart burst with love for this holy little child who wanted so much to live separated from the world, her eyes fixed solely on her savior. He would mention it to Sr. Catherine. If anyone would know what to do with little Mary Clare Phalen, it would be Sr. Catherine.

Meg stood against the cold stone wall of the examining room inside the entrance to the women's ward of the Mayo County Gaol at Castlebar. She was weak with relief to be done with Robert Gilchrist. He had berated her the entire distance from Westport to Castlebar, his vitriol punctuated by fits of coughing. It wasn't until the last leg of the trip as the carriage navigated through the long winding drive to the walled fortress, that he finally stopped talking. His fuming was then replaced by a thin smile of deep satisfaction. When Meg had been ushered into the looming corridor, he had not been allowed to follow. Never had she imagined she would actually appreciate the sound of a prison gate closing behind her.

The white washed walls were much cleaner than the damp gray stone of the Westport Gaol but the floor was as hard and cold as anything she had ever stood on. Meg looked down the cellblock. This small alcove was where they screened new prisoners. She had just endured a humiliating search for contraband and was waiting for the matron to return her clothes. The long row of iron bars revealed several women lying on bunks or sitting staring out from behind their locked cell doors straining to see the newcomers. Meg counted at least seven prisoners and eight empty cells. Somewhere someone was moaning and Meg heard soft crying from the far end.

She was one of three new arrivals. A beefy female guard stood before the next woman and felt her everywhere, looking for money, jewelry, anything possible to justify her vicious probing. The skinny woman swore with contempt at the guard's prying fingers and almost bit her when she forced open the prisoner's mouth. This earned her a clout with the second guard's shillelagh that brought her to her knees. Meg shuddered as the first guard reached down and pulled the prisoner up by her hair forcing her to bend over a chair as she continued her search. Satisfied that the woman had nothing hidden anywhere, she went on to the third prisoner. The shillelagh wielding guard, even bigger than the first shoved the skinny prisoner into a cell and threw her ragged shift in after her, slamming the door closed with a clang.

The last prisoner cried every time the guard touched her, bringing derisive laughter and even rougher probing than the cursing had. By the time the second guard took the poor woman to her cell she was sobbing and desperately trying to cover her nakedness with her hands. When the second guard went to throw the woman's shift into her cell the first guard grabbed it from her.

"Ye'll not be needin' this, love. It's fer yer own good that ye learn t'turn off yer tears in here. A few days naked in this place'll thicken yer skin a bit. Maybe one o'these others'll die and ye can have somethin' new t'wear."

With that she stood before the wailing woman and tore her only possession into shreds. Now she was going to do hard labor for stealing a tattered dress she'd never wear again.

Meg stood paralyzed with fear, not knowing what response would turn the guards' mood toward or against her. Knowing what had happened to Andrew she knew she had been very lucky Gilchrist had come for her when he did. She had spent the few hours after Andrew left waiting in rigid terror for the guards to return for their 'little chat' with her. They had missed their opportunity when the man they had brought in that morning suffered a fit and died. They had been busy dealing with the coroner and then Meg was gone.

But these women! She had never seen such big women. When all of Ireland was crawling with thin, wispy, walking skeletons, how did these women stay so stout and strong? Where did they find them?

The guard approached Meg and ordered her to dress. Meg's hands were free but she still wore leg irons. She hastily buttoned her blouse and fastened her skirt. Standing in the cold cellblock, she shivered involuntarily.

The guard shoved her with the shillelagh and she ambled toward the first empty cell.

"This one's in here fer tryin' t'murder a landlord, Gladys."

The other guard let out a low whistle. Meg had never heard a woman whistle before and turned her head at the sound. Immediately the first guard rammed the shillelagh against Meg's ear and forced her to look straight ahead.

"Open up, murderess. We fergot t'check yer mouth."

Meg opened her mouth and the woman stuck her filthy finger so far back Meg almost gagged.

It was her turn to let out a whistle.

"Gladys, will ye look at them teeth! Not a bad one among 'em! Well, ain't ye the Duchess o'Kent! Maybe we should have her bend over again. Maybe we'd find some o'the crown jewels!"

Gladys hooted and snorted at this remark bringing a grin filled with blackened teeth to the first guard's face.

"Glenda, you slay me!"

Meg silently submitted to the vile remarks, praying that if she said nothing she would be found pleasing to the two guards.

Gladys let out another snort and fawned mockingly in front of Meg as Glenda prodded her along the cellblock. When she and Glenda had finally had enough sport, Glenda shoved Meg hard in the back with her shillelagh. When they reached the last cell, Glenda kicked Meg from behind and she staggered and fell on the concrete floor. Glenda turned toward Gladys and grinned.

"I guess this one niver learned that 'book on th'head' way o'walkin, eh?

Gladys chuckled as she watched Meg struggle to stand up in leg irons.

"We think yer majesty'll be happier down here. Not t'be mixin' with th'riffraff. At least it'll be a wee bit more private, right Glenda? I think the Duchess would like any future necessary visits t'be more private. Just in case she might have any state secrets t'share."

The two guards left the prisoners and Meg dragged herself to her cot. The mattress was as flimsy and worn as the one in Westport Jail but in general the whole place seemed cleaner. This was probably an illusion created by the whitewashed walls. The truth would be revealed when the cellblock was plunged into darkness later that night.

Meg lay down on the miserable cot and turned toward the wall. She knew the guards put her down near the end of the cellblock for their own reasons. Her eyes filled at the thought of them visiting her and humiliating her. She wasn't sure what women did to other women other than touching but she knew they would be back. As afraid as she was of the male guards in Westport, something told her she should be even more afraid of these two huge women who had just slammed the far gate behind them and went cackling off to their post.

Beverly sat still, her fork resting next to her half-eaten supper. She gestured for Moira to take it. Somehow, her appetite had left her. She knew she should say something to Tom Phalen. She could feel the heaviness of his body waiting in the chair next to her. Finally, she took a deep breath and spoke.

"Well, that's quite a tale, Mr. Phalen. Moreover, I believe it. But I'm afraid you have been on a fool's errand. You are correct to say that my brother Robert is the man to help Lady Meg. However, my brother Robert is not here."

Tom let out a groan and threw back his head. Tearing his fingers through his hair he spoke to the ceiling.

"He's not here! Dear God, what d'ye want from me? Dear Jaysus in heaven what am I t'do? Dear Virgin Mother, where do I go next?"

"Mr. Phalen! If you will stop blaspheming in my own home, I will try and help you! What you need is a fresh horse and you can leave right now for GlynMor Castle. There are still a few hours of good light. You could be to Galway by dark and GlynMor by late tomorrow. I expect you will find Lord Robert still there. The days are long and you'll have Bay Rum, as you know, my strongest horse."

Tom was out of his chair and heading through the kitchen door before Beverly was on her feet. Within minutes he was back in the saddle charging north to Clydagh Glyn. He hoped to arrive at GlynMor castle by nightfall tomorrow. He had Bay Rum, indeed, Beverly's strongest horse. He had wanted to ride straight through but Lady Beverly refused to allow the old horse to ride through the night. He had been shocked that Beverly had given him her prize stud to ride but he knew Bay Rum like no other horse and the huge animal recognized him at once. As soon as Tom slipped into the saddle, Bay Rum and he became one animal. Tom's legs, sore as they were from his earlier ride, felt comfortably at home astride the broad back. The power emanating from Bay Rum's flanks as he raced down the yew-lined drive exhilarated Tom.

Charles Hanes, Lord Cushing's head groom, had mapped out a route using the coach road to Galway where Tom could rest the horse and spend the night. Then he would have to cut northeast through Cong where he would leave the coach trail and follow the shepherd's road north until he picked up the southern arm of the Clydagh River. Once he got that far he could follow the river to Clydagh Glyn. He would have to ride hard as far as Galway. He was tired and sore after the long ride from Marie's but no one even tried to convince him to delay his start until morning.

Beverly watched with tears in her eyes as horse and man rounded the last stand of yews. She wanted Tom to free her daughter. Beverly had failed Meg miserably the last time she had needed her and she wanted more than anything to redeem herself. She had ordered Charles to saddle up Bay Rum without a moment's hesitation. He was old for such a long arduous journey but he and Tom would be fine together. She just hoped Robert would still be at GlynMor when Tom arrived.

She returned to the dining room and saw that Moira had cleared her place. Now that she had seen Tom off, her appetite had returned. She wanted to finish her supper and enjoy her pudding with a nice pot of tea. She rang for Moira and immediately she found herself enjoying a second helping of the fricasseed chicken. As she buttered a cold biscuit, Beverly toyed with the idea of traveling to Clydagh Glyn herself. She decided to ask Reina's opinion when she returned.

⁜

George tiptoed out of the dimly lit room and shut the door gently. He had just administered a shot of laudanum to his lordship. The shots were growing less effective, especially in the last few days. Lord Wynn had begged and pleaded for relief only an hour after the last shot. George had taken pity on his master and friend and had given him another half dose within thirty minutes of his asking. He knew to much of the stuff could kill his lordship but he wouldn't be the one with his blood on his hands. But he truly felt sorry for his lordship and hoped a little more would do no harm. George had hardly slept since Lord Cushing had arrived. His soul was tormented by his complicity in the deaths of Lady Meg's children. He wondered if he would ever sleep soundly again. The last thing he needed was to overdose her father.

He was just about to knock on Lady Wynn's bedroom door when it opened and her brother came out. Lord Cushing had been at GlynMor three days and didn't seem in any hurry to leave. George was glad for the company. After the first difficult conversation with his lordship, George had found him a most amiable and compassionate guest. He had even taken to seeking his advice on Lord Wynn's care.

"Good Morning, George. How are you faring today?"

Lord Cushing shrugged into his morning coat and adjusted his cravat as the two men headed toward the dining room.

"Fine, sir. Thank you for asking."

"And Jeffrey? The same?"

"Well, sir, I was actually coming to ask your help. I hope you don't mind, sir."

Robert did mind and had to force himself to keep from scowling. He felt himself in a precarious position as Beverly's benefactor secretly living in her husband's home. The last thing he needed to be doing was deciding matters of his brother-in-law's care.

"What is it, George?"

"Well, sir, he wants the laudanum more frequently than it's been prescribed. I mean he always has but now he wants it within an hour. I fear for his life, sir."

Robert took his seat at the dining room table and gestured to the maid Molly to pour him his coffee. George stood at his side obviously expecting him to instruct him.

"How far is Lord Jeffrey's physician?"

"He's being followed by Dr. Simmons in Castlebar. He prescribes the laudanum every month and I pick it up myself at Swan's Apothecary on King St. He's actually in danger of running out before the end of the month."

Lord Robert gently cracked the shell of a boiled egg placed before him by the maid. She poured him a second cup of coffee, lingering to hear this most tantalizing conversation.

Lord Robert asked her for some oatmeal and toast hoping she would remain in the kitchen until he was done with George. He waved her hand away from his cup.

"Just leave the pot, Molly."

"Yes, sir."

Disappointed, the girl left his side immediately.

"George, I want you to fetch this Dr. Simmons. Leave now and tell him it's urgent. Have him bring more laudanum or write you a prescription for some. From what you tell me, Lord Wynn's health is extremely compromised. The situation is critical and must be handled very delicately by his trusted physician. Who else knows how to give him his medication while you're gone?"

"Well, he's never let anyone but me or Sharon give it. She hates going up there but if I leave the needles ready, she'll do it."

"Good. Get going and please God, you'll be back before supper."

"Oh, without a doubt, sir. I'll have the doctor here by mid-afternoon."

George almost collided with Molly in the kitchen

doorway as she brought Robert a steaming bowl of his favorite cereal and toasted soda bread on a silver tray.

Meg awoke to the sound of metal scraping against metal, punctuated by the loud rapping of Glenda's shillelagh along the bars of the cells.

"Come an'git yer supper, ye sows. Ye'll not be turnin' down an invitation from th'queen!"

She reached the cell door just as the ugly matron shoved a tin bowl of swill through a rectangular opening between the center bars.

Gladys clucked her black teeth and made a sour face when Meg reached for her meal.

"Duchess, I sincerely apologize fer th'humble fare. It's not every day we have inmates with good teeth. I hope ye understand that most of our ladies have no teeth 'atall. Sorry fer th'soft slop."

Meg took the bowl and looked with horror at the thick, stinking stew. She hadn't eaten in two days and she was hungry but she had no idea what this was.

Gladys grinned at Meg's expression.

"And, again me apologies. Ye git no implements. Ye'll have te use yer hands."

Glenda followed along behind Gladys with a cart filled with tin cups of water.

She handed a cup to Meg through the bars.

"Ye can drink it or wash with it. Yer choice. But it's all ye'll be gittin' till mornin'."

Meg took the water gratefully, suddenly realizing how parched she was. Gently she sat down on the edge of her bunk and touched the greasy film that lay on top of the dark brown pile in her bowl. She stirred the mess with her finger and found it to be lukewarm. There were a few vegetables in the stew but no sign of any meat. She gagged at the thought of what meat these wicked people would put in a stew and was grateful not to find any.

Feeling the old familiar hunger pangs from her starving days, Meg knew she had to eat this. Her healthy appetite had never returned and the growling pains in her belly surprised her. She stared at the food, unable to bring it to her mouth.

"Eat it."

Meg turned to the source of the voice. There was a bald-headed hag a few cells away watching Meg's hesitation. The woman had already wolfed down her supper and was licking her bony fingers.

"Eat it or they'll punish ye. Eat it or they'll put ye in the middle o'the cell block and force feed ye a live rat. And they'll make us watch. So, fer Christ's sake, eat it."

A thin street walker sressed in a slinky red rag of a dress, her makeup still intact leaned toward Meg as she spoke over her shoulder at the bald wretch making the threat.

"Maude Devlin, stop yer lyin' talk! Don't mind her Chickie, she's bats. They'll not be feedin' ye rats. They treat the rats better than that around here. Why, they treat the rats better than they treat us around here!"

This brought cackling laughter from the other cells.

Meg sensed that the other women looked to the hooker as their leader. They all dutifully laughed when she chuckled at her own remarks and stopped when her tone grew serious.

"But they will punish ye. They'll single ye out fer th'hardest labor in th'noonday sun, they will. And if ye don't eat yer meal they'll cut yer water ration. That's th'real torture. That moanin' ye hear? That's th'sound o'thirst, girl. Ye don't want t'piss 'em off or they'll just let ye lay there and shrivel t'death. So, eat yer puddin, Chickie. Pretend it's right from yer mammy's table and gulp it down. The quicker th'better so's ye don't taste it."

Meg closed her eyes and prayed an Ave. Without opening her eyes, she lifted the bowl to her lips. She would do this. She would eat the disgusting mixture because she had a husband and children who waited for her return. She would swallow the foul smelling lumps whole if she had to. She would do it for them. For Tom, whose agony at their separation would match her own. For Denny, who may at this very moment be forced to eat worse as he hid beneath the floorboards of the Marianna. For her little ones who would miss her so badly they wouldn't eat at all.

Before she could change her mind, Meg poured as much of the stew as she could into her mouth, swallowing most of it without chewing. The larger chunks she mashed with her teeth bared trying to avoid the slimy texture and gamey taste. It took three tries before it was all gone and Meg had to force herself to keep it down but she did it. She opened her eyes to see the whole line of wretched faces looking at her. Even the skinny girl who had defied the matrons and been left to die of thirst was on her knees staring out of sunken eyes at Meg.

Meg drank most of the water and set down her cup. She wanted badly to pass the rest to the dying girl but the matrons had isolated her between two empty cells. No one could help the poor girl and she slipped back to the floor and resumed her moaning.

When Meg finished the last of her water, the place erupted into a cacophony of tin cups banging on iron bars. The other inmates were applauding her! She had passed the first two tests; the strip search and the first meal. She had achieved membership in the sisterhood of Castlebar Gaol. When her noisy reception was done, Meg sat on her bunk and wept.

Tom sat in the far corner of Brennan's, a dim, smoky pub across from the livery on Galway's main thoroughfare. He had just seen to his horse and booked a room at Mrs. Flattery's Rooming House and Inn. She had been a bit put out that he was only staying one night but Duffy had given him a generous portion of the takings and she didn't refuse his money.. Tom actually had more money on him now than he'd had since Robert Gilchrist had stolen his cows.

So, this was Galway. He watched as a waiter piled sliced ox tongue and onions on a plate and added two thick wedges of soda bread to mop up the spicy broth. The ride from Killarney had gone well and he had made good time. The sun was just setting when he arrived at the pub and he had just made it in before the kitchen closed.

Bay Rum had served him well, proving himself to be as strong and powerful at the end of the trip as he had been at the start. Tom's thighs and knees throbbed with the strain of the ride but he was glad to feel it. His heart cried out for Meg and he tried desperately to shut out the images that swirled around in his head of her in prison. How could he have allowed this to happen to her? How could he have prevented it?

That morning, only a few days ago, when they had stood together in the vestibule of St. Peter's Church they had held each other as though nothing could separate them. Not knowing she had been moved to Castlebar, he imagined Meg shivering in the bowels of Westport while he chased down the only man who could save her. How he wished he could travel through the night! He would have sacrificed himself to do so but the livery stable had no fresh horse for him to hire.

Every moment she spent behind bars was like a whiplash across his heart. He tried to stop his knowledge of bailiffs and guards from plunging him into complete despair. The thought of his Meg at the hands of those brutes was more than he could bear.

He signaled the waiter for another pint. He doubted he could blind his mind's eye with drink but he already felt the mellowing effect of his first two glasses. At least he'd sleep well tonight. Mrs. Flattery said she locked the door at ten o'clock. The big clock behind the bar was just chiming nine. He had plenty of time to get drunk but he thought he'd have just one piece of the rhubarb pie before he filled up on another stout.

Robert Gilchrist blinked at the bright sun creeping around the heavy gold drape. Damn his bad luck! He would have to be assigned a room with an east window. He felt lousy and here was the sun waking him at the break of dawn. He sat up on the edge of the feather bed and immediately began to cough. What a night he had spent!

First he had been denied the opportunity to see the solicitor assigned to defend Meg Phalen. He had wanted to be sure of the man's incompetence. Then he was denied a visit to her cell. What did he care if the place was home to other female prisoners? A pox on all of them! Especially that huge bulldog bitch with the black teeth. Where did they ever find her? Probably some madam from a raided whorehouse.

He tried to hold his head in his hands but as soon as he lowered it his temples began to throb with an awful pain. He lay down again on his damp pillow and shivered with the chill of it. How was he to pursue justice if he couldn't even raise his head? How he wished he were home in his own bed with Mrs. Gilchrist to soothe him with a nice poultice. That damn woman was never around when he needed her.

He reached over and yanked the bell pull. Within seconds there was a knock on the door.

His voice came out in a croak.

"Enter!"

A maid came in, an expectant look on her face.

"Sir?"

"I want a pot of coffee brought to me. Turkish. Two eggs, soft boiled and a bowl of porridge with plenty of sugar and cream. I want someone to prepare a hot poultice for my chest and I want a whore. A young one."

The girl gasped at the last request and began to protest that the Wilburforce Arms Hotel did not allow that type of activity.

Mr. Gilchrist waved away her concerns.

"Either a whore or a nurse, I don't care which. I just want someone to look after me. I'm very ill and no one seems to give a damn. Just find me someone who knows how to apply a poultice and give a bath. Now get out of here before I throw something at you."

The girl turned and was gone in a flash.

A few moments passed and there was another knock at the door. This time a man in formal livery entered without being bidden and stood aside as the maid set Mr. Gilchrist's breakfast tray on a delicate little table by the fireplace.

"Bring it here, you stupid brat. Can't you see I'm too weak to walk over there?"

He looked with contempt at the astonished man in the doorway.

"Who are you? I asked for a whore or a nurse. You, pray God, are neither. What do you want?"

The man cleared his voice.

"Sir, I am Henri DuBois, concierge d'hotel. Monsieur Wilburforce asked me to look in on you. He has sent for his own private physician, Dr. Simmons. I hope you will find him satisfactory. Giselle will be most happy to place your tray closer to your bedside, monsieur but I must warn you. If you behave in any way rudely to her, you will be asked to leave the hotel. Monsieur Wilburforce is very strict about these things."

"Of course, of course. I don't know what her complaint is. I've done nothing to her."

The concierge nodded at the maid and she brought the table and tray over to the bedside.

Gilchrist waved them both away and they left him alone. He sat up again and felt the room spinning around him. What a development! He poured his coffee with a shaky hand, slopping it onto the saucer. Maybe a good meal would help if he could get it to his mouth.

Chapter Sixteen

The Marianna had been at sea for forty eight hours and Duffy and Denny still had not seen the light of day. Marie had been right. There were no open berths available on the little ship and they had had to stow away below decks. Duffy knew they were lucky to have even this dank, tiny space to cross the ocean. Before they left the harbor, the sailor had demanded the stolen sausage as payment for his help but Duffy wouldn't part with it. He and Denny needed every bite of food they brought with them for the long journey ahead. Instead, the sailor, a Scot named Fergus McPhee, accepted a quick free trick from Peggy and Duffy gave her the money to cover her fee.

He had taken them deep in the hull and shown them to a small storage space stacked with bolts of fabric and crates of lady's shoes and accessories. Duffy was grateful. At least the cargo was dry and odorless. The rats would leave them alone too. There was nothing there to interest them. Hopefully by the time the creatures realized they smelled sausage and cheese, it would be gone.

The biggest drawback to their little hiding place was the darkness. The sailor refused to give them a candle or even a storm lantern because of the danger of fire. He had brought them a jug of fresh water and another empty one to pee in along with a tin bucket with a lid to use for other waste. He stayed long enough to see them settled and then slid the door closed leaving them in total darkness. He said he would return for them after dark when he would take them on deck for some air.

Denny had immediately tripped over a crate and fallen behind it. His fall was broken by several large sacks filled with something soft. Denny tossed them over the crate and Duffy piled them together making a fine bed. He couldn't tell in the dark what was inside the sacks but he thought they might be full of eiderdown pillows or featherbeds. He could not believe their good fortune. They would be comfortable even if they couldn't see anything.

The first night, Fergus returned for them around midnight. Duffy and Denny were glad to stretch their legs and gulped the fresh, cold sea air. The stars lay across the sky like a big, lazy lizard with scales glittering and shimmering against the black. Duffy loved the night sky and the stars at sea were like nothing he had ever seen. Denny was transfixed by the glorious spectacle above him. The two stayed on deck until the last minute before the sailor was to be relieved of his watch. He wouldn't be on the night watch again for two days so they would have to stay below. He would try to see them at least once a day but he couldn't promise anything.

Just before Fergus McPhee closed the door, Denny turned to Duffy, a look of raw fear on his young face. This was certainly not the adventure he had expected. Duffy put his arm around the lad and together they settled onto their cushions. He pretended not to hear Denny crying himself to sleep next to him in the dark.

Long after the boy had finally begun to snore rhythmically, Duffy lay awake, thinking. They had no way to mark time. They would have to eat only when they were hungry and drink the stale water sparingly over the next two days. He pulled out his rosary and began a litany of Aves. Mary, sweet mother of God help them. Duffy had begun to wonder if they'd even survive this journey. He knew if they did, it would be by the grace of God and the kindness of strangers.

Hours later, the sound of the door sliding open startled Duffy, and Denny let out a little squeal. They had been wrapping the rest of the sausage in its cheesecloth and had just drunk the last of the water. They had no idea how much time had passed or whether they had eaten and drunk more than they should have. Duffy needed to talk to young Fergus about making some other arrangement for them to get out of this box.

The sailor had come back the afternoon after he took them on board. He had exchanged their jugs and bucket for new ones but he had not let them out. He had not been back since. Duffy had thought by the number of times he and Denny had felt hungry enough to eat that at least a full twenty-four hours had passed since they saw the sailor. They could tell nothing by their sleep pattern. It was so dark they never knew whether it was night or day so they slept like babies, in short naps interrupted by meals. Duffy believed it to be the strangest experience he had ever had.

Now it was again daylight and the brightness of the afternoon sun almost blinded the two stowaways. Fergus stood with another man, their backs to the sun. Duffy felt fear surge through his bowels when he saw the other man. He was sure they had been discovered somehow and would be flogged and shot before being thrown overboard.

Fergus spoke in a hushed voice, his thick Scottish burr almost impossible to understand.

"I haive a frund o'yers hare. Hu'll be jinin' ye sence his oon pleece is a wee bit too pooblic. He cumes beerin' mare pruvisions. Ye laddies are amizin'. Doon't knu whar ye gut it all."

Andrew Feeney ducked through the low doorway bending his long, lean body almost in half. Duffy and Denny both were thrilled to see him despite the prospect of sharing their tight quarters with another person. Just having another companion to pass the time was a godsend.

Fergus exchanged the bucket again and promised to come back in a few hours to take them on deck.

Andrew accepted two of the plump sacks and plopped down on them.

"Oh, sweet Mither Macree does this feel good! Ye lads must be sleepin' like kings on these soft beds."

Duffy tried to plump up his remaining cushions realizing that neither he nor Denny would be as comfortable as they had been.

"Suren' it's all we're doin'. The dark don't afford us nothin' else."

He suddenly felt irritable despite his initial gladness at seeing another brother with whom to wile away the time. They had little enough comfort without spreading it thin. Trying to rest his arm, he bumped the sack of food and felt the bulk of the sausage and the hard edge of the cheese through the thin burlap. His crankiness was replaced by shame as he remembered whom they had to thank for their food.

"We are that grateful fer yer foresight, Andrew. Stealin' all this food from Browne's. 'Twas brilliant. With what ye just brought, we should be set fer the whole trip."

Andrew shifted on his cushion. Duffy's words were high praise and he was proud to hear them.

Denny piped up and asked what he had brought them.

"Well, there's some more sausage, some kippers, three bottles of whiskey, a pint o'cider, a couple more cheeses and a little jug o'honey. I heard somewhere honey was good fer ye so I grabbed it."

Duffy turned to him in the dark.

"Where were ye hidin' that ye had to move?"

"Up near the deck. There was a little space behind some ropes. I just fit beneath the big anchor and figured they wouldn't be lookin' there till we were already where we're goin'. It wasn't the best place but I had t'duck fer cover quick. I bribed a sailor with a snort of Browne's finest scotch but he left me on me own t'find a place. Before I could git below decks, didn't th'captain himself come trottin' right toward me. I took me bundles and disappeared behind the anchor ropes just as he strolled by. Good thing he was busy talkin' t'some pretty miss. Niver gave me a second glance."

Duffy sat up straight.

"D'ye mean there's another sailor on board that knows about us?"

Andrew felt queasy and defensive.

"Well, sure, Duff. How d'ye think I got on board?"

"No, I'm not sayin' it's a bad thing. 'Tis actually a good thing. If we play our hand right we might be able t'git on deck more often. How much whiskey do we have?"

Andrew checked his sack again though he knew there were three bottles.

"And the one in our sack makes four! Praise God, Feeney, you're a genius! Now, listen up. This is what we're doin'. We'll not be givin' away any free bottles. But we can be givin' away free drinks. The price of a nice shot will be a trip to the upper deck. We can git out o'this hole at least every other day if we go once with Fergus and then with yer lad. Fergus says he's the lowest ranker and always gits night watch. He's only on every third night but yer lad must be on some too. I'm not fer lettin' too many fingers in th'pot, that's dangerous. Somebody might git greedy but maybe jist the two t'start with."

Andrew said nothing but lay back on his cushions with a smile on his face. He was a brother after all. God, it felt good t'be one o'the boyos.

Lord Robert hurried through the kitchen door and across the yard to the stables. Good God! He could hardly believe his ears when George told him Tom Phalen was on the property and he wanted to see him on urgent business. What could this mean?

George led the way through the stable to the big double doors at the back. He did a double take when he saw Peter brushing down Bay Rum while the big horse munched from a feedbag. Bay Rum! What was this subterfuge? He followed George up a set of rickety stairs to a small dingy room completely unadorned except for a bed, a rocking chair and a small ewer and pitcher set on a worn table under the tiny window. Ben sat in the rocker while Tom Phalen paced back and forth just clearing the ceiling with his big frame. He turned when he heard Lord Robert approach.

"Thank God yer here, sir! Me wife, yer niece, has been arrested for attempted murder. I've ridden over half of Ireland t'find ye. I'm at me wit's end, I don't know which workhouse me children are in and I have no one else t'turn to! I know ye offered t'take me family t'yer place and I was none too happy t'have ye do it but I'm a desperate man, M'Lord and I'll do anything ye ask jist to have 'em safe again."

Robert stood agape as he tried to assimilate this latest news. George had turned completely white and staggered to the edge of Ben's bed where he sat down with a thud. He looked like he was going to faint dead away.

For a second there was no sound except the creaking of the ancient rocker and Ben's heavy boots tapping out a rhythm as they met the floor.

George looked at Lord Robert, his face stricken.

"I know where she is, M'Lord. Her ladyship is imprisoned right down the road in Castlebar Gaol. It must be her! All the talk at Swan's this morning was about the woman prisoner from Westport who tried to murder a landlord. There were those who cried for her to hang and those who want to make her a national hero but I have no doubt it's her ladyship. Who else would it be?"

Tom stared at George, his own face frighteningly void of color.

The first to speak was Ben.

"Tom, who did Meg try to kill?"

"She tried t'kill no one! That weasel Gilchrist attacked her and she defended herself is all. Denny saw the whole thing and God bless his brave little heart he joined in the fray taking the son of a bitch down in one blow. He's gone from me too, now. On a ship t'the States with the only friend I ever had. The two of 'em fugitives o'the law because of that little bastard. But he won't be lookin' fer 'em. He's got his prize."

"All because o'me, he's got Meg. Christ on the cross, I wish it were me! Meg lied to him, told him I was dead. That was when he first came. Before Reek Sunday for the landlord's meeting. Duff and Meg wouldn't let me face him then. Made me hide at the rectory. Ye'd think I was the bloody crown prince, the way those two protected me. Now she's in Castlebar Gaol and me thinkin' she's still in Westport!"

He looked at Robert, his face a mask of pain and anguish. Robert had to look away. He couldn't bear to witness the man's shame.

Tom raved on, "Tried to git me fer thieven' horses but couldn't make a case of it. He came fer me again. Somethin' about that damn land in America. Claimin' I stole a deed from Lord Jeffrey. This time they hid me in a whorehouse. Me and Duff together this time because o'Duff's cousin in th'Brotherhood. When Denny showed up I thought I'd lose me mind."

"Now what? I had no choice but t'let him go! D'ye see that I had no choice? That snake had th'law after him! Same as his mam! Attempted murder! He's just a boyo! Attempted murder on a lad of twelve! "

Tom's last words came out in a soft, dry sob that brought both Ben and George to tears. Robert looked around and saw that this situation had deteriorated dangerously close to hysteria. He reached for a bottle of cheap whiskey that Ben had on his windowsill. Popping the cap, he handed it to Tom.

"Drink your fill, man. You must calm down. If Meg is in Castlebar that's a good thing. It puts her closer to us and also places her in my legal jurisdiction. It is to this address that I'm licensed to practice law. I've never practiced in any other county so I can only help her if she stays here."

Tom took the bottle and swallowed several gulps of the bitter, stinging booze. He wanted to be drunk. Maybe if he were drunk the noise in his head would stop clanging. The strong drink made his face flush and he felt strangely alive.

"So, ye will help me. Fer that I am truly grateful. I don't know if I have any use in all this. To be sure, I don't even know where the hell t'put meself. If I knew where me children were I'd be off t'git them but I don't know where they are."

"I need to think about that. Stay here for now, Tom. I'll try and find out where the children are and if it's safe for you to leave here. Lord Wynn is dying and has just had the doctor from Castlebar this afternoon. He says it's just a matter ofweeks, maybe days. I don't know if the magistrate in Castlebar has set bail for Meg or not. She is just a poor peasant to them so I don't suppose anyone has even thought of it. I will go there tonight and post bail for her if I can. You could have her at your side as soon as tomorrow morning. Just pray that the magistrate will release her."

He turned to George.

"Have Peter prepare a carriage for me. Don't use my horse. I want one that will find its way home in the dark. My horse doesn't know these roads that well. And get Sharon to feed this man. He looks like he could use a good meal."

George stood up and unceremoniously took the bottle from Tom's hand. Without a word he tipped it up and drained the last of the whiskey. The flavor was so bad he shook his head and let out a soft yelp. He had been spoiled for a working man's belt after all these years drinking his lordship's fine, smooth scotch. He ignored Ben's beseeching eyes as he watched his precious craither disappear.

Lord Robert put his hand on Tom's shoulder.

"Where do you want to stay? You know you can stay right here if you like. Lord Wynn is so bad he spends hardly any time awake so you have nothing to fear from him if you stay here. I'm sure Sharon will get Molly to turn down a bed in the east wing for you. That's where I am. Or if you prefer, your family home is available too. It's been vacant for all these years so you can imagine its condition but it is your home after all."

Tom could hardly choose. He knew if he went to his da's house tonight he would just about lose his mind. His other option was just as bad. How could he ever sleep in this drafty old barn after what it had meant to him and Meg?

"Let me think on it, sir. I would be grateful fer the meal though. But let me think on the other."

One by one they left the little room above the stable, until only Ben remained. The old man continued to rock back and forth, back and forth, occasionally reaching up to wipe a hot tear from his wrinkled cheek.

"Mr. Gilchrist I have had a very long day. I am here at the request of my good friend Mr. Wilburforce and for no other reason. Were it not so I would see you in my office on the morrow. Now if you would prefer I not stay, I have a wife and hearth waiting for me, both offering me a hot meal!"

"Oh, stop sniveling and do your job, Simmons. I am a sick man and you have pledged an oath to take care of me. I want a poultice for my chest. What is so hard about that? And I'm even willing to allow that shriveled monkey you call a nurse look after me tonight. You'll be paid for your time. What is your problem?"

The doctor sat down in the stiff brocade slipper chair next to Mr.Gilchrist's bed. Why did this man smell so of camphor?

"I told you. For me to produce a goose grease poultice, which is the best thing I can prescribe for your ailing chest, I must have access to a butcher. Given the late hour, this is impossible. The best I can do is try in the morning. Until then you must be content to soothe your cough with the elixir I have left by your bed. It will help you sleep through the night and bring down your fever. You will probably wake up tomorrow a new man. What you have is a cold. A miserable summer cold but nonetheless nothing more than a cold. I will not assign Miss Phibs to your bedside because you do not need her and she has a family who does."

"So, I will leave you now to the capable staff of this fine establishment. God save them all. You can expect me to stop by around ten to check on you. If you have not improved, I will order up the poultice and you will have it on your chest by noon."

Gilchrist pouted like a child and reached for the cough syrup.

"Mind you, sir, that is a strong potion. You would be wise to restrict yourself to the prescribed dose. I will not be held responsible for your demise if you take too much. Good night, Mr. Gilchrist. Pleasant dreams."

Together the doctor and nurse swept out of the room.

Gilchrist threw the spoon after them realizing too late that he would have to get out of bed to retrieve it. The capable staff had stopped answering his bell hours ago. No use trying to get one of them up here to pick it up. None of them cared about a sick man who could die during a paroxysm of coughing.

None of them knew how powerful he really was. As he padded across the floor in his bare feet, he plotted various ways to bring down this pompous doctor and that miserable Frenchie, Henri. He would bet money on the fact that Mr. Wilburforce had no idea how incompetent and rude his staff really was. Well, once Robert Gilchrist was through with them they'd all regret treating him like trash.

"Yes, Lord Robert Cushing. Earl of Bantram. I am here to see Lady Margaret Wynn Phalen."

Robert looked respectfully at the fat matron, despite her

grubby appearance and her slatternly posture.

"Well, yer in the wrong place. sir. We ain't got nobody that fits that ladyship type."

Gladys nervously played with a pencil. Where was Glenda when she needed her? Who was this gentleman? Lord Arse and Hole? Earl of Snob? She sighed with relief when she heard Glenda clanging the gate closed behind her.

"The little loves are all accounted fer. Everybody's down fer the…well, well, who do we have here?"

"As I already told your esteemed colleague, I am Lord Robert Cushing, Earl of Bantram and I represent your prisoner, Lady Margaret Wynn Phalen. I wish to see her now."

Lord Robert was losing his need to display good manners. He struck his tall beaver hat on the palm of his hand with a snap for emphasis. Leaning across the desk only inches from Gladys's black teeth, he repeated with precise enunciation.

"Now."

"Well, yer lordship, we ain't got yer client. Nobody named Lady anybody here. What is it she did?"

"She did nothing. She is accused of attempted murder. She is innocent and I intend to post her bail tonight and return to her whence I came with her in my custody. But first I will see her. Now!"

Glenda's face flushed deep scarlet as she realized he was talking about the duchess. That would explain the good teeth! God above she really was a duchess! The matron began fumbling with her papers and found the name Meg Phalen. There she was.

"Sir, did she go by any other name, ye know, an alias?"

"Her married name is Phalen. Her family refers to her as Meg. But she is titled. Her father is the Earl of Cantwell. Where are you holding her?"

Glenda gulped at the cold authority in the man's voice. Gone was any semblance of respect and courtesy.

"Well, sir, ye can't go into the cell block. That's against

policy but I can bring her up here if ye please."

Gladys shot her supervisor a look of panic. No one had ever said it was permitted to use the visitor room. Gladys had been at the prison a year and no one had ever asked before.

"I please."

"Certainly, sir. Let me show ye in and I'll have the lady here in a jiff."

She hoped the gentleman wouldn't notice her hands shaking as she opened the door. She called over her shoulder.

"Gladys, get his lordship a lamp."

Once he was seated in the musty little room and Gladys had set an oil lamp on the table, Glenda left to get Meg. She turned to Gladys and whispered in a loud hiss.

"Git yer ass over t'the judge's house! I don't care what time it is. I ain't takin' th'heat fer this. I want him here. This case is about landed folks and I'm not goin' t'the workhouse so the judge can git his beauty rest. Git him over here or don't come back."

Gladys scooted out the front door and ran as fast as she could the five blocks to the magistrate's house. She could hardly keep from wetting herself as the cool night air mixed with her panic to create an impossible urge to pee down her leg.

Glenda walked directly to the last cell and rapped her shillelagh gently on the bars. No use waking the lot of them. Better they didn't know who they had in here.

Meg sat up and squinted in the dark to see what the matron wanted.

"Ye're comin' with me."

She opened the cell door and reached in to grab Meg by the wrist. Thinking she was going to be molested by the guards, Meg resisted, pulling away with whispered pleas.

"Please I beg you, no. Please have pity. I promise I'll do whatever you want, just not that, please. I beg you, please don't hurt me."

"Just shut up and come! Ye have a visitor."

Glenda turned Meg around and roughly snapped the

handcuffs on her wrists. Better not take any chances with the judge on his way. Now that she finally said something Glenda thought she sure talked like a duchess.

Dragging the heavy leg irons, Meg walked slowly through one gate after another prodded by the shillelagh at her back. Each gate was closed and locked before they moved on to the next. Finally, they emerged into the guardroom. Meg blinked in the bright light of several wall sconces holding fat sputtering candles. The candles made the room hot and smelly. What a place this was. What a terrible place.

Uncle Robert rose from the table and approached the door before Meg even came through the last gate. When she saw him, she let out a gasp and fainted to the floor. At first, Glenda thought she had died and began to perspire profusely. What now? The judge on his way, the prisoner on the floor and the gentleman towering over her demanding smelling salts. Never had she had so many things go wrong at the same time!

She did find a vial of ammonia kept in the desk drawer for women on their way back from the quarry. Sometimes they worked them so hard out there that they fainted dead away before they could get to their cot. The matron snapped the vial and waved it under Meg's nose. She stirred immediately and Glenda went to help her stand up. But the gentleman got to her first.

"Meg, dearest, let me help you. How did things ever come to this?"

He turned to Glenda and ordered her to fetch a glass of fresh water.

Gently he led Meg into the visitor's room and sat her down. She was still dazed and looked right through him. Glenda brought the water and he coaxed Meg to drink some of it. Gradually, she focused her gaze on him and began to cry. He took her in his arms and let her sob against his chest. Tenderly he wiped her face with his handkerchief like he had when she was a little girl. When she finally calmed down, he sat back in his chair and just looked at her.

He could not believe his eyes. His dear niece, in shackles, her slender ankles rubbed raw and bleeding, her hair matted and filthy, reeking of sweat and vomit. What could he do for her? He had hoped to take her home in the morning but he would not allow her to spend another night in this hellhole. Whatever it took, he would have her at GlynMor Castle tonight.

He stood and looked out into the guardroom. Glenda sat at her desk filling out a form. Before he could demand to see the magistrate, the door burst open and a round beefy fellow with old fashioned mutton chop whiskers barged into the room. He was fuming at having been pulled from his bed not ten minutes after he put on his nightcap.

"Sir! I say, this is an outrage. This matron claims that you are an earl and I must attend to you immediately. I am His Honor, Judge David Sessions and I must insist on a full explanation of this most egregious behavior. What have you to say for yourself?"

Robert introduced himself and explained his reason for being there. He had no proof of his relationship to Meg but he did have her baptismal record found among the documents the other night. He also had his license to practice law and enough cash to post at least part of her bail.

Once the judge realized that Robert was a legitimate barrister and Meg was indeed Lady Margaret Wynn, he asked Lord Cushing what he wanted to do. The woman was charged with attempted murder, after all. Robert offered to post bail and promised to keep Lady Margaret in his custody until her trial could be scheduled. Judge Sessions accepted Lord Cushing's offer of bail and directed Glenda to release the prisoner immediately.

"She may not leave the county for any reason, Lord Cushing. Where do you plan to house her?"

"Her family home is GlynMor Castle in Clydagh Glyn up near Derryhick Lough. She'll have no reason to go elsewhere. God knows she will barely be able to walk about the grounds!"

The judge raised an eyebrow in mock sympathy.

"Very well, then. I'm sure you know the consequences for disregarding the conditions of her release. The court will notify you when you need to bring her to trial."

Robert kept his counsel and merely nodded. He had no intention of this ever going to trial. Lord Robert's intention was not to have Meg stand trial but to have her accuser brought to justice.

Within minutes they were in Beverly's old brougham with Peter driving them home. Meg sat looking out the window at houses and trees flying by. Pretty soon they were far enough from town that it was too dark to see. The carriage lamps swayed and bobbed, shedding eerie splashes of light as they sped along the dusty road. A light rain started just as they made the turn into the long sweeping drive up to GlynMor Castle.

Meg had said little on the ride home and Uncle Robert had respected her silence. She had thought many times about what it would be like to come home but never had her thoughts been as jumbled as they were tonight. It wasn't until they pulled up to the front door that her uncle told her that Tom awaited her inside.

Suddenly the fleeting thought left her and she had but one thought. Tom! Tom waited for her inside. Then Tom was running down the front steps and Tom was scooping her out of the buggy, holding her against his broad chest. The last thought Meg had before they reached the door was that Tom was carrying her back through the very door that had slammed behind him the night that had forever changed their lives.

Rose Phalen broke the last of the crumbling soda bread into a bowl of milk and tried to persuade Martha to eat it. The baby just cried and spit it back at her.

"Come on Martie, have just a wee bit. Look at Sr. Mary

Louis. She cut ye sich a nice piece o'bread and gave ye some o'her own milk. Be a good girl now, and eat."

Martha just wailed and shook her head wildly from side to side. Finally, she climbed down from the bench and toddled through the refectory. She went howling into the courtyard and plopped down on the flagstone walk. Three of the older sisters were walking the Stations of the Cross and stopped to look sternly at the miserable baby. The presence of this family in their usually silent monastery was very disturbing indeed. It had been three days since Fr. Finnegan had deposited them here and he still hadn't returned for them as promised.

Sr. Mary Louis, the novice mistress, was in charge of the kitchen. Her crew of a dozen young sisters was polishing the pans used for breakfast and setting up the long refectory table for lunch. Seeing Rose's failed attempt to feed her baby sister brought her over to the bench by the door.

"Here. Take this damp rag and clean up that mess. Babies do bring messes with them don't they?"

Rose nodded and obediently wiped the soggy bread and milk from the tile floor.

"I'm sorry, Sister."

"There's nothing to be sorry about, child. She won't eat. I'm more worried about her starvin' herself than a little spilled boxtie. The poor thing wants her mam and that's the all of it. Now, take care of her. I can see she's disturbin' the other sisters. Maybe she'll play with yer brother. He always seems to make her laugh. Where is Francis? Find him and see to it that he doesn't get into the chapel again. Yesterday's accident with the wine was most unpleasant."

"Yes, Sister."

Rose didn't like nuns. Their mouths were always smiling without showing their teeth and their eyes never smiled at all. Why would Mary Clare want to live in a place like this? All that praying and bells for everything! Bells to wake up, bells to sit down, bells to walk to chapel, bells to kneel, bells to stand! Was there no end to the ringing?

And the meals! The food was plain but good enough and the nuns had their own cow and vegetable garden so there was plenty to eat. But they couldn't talk! At home and even at Mr. McGee's they all talked around the table. Here they had to keep silent while some nun read from something according to someone at every meal. Ellen had been very naughty about that and, yesterday after breakfast had gotten her knuckles rapped good. Then at lunch she had to stand in the corner after she stuck her tongue out at Sr. Agatha Marie. Last night Rose had tried to talk sense to her but she just pushed out her lip and refused to listen.

Francis loved it here. He was forever messing around in the garden with Sr. Fiacre and she even let him catch bugs in a little jar. Last night after Compline, Sister took him out to the honeysuckle to watch fireflies while she and Mary Clare got the girls ready for bed. The nuns wouldn't let Francis bathe with his sisters because he was a boy. Rose had to get him dressed and undressed by himself.

She turned and looked for Martha. Where had she gone? Just a minute ago she had been sitting on the gravel path wailing. Now Rose couldn't see her anywhere.

"Martha, where are ye? Martie, come t'Rosie! Yoo-hoo! Where's Baby Martie? Where has Rosie's baby gone?"

There was no sign of the little girl though Rose's calling brought Francis and her other sisters running. Ellen, as usual, was pouting about something and Francis, ever the peacemaker, was trying to cheer her by sharing his precious Japanese beetle in a jar.

Ellen stomped up to Rose and shook her finger toward the back of the garden.

"Rose, that sister is givin' Martie berries and beans right off the bush and she wouldn't give me any. She says I'm a sassy fanny and don't deserve any beans."

Francis piped up.

"Sr. Benedict says me full o'beans."

Gracie put her hands on her skinny hips and scowled.

"Martie stinks and Sister says she likes her best anyway.

320

'Tisn't fair! Sister likes stinky Martie better than us even after our bath!"

Rose rolled her eyes and left the children to squabble about which nuns they liked and which were nasty. If Martie stunk, she needed Rose. The nuns drew the line at changing nappies. At least they had been generous in supplying Rose with pieces of soft rags to put on her baby sister.

Just as Rose rounded the path toward the vegetable garden, she was stopped by a wall of black. A very fat nun stood with her back to Rose, blocking the path completely. She could hear Sr. Gerald, the Mistress of Postulants, gently scolding someone. Ducking behind a tall trellis covered with late climbing roses, Rose listened with rapt interest to the conversation.

"Dear, ye're simply too young. Givin' yer life t'Christ as his bride forever is not a decision t'be made lightly. Ye need t'taste life first. That way, ye'll know what ye're sacrificin' when ye enter the monastery walls. Ye must wait until ye're older. What would yer parents say if we just took ye in and they never saw ye again? How old are ye, child?"

A little voice answered.

"Ten. But I'll be eleven in January. Please Sister, 'Tis all I've ever wanted. Even Fr. Finnegan said I have that look about me. Can't ye see it, Sister? Do ye think I have that look?"

Rose was shocked to hear Mary Clare pleading with the nun. Peaches had always wanted to join a convent but Sr. Gerald was right. Da would break down the doors of this place if they took Peaches away from him.

The big nun pulled out a clean white hankie from her pocket and Mary Clare blew her nose.

"Jesus must love ye very much, darlin', if Fr. Finnegan said that. To carry the look of piety at so young an age is a great gift indeed. But ye're still too young. When yer stay here is through ye must go back to yer family. When a few years have passed, if ye still wish to live here with us, ye can come back. Remember child, Jesus returned to his home in obedience to His Blessed Mother and St. Joseph when they found him in the temple of Jerusalem. If ye're to be a bride of Christ someday, ye must sacrifice yer will to His in all things. Ye can begin now by acceptin' His will for ye to be young and free in yer own home with yer own family. He will show ye when the time is right t'return to us. Until then, I will pray very hard fer ye to make the right decision. Do ye promise to pray fer me too?"

"Of course, Sr. Gerald. I really like ye! Of course, I'll pray fer ye. I'll even pray fer Sr. Agatha Marie, even though I don't really like her much."

Rose winced at her sister's bluntness. Fortunately, Sr. Gerald didn't seem to mind. She put her arm around the little girl and together they turned and walked back toward the kitchen.

"What d'ye say we see if Sr. Mary Louis has any of those wonderful sweet rolls left over from breakfast? Sometimes she saves some fer th'poor beggars. I'll bet she might let us be poor beggars if we show up at her door. What d'ye think?"

Mary Clare didn't answer but there was a skip in her step as she headed down the path to see.

Rose was glad Martha had eaten her fill from Sr. Benedict's basket of pickings. She wiped the berry stains from around the baby's mouth and went to rinse out the dirty nappie. She hurried to finish her task because one of the postulants had just told her Mother Catherine wanted to see her in her office. The young nun scooped Martha up and marched off to the front of the building where the Mother Superior waited.

Da! Da must be here to take them all home! He came! Rose knew he'd come. He would never leave them all alone! Rose smoothed her ragged dress and tried to tuck her frizzy curls behind her ears. She wanted to look her best when Da saw her. She was his Lovie after all!

Rose heard Martha fussing before she even entered Mother's office. The nervous postulant was happy to hand the baby over to her sister and at Mother Catherine's nod, bowed slightly and gracefully backed out of the room.

Rose felt her heart sink when she looked around and Da was not there. But her face brightened when she saw her jolly friend from Mundy's Bluff. She hadn't seen him since she had last begged fish from him.

"Mr. Fellowes!"

Rose stopped short and covered her mouth. Mother Catherine had warned her about speaking before she was spoken to. The stern look on the nun's face told her she had been very bad.

Mr. Fellowes didn't seem to mind Rose's greeting one bit. He swept his hat off and bowed before Rose with great drama.

"Miss Phalen! What a pleasure to see you again. You're looking very well, my dear. Much better than the last time we met."

Mother Catherine cleared her voice and glided out from behind her desk. Francis had asked Rose if sisters had legs and she had confessed that she really didn't know. Looking at Sr. Catherine move, she decided that they probably didn't.

"Rose, Mr. Fellowes is here to take you and your siblings to stay with him and Mrs. Fellowes until you can be reunited with your parents. Please gather your brother and sisters and whatever few things you will be taking with you. Of course, you must take anything you brought."

"Yes, Mother."

Rose curtsied politely to Mother Catherine and Mr. Fellowes and awkwardly tried to back out the door like the beautiful young nun had moments before. She crashed into a tall planter filled with ferns and watched in dismay as it began to topple. Mr. Fellowes quickly reached out and caught it but not before a large clod of soil had landed with a plop on the polished floor.

Rose looked up at Mother Catherine, her eyes wide. Mother simply nodded, a look of disdain on her face.

"You will be allowed time to clean that up before you leave, Rose."

"Yes, Sister. Thank you, Sister."

Tearing down the hall toward the kitchen, Martha bouncing in her arms, Rose thought Mary Clare was absolutely insane to want to live in a place like this. Never mind the silence! The look on Mother Catherine's face would freeze stone! Who needed that face souring your milk?

Within the hour they were all bundled into Mr. Fellowes's phaeton and careening through the streets of Castlebar. By three o'clock they had all been scrubbed and were lined up on a bench in the yard wrapped in Turkish towels while their hair dried in the afternoon sun. When Mrs. Fellowes saw the rags they wore, she immediately sent them to be burned and dispatched her two upstairs maids to Gifford's for new clothing for each child. The local cobbler had just finished measuring their feet for shoes and as soon as the girls returned with their new outfits, they were all promised supper in the kitchen.

By nine o'clock they were all tucked into eiderdown featherbeds. Francis and the three little girls were lined up like logs in a huge brass bed while Rose and Mary Clare giggled together under a satin counterpane in a trundle bed filled with plump pillows.

The little ones fell asleep immediately and Rose grew drowsy listening to Mary Clare praying on the beads Sr. Gerald had given her, but she couldn't sleep. The big grandfather clock at the foot of the stairs rang ten and Rose still lay in the dark wondering what would happen to them. She had been so sure Da had come for them she couldn't believe she had been wrong. Mr. And Mrs. Fellowes were very kind but Rose wanted Da and Mam.

So much had happened since she last sat on her father's knee in the rectory of St. Peter's. They were so far away from Westport how would Da ever find them? She knew she should have stayed hidden. Who was that old Mrs. Trent to just haul them off like so many sacks of corn? Then she just goes on to her sister's and leaves them in this strange city so far from home. She began to pray in a soft whisper.

"Dear God, please help Da find us and Mam too. Please, dear Jesus, make Mam all right. Please git her out of jail so we can have her back. And, Jesus, you can kill Mr. Gilchrist if you want to. He's very bad and we don't need him 'atall. You can even send him to hell if you like. Amen."

Mr. Fellowes had said his grandson Jimmy Malone was coming tomorrow to see her. That thought brought Rose a small bit of comfort. Mary Clare had said many times she knew Rose and Jimmy Malone would marry some day. Rose smiled, remembering how she cuffed her sister every time she chanted 'Rosie Malone, Rosie Malone'.

Finally, as the big clock chimed eleven, Rose fell asleep. Her last thought was of kissing Jimmy Malone the way she had practiced on her mother's old looking glass. She was very glad Miss Marie hadn't accepted her offer to kiss the sailors. Saving her kisses for Jimmy Malone seemed like a much better idea.

Chapter Seventeen

"So, you're sure ye don't want yer uncle t'send fer Dr. Simmons."

Tom watched Meg as she sorted through the closet full of old clothes looking for something suitable to wear.

"Tom, I'm fine. My ankles are bruised and I'm tired but otherwise, I'm perfectly fine. I just want to find the children. That's the most important thing."

"Well, ye'll not be able t'do that yerself. And we might as well hear what yer uncle has t'say. He's the man in charge, now isn't he?"

"Tom, you can't still hold it against him that he's a wealthy gentleman. My heavens, he's saved our lives!"

"No! I'm not sayin' that 'atall! I'm that grateful, really. If I thought less of him than I do, I would niver have come t'him fer help. I'm jist sayin' he's the one in charge. Ye're in his custody. I don't even have clothes t'wear now that Sharon went and burned everythin' and yer lookin' at duds that are almost fifteen years old! T'be sure, it's not likely anyone would release our children t'me in this silly silk nightshirt o'yer uncle's! Not even Fr. Finnegan! I'm jist sayin' we need t'talk t'yer uncle and see what he says. And the invitation has been extended t'join him fer breakfast so I'm plannin' t'go.

No reason t'be hungry while I'm waitin' fer the loan of a proper pair of trousers, now is there?"

Meg fastened a belt around her slender waist and smoothed the burgundy silk skirt with her hands. The ruffled fluting at the throat of her pink chiffon blouse was very old fashioned but she didn't care. She could not have told anyone what the current fashions were. It was amazing how little that mattered to her anymore.

She slipped on a pair of house slippers. Her ankles were too sore from the shackles for boots and none of the shoes in her closet fit her after years of going barefoot.

Sitting at her vanity, Meg ran her old boar's bristle hairbrush through her thin, limp curls. The worst spots had started to grow in since they had been eating at Browne's but it would be months before her hair looked even remotely attractive. She rummaged around in a drawer full of lace and sundries. Finally she pulled out an old fashioned mob cap she had brought back from London when she returned after caring for her grandmother. Pulling her hair into a bun on top of her head, she positioned the mob cap to cover the thin spots. Pushing the front into a soft wave, she actually looked nice. Odd but nice.

"There you are, my love. I am officially an old lady. I know now why old women wear these things. They hide a lot!"

Tom approached Meg from behind.

"It's lovely. Really. You looked wonderful to me even when we were starvin' on Achill, Meg. And last night when I carried ye into the drawing room I cried fer the feelin' of ye in me arms. Meg fallin' asleep against yer back last night, all bathed an' smellin' o'lavendar soap, nuzzlin' against me between soft, clean sheets was a little bit o'heaven. But as long as I live, nothin' will ever compare t'the feelin' that went through me when ye fell into me arms, dirty and ragged and cryin' yer heart out before th' door yer father threw me out of all those years ago."

He talked to her reflection in the big gilt mirror.

"Look at me Meg. I haven't laid eyes on me face in five years. I don't even know the man in this mirror. I feel like I'm lookin' at me Uncle Terrance! I'm almost fifty years old, Meg. Look at me with me gray hair and me bony jaw. Yer handsome prince is turnin' into a bit of a frog! Shite, I look older than yer Uncle Robert! Starvation'll do that to a man!"

"But Tom! You still look wonderful to me!"

He laughed and placed his hands gently around Meg's neck, caressing the soft spot below her ears.

"I rest me case. Shite, I shoulda' studied law."

Picking up a maroon silk dressing gown, another loan from Uncle Robert, Tom turned to Meg.

"Come on, Darlin'. Let's go t'breakfast. We may not be fashionable but we'll be a matched set, at that. Don't we have a few children we need t'pick up at St. Brendan's church in Castlebar? Well, I'm fer doin' it on a full stomach."

Uncle Robert stood up when they entered the dining room. Stiller pulled out Meg's chair and she slipped into it as though she had never sat any other way. Molly O'Brien could hardly contain herself as she served them steaming porridge and yellow scrambled eggs. The smell of bacon was enough to make Tom's mouth water. Meg had been able to fry bread in bacon grease at Browne's but it had been years since Tom had actually savored the feel of a rasher in his mouth.

Uncle Robert was almost finished with his meal and stirred sugar into a cup of aromatic Kenyan coffee laced with cream. Setting down his spoon, he turned first to Meg and then to Tom.

"How are you? Did you sleep well? I hope everything was satisfactory."

He smiled at Tom's outfit, noticing that even his loose fitting nightclothes were a bit tight on Tom.

"You are broad in the shoulders aren't you? Today we'll find you something more suitable to wear, though I'm not quite sure how. Perhaps something of Peter's. He's a pretty big lad and might have something you can have until we get you something of your own."

Tom shifted uncomfortably in his chair. He wasn't sure what he ought to wear. Was he about to be dressed as a country gentleman or should he expect to wear livery? It was obvious Meg would find plenty to wear in her old clothes press and dresser. No one had touched any of her things since the night she left.

While Meg had bathed in the kitchen in the big copper tub, Sharon had the upstairs maids scurrying about making up her old room for them. The few pieces George had taken when Meg left were of little consequence and once the room had been aired and fresh linens put on the bed, it was as if she had never been gone.

While Meg sipped tea in the drawing room, Tom bathed. Sharon would have no filth in her house and he almost died when she took a scrub brush to his feet.

Tom was apoplectic relaying the scene to Meg later that evening. He sputtered around a mouthful of nutmeats from the big silver bowl on the table.

"This one was worse than Mrs. Carrey! She had no shame 'atall. Imagine a married woman washing the grimy feet of a man married t'someone else! And me naked as the day I was born! Twas no wonder I didn't drown with the shame of it all."

He smiled at Meg's pleasure in hearing his tale.

"At least I had a fine big sponge t'cover me pride with."

"Well, you certainly would need that and don't I know it."

It was Meg's turn to smile as she ducked a walnut, unceremoniously thrown in her direction.

Tom continued his tale, washing his snack down with a cup of lukewarm tea. Once he had his feet safely under the water, as he soothed his frayed nerves and achy muscles with salts and sweet soap, Sharon had tossed his only clothes onto a bonfire Peter had built in the yard. He thrashed like a madman trapped in the tub until George presented him with the biggest clothes in the house.

So it was that he sat half-listening to Uncle Robert,

wearing the man's own nightshirt and robe as he smiled to himself at the memory of his fine bath in the kitchen of GlynMor Castle.

"I have a plan but I want to hear what you think of it. I intend to turn the tables on Mr. Gilchrist but I have to do it very carefully. He is trying to have you hanged for stealing the deed to the American land that my brother-in-law won some years ago. He has no evidence and the statute of limitations has passed; a fact that I'm sure Mr. Gilchrist has overlooked."

"Gilchrist doesn't even have proof that you ever possessed it. He only knows Lord Jeffrey won it, put it in the pocket of his jacket and never saw it again after you left Clydagh Glyn."

"Also, there is the attempted murder charge. Now, he must be inside out with glee to think he has the power to destroy you both. He is relying on the supposition that because you have been under his authority for so many years you will be the little curs in this dogfight and he will be the big cur. Well, he's making a fatal assumption and he's about to see what happens when a wolf joins the game."

"Time is of the essence but before I can force him to drop the charges against either of you, I have to prepare my case against him. Of course there are other equally urgent matters. The children. We must bring them here as soon as possible."

Robert looked at his niece seriously.

"And your father is failing every day. George told me this morning that someone should probably sit with him around the clock now. He hasn't much longer and your mother needs to be notified. I have thought about all of this and I think I've come up with something that works."

Turning back to Tom, he continued.

"I need you to tell me everything you can remember about all of your dealings with Mr. Gilchrist. Everything: things he said, promises he made, lies he told to and about you. If you can, you must recall any dates, witnesses, documents or anything you can remember to develop a pattern of abuse and evidence of cheating. I couldn't sleep last night so I drafted a letter to Lord Lucan laying out my suspicions that Mr. Gilchrist had malice aforethought when he approached you about paying the rent with your cows in the spring of last year. I want to see if Lord Lucan ever received that rent money. I want to pay a visit to Newport where Mr. Gilchrist conducted business with you but I need to see Lord Lucan first. I know he's residing at his estate outside Castlebar."

Meg sat very still, tears forming in her eyes.

"What about getting our children?"

Tom spoke with firm resolution.

"Don't worry about the children, Meg. I'll retrieve them and have them on your lap by tonight."

Lord Robert stood up and began to pace.

"That won't be easy, Tom. You're supposed to be hiding, remember? As long as you're free you can do anything but you must not risk being seen in Castlebar. We don't know where Gilchrist went after leaving Meg at the prison."

"Well, if ye think I'm goin' t'sit here on me hands."

"No, no! Of course not! I don't expect you to do that. You could be the man to ride to Cushing House and bring my sister to her husband's deathbed. I had thought of sending you to Lucan but Gilchrist could use that against us in court."

"I'm not that keen on doin' yer runnin' fer ye. If yer sister wanted t'be here she would. How do we even know she's not on her way t'see her daughter? She knows from me that Meg's been arrested."

Tom was beginning to get steamed and Meg put her hand on his arm.

"Uncle Robert, how much time do we have to put together the facts you need?"

Meg's uncle looked hurt by Tom's outburst but he couldn't afford to let Tom's ragged nerves waste precious time and energy.

"Well, an hour maybe. I'm thinking George should go to see Lucan with me. I don't know if Gilchrist might return home once he finds out Meg has been released. At this point, I really don't want to encounter him alone. Tom, I apologize for sounding like I was sending you on an errand. I know you want to help. Of course you want to be the one to get your children but you must see the danger."

"I do, I do see th'danger. Our lives have been nothin' but danger since we left Clydagh Glyn in the first place. I suppose I could go t'Cushing House fer ye. I need t'return Bay Rum anyway and git Marie DeVianney's horse back t'her. But I can't do that either, her bein' in Westport! I'm a terrific help, that I am! Especially in me nightie here!"

They all turned when they heard Stiller clear his voice in the doorway.

"Sir, a gentleman to see you. He has a priest with him."

"Who? Me?"

Tom and Robert asked the question in unison.

"Actually he wasn't specific. He simply asked to see the man of the house. I knew he would not be referring to Lord Wynn. He's with a Roman priest, sir."

"Very well, have them wait in the drawing room."

"Yes, sir."

Uncle Robert stretched out his arm toward Meg and Tom.

"Shall we?"

The three crossed the foyer to see what the men wanted.

Robert Gilchrist stood in rigid silence. He could not believe what he was hearing. After waking this morning convinced he had pneumonia, he had barely managed to dress himself and take nourishment. His chest was raw with coughing and he would swear he had broken a rib. His fever had left him in a pool of sweat around dawn but if the horrendous chills creeping up his spine were any indication it was climbing again. And now this imbecile with the blackest teeth he'd ever seen, was telling him Meg Phalen was gone.

"Gone! What do you mean gone?"

"I mean gone. Some rich dandy posted bail last night and she's gone."

The ugly matron looked up from her papers and shot him a grisly black grin.

"Sorry. Now if ye don't mind yer standin' in me light."

Robert Gilchrist could hardly contain himself. If blasting this insolent woman to hell and back wasn't such an effort she'd be on her way. Instead, all he could muster was a snarled question through clenched teeth.

"Do you know where she went?"

She didn't even give him the benefit of her foul teeth this time as she continued shuffling forms.

"Sorry. That's privileged. If ye like we can deliver a message t'her barrister fer ye."

"She has a barrister?"

"Yup. Same gent who posted her bail. Now, I suggest ye leave. Ye don't want me t'be callin' me supervisor d'ye?"

"Don't be insolent. I demand to speak to the judge. Who is handling this case?"

"Sorry. Privileged."

"Listen you piece of trash! You are obviously enjoying this. Now, you will do as I say or you will be looking for another position. I am not a well man. I have filed charges against Mrs. Phalen for attempting murder on my life. I will see her or I will know why not. Who is the judge on this case? If you won't let me see him here I will see him at home. Look at me when I address you!"

Gladys stood up as Glenda entered the room. This was their silent warning signal.

"Trouble Gladys?"

"This here gentleman insists on seein' th'duchess or th'judge and won't take no for an answer on either count."

Glenda had just found a prisoner dead in her cell and was not in a mood to discuss Mr. Gilchrist's rights.

"Let's go. 'Tis goodbye t'ye, now."

"I am not leaving until I see the judge! Now see here!

Take your filthy hands off of me! I am not well! Put down that baton or I'll have you arrested for assault. What are you doing? See, here, you're hurting me!"

Gilchrist's last words were spoken to the outside of the massive iron door to the guardroom of the Castlebar Prison. He stood staring at the black barrier as he heard the bolt inside turn. He couldn't believe it. He had been hustled out the door by two women! This was an outrage! He thought of going back and pounding on the door until he was allowed back in but he was too weak. The exertion of his forced departure threatened to start a fit of coughing. He started toward his hotel and remembered that he had checked out. He had intended to head home after stopping in to see Meg Phalen. He wanted to remind her of how long death by hanging actually took.

Now she was gone. But who would bail her out of jail? No one even knew she was here. What rich man had done it? The thought occurred to him that it may have been her father but that was ludicrous. What about that uncle of hers? No, Gilchrist distinctly remembered him saying he was off to Killarney and home. Gilchrist sat on a bench in the public garden across the street from the prison.

Carriages and bustling people sped by. Nannies with their charges in prams and wagons strolled along the walkways. Constables shooed away the dozens of hungry beggars that littered the place looking for a free meal. Gilchrist kicked dust in the face of a man he thought slept in the grass at the end of the bench. When the man never even flinched, he realized with a start that he was dead. How disgusting these people were. Didn't they even have the decency to find a secluded place to do their dying? Shaking his head, he went to another bench.

He supposed he might as well go home. Mrs. Gilchrist wouldn't be there but the servants could take care of him. Henry hadn't gone with the family and he supposed someone stayed to cook for the gardeners and the rest of the staff left behind.

He was so tired. He could go to GlynMor Castle. Maybe Meg Phalen was there. But he had just been there and they wouldn't even let him see Jeffrey. They certainly wouldn't tell him if she was being hidden there. Besides, he wasn't sure how Jeffrey would take to him pressing charges against his daughter. He was disgusted and angry with her but Jeffrey was weak and weak men could sometimes harbor sniveling sentimentality. No, it wouldn't be worth his time to go there.

Damn! This was not working out as he had hoped. He couldn't see Meg Phalen hang if he had no control over her solicitor. No one would tell him anything, so he could only assume her children had been dispatched to the workhouse in Westport. He could only hope that at least that part was settled. Damn them all. He really didn't care anymore.

He could return to his uncle's nearby country home but his uncle would probably want him to entertain his insufferable Aunt Bea. And his mother was there too. It never ceased to amaze him that such a silly woman could have given birth to a man of such ambition and promise as Robert Gilchrist. He never knew his father. He had died when Robert was a baby but he must have inherited his brains from the Scots side of the family. His mother's head was surely full of stuffing.

No, he wouldn't want to return to his uncle's. He couldn't face the fawning and fussing over his fine position as Uncle George's undertaker. He could go to Tipperary and reunite with his family but all those squealing girls were such a penance. Robert Gilchrist found himself in a quandary. He had no immediate plans and could think of nowhere he wanted to be except bed.

He headed for the bank. He needed to withdraw some funds and try to decide whether to book another room here in Castlebar or purchase a coach fare to Newport. As he crossed the parkway toward Butler St. and the financial district, a phaeton carrying a big rowdy family passed by. Just as they rounded the corner the horses trotted through a deep puddle left after last night's rain. Mr. Gilchrist waved his walking stick and cursed them all as he wiped the muck from his chin and surveyed the blotches of slimy black ooze that dribbled down his gray silk vest.

Lady Beverly gently prodded Sunday Morning along the bridle path guiding him away from the low hanging branches of the monkey trees. The storm that had blown in from the north during the night had drenched the Killarney area while she slept. Now, the tall yew trees and shorter, fuller monkey trees along the banks of the lakes dripped in a staccato melody all around her.

What a glorious day! She marveled at the clear white rays of the morning sun piercing the forest and dappling the path before her. The storm had moved on hours ago but the dense canopies of the trees shed their soggy raiment in spurts of droplets flung from their branches on the gusty breeze.

Beverly loved this ride, especially in late morning as the sun climbed to its pinnacle over the serene panorama of the Lakes of Killarney. The sun dipped in and out of the low clouds, changing the smooth surface of the lake from clear green to silver, inviting the observer to plumb the secrets of her depths. Tiny islands seemed to float on the surface, seemingly ready to peel away and float heavenward in the next good wind. Strong, hard rock formations reached far into the center of the lake grasping the cool, deep water and clasping it close to shore in secret eddies and inlets filled with fairy life and mythical night creatures.

She gave the horse his head, allowing him to wander off the path at will. Sunday Morning, himself, apparently recognized the rare beauty of his surroundings. He trotted contentedly along the path until a bucolic vista opened up before him and then stopped, facing the lake.

Anglers launched their lines deep into the clear silver water, breaking the stillness with gentle ripples that lapped against the low overgrown shore. Herons swept across the reeds and tended their nests deep in the cattails. Hawks circled overhead, swooping and diving on the air currents high above the treetops. Beverly sat upon Sunday's broad back and soaked in the healing peace of the place until the horse decided it was time to move on.

When they finally reached the end of the path where it turned at the stone bridge near the waterfall, Beverly dismounted. This was her favorite spot to sit and think. A large square rock sat only feet from a low bluff that formed the shore of the brook that fed the lower lake from the tumbling water of the higher elevations. The green palace formed by the mountains of Kerry's Ring was surely one of the most beautiful in all Ireland. With the ring of emerald coated highlands falling down into the deep shadow of the valley and the lakes below studding the landscape like huge glistening diamonds, surely there could be no other place so gorgeous.

Beverly sat down on the rock and pulled off her riding gloves and bonnet. She loosened her hair as she watched her horse pick his way down to the water. He drank his fill and she soaked in the view. The stone bridge was old and speckled with lichens and patches of lush green moss. The water bubbled under the bridge's three low arches, tumbling over rocks to form tiny waterfalls and swirling eddies all the way to the lake.

Beavers had built dams along the way and water spiders created tiny circlets and rings that spread out in ripples hardly visible to the eye. It was no wonder that the common folk believed that fairies inhabited these waters. Look at the evidence. Their very breath beneath the surface sent tiny bubbles skyward and the stick villages abandoned by beaver families gave them a perfect dwelling place.

Sunday Morning came over and nuzzled her hand. She dug a sugar cube from her pocket and treated him to his favorite snack.

"What shall I do, Sunday? Shall I go home? Leave these cool waters and head back to the home I grew up in? Should I try to reconcile with Meg? Could I even hope for that?"

She stroked the soft gray nose and let the horse lick her palm. Tears spilled over her cheeks as she thought about her life.

"You know, Sunday, I haven't been a very good person. Long before you came to me, I spent most of my life pitying myself and wishing I had never married and borne a child."

She sniffed loudly and blew her nose in a white lace hanky.

"I was so well loved as a child I couldn't help expecting that of a husband. Oh, Sunday, I made such a bungle of the whole thing! Jeffrey was so terribly disappointing as a lover and such a tyrant to live with, I simply folded up my tent and gave up. But Meg never deserved the coldness I gave her! It's just that I was in so much pain! And it all started when she came along. Sunday, oh sweet Sunday Morning, how was I supposed to feel? My husband no longer wanted me and it was all because of her!"

Beverly sat alone in the woods, crying out years of pain and self-loathing into the little hanky until it was nothing more than a limp, soggy wad in her hand. When she finally cried herself dry, she leaned her head against the smooth gray shank and wrapped her arm around the horse's leg. He stood still and let her lean on him, responding to her sighs with tender whinnying.

Finally she stood up and fished around in her pocket again. Another sugar cube was Sunday's reward for his gentle friendship. She pulled on her gloves and tied her bonnet to the saddle. She wanted her hair to blow free. Nobody cared how she looked anyway. Together she and her horse turned and started the winding walk home.

They cantered along the path until they approached the ruins of an old Franciscan monastery. Beverly dismounted again and led the horse by the reins. Together they wandered through the tiny graveyard filled with crosses of all shapes and styles. Large Celtic crosses carved from stone or wrought from iron marked many of the graves, while some of the humble friars had nothing but crumbling heaps of loose stones to mark their final resting place. The graves were all overgrown and most of the inscriptions were caked with lichens and completely unreadable.

Beverly wondered who the people beneath the soft green grass were. They had all had lives filled with pains and sorrows, joys and triumphs. Certainly the friars had achieved the glory of heaven. What of the others? What had been the deeds that merited the big stone cross or the large sarcophagus? In the end, who really deserved any of the trappings of the dead? Moreover, who really cared?

She came upon a grave that was in remarkable condition given the fact that this cemetery had obviously been abandoned for years. The gravestone had sunk almost half-way into the ground but what remained in view was maintained with painstaking care. The moss and lichens had been carefully scraped off and the chalky stone gleamed in the sun after last night's rain. There was a short, white wrought iron fence all around the little plot. Planted along the inside of the fence were beautiful deep purple shamrocks that had produced showers of tiny pink blooms that bobbed in the breeze. Beverly had never seen leaves that color on a shamrock. They were almost black and the delicate pink blossoms were so dainty they appeared to float above the thick clusters of leaves. She noted one spot to the left of the gravestone where the plant had withered and died. What a shame. One sad little spot marred the beauty of the rest.

Beverly bent to read the inscription on the small humble stone. It read, simply, 'Beloved Mother'. The rest, the name and even the birth and death dates were buried beneath the well-clipped grass. She would never know who the beloved mother was! She found herself on her knees, pulling at the grass, trying to peel it back so she could read what was written below but she couldn't do it. Sitting before the little white stone, Beverly began to cry again. Sunday Morning had wandered off to graze in a patch of clover and there was no one to hear her now.

She cried for her own mother, for herself and Jeffrey's mother who had been her friend. She wept for Adelaide and little Madeleine. She cried for Meg and the loss of her sons, grandsons Beverly would never know. She cried hot stinging tears of remorse and the knowledge that someday she too would lie beneath a white stone in a cemetery filled with dead strangers.

What would be written on her grave? Would Meg ever be able to stomach placing the words 'Beloved Mother' on a stone bearing her name? Would she ever forgive her for all the times she needed her and Beverly was not there?

No. It was hopeless. Given what Robert said, Meg may not even outlive her! No one would ever put 'Beloved Wife' or 'Beloved Mother' on her grave and she didn't deserve either. All she could hope for was 'Beloved Sister'. That she could count on though it was cold comfort indeed.

She rose from the sod and brushed the grass from her black serge skirt. As she and Sunday Morning started to pass the crumbling ruins she heard a scraping from behind her. Turning around she saw through a blur of tears, a ragged old man dragging a spade along the path to the pretty little grave. In his other hand he carried a sack from which bobbed the tiny pink blossoms of a deep purple shamrock, the likes of which Beverly had never seen before today. As she watched the man reverently scoop out the dead plant to make room for the new one, she new what she must do. She and Sunday Morning hastened back to Cushing House. Lady Beverly needed to dispatch a messenger announcing her impending arrival at GlynMor Castle.

Meg and Tom rushed to the drawing room knowing the priest must be Fr. Finnegan. After all, Andrew had told her the plan. But who was the other man? Neither of them spoke. Fear had gripped their throats as they prepared for the worst.

Stiller threw open the double doors of the drawing room

and the two men stood up. Smiling broadly Fr. Finnegan approached Meg and Tom. Meg let out a sigh of relief at his expression and Tom went to shake his hand.

"Oh, my dear friends, I have such good news for you! This is Mr. Joshua Fellowes, a parishioner at St. Brendan's. He and his wife have your children in their custody. They are safe and being cared for most lovingly by his household. We weren't certain we would find you here or we would have brought them directly. Fortunately Mr. Fellowes's home is on the outskirts of Castlebar about half-way between here and there."

Meg's knees gave out and Tom scooped her in his arms. He deposited her in Robert's favorite leather chair and turned to embrace Joshua Fellowes. Pulling back he stood with his hands on the other man's shoulders.

"How does a father thank a stranger fer the lives of his children? May God bless you and yers ferever. I can think of no better gift to wish on ye."

His voice cracked as he tried and failed to say more.

Uncle Robert offered the two men refreshment and Stiller arrived in moments with a tray laden with pastries and coffee.

The two men had much to tell and enjoyed the rapt attention given them by the grateful parents. Once they had reassured Meg of the health and well-being of each individual child, they asked what the grateful parents wished them to do next. Uncle Robert suggested that Meg and Tom both go with Fr. Finnegan and Mr. Fellowes to retrieve the children. He would have Peter prepare the Phaeton for them immediately.

Tom stood scowling at his wife's uncle.

"Have you forgotten me nightie or is it now fashionable t'traipse around the countryside dressed fer bed?"

Meg burst out laughing and Uncle Robert couldn't help smiling.

"Tom, I am so sorry. I forgot you are compromised in your attire. We must get you something that you can wear for the trip. I just don't know anyone as large as you. Anything you wear would certainly be uncomfortable if not impossible to move in."

Mr. Fellowes looked Tom over and spoke up.

"What about me? I'm about the same breadth in the chest though my trousers would be way too big. I do have a second outfit in the buggy. I always keep a satchel packed for travel between Castlebar and Westport. You're certainly welcome to whatever pieces fit."

"Thank you, Mr. Fellowes but…"

Meg stood up.

"I'm sure it would be most satisfactory, sir. If we can find trousers of a suitable size, we can leave right away."

Uncle Robert circled Tom checking out his dimensions in the tightly cinched dressing gown.

"My trousers will fit you Tom. You're really quite slim through the waist and hips."

Within moments they had cobbled together a respectable outfit for Tom to wear. As they all walked to the front door, Lord Cushing asked Fr. Finnegan a question.

"How did you know Mrs. Phalen had been brought to GlynMor?"

"Oh, I simply asked the matron at the desk. She was happy to tell me anything I needed to know."

Lord Robert nodded.

"Yes, I found them to be quite reasonable myself."

While Meg and Tom got ready, Uncle Robert made arrangements with Mr. Fellowes to return Marie DeVianney's horse. He had assured Lord Robert that he would have his own groom retrieve the animal from Cushing House and return her to Westport.

They said their goodbyes and Meg and Tom were off to get the children. Shortly after the big Phaeton pulled away from GlynMor Castle a rider approached with a message for Lord Robert Cushing from his sister. She was due to arrive within three days. If he was going to see his friend Lucan in Newport, and be back in time for her arrival, he had better leave at once. Within a half hour, two more horses galloped down the long drive beneath the towering yew trees. George and Robert were off to Newport to bring justice to the family they loved.

Rose Phalen pulled away from the boy who shared the bench behind the booley with her. The empty basket she had been holding rolled away under a bush. Jimmy Malone had just mashed his closed lips against hers in what was her first kiss. Her only thought was how hard it was to believe sailors would pay good money for such a bland experience.

He put his arm around her shoulder, drawing her near to his side. Together they gazed out over the fields of wheat and barley on his grandfather's farm. High above the golden fields, sheep grazed against rugged, stony outcroppings dotted with short gnarled trees.

"Rosie Phalen, ever since I first laid eyes on ye I've known ye're the lass fer me. Tell me ye feel the same and I'll wait fer ye ferever."

Rose said nothing. At almost thirteen she felt a bit differently than she had a year ago when the only thing she did to Jimmy Malone with her mouth was stick her tongue out. She had missed him and his round smiling face. After they moved to Westport she had never seen him despite the fact that his grandfather owned that big inn up on the Louisburg Road. She had been busy enough helping Mam at Browne's Inn at the bottom of the hill. There was no time to go exploring anybody else's inn.

"Rose?"

Still she kept her tongue silent. She did like Jimmy very much. He was very cute and had loads of freckles on his face and arms. He was strong and muscular from lugging kegs of beer and creels of fish for his granda. He had curls like her but they were sandy colored and at sixteen, his beard hadn't grown much. He had big feet and hands but he wasn't much taller than she was. She doubted he would ever be as big as

Da. But then, almost nobody was as big as Da.

"Rose, answer me! D'ye think ye'd like t'marry me some day? I sure would like t'marry you."

Rose didn't want to answer him. She had just reached the end of Miss Jane Austen's book, *Pride and Prejudice* and her heart belonged to Mr. Darcy. How could she love this boy whose kiss was not much different from the ones she had shared with her mother's looking glass? Now, Mr. Darcy; Rose supposed he could really kiss.

"Jimmy, I like ye. Lots. But ye can't expect me t'know anythin' about gittin' married, saints alive! I'm only thirteen! Besides. Ye need some practice with th'kissin'."

Jimmy blushed all the way to the roots of his sandy curls. When he turned Rose's face toward his, she thought his light brown freckles looked sort of green against the vivid pink of his face. But Jimmy wasn't about to give her much time to look at his green freckles. He took her face in his hands and kissed her again.

This time he pushed her lips apart with his own and ran his tongue across her lower lip. He pulled her into a tight embrace and let his mouth linger maddeningly over hers, tasting and exploring her sweet lips. He kept her mouth captive to his until he could feel her breathlessness against him. Pulling away slightly, he gently kissed her cheeks and eyelids. Then he let her go and stood up.

As Rose gasped for breath and tried to steady herself on the stone bench, Jimmy walked away toward the booley. He swept the basket from under the bush and ducked into the little stone hut, scattering squawking chickens as he bent to gather eggs. He peeked at her through a tiny louvered window and smiled to himself. She still sat where he had left her, stunned at the sensations aroused by her second kiss.

"Tis that glad I am ye like me, Rose. Now, fer the kissin' part. I was only tryin' t'break ye in slowly, 'tis all. I'm not about given ye the wrong impression, now am I? I mean ye're a lady and I'm a gentleman and all that. So, now that ye know what I can do, I'm more than willin' t'go back to the other way while ye decide whether ye liked the second kiss or not. Then if ye decide ye want more of that kind o'kissin' well, it'll be there once we say 'I do'."

Rose had quite recovered her equilibrium when she heard the taunting in Jimmy's voice. Furious that he had teased her so effectively, she balled her fists and stormed off toward the house. Spurred on by the sound of his chuckling, she blew through the kitchen door and marched straight to Mary Clare's room where she sat down with a thud on the cushioned window seat.

Gracie looked up from a puzzle she was working with Ellen.

"What's put th'bee in yer bonnet?"

"Oh, Bother! Can't you children ever leave me in peace?"

She turned on her heel and stalked off to the other bedroom where she had been sleeping with Francis and Martha.

"Peaches? Where are ye? I'm wantin' t'tell ye somethin'!"

Grace looked at Ellen and shrugged. Sometimes their older sisters were impossible to figure out.

George and Robert made the trip to Castlebar in record time. It had been a long time since George had ridden so hard and he knew he would be sore but he didn't care. He had found the thundering hooves and rippling flanks of the huge black stallion beneath him a most exhilarating experience. He rode Jet, the son of Lord Wynn's old horse Angus. The animal was so black he looked blue in certain light. There wasn't a spot of any other color on him. Even his eyes were black. Robert had taken Chester, who had been raring to go after his rest. Together they traveled the coach road not far behind Meg and Tom and the men who had rescued their children. They arrived at Lord Lucan's estate outside Castlebar by mid-afternoon. The house was set much closer to the coach road than most estates. There was a high wall adorned with two wrought iron gates that stood open to let a small, open buggy carrying two women exit the grounds. Before the gatekeeper could stop them, Robert and George had galloped through and were already dismounting.

When they arrived at the front entrance, liveried groomsmen took the sweaty horses into the stables to be rubbed down and rested. George stood at the door waiting to be admitted with Lord Robert. He felt strange entering this massive home by the front door. He couldn't remember ever entering GlynMor Castle by the front door. The breathless gatekeeper arrived to apprehend the intruders just as Lord Robert handed his calling card to the stone-faced butler. Before he could object, the two men had been admitted into the foyer and the door closed in his face.

The butler showed them to a small sitting room and went to announce them. Lord Lucan was just sitting down to lunch in the massive dining room and invited them to join him.

"Robert! What a pleasant surprise!"

The rotund gentleman stood at his place and waved Robert and George to places at the long polished table. Two menservants pulled chairs out for them on either side of his lordship.

"Thank you for seeing us Lucan. It is really quite rude to be barging in on your midday meal like this. Forgive us but our mission is rather urgent. Please let me introduce you to my friend George Spiner. George, His Lordship, George Bingham, 3rd. Earl of Lucan."

George bowed deeply.

"The honor is mine, sir."

"Nonsense!" Lucan bellowed, "Any friend of Cushing is a friend of mine. Sit, Sit. I insist you dine with me."

He snapped his fingers.

"Gertrude! Evelyn! More soup for our guests."

Two maids stepped away from their respective positions against the wall. One was thin and pale, about fifteen and timid as a rabbit. The other was a woman of about forty, plump, rosy and obviously the experienced superior to the other.

Turning first to Robert then to George, Lord Lucan smiled.

"You've barely missed Lady Lucan. She and her sister just left to take tea in town. But that suits me well, Robert. My wife always had a sweet spot in her heart for you. Best not to make me jealous! My physician says I must watch out for too much excitement. Missed you at the hunt. Didn't realize you were at Killarney now. Sent the invite to the wrong place."

Robert began to sip his broth and took a thick slab of warm soda bread from a sterling silver basket proffered by the young maid. George followed suit, nervous about making the wrong move.

"Tell me, Robert, how are things with you? How is your sister and that handsome devil she married? My word, I haven't seen them in fifteen or twenty years. He had some sort of accident awhile back didn't he?"

Robert thought his friend would never shut up long enough for him to plead his case.

"Well, George, that's partly why I'm here. There has been a bit of ugliness and I need to know some things from you."

George sat in rapt admiration while Lord Cushing gave Lord Lucan every bit of information he needed without ever once revealing the scandal that accompanied Meg Wynn's marriage to Tom Phalen. Equally adept at the politics of gentrified living, Lord Lucan behaved as if titled ladies married peasant Irishmen every day. George was amazed at the delicate dance these men did around the facts of the situation, never offending, never prying but always frank and honest in their remarks.

By the time the three men had indulged in two servings of raspberry fool and had drunk several demitasse cups of strong coffee, all of the cards were on the table. Lucan thoughtfully sipped a glass of sherry, mulling over the deftly veiled accusations against his nephew. Robert discreetly looked out the window as he stirred his cold coffee and politely waited until his friend could reply to the shocking possibility that his nephew had robbed not only Tom Phalen but Lucan himself. George Spiner simply focused on his right index finger as it traced its way up and down the satin stripes of the white damask tablecloth.

Finally Lord Lucan spoke.

"Robert you have my full permission to investigate any and all of Robert Gilchrist's property. I am simply appalled at the things you have told me. The man, if he indeed swindled Tom Phalen out of his livelihood, then he directly caused the death of his two sons. And if you are correct about his assault on Lady Meg, and I have no reason to assume otherwise, then he is guilty of subjecting a fine member of the gentry to the incomparable humiliations of the jailhouse. If he is found guilty of these other heinous crimes, he must also be found guilty of causing the indelible wound to Lady Meg's heart at the loss of her eldest son to the high seas."

"And that doesn't even address his offenses against me. Anything he did to Tom Phalen while the man was my rental agent is a punishable offense against me and I will see him prosecuted! Is there no end to his avarice? I am ashamed to call him my kin, Robert. I am sorry for his mother, my wife Beatrice's dear, lovely sister, Bernice."

He turned to the older of the two maids.

"Fetch Grimes for me, Evelyn."

When the butler came to the table, Lord Lucan told him to go to his office and bring him some of his heavy vellum and a pen. He also demanded his seal and fresh wax.

Robert and George excused themselves while Lord Lucan wrote out an order to the constable in Newport to allow Mr. Gilchrist's premises and belongings to be searched. He instructed the constable to assist the two bearers of this missive in any way he could, giving them complete authority to confiscate anything they found. He requested Lord Robert be given every opportunity to view any and all evidence collected in order to build his case against Mr. Gilchrist. When he was finished and the seal was in place he sent Evelyn to summon them from the garden where they had taken a stroll.

The two men had walked to the far end of a long row of cypresses and Evelyn was flushed and breathless as she delivered her message. When she curtsied, George noticed how her crisp white mobcap bobbed against the thick auburn braids that wrapped her head. He found himself smiling as he absently admired the way her skirt swished as she hurried ahead of them back to the house.

Two hours after they arrived at Lord Lucan's home, George and Robert galloped out the way they had come in. As the gatekeeper closed the big iron gates behind them, he had a feeling he would be seeing those two again.

No sooner had Rose stormed into the Fellowes' kitchen and raced up the stairs, did the bell chime to announce someone at the front door. The maids were all doing laundry and the cook had her hands in a gooey batch of pie dough. Again the bell chimed and Rose started down the stairs. Mary Clare got there first. Using both hands, she pulled open the heavy oak door.

Rose saw that it was only Fr. Finnegan and Mr. Fellowes. She sighed and turned to go back upstairs. Then she heard her sister squeal.

"Mam! Da! Oh, Father! Mr. Fellowes! Look, look everyone they're here! They aren't dead after all!"

Tom bent and scooped Mary Clare into a tight embrace.

"Dead is it? Who's been sayin' I'm dead? Ye can see fer yerself I'm as fit as a fiddle. And if I had me fiddle we'd all dance a jig!"

Rose almost collided with Fr. Finnegan trying to reach her mother.

She buried her face in her mam's soft blouse and bounced up and down like a little child, her arms wrapped tightly around her mother's waist.

Mrs. Fellowes, who had been writing letters upstairs, now

descended the stairs with the little ones. Only Martha, sound asleep on the Fellowes' big bed, was left out. Francis tried to act as though he didn't care that his parents had returned. He hung back in the shadow of a potted cactus and pretended he couldn't be seen. When his da reached around and grabbed him in an embrace, he balked and resisted being lifted up. Gracie and Ellen clung to their mam's skirt clamoring for a hug. They had to wait their turn as Rose and then Mary Clare had their moments. Once Meg was able to release Mary Clare, she knelt on the floor and scooped up her little girls and Francis, who finally decided he wanted hugs too.

Tom took Lovie by the hand and together they walked over to a settee and sat down. He held her close and told her how proud he was of her courage at Miss Marie's. For the first time, Rose felt awkward in her father's arms, the memory of Jimmy Malone's kiss so fresh in her mind.

Suddenly shy, she blushed and had trouble meeting Da's eyes. He thought nothing of it, believing it to be the result of Rose's bashfulness over having been at Marie's. He was simply overjoyed to see all his children looking so well, he could think of nothing but hugging them over and over.

Without warning, Francis looked around, his face screwed up, ready to cry.

"Dinny!"

He ran outside calling his brother's name.

"Dinny, time to come home!"

His little sing-song voice carried over the lawn to the street.

He ran over to the iron fence and climbed up on the first rung.

"Dinny! Dinny! Come home!"

When his big brother failed to appear, he turned away from the fence. He stood in the center of the gravel path, his little body folded in half at the waist. In this posture he emitted a wail filled with such grief that Meg left Gracie and Ellen on the walk and gathered him, shaking, into her arms. There on the walkway she knelt, enfolding her little son against her bosom, crooning and rocking him against the pain they shared, knowing that Denny wasn't going to come home. Poor Francis! He had no understanding of what was going on but was old enough that it mattered.

Mrs. Fellowes, who had taken a great liking to his charming mannerisms and perpetual smile, was deeply moved at his sad little realization that his only brother was missing. She quietly urged Tom and Meg to consider joining her and Mr. Fellowes for lunch. It would give Martha a chance to have a good nap and the rest of the children to adjust to all the excitement.

They all piled into the Fellowes' dining room and eagerly tucked into a splendid vegetable stew and popovers dripping in butter. Cook had baked two rhubarb pies and served them warm with thick yellow cream. Young Jimmy Malone joined them for lunch. Only Mary Clare was aware of the change in the air between him and Rose. She knew something was up and smiled to herself every time Jimmy looked at Rose and winked. He was the freshest boy Mary Clare had ever met but she loved the way he looked at her Rosie. In fact, if Mary Clare hadn't already decided to enter a convent, she might have wished he'd wink at her.

They left around three o'clock. The cobbler who was commissioned to make the Phalen children shoes had only finished Rose's and Mary Clare's but Mrs. Fellowes promised to have them delivered to GlynMor castle as soon as the order was completed. There was absolutely no arguing with her about payment. She was adamant that she and Mr. Fellowes had taken on the children and had been delighted to do so. The shoes were just a small part of that commitment. Joshua Fellowes bundled up a few shirts and a vest for Tom until Tom could have some clothes made. He was equally impervious to Tom's protests about that.

They were already to go when they realized Rose wasn't in the buggy. The adults called and went back into the house to find her but she was nowhere to be found. Tom was growing impatient to leave before the Fellowes' found more things to give them.

Mary Clare thought she might know where Rose was. Before her parents could protest, she had started down the path to the outbuildings. As Meg watched her run along the stone fence she suddenly felt as though she had seen this place before.

High behind the house and garden rose a row of hills dotted with sheep grazing. Wash hung on the clothesline stretched between the house and one of the boolies out back. Another line was tethered between two fruit trees. Small hillocks of hay were mounded neatly in the field and boxes of pretty summer flowers decorated the windows.

Meg scanned the property. What was missing here? She knew she had been here but there was something about it that wasn't complete. Suddenly she heard a shrill whistle from the foot of the hill and two border collies began the round up of the sheep. Meg realized with a start that she had indeed seen this place before! This was the lovely farm she and Tom and Maureen had passed on their original trip to Turlough and Newport. She remembered clearly the man waving to them from that very door on the side of the house. Over lunch, Joshua Fellowes had said that this farm had been in his family for three generations. The man who waved must have been him!

How strange that she had exchanged greetings with him, a stranger, only to have him save their lives toward the end of their stay on Achill by generously giving them fish from his own stock. Then in an even more bizarre twist, he saved these same children again by taking them into the very house Meg had passed so many years ago. All those coincidences gave Meg a chill. She wondered if fate had any other plans for encounters between them.

Mary Clare found Rose behind the booley with Jimmy. They were just sitting staring out at the high grazing sheep, saying nothing and looking forlorn. Rose shot her sister a look but left the bench and followed her without saying anything to Jimmy. She had heard them all calling her but he was kissing her again and she didn't want him to stop. His goodbye kiss wasn't like the first one or the second one. Instead, he took her mouth in his with sadness and a longing that brought tears to her eyes. Neither of them had said anything. Everything they wanted to say had been in that kiss. For all either of them knew they would never see each other again. As she turned away from him, she thought at first it was the wind in the trees, but then she distinctly heard him whisper to her back.

"I will wait, Rose Phalen, I will wait."

Robert and George again rode hard this time along the coach road to Newport. They weren't sure if they'd find Gilchrist at home and wanted to get Lord Lucan's order to the police as soon as possible. If he were not at home, the search would be easier but they had to have the warrant to legally search Mr. Gilchrist's property. Once the police had his lordship's order in hand they could have a judge issue the warrant immediately. In the meantime, the two men could use a hot meal and a good night's sleep.

They arrived in Newport shortly after dusk and went immediately to the station house. The chief of police was the son of a judge and was able to get a warrant signed within the hour. While he did this, Robert and George registered at the local hotel and supped in the hotel dining room. The food was plain but hearty and by the time the constable approached them with the signed paper, they were full of salmon and Irish Apple Cake and enjoying a glass of port together.

The two men hadn't had much to talk about during dinner. They were both fatigued from the events of the last few days and their hard ride had left them bone weary and ready for an early night. The message from the police chief was for them to meet him at the station house at their earliest convenience. They decided to rise early and commence searching for the deed to Tom Phalen's property and any other evidence of Gilchrist's chicanery immediately after breakfast. As soon as they retired to their rooms, the exhausted sleuths were sound asleep.

George awoke to the sound of thunder and the chill of the sea breeze across his chest as a storm blew in across Newport Bay. He sprang from the bed and cranked the casement window shut just as the first big drops began to hit. Returning to bed he closed his eyes and listened to the storm. He wondered how he had ever arrived at this place in his life.

When he first took the position as Lord Jeffrey Wynn's manservant, he had no idea that someday, at the beginning of his twilight years, he would be involved in a mission of such queer subterfuge. Here he was, his master dying, very likely calling for him, miles away in pursuit of proof that one of his friends had committed grievous crimes against his family. Some twist of fate for a man who preferred the tasks of polishing shoes and lining up trousers in a clothes press!

He thought of the night Lord Cushing interviewed him behind the old Phalen house. Lord in heaven he had been scared! George had always thought of himself as a man not easily ruffled. He certainly had never been one to scare easily. Hadn't he been the one to take the situation in hand the night of the accident? But he admitted to himself that he had been afraid to meet Lord Cushing. That encounter had had legions of possibilities to destroy his tidy predictable life at GlynMor Castle. He still marveled that he had been able to do justice to Lord Wynn and still give Lord Cushing what he needed to know.

He felt rumblings in his belly and looked at his watch, lying on the bed table. Time to get up. He walked over to the ewer and bowl and took out his shaving gear. The sun cast a bright yellow streak across the marble top of the commode and he shook his head. The storm was over. If it hadn't awakened him he wouldn't know it had ever passed through. On the right side of the porcelain bowl George laid out his razor and mug, comb and a small scissors. His hairbrush and pomade he set neatly on the left, alongside nail clippers and moustache wax.

He looked at himself in the mirror as he mixed up a nice lather in his shaving mug. Trim and lean in his nightshirt, he cut a handsome figure for a man his age. His hair was only touched by gray and his skin was barely wrinkled. He scowled at his moustache. He had never noticed how gray it was and even faithful waxing couldn't control the unruly stray hairs that spoiled it. George had had his moustache since he was a young man. He had fancied it as a sort of companion to his face, a manly fringe that gave him dignity and an appearance of intellect and reflective thought.

He picked up the scissors, planning to trim a few stray hairs but he reconsidered and set them down. The image of Evelyn's sweet round face flashed across his mind's eye. Picking up his brush, he dipped it in the lather and coated his cheeks and chin as he had for forty years. Suddenly, he took the brush and smeared a dollop of foam across his upper lip. Within seconds he had shaved his moustache into the bowl. He finished shaving and splashed cologne on his cheeks catching his new reflection in the mirror. He smiled at himself and tossed the little tin of wax in the wastebasket. He was suddenly very keen to be done with this searching business and on his way back to Lord Lucan's.

Lord Cushing was waiting in the dining room when George arrived. He looked up pleasantly at George and motioned for him to sit down.

"Good Morning, George. I hope you slept well."

"Yes, sir, like a baby."

Lord Cushing closed his paper and gestured to the waiter.

"Coffee, George?"

"Actually, sir, I prefer tea."

"Then tea it is."

They gave the waiter their orders and ate quickly. Soon they were in a cab on their way to Dublin Street. Lord Cushing kept looking over at George and returning to his paper.

"You're looking hale and hearty today, George. Are you warming to the role of private investigator?"

George couldn't help smiling. A man's visage was not the kind of thing another man noticed and he had a feeling Lord Cushing was trying to figure out what was different about him. He decided to relieve his lordship of his curiosity.

"Yes sir. I have even shaved my moustache as an assumption of disguise. One must be careful when one is nosing about the chambers of powerful scoundrels such as Mr. Gilchrist."

Lord Robert laughed out loud.

"I thought there was something different in your demeanor, George! I say, a clean shave does lend your face a bit of daring-do. Perhaps you should look to Scotland Yard for a future appointment. Never too late to change careers, eh?"

"Not at all, sir. Given the state of affairs at GlynMor I am forced to consider my future very seriously."

Lord Robert folded his newspaper.

"George you and I are about the same age. I must say, I have the same energy and ambition as I did right out of University. Neither of us has ever borne the responsibility of rearing children, a sad development for me; perhaps for you as well. But I do think we have some very good years ahead of us. This turn of events has infused me with a new sense of purpose, indeed."

George sat quietly and thought about Lord Cushing's remarks. He too felt strangely alive and excited about life in a way he hadn't in years. As the cab pulled up in front of the stately seaside house, Evelyn's face again flashed across his mind.

Beverly closed the gate between the stable yard and the

herb garden and headed toward the kitchen door. She was all ready to leave for Clydagh Glyn. Her trunks were packed and Reina was overseeing the loading of the Clarence double brougham carriage. She had requested the larger double brougham to accommodate extra luggage. She had a feeling she'd be staying at GlynMor for a while.

Gilded Lily had begun to deliver her foal early that morning and Beverly would not even consider leaving until she was sure both mother and baby were going to be alright. She shook her head at Reina as the maid held open the door for her in the twilight.

"Nothing yet, Reina. It looks like it's going to be another night delivery. I don't expect to be leaving for Clydagh Glyn for another day or so."

"Can I refresh Madame with a cup of tea, perhaps?"

"Certainly. Thank you. I'll take it in my bedroom."

She climbed the long staircase to the second floor. Standing at the landing, she clutched the round dome of the carved newel post. How tired she was! It would be good to be done with foaling but Beverly knew even then she would not be done with sleepless nights. There was much in her life right now to keep her awake.

Reina set the pot of steaming tea on the table next to Beverly's chaise lounge and poured her mistress a cup.

"Will you be needing anything else, Madame?"

"No, Reina. I would love to have you loosen these stays but I know I'll be needing to return to the stable sometime during the night. I might as well stay dressed and sleep right here. Please take your rest as you can. I've instructed the grooms to have you wake me as soon as Lily's time gets close."

"*Bonsoir, Madame.* Rest well."

"Thank you Reina, you too."

The next morning Beverly woke to the sound of birds chirping in the monkey tree outside her window. Realizing she had slept through the night on her chaise, she sat up with a start. Why had no one called her? She slipped on her boots and hurried to the stable where she found Charles dozing next to Gilded Lily. The big mare slept soundly, never even stirring when Beverly rousted Charles from his sleep.

M'Lady! 'Tis early fer ye t'be out here."

"Why didn't you call me?"

"Well, M'Lady there was no reason t'wake ye! Everythin' stopped around one o'clock and she's sleepin' like a baby."

"Hmm. Well, let me know when things start up again."

By two o'clock that afternoon, Beverly and Reina were on their way to Clydagh Glyn in the big Clarence. Gilded Lily had delivered a fine filly around nine o'clock and all was well in the stable. Beverly planned to breed Gilded Lily again. Foaling for that horse was easier than for any other mare she'd owned. The afternoon was perfect. As they sped along the coach road to Galway they remarked on the high wispy clouds and clear blue sky. They stopped in Ennis for lunch and by late evening were checked into a lovely inn in Cong. From her window, Beverly could look out on the ruins of an ancient abbey. As Reina laid out her mistress's nightclothes, Beverly watched the moon shimmer low in the sky casting the ruins in her eerie light.

She climbed into bed, grateful for the crisp fresh sheets and smooth silky counterpane. She had a feeling she would need a good night's sleep, knowing that tomorrow might bring unpleasantness.

Lord Robert and George Spiner waited in their rented cab until the constable and two police officers joined them. The morning was warm and the gardeners had been working in the shady part of the yard. The men had been watching from their posts, every so often leaning on their spades and shrugging to each other. They obviously had no idea what the two gentlemen in the hired taxi wanted with Mr. Gilchrist. When the police arrived a current passed from one to the other and they clustered together near the walkway to see what this was all about.

One of the men approached the constable and introduced himself as Alexander Briggs. He said the Master was away on business and offered to help. Robert and George walked up just as the Constable handed the man the search warrant. The gardener handed it back without looking at it. It was clear the man couldn't read it. The constable was growing impatient and seemed to think the illiterate gardener was trying to obstruct his investigation. Lord Robert stepped in before the poor man found himself under arrest for being unable to read.

"Please let me help here. I'm Lord Robert Cushing of Cushing House, County Kerry and GlynMor, County Mayo. I represent the interests of Lord Wynn, Earl of Cantwell and Lord Bingham, Earl of Lucan."

Relieved to be out of the hot seat, the gardener bowed slightly in Lord Robert's direction.

"Alex Briggs, sir. I'm the head gardener here, sir."

Lord Robert acknowledged the man's position with a nod.

"Mr. Briggs, what the constable has here is a search warrant that permits us to legally enter these premises and search them and any property within these premises."

Alexander Briggs shifted nervously from one foot to the other.

"But Mr. Gilchrist is not at home, sir."

The constable pushed him aside.

"Don't matter! This here paper gives us the right. Now git outta' the way."

The constable and his men barged up to the door and rang the bell as Lord Cushing turned to address the gardeners.

"Please carry on. This has nothing to do with you and you're not in any trouble. This is a legal matter between gentlemen."

George said nothing. As he followed Lord Cushing past the sputtering butler, he was just glad the constable wasn't after him.

The search for the deed was very simple. Mr. Gilchrist had the keys to his safe in his top desk drawer and the deed to Tom Phalen's property was right there along with ten tidy ledgers stacked in a neat pile. There were some private papers as well as a tintype of Meg and Daniel Parker that Robert remembered having been on the table in the foyer at GlynMor. He wondered at that particular discovery as he slipped it into his waistcoat pocket. They emptied the safe and the desk drawers, filling several crates with evidence that might prove useful in making a case against Gilchrist.

Within two hours the police had catalogued all of the evidence and pronounced their work done. The evidence was collected and taken to police headquarters. Lord Robert had dismissed the cab when the police arrived at Gilchrist's house. Now he and George tried to sit low in their seats as they rode for the first, and hopefully the last time, in a police wagon.

Robert and George sat at a long table in the back room of The Newport Municipal Building where police headquarters was located. Aside from the constable's brusque manner, they had found the officers to be polite and helpful. By suppertime he and George had filtered through all the ledgers and bank statements. What they found was strong evidence that Robert Gilchrist had kept two sets of books, only one of which had a record of the sale of Tom Phalen's cows. He was certain they had enough evidence for the police to book Gilchrist for the theft of both the deed to Tom's property and the cattle and for embezzlement of Lord Lucan's rent. He would also try to build a case against him for the death of the boy,Thomas Phalen, indirectly attributable to the poverty resulting from the loss of his father's income. This would be a much more difficult matter which he would have to discuss with Meg and Tom. He and George needed to return to Lucan's and check his rent records to compare them to the figures they had found in Gilchrist's.

He stopped at the constable's office on his way out. He knocked on the door. A clerk opened it and the constable grunted permission to enter. Lord Robert bowed slightly and

informed the constable that George would be leaving for
Castlebar as soon as he had something to eat. He also advised
him to have his men arrest Mr. Gilchrist for grand larceny and
embezzlement as soon as he returned to Newport and to
notify him at the hotel when they had him in custody. He
wanted to be there for the arraignment. This man should be
remanded without bail. Lord Robert was concerned that he
might try to run. He was just that sort of a coward.

The day after the children were found, Meg sat on an
upholstered bench, soaking in the warmth from the afternoon
sun beaming through the big bay window in the upstairs hall.
She looked around at the silk-clad walls, the sconces with
neatly trimmed candles, the high ceilings and carved
doorframes. In this light the corridor that led from her old
bedroom to her father's chambers around the corner looked
bright and pleasant.

There was no trace of the sinister doings that surrounded
her the night she fled her father's house. Even the paintings
of centaurs and maids appeared benign, faded over the years,
more whimsical than threatening. Meg wondered how much
of what we perceive is truly present and how much we must
attribute to our inner expectations. She knew from the
experiences of her years away from this house that she had
weathered far more danger than this hallway had ever
presented. She also knew that the night she and Maureen
escaped there had been no more dangerous place on earth.

Now she sat trying to muster up enough courage to go
again into her father's room. She knew she had nothing to
fear from him. Even the prospect of having to see his
horrible injuries and look into his dim eyes brought her no
revulsion. She wondered at this seeming distance from the
prospect of seeing her father so disfigured. She wondered if
she would be so calm if he were fit and mobile, able again to
beat her and lock her away. Had she gained nothing, then, of

courage or fortitude since she left these walls? Was her serenity born of her ability to flee again if need be? Or had she really grown up, matured beyond her need for his approval, his love?

A single tear coursed down her cheek. Impatiently, she brushed it away. For fifteen years she had had nothing but contempt for the bully behind the big mahogany door. Seasons had come and gone without her ever missing him, pitying his fate or caring a fig what he did day in and day out. Her anger had shielded her completely from feeling anything but relief that he was far away and unable to follow her. She hadn't cared whether he suffered, whether he had regrets or whether he spent one moment or thousands, thinking good or ill of her.

This sun-dappled hall had simply vanished from her consciousness and with it the man she had once called Papa. Had he ever loved her? Did it matter? Meg knew it did. Seeing how Tom loved his Da and how his children loved him showed her how it should have been between her and her father. Had it ever been thus? She tried but couldn't remember.

Holding her head in her hands, she closed her eyes against the brightness. Why could she not remember? She wanted to remember more than anything a moment of tenderness, a lesson gently taught, a claim proudly made. Her mind remained closed to even a single memory of her childhood. It was as if her old self had died the moment his whip touched her flesh and had been reborn the instant she had fled into the fresh night air of the stable yard. The woman she was had no connection to the child and girl who grew up in this house.

But there had been life before that awful day! There had been meals and parties, church services attended, Christmases and summer evenings in the garden. There had been sunny mornings and thunderstorms in the night. Where had he been then? Where did her father fit into those moments? Was he always a tyrant, always a beast? She wanted to believe it wasn't so. Or had he just been more skillfull at hiding his real nature from her and her mother?

She thought of her brother Andrew. When he was torturing her in her own yard, his eyes ablaze with hate, could anyone have convinced her that he would be the one to save her and her children? How did that happen? Oh, sweet Jesus, why did he have to be the one? Why couldn't he have stayed hateful and demonic? Why did his noble act of filial loyalty have to blur the terrible pain of that night when she knelt half-naked in the dust?

What had been the great equalizer? Was it her descent into the gutter or his abuse at the hands of his own countrymen? That day, when they both looked across a filthy cellblock at each other, was that their resurrection day? Would he now be a changed man? Would compassion forever temper his quest for justice? Or would he slide back into hate and brutality the first time he encountered the prejudices of the gentry again?

What about her? Meg was already enjoying the return to comfort. The feel of silk and velvet was wonderfully familiar to her, the sound of servants in the kitchen and the sheer pleasure of plentiful food was rapidly erasing the years of starvation. With every mouthful of rich egg crepes, the memory of thin gritty tortillas faded a bit and miniscule dabs of honey, once so vital to her family's very survival, paled at the sight of chubby fingers sticky with gobs of the golden treasure.

She wanted to forget! She wanted Tom and her children to forget, too! They had scratched in the dirt and groveled in the soup line and now they would never have to do that again. Why would she ever want to remember? How could she ever miss the night Thomas died or Tom's screams of fury the day Mary Clare's hair was torn out? There had been so much pain! Of course she wanted to forget.

She swiped furiously at her tears but they would not stop. How simple it had seemed when she had told Tom she wanted to see her father. He had been skeptical about the wisdom of seeing him alone and offered to go with her but she had insisted on doing this herself. The little ones were in her bed napping and Tom had taken the older girls to see the place where he had been a lad. This would be the perfect time. And here she sat, sobbing outside his room unable to remember why she wanted to see him.

Was that how it worked? If we are willing to face the past, we can live in the present? If we ignore the past, we are doomed to live in its shadow, never able to fully step into the light? Meg was very troubled by the thought that putting the terrible events of her past aside was, in the end, impossible. No matter how far she ran from them, they followed her. No matter how deeply she buried them, they had the power to haunt her like specters in the night.

What then, was the benefit of remembering our pains and sorrows? It didn't make sense that true freedom was born of carrying our past with us and building new joys upon the foundation of old sorrows. It just seemed too burdensome to handle. But burying her difficult childhood hadn't freed her at all. Rather, what she remembered was the pain and what was good had been lost.

How unfair that was! She only wanted to see her father; to tell him she loved him, though why she loved him was too hard for her to understand. She had the right to forgive him, to free herself from the anger and fear that had driven him to the edge of her mind for years. Yet, how could she face him if she had nothing good to remember?

Meg knew she must see her father before he died. If he died without any effort on her part to reconcile, she would never know if there had ever been any good in all her years in this house. She heard him call out for George. He must want more laudanum. Should she get Sharon? George had left the filled syringes on the dresser but Meg had no idea how to administer this medicine. Her father called out again, fear clearly audible in his voice. Without thinking, Meg was on her feet. Within seconds she was standing at the foot of her father's bed.

Lord Jeffrey lay propped against several plump pillows, his eyes closed. He had called out while asleep and was unaware of Meg's presence. Despite Lord Jeffrey's demand for complete darkness, George had left one of the windows undraped so he could see what he was doing. Meg knew her father's eyes were sensitive to the light and looking at his face, she could see why. Silently she surveyed the sagging left cheek, the stub where his left ear had been and the stringy hairs that her poor father imagined would pass for a beard.

Meg was astonished at the sight before her. This was no one she knew. Here lay a man she neither remembered as the man who taught her to play piano nor as the monster she witnessed raping Maureen. Her father, who could have bred terror in a strong man's heart, was nothing but a pile of sagging flesh and broken bones. He was no less a prisoner than she had been when he locked her away in her room.

The man in the bed had only half of his face. The other half was a mass of silver scars that looked like melted wax in the dim light of the distant window. The place reeked of body odors of all kinds but the predominant smell was of the sickening sweet opium that hung on her father's breath when he exhaled. Her head swam as she tried to find her balance in the heavy, putrid air.

Meg looked around her. Gone was the hellish red glow and the elongated shadows on the wall. The evil energy that had filled this room like a living organism had disappeared. The floor no longer moved like vermin beneath Meg's feet. Instead, nothing moved. A smothering heaviness enshrouded the whole place.

Meg's father, enthroned in the center of this dark, lifeless womb seemed entirely diminished. He had never been a big man but now he was no bigger than a boy. He slept fitfully, picking at his bedclothes and absently swiping at his head. The flat stillness beneath the sheets was so strange to Meg that she could only stare at the outline of his legs and imagine them straddling a horse or charging up the sweeping staircase in the foyer.

Here was no threat. Meg could feel anything, say anything or do anything and her father would be helpless to do anything about it. He snored quietly as Meg stood at his feet, unable to move away from the bed. She marveled at the power he still had over her in his helplessness. He could do nothing to stop anything Meg could dream of doing. That alone rendered her as powerless as she had been beneath his whip.

Meg could do anything or nothing and still it could not change him. She could beg and plead with him to take her riding again. She could cajole him into buying her a new gown or bonnet. She could parade her family before him and demand his acceptance of her life. But none of it would matter. All that her father had, all that he cared about was contained in the syringe on his dresser. Even if she were cruel enough to withhold his comfort from him, someone else would provide it. That was the reality Meg faced as she stood in the dark, looking at her broken father on this warm sunny afternoon. She had never mattered to him. His indifference had been the cruelest blow of all.

Slowly, Meg turned and walked back into the hall. She knew she would be back. She knew she must speak to him despite the very real possibility he would simply spew poison at her. He was dying but there was still time. Meg dried her face and went to see who was ringing the front doorbell. She heard Tom and the girls coming in the kitchen door at the same time she heard Stiller's footsteps crossing the foyer. If her father's room had been devoid of life then perhaps the antidote waited for her at the foot of the marble ballistrade.

Lord Robert chuckled as he ducked into a pub not far from the Newport Police Department station house. The owner certainly had a sense of humor. On the sign outside was painted a headless woman in a fashionable dress. Where her head should have been were the words, painted in bright blue, *The Silent Woman*. He stood in the dim smoky taproom while his eyes adjusted to the subdued light. He peeked around a richly carved lintel into a handsome lounge.

The focal point of the room was a fireplace as big as the one in his drawing room but more rustic in design. Two heavy andirons dwarved a small turf fire laid more for ambience than warmth on this sunny, late August day. There were small round tables and intimate clusters of leather club chairs for friendly visiting and two overstuffed divans for serious lounging. Beyond the lounge was a gaming room with a billiard table and several smaller tables for the gambling crowd. Stacks of chips in little round holders sat in the center of most of the tables but there was one large square table in the corner where a jigsaw puzzle awaited anyone interested in placing a piece or two.

Stepping back into the taproom, he and the barkeep spotted each other at the same time.

"Help ye, sir?"

"Yes, a double Jameson's please, neat. I'll take it in the lounge. And if you have some nutmeats and perhaps some fruit and cheese."

"Certainly, sir. Sit anywhere ye like."

Robert eased his tired body into one of the club chairs, finding it to be very comfortable. This chap knew how to run a business. This was definitely a cut above the average pub. It was more like a London gentleman's club. Why, he even had gas lamps in here! Despite the fact that gaslight had been around for over twenty years elsewhere, this was real progress for Ireland.

He pulled the briefs about the Gilchrist case out of his leather satchel. It had been a long time since he had tried a case but he felt confidant that given the evidence, Mr. Gilchrist would easily be convicted. It would be simply a formality to have him drop the charges against Meg in exchange for a lighter sentence.

If the little weasal wanted to pursue his vendetta, let him. He had Rose Phalen and Leona Trent who witnessed his attack on Meg. There would be no doubt she acted in self-defense.

Robert doubted Gilchrist would argue much, once he saw that Robert and George had confiscated his books. Of course, his uncle, Lord Lucan would have to press charges against his sister-in-law's son. That could be a sticking point. Robert would be happy to have Robert Gilchrist either shipped off to Australia or jailed in London. He cared little whether the little fool slaved away in the hot sun harvesting sugar cane for the rest of his life or simply rotted away in Old Bailey prison.

He had left instructions at the station house for a deputy to fetch him at *The Silent Woman* once they had Gilchrist in custody. He smiled to himself. This promised to be an interesting afternoon. The whiskey had made him very relaxed and the notes he had taken from Gilchrist's ledgers began to jump around on the page as he dozed off. Realizing how exhausted he was after yesterday's long hard ride, he decided to nap. With a sigh he stretched out on one of *The Silent Woman's* wonderful couches. The man who built this place was indeed a brilliant businessman, a brilliant businessman indeed.

While Lord Robert Cushing slept in blissful comfort, Mr. Robert Gilchrist sped home by the coach road in a rented cab. Too impatient to wait for the afternoon coach, he reluctantly hired the much more expensive private cab. At least he wouldn't have to put up with some sour smelling old woman.

He couldn't wait to get home. Every time he coughed, his chest felt like he had swallowed razors and he had almost entirely lost his voice. Oh, to be in his lovely bed! He felt so terrible he had almost forgotten about Meg Phalen and her little gaggle of bastards. He still puzzled over Tom Phalen's whereabouts. He could have sworn by her reaction to his threats that the big lummox was still alive. And those gossiping maids! Could they have been lying? He thought he would have surfaced by now, though. A man can only hide for so long. The boy, too. Where had that shitegob gone? He'd see him swinging from the gallows too! The lot of them weren't worth the rope it would take.

The buggy wobbled as its wheels hit the cobblestones of Dublin Street. Ah, sweet homestead. A few more minutes and he'd be shoeless before his own fireplace enjoying the tender mercies of one of his parlor maids. Yes, Dolly could rub his aching feet while Genevieve prepared a fresh poultice for his chest. Let Mrs. Gilchrist abandon him for her sister's farm! He could manage quite well in her absence.

Suddenly the cab slowed to a stop. Oh, please! What was it now? He was within yards of his front door and going nowhere. He rapped his cane impatiently on the ceiling of the cab. This impertinent driver was ignoring him. He was beginning to regret paying his fare ahead of time. He was just about to rap again with his cane when the cab door flew open and two strong hands grabbed him.

Good Heaven's! Highwaymen! On Dublin Street.? As the police hauled him out of the buggy, Mr. Gilchrist tried to protest but made no sound. Damn this chest cold! In his confusion he tried to smack the intruders with his cane. Within seconds he was subdued by the officers and found himself rammed up against the cab with a shillelagh pressed hard against the back of his neck. His hands, in their grey kid gloves were behind his back and being snapped into handcuffs. The next thing he knew, he was in the back of a police wagon. He was no longer on his way to his bed, under his covers, but to the station house under arrest.

It wasn't until he was planted firmly behind bars that Robert Gilchrist realized fully what had just happened to him. He sat on a filthy bunk, rubbing his wrists and trying to tell anyone who would listen that a grievous error had just been made! An abberation of justice had been committed against an innocent man! Heads would roll!

No one could treat Robert Gilchrist of the Scottish

Gilchrists this way and not feel the pain of recrimination. On and on he ranted but nobody heard. He had no voice and none of the trash that languished in the other cells of the Newport Municipal Jail cared anyway. He would just have to wait until the bailiff came and he could explain that a terrible mistake had been made.

George Spiner stepped gingerly toward the kitchen door of Lord Lucan's huge manor house. He was so saddlesore after the last two days he could hardly bear the thought of getting back on a horse again tomorrow. He had even needed help dismounting.

The groom had recognized the problem at once and offered to prepare him a mineral bath whenever he was ready. He gladly accepted and headed into the house to find Lord Lucan.

He was shown at once to the library where Lord Lucan was perusing some new volumes he had ordered from the United States. He had a passion for good writing and was very interested in some of the recent works coming out of the colonies.

"Well, George, come in, come in. Let me show you my new acquisitions. Are you a man of letters, George? Enjoy a good read, now and then?"

"Yes sir, absolutely sir."

"Well then, come and see what I have purchased from our rebellious little brothers across the sea. Let's see, we have a couple of older ones by Emerson entitled *Nature* and *Essays*. Both are about ten years out but I've never read them. Then we have *Two Years Before the Mast* by a fellow named Richard Dana. I dare say I was captivated by the title of this next one: *Tales of the Grotesque and Arabesque* by that Poe fellow. A bit macabre, that one, but I like his work for a cold winter night by the fire. The last two are new releases. One of them is by a woman named Brontë. I still can't get used to women authors but Lady Lucan likes the Austen novels. I thought I'd give her Miss Brontë's *Jane Eyre* and *Vanity Fair* by Thackeray as a late gift her birthday last week. I'm delighted the shipment finally arrived.

Looking up from his purchases, Lord Lucan squinted at George through his monacle.

"What have you for me? I can tell you have something more important than literature to discuss. And, you look like you could use a drink."

A manservant appeared from the shadows and silently approached a heavy Italianate sideboard. Lord Lucan nodded in the direction of the Russian crystal decanter.

"Marcus will pour you a glass of sherry. Or, if you wish stronger spirits, ask for anything you want."

"No sir, sherry will be most satisfactory. Thank you, M'Lord."

"Sherry for me too, Marcus. And have Cook send over some lunch. I seem to have lost track of the time in here."

He looked at George again, his monacle glinting on his nose.

"You must be starving after your long ride."

"Yes, sir. Thank you, sir."

George thought about the hundreds of dying people he had passed on his way to and from Newport. He was hungry and lunch sounded wonderful. But he wasn't starving. Starving was what he saw in the stumbling gait, the haunted eyes and the dead children by the side of the road. For some reason the first ride to Lord Lucan's hadn't been as bad but once he and Lord Robert had approached Castlebar and when they had gone north to Newport the throngs of suffering people had sickened him almost to vomiting.

Returning here this morning, he had found himself behind a crowd of ragged beggars who had tipped a grain wagon and were literally killing each other for the kernels dumped all over the road. They were stomping on the driver but were so weak that he escaped without serious injury. A mounted patrol of Her Majesty's finest ran at them from the field where the grain had just been harvested and scattered the crowd, firing their sidearms over their heads as they limped away as fast as they could.

He was grateful that the soldiers didn't shoot any of them point blank. They had orders to do so and perhaps it would have been the merciful thing to do in the end but he was grateful anyway not to have witnessed such carnage.

He found himself nodding in agreement at Lord Lucan. He accepted the sherry from Marcus as Lord Lucan gestured for him to sit down.

"So, what have you to say about my nephew?"

George took a long sip of the sherry and cleared his voice. It wasn't going to be easy to deliver this message.

'Well sir, begging your pardon, sir, the news isn't good. Lord Cushing and I discovered that Mr. Gilchrist kept a double set of books. The first set had all of the revenues and records of his personal bank transactions. The second set was the set he showed you. There weren't too many discrepancies in the early records. Some skimming of the rents but only in small amounts. But after the hunger started, the revenues in his books were substantially more than the second set of figures reflected."

George took another sip of sherry and a deep breath.

"Then in '47 according to your set of books the spring rents were paid in full but he also has recorded in his own accounts a very significant deposit, after which is the notation *cattle*. . Tom Phalen has told us that Mr. Gilchrist took all of his cattle as prepayment of the spring rents for '47. After that, the rents were short by two-thirds for fall of '47 and there were no rents collected at all for '48."

A maid, not Evelyn brought in a tray. Two bowls of late summer fruit and a wedge of crumbly Stilton cheese were accompanied by a basket of buttered bread. Behind her, Evelyn arrived with a tray filled with a huge silver coffee service and a platter of cakes. The delicious aroma wafted across the room as Evelyn set the tray down. George tried to catch her eye but she was quick about her task. Before he could even thank her she was gone. Disappointed, he cleared his voice and went on.

"What we need from you is your book of receipts, sir. The period in question is that spring payment for 1847. According to Tom Phalen, he had subsidized the rents for years to keep the village in good stead. If you wish, we can look at all your receipts to see if you actually received the full payments right along. If not, then it's very likely that we'll find Tom Phalen's money in Mr. Gilchrist's bank account for all of those seasons as well."

The manservant again appeared at Lord Lucan's side and fixed each man a plate. He served the coffee and assembled a small plate of dessert for his master and his guest before retreating into the shadows again.

Once the man was out of earshot, Lord Lucan drained his sherry and tucked into his lunch. George also ate, willing to wait patiently for his lordship's reply. Why wouldn't he? It wasn't often he got Stilton of this quality.

George felt for the older man. He could see in his deliberate chewing and sipping that he was embarrassed to be made aware of his nephew's treachery by this untitled stranger. He looked like he would cry! George concentrated on his plate and waited silently.

Finally, Lord Lucan spoke.

"I will certainly provide Lord Cushing with my records. I want to do the right thing by Tom Phalen as he is a member of the family by marriage. I will fully compensate him for his losses and see to it that my nephew bears the expense. But I cannot see how I can allow him to be prosecuted like a common swindler. He is after all, my dear wife's sister's son. It would destroy the deep affection they have for each other and I simply could not allow that to happen. I'm sure I can make some arrangement for Lord Cushing to speak to the magistrate on his behalf. Once Mr. Phalen has his just recompense, we can all forget this ever happened."

He extended the plate of little cakes.

"More, Mr. Spiner?"

George was shocked at Lord Lucan's turnabout from their last conversation. How was he going to tell Lord Cushing of this new development? George was no student of the law but he knew they had no case if Lord Lucan failed to press charges against his nephew. No court would even consider Tom Phalen's stake in all this.

"No thank you sir. With Your Lordship's permission, I will take my leave. I expect to return to Newport tomorrow morning, unless Your Lordship prefers me to copy the originals and take the copies to Newport."

"Not at all! Marcus, have Grimes assemble my bank records from the last five years. Mr. Spiner will be requiring them by tomorrow morning. And then you can show him to his room in the west wing. I wish I could invite you to join me again for supper in the dining room but I have another engagement tonight. A rather tedious meeting at my club, I'm afraid."

George's voice sounded hollow to him as he responded with the words he was expected to say.

"Please sir, you have been way too generous! I wouldn't think of imposing any further. I'll perhaps take a light supper in my room. Think nothing of it, please."

George was so uncomfortable with this new development that he was deeply relieved that Lord Lucan was going out to eat. He could just hole up in the kitchen where he belonged. Besides, now he would be free to get better aquainted with a certain maid named Evelyn.

"Very well, then. Marcus? Mr. Spiner is ready."

He smiled stiffly at George.

"Until tomorrow, then?"

"Yes sir. Tomorrow, sir."

Marcus led George up the servant's stairway to his third floor room and Lord Lucan returned to his new books. It was George's turn to be embarrassed. When Lord Robert and he had stayed the other night, they had both been put up in second floor guest rooms in the east wing. Now that he was here alone, and the bearer of humiliating news, Lord Lucan was very clear on his diminished status. The west wing housed the kitchen and utility rooms in the basement, the dining room and conservatory on the first floor and the ballroom on the second floor. There was only one floor for sleeping in the west wing. It wasn't likely that anyone would be bringing him Stilton cheese up there.

"Madam, how good to see you."

Stiller could have been greeting the grim reaper for all his enthusiasm. Meg could only imagine who might be the unfortunate recipient of his stale, almost deathly greeting.

Then she heard a voice from her past that almost took her breath away.

"Well, Stiller, you might say I've been away too long if you're actually glad to see me! But then again, you'd say that if I were a snake sticking my head out of a basket on the doorstep."

She gestured impatiently to the footmen laden with her trunks.

"Upstairs to my rooms. And be careful, I have some very fine hats in those boxes. Let Reina handle those lighter things. I'm not having you fools dropping my jewelry and fur collars."

Stiller cleared his voice.

"Madam, I'm afraid Lord Cushing is occupying your room. However, he is in Newport at present. If you like we can relocate his things and have your rooms ready momentarily."

"No, don't disturb his belongings. I'll stay in my daughter's old room."

"Ahem, Madam, um, I'm afraid that room is also occupied."

Meg stood frozen at the top of the stairs. She couldn't believe she was hearing her mother's voice after all these years. Her mother had sent word that she was coming but

Meg had had no time to prepare for this. After just seeing her father, she was not ready in the least to see her mother too. She literally did not know what to do.

Her decision was made for her by the sound of Martha crying followed by the sound of the other young ones getting up from their naps. She turned and dashed to her room closing the door behind her. There she stayed with her little ones until Tom came upstairs and knocked softly on the door.

Meg had known that she would eventually have to face her mother. The actual encounter was as hard as she had expected and no less disappointing. Her mother had already met Rose and Mary Clare who sat primly across from her in the drawing room. Sharon had fixed tea and Lady Wynn had invited her granddaughters to join her. When Meg entered they were making stiff, polite conversation. She heard Rose breathe a sigh of relief.

Taking in the scene, Meg was struck by her daughters' dignity. They were dressed nicely, thanks to the Fellowes' generosity and sat properly at the edge of the settee like little ladies. Meg took in their thin faces and the unmistakable signs of their long hunger. Her mother couldn't help but see what Meg saw, perhaps even more with her discriminating eye. Despite their white eyelet dresses and blue sashes, the girls' bony wrists and lank curls gave evidence of their ordeal.

Despite their appearance, Meg was very proud of them. She carried Martha and ushered the younger girls into the room ahead of her. Francis, usually the sociable one, clung to her leg.

Meg stood before her mother, much as she had before her father. Her anxiety at seeing her again had built itself into a state of panic and waves of nausea had assaulted her as she dressed her little ones in their new finery. Now that the moment had arrived, Meg saw her mother as much smaller than she had remembered.

Lady Beverly sat ramrod straight on a small gilt Louis XIV chair, her deep, green silk skirt spread out around her.

Her pale pink blouse peeked out from behind a bolero of plaid satin in soft shades of pink and green. Meg noticed the subtle graying of her mother's blond hair and the fine wrinkles around her mouth.

Seemingly reluctant to turn and face Meg, Beverly deliberately continued engaging Mary Clare in a conversation about the furnishings of the Fellowes house. Rose stole a glance in Meg's direction and caught Francis's eye. The little boy darted away from his mother and climbed up into his favorite sister's lap.

This broke the spell and Lady Beverly looked up at her daughter.

Meg nodded.

"Mother."

"Hello, Meg. Please, won't you join us for tea? I was just getting acquainted with young Rose and Mary Clare."

She passed her eyes over Grace and Ellen and shifted them to Francis as he squirmed into a comfortable spot on Rose's lap.

Meg knew that look. Her mother was really very transparent. Her scrutiny, thinly disguised as a casual glance was no less the intense inspection she had given Meg at the breakfast table every morning of her childhood. Meg could only imagine how she looked to her mother with her own thin hair and her outdated outfit.

Beverly observed the two little girls who stood stock still in front of her saying nothing. Meg knew she hadn't been able to teach her younger children any of the social graces. God knew she had barely been able to keep them alive. Taking each of them by the hand, she walked them up to where her mother sat waiting for them to curtsy or something. Well, she would have to wait a long time for bows and curtsies from children who had known only grubbing for garbage for most of their short lives.

"Mother, this is Grace. She is six years old. And this is Ellen who will be five next month. Girls, this is Lady Beverly Wynn, your grandmother."

Beverly held out her hand like a bishop for them to kiss.

Meg was furious that her mother would expect these two babies to perform like trained pooches. Had she no idea how they had been forced to live, thanks to the machinations of the landed class against the poor Irish laborers?

She held tightly to their little hands preventing them from being forced into failing to meet their grandmother's expectations.

Lady Beverly straightened up in her chair and withdrew her hand.

"Hmmph. They are too shy to display proper manners to their Grandam? How odd. Meg, you were never shy and looking at the size of your family, your husband certainly never curbed his sociable nature. How strange that these young ladies do not deport themselves as they surely must have been taught. I found the same lack of response from their older sisters, though I must say, they at least, have been able to make polite conversation. Perhaps island living is simply more casual, what with all that sand and sea air."

Meg's mother turned her hard gaze on her daughter.

"Let me look at you, my dear."

"All these babies and still you fit into those old clothes! How you must have been the envy of the peasants around you! And who is this? You fail to introduce me to whom I assume is your youngest."

Meg could hardly contain her rage at her mother's nastiness. How could she, after all these years, be so harsh? How she wished Uncle Robert were here! Or Tom. She had spurned his offer to join her in the drawing room, believing this would actually be easier without him there. She realized too late that she had been badly mistaken.

Nothing had changed between her mother and herself. Meg hadn't expected to be warmly welcomed in her childhood home but she would not tolerate her mother treating her children like trash.

"This is Martha, Mother. She is obviously too young to absorb your insulting condescension as is Francis, our young son, about whom you have not yet deigned to ask. Let me save you the trouble. Francis is three and unless God blesses me with another son in my old age, he is my only remaining son. Dennis, our eldest son has been forced by the same unjust accusations that were leveled at me, to flee the country. I have not even begun to grieve his loss. Our other two sons starved to death at the hands of wealthy landowners and politicians who regarded their deaths as God's will. I'm sure you must know all this from the reports of your spies. No doubt Rev. Nangle has kept you informed of my family's demise."

Meg took a deep breath, fighting back tears of fury.

"I had hoped that this reunion would have been more pleasant but I see that you still hold me in cold judgment. I am sincerely sorry for you that you can't enjoy these beautiful children who have survived unspeakable hardship and as recently as three months ago were at death's door. Rather than being ashamed to call myself their mother, I am ashamed to call myself your daughter. Your ridiculous expectation of hand-kissing and formal address after what they have been through mocks true gentility and insults the integrity their father and I have instilled in them."

"Have no fear. We will not be a burden to you. Uncle Robert has very generously offered to take us in but that won't be necessary. We will survive. None of us is afraid to work. Mr. And Mrs. Fellowes in Castlebar have already offered the girls positions in their home and Uncle Robert can certainly help Tom find work. As for me, I had fancied myself more content returning to the comfort of life in the manor house but I see that the price is far too dear for me. I too will find honest work. No, you needn't fear the humiliation of grandchildren who fail to kiss your hand."

She turned toward Rose.

"Bring the others along, Rose. Mary Clare, take Martha for me, please. Grandmother seems a bit fatigued after her long journey. Let's not keep her from her tea."

At the door, Meg looked back to see her mother turned

away from her, leaning over the tea tray, helping herself to a sweet bun. She spoke quietly to her mother's back.

"Uncle Robert agreed to house me here until my trial is over. You can ask him yourself when he returns from Newport. Of course, given the strain of living here with all these unruly children, I'm not sure how that might change your plans. I'm sure you can understand that my children will be with me wherever I am."

Lady Beverly spoke without turning around.

"Don't worry, my dear. You and your children and your servant class husband can stay here. I will have your things moved to the Phalen house. I'm sure you will find it suitable. As for honest employment, I will speak to Sharon about that. No doubt she could use scullery maids. It is coming on harvest time after all and there will be much work to keep you and your girls very busy indeed. I don't imagine you will want wages. Your room and board should suffice. But I will expect all of you to work. Your children may be young but I'll have no freeloaders on my staff."

Chapter Eighteen

August 24, 1848

Denny Phalen leaned on the railing near the prow of The Marianna. His skinny frame reflected the strict rationing of the food that he, Andrew and Mr. McGee had had to share over the last three weeks. His stomach growled with hunger as he waited to see if Andrew had been able to bribe any of the sailors for anything edible. Andrew had portioned out the whiskey very carefully throughout the trip across the sea and tonight as they were within sight of shore, he was about to bargain the last of it away. Denny knew he could never rely on Andrew the way he could Mr. McGee, nor did he respect him as much but his admiration for his friend had risen to new heights as he observed him at work.

Mr. McGee stood next to Denny, savoring a bit of sponc won in a secret poker game last night. He puffed his pipe quietly, the aroma reminding Denny of Da and the land he left behind.

Denny had wept silently in the dark for the first several days of their voyage. The hardship of their cramped quarters, the scarcity of food and fresh water and the fear of being discovered had made his yearning for his old life unbearable. He longed to see Da and feel his heavy hand rest reassuringly on his shoulder. Mam, he could hardly think about without tearing up. If he could just hear her voice one more time! If he could only know that she was all right. He missed Francis and his sisters far more than he thought he would. He even missed the hard work at the inn and wished he could carry barrels up ten flights of stairs for just one piece of barm brack and a comfortable place to sleep.

The night was crisp and cool with a blanket of stars so low they looked like he could reach up and pluck one right out of the sky. Denny had grown to love the night. After weeks of hiding all day he had almost forgotten the feel of the sun on his back. He knew this would all change once they arrived in New York harbor but for at least one more day he would live the life of the night owl.

New York harbor! The thought was overwhelming to him. The biggest place he had ever seen was Westport and he had only ever seen part of that city. What would New York be like? Neither Andrew nor Mr. McGee could tell him and the sailors just shrugged and said it was nothing like Paris or London. Mr. McGee said he didn't plan on staying there long anyway. He hoped to get work on the railroads or maybe open an inn along that new canal that ran across New York State. Denny knew he had to go wherever Mr. McGee took him. He didn't mind. Mr. McGee had treated him like a man ever since he arrived at Miss Marie's. He knew he would take good care of him until he got old enough to take care of himself.

Andrew had been very careful with the whiskey but because it was so dark in their cubby, he couldn't see much. He kept saying he thought it was going faster than he expected but Mr. McGee kept telling him it was fine. What Andrew hadn't known until tonight was that they actually had one bottle left. Fergus had told Mr. McGee he would show him where to exchange his money and where they could get a good cheap room with meals.

Mr. McGee said that was why he was saving the last bottle of whiskey. Insurance, he called it. Fergus thought the whiskey was almost gone. Once they landed, Mr. McGee planned to show him the remaining bottle and extract the sailor's high-seas promises for the luxury of several free drinks.

The contraband had bought them almost nightly trips to the deck. This morning they had eaten the kippers and most of the remaining cheese. They had saved a small bit of sausage and the rest of the cheese for their evening meal. Fergus had brought them some hard tack and they planned to finish off the honey with that in the morning. After that, they hoped to be buying their next meal onshore.

When Andrew first felt the full bottle of Jameson's buried beneath Mr. McGee's cushion, he was angry and hurt. He had accused Mr. McGee of not trusting him and of hoarding the whiskey for himself. Denny had been shocked to hear the hurt and disappointment in Andrew's voice. He would never think those things about Mr. McGee. He had quite forgotten his own resentment of Mr. McGee's authority from his days at the inn.

Mr. McGee simply reminded Andrew of his higher status as a Brotherhood member by virtue of his blood relationship with D'Arcy McGee. Andrew said no more but Denny could feel his resentment fill the tiny space as he sulked in his corner.

Now, Andrew returned from his last foraging expedition with a few scrounged treasures. He had been able to trade one shot for a cup of drinking water and some more hard tack. The second and last shot in the bottle had brought some salted cod and some greasy fried bread. It wasn't much but it tasted like heaven as the three friends shared it under the stars.

They returned to their hiding place just as the rising sun began to cast long shadows across the deck. Fergus said they would be in port by noon tomorrow. Before they ducked into the low door leading below decks, they looked west toward their new home. The sun behind them cast it's light along America's eastern shore. From where they stood it surely looked like the whole great stretch was paved in gold.

Lord Lucan had at first refused to bring charges of embezzlement and malfeasance against his nephew. Lord Cushing however, as his peer, was able to persuade him that the police had enough evidence from the altered books and Lord Lucan's own financial records to convict Gilchrist. He also hinted that Gilchrist could be held accountable for the deaths of Thomas and Patrick Phalen if he could prove that they died as a result of Gilchrist's theft of Tom Phalen's livelihood. Robert strongly appealed to his friend's sense of self-preservation in lobbying for charges to be brought. In the end he was able to convince him that he could and probably would be charged as an accessory to the crime if he failed to cooperate.

So it was reported to George, by his new friend Evelyn, that last evening, shortly after he presented her with her new novels, his lordship broke the news to her that her nephew would probably spend a long time in prison if he wasn't hanged or sent to Australia. Poor Aunt Bernice had dissolved into a puddle of tears and George Bingham, 3rd. Earl of Lucan exited his dining room to the sounds of wailing and accusations of having ruined his wife's birthday present.

Tom cared little for any of this. He had just returned from a long dusty ride to Ballaghey where he had served papers to Mrs. Leona Trent. She would be present to lend witness to Meg's defense on 12 September, the day her trial was set to open. He was dirty, tired and hungry but most of all, angry. Shortly after Lady Beverly had arrived at GlynMor castle, Lord Robert returned from Newport with the ridiculous, terrible news that Robert Gilchrist refused to drop the charges against Meg despite the compelling evidence against him for his crimes against the crown. He and Meg both had been so shocked when Uncle Robert broke the news to them that there would indeed be a trial that it had taken him until Newcastle to realize he would be passing through Swinford. He could actually get to see Davey and, God willing, Da!

Their reunion and the grip of his father's handshake had given Tom more hope he had felt for a very long time. The hunger had taken a toll on his da and his brother and Molly. Da was completely bald and had lost all his teeth but as frail as he appeared, Tom's father still had the strength of two men and a kind word of encouragement on his lips. Leaving him and Davey had been hard but he promised to fetch Da for a visit to his old home as soon as the trial was over.

He trudged across the stable yard the way he had a thousand times in his former life and stopped in the kitchen to see if Meg or one of the older girls were still working. They had fallen quite easily back into their roles as servants. The one person who had the most trouble adjusting was Sharon. George didn't like it either but he had been working away from Clydagh Glyn with Uncle Robert. He didn't have to see his former mistress dressed in livery and slopping pans of dirty dishwater over her bare feet.

Uncle Robert himself had been incensed when he found out what his sister had done. They had never had such hard words as Tom had heard from behind the drawing room doors. It was no surprise that Meg's uncle had concentrated on the Gilchrist affair. Even if he hadn't had so much work to do in Castlebar and Newport, he would have stayed away.

Tom looked around the kitchen and called Meg's name. No one was there but Meg had left him a plate of cold meat and cheese. A sweet bun and a glass of milk sat next to it. All of it was covered with cheesecloth to keep out the flies. He ate and drank his fill, leaving the dishes in the sink. Grabbing a couple of pears, he headed home.

It was very strange to be treading the old familiar path to his father's house. His heart had sunk in his chest when he heard that Lady Beverly was giving them the old place as their living quarters. How could she expect them to live in that tiny house with a roof half caved in and nests of every kind of creature in the thatch? He had never thought of her as cruel but she was behaving like a madwoman now.

It was that decision that had made Uncle Robert howl with fury. Tom remembered how he bellowed at Meg's mother and how she had run from the drawing room sobbing. Later, she had relented and allowed the Phalen's to stay in the manor house upstairs with the servants until the old house was rethatched and cleaned up. Within days, Tom and the local thatcher had a new roof on it and Meg and the girls had scrubbed and whitewashed the place from top to bottom. Sharon had given Meg some extra cooking pots and utensils. She even passed on a tin oven she had found in the root cellar. Meg had helped herself to all of her old clothes and stripped her old room of all of its furniture and bedding. She even took the carpet from the floor. The cramped little cottage had taken on the appearance of a cozy little nest and Tom actually looked forward to seeing what Meg had done while he was gone.

Meg had covered the floor in Tom's old room with her old Oriental carpet and filled the little room with her big bedstead. Once it had been cleaned out and the bed put in place there was hardly room to turn around. There was a loft where she set up two tester beds found in the third floor room that had been her nursery. After she threw some plump feather beds and pretty counterpanes across them, they looked quite inviting.

Tom had never seen Meg work so fast. Fueled by her rage at her mother's insensitive behavior, she was like a dervish. She repaired the old spinning wheel and Sharon set her up with wool and carding supplies to make homespun. She had her own sewing basket filled with delicate tatting needles and every kind of silk thread and embroidery hoops. Before Tom left for Ballaghey, Meg had taken an old petticoat and made curtains for their bedroom and the kitchen. The remaining lace she hung across the tiny window in the loft upstairs. He found a good sturdy ladder in the stable and placed it so his children could climb up safely to their beds. He painted it green with the paint he had left over after he finished putting a fresh coat on the doors and the kitchen dresser. Meg missed her settle but the hearth was designed with two stone seats the way she had been used to in Doeega.

As he approached the little house, he saw smoke coming from the chimney and light in the window. His eyes misted over when he thought about the miraculous transformation they had made to his humble boyhood home in a matter of weeks.

When he opened the kitchen door he was greeted by Meg's radiant smile. She had just finished hemming a shirt for him from the rest of the old petticoat and held it up for his inspection. It had been a long time since he had worn anything so fine and he folded her into a grateful embrace. They were going to be just fine here. As he closed the door behind him he wished he had his fiddle. That was one thing that he hadn't been able to take from Westport. He would have to get it from Fr. Timon. They would eventually get the rest of their belongings from their old house and in the spring they would put an addition on the house where Meg could have a nice little parlor.

As he held his wife in his arms, the one thing that cast a shadow over Tom Phalen's face was the very real possibility that none of this would matter in a few weeks. If a jury found Meg guilty of attempted murder on the life of Robert Gilchrist nothing in his life would ever matter again.

Lord Cushing was losing patience with the little man on the prison cot.

"You fail to comprehend, sir, the seriousness of these charges. You stand to spend the rest of your life in prison or hang for your crimes. Yet you still insist on carrying on this ridiculous charade of charges against my niece. You are outranked, completely outstripped by the evidence against you and your foolishness can only lead you to the gallows!"

"Look at me you ass! I'm trying to offer you a bit of leniency here. How can you be so unreasonable as to risk your own neck in a noose for these trumped up charges?"

Robert Gilchrist turned away from Lord Robert Cushing and cast his rheumy gaze on his lawyer, Harry Franklin. Mr. Franklin sat with his head in his hands. He had given up trying to talk sense to his client. The man was impossible. Here he was being offered his life and all he wanted was something to soothe his chest cold.

Harry Franklin was sorry he ever took the case. If he weren't obliged to the man's wife for her discretion over an incident that had happened many years ago he wouldn't even care about the case. She had caught him in a compromising position in the sacristy of St. Alban's Presbyterian Church with the charwoman. At the time, he was a trustee of the church and had pleaded with Mrs. Gilchrist to keep his indiscretion to herself.

When Gerald Pritchard, Mr. Gilchrist's own lawyer, had found out the nature of the charges against him he had immediately dismissed him as a client. Mr. Pritchard had been outraged that Mr. Gilchrist would toy with his reputation by keeping secret books and cheating honest men while his name appeared on Gilchrist's legitimate legal documents.

Mrs. Gilchrist returned home to find her husband in jail without legal assistance. That was when she had called Mr. Franklin. It was time for payback. Of course he would take her husband's case. Yes, of course he would wave his fee.

Now, here he sat his head pounding as Lord Cushing tried to convince his blockheaded client once more to save his skin by dropping his charges against Lady Meg Phalen. The pounding got worse as he heard the voice of his client start whining again.

"Well, Lord Cushing, as I've told you several times over the last fortnight, I am convinced of my case. She and her son attacked my person with the intention of doing me serious bodily harm. It is my belief that they would have done murder had I not been the tower of strength that I am. I will not let a madwoman like her walk the streets! As for the term 'trumped up charges', I dare say your case is so weak it needs crutches. You too will feel the consequences of browbeating my poor uncle Henry Bingham when this is all through. I intend to have the last laugh as I stand on the outside and you stand on the inside of this very cell."

Lord Robert had had it.

"Very well, Mr. Gilchrist. I will not make this offer again. Your trial has been set for two days from now, September 4. Mrs. Phalen's is almost a fortnight away. You will be found guilty of all charges and you will face the wrath of the court. As you are being hauled off to the gallows, as you well may for the death of Mrs. Phalen's two young sons, then you can gloat that Mrs. Phalen will be tried in the same court. However, it will be your loss that you won't be around for her acquittal."

"Conviction, Mr. Cushing, conviction. And after a jury of my peers finds me innocent of your silly charges, I will gloat from the audience as she is taken away. And when you are finished I and my uncle will sue you and take your house, your townlands and your precious horses."

Robert Gilchrist hollered the last statement to Lord Cushing's back as he stalked out of the Castlebar Prison and hailed a cab. When he arrived at *The Silent Woman* he went right to the lounge. He had found out that there were two rooms above the pub that could be rented and he had rented them both. He needed a quiet place to stay and when George returned he could stay in the other room. The barkeep knew him well enough by now that he just brought him the Jameson's without being asked.

Lord Cushing shared his sister's ability to eat heartily despite his agitation. He devoured a whole trout for dinner and was finishing a big piece of blueberry tart for dessert when George entered the dining room. He carried a stack of ledgers and a sack of notebooks. Lord Robert bought him a drink and he gratefully accepted. They took Lord Lucan's records upstairs and George ordered supper and a pot of coffee in his room. Spreading the mess out on two large tables, the two men drank coffee and assembled an airtight case against one of the most arrogant fools either of them had ever known.

Within forty-eight hours they were packing their bags to return to Clydagh Glyn. Mr. Robert Gilchrist's trial was over. The two men would be stopping at Lord Lucan's Manor to deliver their report. They expected to stay the night in Castlebar and then hasten home to tell Tom and Meg their news.

Lady Beverly had moved Robert's things into a large comfortable suite of rooms at the far end of the east wing. She had ordered her suite and Reina's room cleaned from top to bottom and all the bed linens washed and aired. Meg's older daughters worked side by side with the O'Brien girl and three other girls from the valley. She purposely ordered Meg to help Sharon put up the bounty of late summer fruit that still lingered on the trees. She wanted to see how these little Phalens behaved when away from their mother's watchful eye.

Beverly was favorably impressed with the quality of her granddaughters' work. Only occasionally did it occur to her that these little maids, in their crisp gray striped uniforms and white aprons were actually of her noble flesh and blood. When this realization crossed her mind, she simply dismissed it as so much sentiment and concentrated on their unmistakable Irish features.

They were actually quite pretty in very different ways. Rose's eyes were startlingly blue and her dark curls offset her creamy skin and rosy cheeks. When the girl smiled the room lit up as her full lips curved over her beautiful white teeth. She was certainly her father's daughter, inheriting not only his looks but the playful, sly smile that teased her face at times. Like Tom Phalen, Rose could find humor in obscure places where Beverly simply could not. This kept Beverly on guard even as it caused grudging admiration.

Rose was a big sturdy girl, the kind who works hard and plays hard. Beverly could imagine her on horseback fearlessly taking jumps and racing across the rough countryside. She also imagined that she would be quite capable of effortlessly bearing children and working tirelessly at the task of rearing them.

Mary Clare, on the other hand, was all delicate bone structure and dreamy eyed gentility. Her auburn curls were always gathered in a top-knot on her head or braided in tidy plaits with tiny tendrils escaping around her face. Even in the throes of hard, sweaty work, Mary Clare was never wrinkled, never cranky, never unkempt. Her smile was as shy as Rose's was bold and her soft eyes always seemed to probe until they found the sweetest image on which to rest.

Beverly grudgingly admired Rose's ability to command the respect of her younger siblings. Even the veteran maids tolerated her bossiness. After all, she asked one afternoon, hadn't she practically run Browne's Inn in the great city of Westport? Francis clearly adored her and the two little girls followed her around like sheep. Beverly originally thought Grace and Ellen would simply be in the way of the housecleaning but Rose found real work for them to do. While Rose and Mary Clare dragged the heavy silk draperies down and passed them off to be aired, the two children were assigned the task of sorting and polishing candlesticks.

Francis had been commissioned to gather them from all of the bedrooms in the east wing and from upstairs in the servants' quarters. His task took the better part of a day and once his sisters were finished chipping away the old wax and polishing them to a high sheen, it was his job to return one candleholder to each room he had emptied. She watched as he nagged at Grace to hurry. Beverly couldn't help smiling to herself at the warm memories of her own little brother bothering her at that age. Francis was indeed a rambunctious little fellow.

He approached her once as she sat observing the washing of the hundreds of panes of glass that made up her windows. It had been years since they had been cleaned and the job was going very slowly. She had had to recruit Reina to supervise and her friend was very unhappy with the progress. Reina had been cross with Francis after he threw several drying cloths into a bucket of water. She bellowed at him in French and sent Grace and Ellen to the kitchen for more rags. Thoroughly chastened, the little boy turned to his grandmother for comfort.

Beverly was not accustomed to children but had a soft spot for Francis. He was very bright and talked incessantly to his sisters. While Beverly had never tolerated chatty children, regarding them as badly bred, she made an exception for Francis. She watched him as he approached, chagrin written across his little face. Without warning, he had buried his red curls in her lap and had wrapped his skinny arms around her legs.

Her first instinct was to push him away so as to avoid crushing her sea green striped skirt. Instead, she lifted his little chin and took a long look at him. He clearly resembled his father with his round blue eyes and dark lashes. He had inherited curls from both sides of the family but Beverly wondered at the red hair. Meg had had a reddish cast to her blond ringlets when she was little but Francis's hair was true red, much lighter than Mary Clare's auburn but never blond like Meg's.

"What did you do?"

"I spilled th'rags into th'water. The brown lady hollered at me. I didn't mean to. They fell."

"Were you being naughty with the rags?"

Beverly knew he had been wadding them up and throwing them at Gracie.

Francis looked guilelessly into her eyes.

"Aye."

"Yes, Francis. Say yes."

"Aye. I'm sayin' yes."

"Francis, do you not want to learn how to speak properly?"

He sighed dramatically.

"No, not t'day. I'm that tired from gatherin' candlesticks. Maybe t'morrow."

He never took his eyes from her face. Beverly tried not to smile.

"Your mother speaks proper English. Don't you want to speak like your mother?"

"No, not today."

"Are you not a big boy?"

"No, I'm only free."

Beverly stroked the soft skin under his chin. She was about to say something else when Rose saw him with her and came charging over to retrieve him.

"Francis John Phalen! I told ye about botherin' grandmother, I mean Lady Beverly! Beggin' yer pardon, M'Lady, he's jist little, he meant no harm."

Taking him by the hand she yanked him back to where Grace and Ellen were polishing. She handed him a gleaming candlestick and sent him to put it in one of the bedrooms. Beverly felt a cool draft across her lap where his warm little body had leaned against her. She felt a short pang of regret that she had ordered her grandchildren to use her titled name instead of 'grandmother' when they addressed her. Perhaps she was getting used to the idea that these Irish ragamuffins were actually related to her.

Meanwhile, Francis wandered around the corridors looking for a room to deposit his candlestick. He couldn't seem to find one that didn't already have a clean one on the bed table. He turned a corner and kept walking. Soon he could no longer hear the voices from his grandmother's room. Finally he realized that he was lost and started to cry. He sat on a bench outside a bedroom with the door ajar and looked around. As he took in the strange hallway with the pictures of the horses jumping around the sleeping ladies, he began to cry in earnest, calling for his mam in loud gulping sobs. No one came to his rescue. Everyone was busy cleaning. He slid off the bench and began looking for Rose. Panic came over him as he went from room to room crying out first for Rose and then for Mam.

Room after room yielded nothing but empty space. He was all alone and didn't know how to find his way back to Rose. He checked all the rooms up and down the hall and found himself back where he started. Pushing open the door, he looked for a spot to set the clean candlestick. There was someone lying in a bed, facing away from the door. Maybe this person would know where Mam and Rose were.

Lord Jeffrey slipped in and out of a restless sleep filled with sad, fleeting dreams of his mother. He was a little boy and had just arrived home from school. Jeffrey hated school. It took him away from his sweet mummy and put him in the midst of stern, demanding men who insisted on speaking Latin. As he wandered through the rooms of his childhood home, young Jeffrey called out to his mummy and tried in vain to find her. Why didn't she answer him? Where could she be?

Little Jeffrey sobbed as his calls became more frantic. She was always here! She always waited for him and hugged him hard when he came home. Where had she gone? Who would hug him now? He came upon her bedroom door and could hear her inside. He pushed the door but it wouldn't move. He called her over and over but she couldn't hear him. He could hear her laughing and talking silly talk on the other side of the door. Pounding on the door he realized the laughing had turned to moans. Someone was hurting Mummy! Harder and harder he pushed against the door until finally it few open. There he was! Tom Phalen was pushing Mummy against her bed and Jeffrey had to save her.

When he reached for her he felt the huge hand of the big groom grab his shoulder in a hard grip. Down, down down, he fell, all the while taking blow after blow from the evil Irishman. When he finally hit the bottom of a deep black pit he awoke with a start. He realized immediately that his old familiar nightmare was somehow different this time. He knew he was awake but he still heard himself crying. Someone's hand still shook his shoulder. He knew he was in his bed in his old familiar room but he felt somehow like he wasn't alone. He really wanted a shot of laudanum. He had no pain but had long since become very agitated when it wore off.

"George? Is that you?"

The crying stopped and a little voice answered.

"No, me. Francis."

Jeffrey started at the child's voice. For an instant he thought he was dead and this was somehow an imp ready to lead him to Hades. He wondered absurdly how any imp in the ranks of Satan could ever be named Francis.

"Where's Mam?" The little voice asked. "Where's Rose?"

"Who are you? Who is your mother?"

Jeffrey couldn't roll over to face this child and he wished heartily for the creature to stop patting and nudging his shoulder.

"I'm Francis. Mam is me mither!"

Jeffrey was losing patience. Which stupid maid had lost her child in the vast corridors of his house? This was preposterous! Where was George?

Again, he bellowed for George. Immediately the patting stopped and the little voice raised itself in a despondant wail. Now he'd done it! He'd gone and frightened the little blighter. Jeffrey recognized the sound as the crying from his dream. He realized that the gripping he had felt on his shoulder had also come from this child's tiny hand.

When Francis finally stopped screaming, Jeffrey spoke again.

"You have nothing to fear, you little fool. I can't hurt you and I wouldn't waste my time. So, Francis or Frances, are you a boy or a girl?"

Francis giggled at the question.

"I'm a boyo, silly. A serious thinkin' boyo."

"A fresh little piece, too. Where's your mam indeed? What are you doing in my room?"

Jeffrey suddenly felt the cold hard thud of a candlestick on his forearm as Francis rolled it over Jeffrey's shoulder.

"What? Are you trying to kill me? What have you there?"

He grabbed the candlestick and righted it on his counterpane. As he lifted it close to his face he saw what it was. A terrifying thought occurred to him.

"You haven't a candle there do you, boy? You haven't any fire there do you?

"No fire. Mam says 'No, no. Hot'."

Jeffrey breathed a sigh of relief. At least he wouldn't be burned to death in his bed. Jeffrey had had enough burning for one lifetime.

"Do you have a father, Mr. Francis?"

"Sure, Da is me da."

"How old are you?"

"Free."

No wonder he was getting nowhere. He was having a conversation with a baby. Jeffrey tried a different approach.

"Francis, what does your da call your mam?"

Francis said nothing for a moment and proclaimed with excitement.

"Meg, Darlin'. 'Cept when he's cross. Then he says 'Whativer ye want, Lady Meg'."

He giggled at the image of Da in a temper.

Jeffrey felt a flush of heat move from his chest straight up to the top of his head. This couldn't be her son? Where was she that her son was delivering a candlestick to him in his bed? He decided to probe a little further.

"Francis, where is your mam now?"

This threatened to bring on another torrent of tears and Jeffrey smacked the mattress in frustration. Francis stopped whimpering immediately.

"I know you don't know where she is right this minute. Where was she the last time you saw her?"

"She was in th'kitchen." Francis said with a sniffle. "'Afore that she was in jail."

"In jail! Now, don't you dare be telling me tales, boy! I won't have it do you hear? Come around here so I can see you up close. I need to see who you are and my eyes are no good."

Francis had climbed up on the bed when he first tried to arouse Jeffrey. Realizing it was along way down, he clambered over Jeffrey and plopped down in front of him. Together they checked each other out in the shaft of light from the doorway.

Francis spoke first.

"Yer face is broken."

"Is it now? Well, I suppose you could say that."

Jeffrey felt the pressure of tiny probing fingers on the thick scars. Other than his own, no fingers had ever actually touched the terrible wounds on his face. George had always used a cloth to bathe him and there wasn't one other creature willing to get close enough to him to touch him. He marveled at how painful that realization was. For almost fifteen years, his face had been nothing but a source of repulsion to the beholder. Now, here was this little boy gently pressing on his burn scars and intently studying his tortured skin. Jeffrey actually wondered if he wasn't still dreaming.

"Hurts?"

"No. Not much anymore. But it hurt when it happened."

"Did someone hurt ye?"

"No, I fell against something very hot and burned myself."

"But yer mam kissed it?"

Jeffrey made no reply to that question. He couldn't believe he was having this conversation. He hated children! Who was this little person who had captivated him so?

"Come close, Francis. I can't see you. My eyes are broken too."

Francis leaned down and placed his face nose-to-nose with Jeffrey.

"Not quite that close."

Francis backed up, losing his balance and almost falling off the bed. Instinctively, Jeffrey reached out and grabbed him pulling him back onto the mattress. Francis thought this was great fun and started bouncing around trying to repeat the maneuver. Where only moments ago, he had been crying his heart out, the little boy was now awash in giggles and playful squeals. Before he could stop himself, Jeffrey too, was laughing. Francis bounced harder and Jeffrey's body was jostled and shaken up and down on the bed. Together the two of them laughed and howled like too naughty schoolboys skipping Saturday chores.

Finally, Jeffrey had had enough and stilled the little body with both hands. Breathless, the two new friends settled down. A voice called from the hall and a look of relief crossed Francis's face. He slid down to the floor and announced his departure.

"I hear Peaches! She's come t'fetch me!"

He scooted around the foot of the bed where Jeffrey couldn't see him. Suddenly, Jeffrey felt panic seize his gut. Where was the little boy going? What if he never came back? He called after Francis.

"Boy? Francis? Come back here, I say!"

But Francis had already disappeared through the door into the hall. Jeffrey wrapped his fingers around the cold, hard pewter of the candlestick. This one was obviously from the servants' quarters. Petulantly, he pushed it over the edge of the mattress onto the floor where it landed with a soft thud on the carpet. He could still feel the pressure of the little boy's fingers on his scars as hot tears trickled across his cheek to soak his pillow. Gut wrenching loneliness engulfed him as he tenderly ran his hand over the warm spot on the bed where his little friend had bounced up and down.

A week after her mother arrived, Meg heard the warm, familiar voice of Uncle Robert carried down the kitchen hallway.

"Uncle Robert! Finally! We've been waiting so long, Please, please is there good news?"

Meg ran from the kitchen the moment she heard her uncle's voice in the foyer. He started at the sight of his niece in livery, her arms red and chapped from washing linens and putting up fruit. From the opposite direction, his sister appeared in the drawing room doorway, her impeccable coif framed by a halo of afternoon sun.

Uncle Robert turned from one to the other, his face a mask of confusion.

"Come with me, Meg. I'm very fatigued and hope to relay the news only once. Where is Tom? I'd prefer him here from the beginning."

Meg felt faint and grabbed the banister leaving the imprint of her damp palm on the gleaming newel post.

Tom came in from the stable yard where George had summoned him from reshoeing horses with Peter.

"I'm here. Ye can start anytime."

"Good. Let's assemble in the drawing room. I can certainly use a drink. George, once you get my bags in my room, please join us. Here, give me my carpetbag. I'll be wanting that."

Lady Beverly, miffed that her brother addressed the Phalen's before he even looked at her, took this opportunity to put George in his place.

"Oh, you, Lord Robert's things have been relocated. I'm sorry, I can't quite recall where. I'm sure you'll find them."

Meg piped in.

"My mother is getting forgetful, George."

Turning to her uncle she smiled.

"You don't mind taking over the guest suite at the end of the east wing do you Uncle? I believe those used to be the rooms where your school chums used to stay, aren't they?"

George lugged the heavy satchels up the long flight of

stairs followed by two of the O'Brien boys with Robert's trunk. Beverly turned abruptly in a swish of taffeta and stalked into the center of the drawing room. She was about to chastise Meg for being rude when Robert held his hand up. He regarded her coolly, still appalled at her treatment of his niece and her family. It obviously pained him to be at odds with his sister but he simply could not condone her behavior. He could barely look at her as he made a slight bow in her direction.

"Beverly. How pleasing to see you looking so well."

Once everyone was seated and George had returned, Robert took his place before the massive stone fireplace. Propped against the mantlepiece, his lean frame reflected the long, difficult days he and George had just put behind them. George brought him a small glass of Jameson's. He silently offered Lady Beverly a sherry and took his place against the wall. Tom and Meg sat rigid on the brocaded settee clasping each other's hands.

Uncle Robert took a deep swallow of the whiskey and began, "I know you all want to hear good news and I am happy to be the bearer of it. I must warn you, I also have some news that may be a bit unpleasant. Mr. Gilchrist has been incarcerated for fifteen years for crimes against the crown. He was found guilty of all counts of embezzlement, malfeasance, petty larceny and grand larceny in the altering of the rental records submitted to Lord Lucan from the Doeega collections."

"He skimmed money from Lord Lucan's assets every year he was undertaker but in 1847 he reported no rents collected and took every cent. He kept every ha'penny of the profits from the cattle he took from you, Tom. I am so sorry for that."

"I was also able to prosecute him for the theft of your land. He had your deed in his safe as plain as day. Lord Lucan testified that he never once placed conditions on your holding of that property. Those three-year performance reviews were strictly Gilchrist's doing. At no time was he legally empowered to hold your land in abeyance."

Robert pulled the deed to Tom and Meg's home from his carpetbag and solemnly handed it to Tom.

"Because the removal of your livelihood led to the demise of your dairy farm and the end of your income I had hoped to prosecute him for murder in the deaths of your two sons. Unfortunately, I had no evidence to connect him directly to those tragic events and those charges were dropped."

He took a sip of his whiskey and inhaled deeply.

"That is a grave disappointment to me, but I knew it was a long shot from the beginning. I am truly sorry."

He walked over to an overstuffed chair and sat down wearily.

"As for the matter of your subsidizing the rent, there was never any record of how much you gave and how much of that Gilchrist actually took. The court is figuring out a fair compensation for your losses and will forward the decision to me as soon as they have one. This amount will be extracted from Mr. Gilchrist's account, of course. I guarantee you they will be generous. My friend Lord Grissom was the sitting magistrate and believe me he was as digusted as I was at our friend Gilchrist. You stand to be a man of some means when the dust from this settles."

He looked up at George.

"Did I miss anything, George?"

"No, sir. I believe you've covered everything, sir."

Beverly bristled at her brother's obvious regard for her husband's manservant. How he must have weaseled his way into Robert's affections! She would have to advise Robert of George's extreme rudeness to her in the early days after Jeffrey's accident.

"Well then, that brings me to the unpleasant news. Meg dear, despite the wonderful outcome of Gilchrist's trial we still have to face the courts next week regarding his charges against you."

Meg gasped and clutched Tom's hand harder causing him

to wince with pain.

"I am sure we will prevail. The fool insists on pressing charges against you and Denny in absentia, for attempted murder. He must be insane with arrogance. I practically begged him to accept the opportunity to plead guilty of lesser charges in exchange for dropping the charges against you. He steadfastly refused which leaves us facing trial in less than a fortnight."

"I have two good witnesses, Rose and Mrs. Trent who will testify that he attacked you and you simply defended yourself. As for Denny, he rightly came to your aid. I hate to have you suffer this even one moment longer but it can't be helped. Grissom will sit for your trial. I am sure the whole thing will be over in one afternoon."

Robert stood up and the others followed suit.

"Now, if you will excuse me, I have a brutal headache and need to lie down. Beverly, perhaps you could order a nice roast chicken for dinner? I have had my fill of rich, greasy pub food. A hearty farm meal with plenty of harvest vegetables would suit me fine."

Beverly seized the opportunity to please her brother. She turned to Meg.

"Now that you've heard your news, I'm sure you have work to do. Please convey Lord Robert's wishes to Sharon. And have her make a nice fruit tart for pudding. With plenty of clotted cream."

Meg stood looking after her mother's sweeping skirt with astonishment. Would she never accept her again as her daughter?

Tom felt Meg's body go rigid at his side.

"Now, Darlin', in two weeks ye'll be free and soon after we'll be comin' into our just returns. I'm holdin' in me hand the deed t'me land. This opens up all sorts of avenues fer us, Meg. Yer mam will come around. Once ye don't need her anymore and she sees what a great mistress ye are in yer own home, she'll change her tune. Jist watch her."

Meg just stood there. There was nothing she wanted to

say. All her hopes rested on the impending trial. Until she walked out of Castlebar Courthouse a free woman, nothing her mother said or did would make a bit of difference to her life.

She returned to the scullery and took her anger out on two fat, headless chickens, leaving a pile of feathers to be cleaned up in her wake. She called Gracie and Ellen to bring a sack and pick up the feathers. When they arrived she asked where Francis was. He loved this job and she hadn't seen him in awhile. The girls just shrugged and began snatching at the floating feathers. Rose and Mary Clare were out in the truck garden pulling carrots and gathering the last of the beans for supper. She decided to stretch her legs and search for Francis herself.

He was always getting into mischief somewhere and as patient as he was; George didn't need a three year old messing about with his work. Ever since his candlestick chore had ended, Francis had taken to playing in the second story bedrooms. She had no idea what, but something had really caught his interest up there but the upstairs maids never minded and he was perfectly safe under their watch.

She went up the servant's staircase calling Francis's name. When she came out at the juncture of the east and north wings, she stood stock-still. There were all the polished candlesticks lined up like soldiers along the floor against the walls! Their candles were strewn all over, obviously not part of his game. She headed down the east wing calling his name but he was nowhere to be found.

The maids had long since finished the beds and she could hear their distant chatting as they washed the windows in Uncle Robert's suite. Meg wondered if Francis had fallen asleep in one of the beds. She went from room to room poking her head into each one and calling him. She even surveyed all the draperies to see if two little feet might give away a secret hiding place.

Turning into the north wing she suddenly heard him call out.

"No!"

Meg realized with shock that his little voice was coming from her father's room!

She ran to the door and threw it open. There in the dim light she could make out her father sitting in his wheeled chair with Francis on his lap facing him.

"No, not over! Tell me agin!"

Meg heard her father's voice for the first time in fifteen years.

"What do you mean, no? I've told you three times about the roses. Why do you need to hear it again?"

"Mam. Tell me th'part about Mam. Please, please, Mam, Mam, Mam!"

Francis bounced up and down on his grandfather's lap.

"No, you must stop that, Francis. Remember what I said about my broken legs. You'll hurt them bouncing like that."

Meg could not believe what she was seeing. Her father holding Francis? Speaking to him with patience and kindness? She felt weak and beads of perspiration rose on her forehead. What did this mean?

Her thoughts were interrupted by Francis's voice.

"Can I hear about th'roses agin? Jist one more time? And about Mam? Pleeaase?"

"Oh, all right! But no more, do you hear? You tire me out boy! After this you must run and fetch George for me. Papa needs to go back to bed."

"Aye, Papa. Jist one more."

"So, when your mother was a little baby much smaller than you, I planted a red rose bush for her in my garden. Then on her first birthday I planted another one, this time white. And on her second birthday, a pink one. Every year after that I planted another one. First yellow, peach, more red ones, more white ones. So, Mr. Serious Thinking Francis, how many did I tell you I have now?"

"Ten hundred!"

"No, silly boy, I have forty bushes. Your mother is forty years old! Now, you must remember that. I've told you many times! You're just a silly, old boy with your ten hundred! Now, tell me who is the Rose of Clydagh Glyn?"

Francis threw back his head and roared.

"Mam is! Mam is th'Rose o'Clydagh Glyn!"

Meg heard her father laugh. She hadn't heard that sound in so many years she had forgotten what it was like.

"Good. Now you must go. You said yourself that I'm all broken and need my nap every day. Get George up here and he can put me to bed. Then you can have your treat in the kitchen. Remember, you must come back tomorrow. Now go."

Francis dawdled next to his grandfather's chair.

"What? Didn't you hear me? I said go get George."

"Does it hurt?"

"Now, Francis, we've been all over that. You know all about it. Now go."

Still Francis didn't move.

"Can I kiss it?"

"Kiss what? What's this about kissing?"

Francis leaned close and whispered something to his grandfather.

"I can't hear you. Speak to me in the other ear. That one doesn't work."

Again Francis leaned in and whispered in Jeffrey's good ear with a loud hiss.

"Your broken face."

"No, you may not kiss my broken face! Nobody gets to kiss my broken face. Now get out of here you scamp! Go get George before I smack your little behind."

Francis slowly rounded the chair and began heading for the door. Meg ducked around into the linen closet just as she heard him say.

"T'morrow I can kiss yer broken face, right Papa?"

Then she heard his little feet scamper down the hall to the front stairs.

Meg waited until George had left her father's room before she emerged from the linen closet. She crept into the room wincing at the strong odor of stale urine. It amazed her that Francis cared nothing for any of the unpleasantness surrounding his grandfather's existence.

She quietly slipped into a chair next to his bed and watched him dozing in his wheeled chair. He was very tired and his face reflected his fatigue and his frailty. Francis could wear out a healthy man. Her father was hardly up to the challenge of his curious prattle much less the weight of the boy sitting on his lap.

Without opening his eyes, her father spoke.

"Go away, boy. I told you Papa needs to sleep. Be a good boy and go away until tomorrow."

Meg leaned toward the man she had once feared above all men.

"It's not Francis, Father. It's Meg. I've finally come to see you."

He opened one eye and looked at her blearily.

"What the hell do you want? Are you taking away my little chum? Afraid I'll taint his innocence with my evil ways?"

Her father's harsh tone, so unlike the way he spoke to Francis, hurt Meg but she persevered.

"Father, I know you just visited with Francis. He found you on his own and he seems to enjoy you very much. Of course, I won't stop you from being friends. I have five other children who would enjoy your stories too."

"No! Francis is my boyo. Leave it alone. I asked you what you wanted. Or is this just a social call after fifteen years?"

"Just a social call? Hardly, Father. I have so many things reeling through my heart and mind right now I can hardly manage social amenities. No, I wanted to see you before you die. Basically, that's why I'm here."

"Oh, that's it. Check out the damage you did. Take a good look Meg. Pretty soon it will be all worms anyway. Gloat over my ruined face and be done with it. Why not parade the others through the room so they can all get a good look? Bring your big ape of a husband in! He'll really enjoy watching me drool into my half-assed beard."

Meg stood up, unwanted tears springing to her eyes.

"Stop it, Father! We have had such hurt between us! I wanted to make an effort to mend things before it was too late. I can see that you haven't the same desire. I'm sorry I tried. Mother and you both clearly hate me and wish I had never been born. Why you planted roses on my birthdays is anybody's guess! I can only imagine you grew them for the thorns!"

As she started to leave, Jeffrey reached out and grabbed ahold of her skirt.

"Sit down, Meg. Just sit down and shut up."

Meg sat down, unable to stem the flow of her tears.

Jeffrey looked at her with heavy lidded eyes. His tone was much gentler now.

"You always were a crybaby. There are hankies in the drawer. Help yourself."

He shifted closer in an attempt to see her face.

"Help me sit up a bit so we can have a proper visit, though I can't promise I'll remember it tomorrow."

Meg stood up again and plumped her father's pillows behind him raising him up enough to really see her.

"What are you doing in that livery? What the hell are you doing dressed like a kitchen maid? Actually, let me ask what the hell you're doing here at all."

Meg explained to him all that had led her to come home. Surprisingly, he paid close attention to her story and only nodded off once. She knew he waited for his dose of laudanum and was growing increasingly uncomfortable waiting for George.had to fight to stay awake. The thought that he was willing to do that pleased her.

When she was finished, he looked at her queerly through one eye.

"Beverly! Your mother would hire you as a scullery maid rather than feed you as the eventual heir to this whole place! I never could figure out what was the matter with that woman."

He peered at her, his lopsided face breaking into a half-smile.

"So, you really were in jail? The little fellow wasn't making it up after all!"

He chuckled to himself and shook his head.

"How the hell did we end up this way? We actually come from very good people, your mother and I. If anyone knew our family secrets they'd run us off our land and certainly bar the doors to the church! Shit. I don't want that little Francis to carry on this mess. Is he your only son?"

"No, you said you have one on the lam. Good way to start a life. And you lost two boys. I'm sorry about that. When your mother and I were married, I thought I wanted a lot of children. But I'm afraid she changed so when you came along, I never had the opportunity to make any more."

Meg sat up with a start at this confession. Her father laughed with a shallow grunt that made him cough. Meg brought a glass of water to his lips and held his head while he drank. Her hand brushed the silver scars on the left side of his face and he grabbed it.

"Feel them Meg. They don't bother Francis, they shouldn't bother you. Feel them. I am forced to feel them every day. Every waking moment I am reminded of why I was so drunk for so many years, why I kept Maureen the way I did, why I hate your husband. Hell, I remember everything, Meg! I have nothing in my brain except memories. Even my dreams won't leave me any peace."

"I'm trapped in this mangled body and no one comes. Not a preacher, not my solicitor, not a tailor or a tobacconist- no one comes to see me unless I call them and demand them to come."

"No one but Francis."

"The day he came in here and started poking around my face was the first real day of my life."

"That little boy loves me! Ha! Imagine that. All my life I've searched for someone to love me the way my mummy did and not my wife, not my daughter, not my manservant, not any of my mistresses not even Reina back in her day!"

"Ha, I'll bet you never knew about me and Reina! Man

alive, now there's a woman! But she never loved me. No. No one ever loved me. Everybody was too busy hating me or being afraid of me to love me."

"But Francis loves me. Just the way I am!"

Jeffrey smiled a crooked wet grin releasing a stream of drool that soaked his chin and neck.

"That little fellow is my friend. He doesn't care if I reek of piss, or spit when I laugh or have the ugliest face this side of hell. He comes in here, practically clobbers me with a candlestick and bounces all over me wanting to play."

"And he comes back every day! I can't get rid of him."

He chuckled again and then suddenly grew serious.

"I don't want him to stop. He makes me feel alive!"

Meg sat very still as her father continued, "You know about the roses. So, you were listening."

"Yes, Father, I heard the story. I always thought it was Graber who said that."

"No, it was I who said it. Don't you remember sitting in your window, leaning out, watching me pruning the final selections for the flower show and saying…"

Meg chimed in.

"This one is the rose of Clydagh Glyn."

"Yes, you do remember! Then I'd look up at your window and point to you with the cut blossoms and say…"

Meg chimed in again.

"Now, there's the real Rose of Clydagh Glyn."

Meg was crying again.

"Father, I always remembered it being Graber who said that to me. Why did I not remember you doing it? Why are my memories wrong? I so badly want to remember the good things. Why do I only remember the bad?"

But she received no reply. Her father had finally succumbed to his drowsiness.

Meg stood up and pushed him close to his bed. For a moment she thought she could put him back to bed but realized that she hadn't the strength. She stood for a long time just looking at him and finally left him to find George.

Leona Trent was eloquent in her praise of Meg Phalen both as a wife and mother and loyal subject of the queen. She looked frail on the witness stand but her mind was sharp and her testimony rang like a bell through the courtroom.

Rose Phalen was remarkably composed for such a young witness. Her dark curls were pulled up in a tidy cascade of ringlets and her pristine white dress was modestly sashed in blue satin. She answered all of the questions clearly until Uncle Robert asked her to describe her feelings in the aftermath of her mother's arrest.

Then, her voice wavered as she spoke of being forced to approach Marie's and finding her brother quaking in the kitchen of that horrible place. The men of the jury were stricken at the thought of this innocent in such a place. When she described the last goodbye between her and her beloved brother, her tears flowed freely. Her account of rescuing her younger siblings from their beds and assisting Mrs. Trent and Fr. Timon was nothing short of harrowing.

Meg took the stand in her own defense, her beautiful green eyes as wide as saucers and her pink and white complexion offset by a bottle green day dress and fashionable bonnet. She described with disarming integrity her encounter with Mr. Gilchrist. When asked by Lord Cushing how she and her family had found themselves working at Browne's in the first place her account of their decline at the hands of Mr. Gilchrist was breathtaking. Tom sat in the gallery, his eyes brimming with pride.

It took the jury but moments to decide Meg's innocence. At Uncle Robert's request, the charges against Denny Phalen were then dropped altogether. Mr. Gilchrist was not in attendance but Lord Robert's friend the Honorable Mr. Grissom promised to convey the news to him post-haste.

Uncle Robert's big landau awaited them and by noon they were on their way back to GlynMor castle where they found lunch set for them in the dining room. Meg was surprised at that development but Uncle Robert had insisted that all the parties involved in the trial be treated to a fine meal. Beverly had not attended the trial and joined them late for tea and pudding. She had excused herself, claiming an appointment with her dressmaker. Robert suspected her tardiness at the table was another fabrication.

After seeing Mrs. Trent to her coach, Uncle Robert called Meg, Tom and Beverly into the library. He had some more business to take care of before he left for Cushing House in the morning.

Beverly was anxious as soon as Robert spoke of leaving. He made no mention of her going with him and she had no plan to stay in Clydagh Glyn. Again, he asked everyone to be seated. Perching on the edge of the desk chair, he opened his carpetbag and pulled out a little leather trunk. The sight of it made Beverly gasp and put her hand to her throat.

"Robert, where did you get that?"

Robert looked at her with both curiosity and relief on his face.

"I found it hidden in the depths of this desk the first night I came here last month. I was actually looking for an old portrait of Adelaide and this was buried deep inside father's old desk. To be frank, I have found the contents to be quite confusing. There are, however, some items of great interest to all of you."

He reached into the box and pulled out the jewels. He laid the two necklaces and the string of pearls on the desk and set the two sets of earbobs next to them. Beverly was on her feet at the sight of the jewelry. Eagerly, she gathered them into her hands.

"Robert! These are my things! My mother-in-law gave me these pieces for our wedding. They belonged in her family for years. Somewhere there's a document that traces them back to Anne Boleyn."

Robert's face registered disbelief and Beverly pouted with indignation.

"You think I'm making that up, do you? One of her ladies in waiting was an ancestor of Rose Wynn's on her mother's side. She gave the woman these jewels when she was sent to the Tower of London. According to the certificate, when she married Henry the VIII he had given them to her. She couldn't bear to see them worn by any other woman so she gave them to her lady in waiting for safekeeping. My mother-in-law told me her mother showed her the the letter in Anne Boleyn's own hand, written the very night she was taken away. That was lost somehow but she gave me the jewelry the night before our wedding. I wore the diamonds on our wedding day. Jeffrey had them placed in the ship's safe when we returned from our wedding trip but claimed they were somehow lost. I was crushed, of course, but I never told Lady Rose. I had other jewelry I preferred and as time went on, I forgot about them. I can't believe he hid them from me for all these years. Why would he do such a thing?"

Robert shrugged at Beverly's question. He went on to share the papers from the trunk.

"There are some lovely mementos here of our childhood Beverly, our baptismal records and the like. I invite you to take them and cherish them along with the jewels. There is also the paperwork describing the purchase of two townlands. Do you remember father talking about acquiring the lands on either side of the Phalen property? We were just newlyweds but I remember how excited he was. Well, I carefully read the deeds and found a clause in there I would like to read now."

"These lands, adjacent to Thomas Phalen's fields on the east and south sides, bounded by the stream we call Derrylick Run to the north and on the west by the easternmost tboundary of GlynMor Castle are to be distributed evenly, upon the occasion of their weddings, among any and all grandchildren God sees fit to grant me in my old age. I leave it to my son and solicitor, Robert Cushing, to be the executor of these properties."

Robert looked up from the page to see Tom and Meg looking back with shocked, colorless faces.

"So, Meg and Tom, Happy Wedding Day! You are now in possession of a great deal of land. I wish with all my heart that I had to ask you to share it with my own children but as God sees fit, there it is. All yours!"

Meg and Tom were speechless. In less than a month they had gone from homeless paupers to wealthy landowners. They needed time to assimilate these dramatic changes in their lives.

Beverly stood rigid and finally spoke up.

"Well, that is apparently that. Tom Phalen you are now in possession of more land than either my brother or myself. Marrying above you has certainly been in your favor. What have you to say for yourself?"

Tom Phalen smiled from ear to ear, relishing his moment of vindication.

"Given yer attitude, Lady Wynn, I'm inclined t'say good riddance t'ye. But given yer relation t'me wife and children, I'll refrain."

Beverly stomped her foot and flounced over to the window where she suddenly found a need to examine the jewels in the light.

Robert, too, smiled as he handed Tom the sheaves. He was enjoying this as much as Christmas. But oh, Beverly could be a penance!

"This certainly calls for a toast. George, a little sherry for the ladies and whiskey for me and Mr. Phalen?"

He winked at George.

"And pour yourself a stiff one too. After all, you had a hand in this development."

"Yes sir, very good, sir."

They all enjoyed their libation and began to disperse. As Meg headed for the door, Robert asked her to stay behind.

He took her hand in his and tenderly laid a small leatherbound book in her palm.

"Meg, I have something for your eyes only. Once you read it I strongly suggest you consider sharing it with your father. I understand you have established a reconciliation of sorts and I think what I'm about to give you will help a great deal to further that effort. At the very least it may bring you some understanding as to your father's behavior the day you told him you were carrying Tom Phalen's baby. Of course, I expect you will want to share this book with Tom and perhaps even discuss it with your father together."

"The book is a diary kept by your grandmother Wynn in the early days of her marriage. I found it among the items buried in the bottom of the desk. The desk was my father's and apparently, so was the leather chest. I suspect Jeffrey found it an ideal place to stash his own things, things too painful to leave in plain sight."

"I imagine he hid your mother's jewels to punish her and that is something she will have to deal with in her own manner. I'm not sure when he might have found the diary. Perhaps when his mother died or later when his father died. Maybe he will tell you."

"As for the townlands, I imagine he never expected you to run away and get married the way you did, and of course he would have no way after the accident to retrieve the deeds even if he wanted to do so."

He closed his hands around Meg's and looked deeply into her eyes.

"I needn't warn you of your father's very frail condition and the effect this discovery may have on him. I have asked Sharon to mind the children for you so you can take your time with these words. Meg, I thought hard and long about giving you this book. Whatever you decide to do once you've read it, please know that I share it with you out of my deep love for you as my niece. You are like the daughter I was never privileged to enjoy and you know you have always had my heart."

Meg put her arms around her uncle's neck and they held each other in a long embrace. Without another word, Uncle Robert left her alone to read the little book.

The big grandfather's clock in the foyer struck four as Meg reached the top of the stairs. She had finished the dairy and hoped she would find her father awake. With her head high and her jaw set she approached her father's room.

Standing outside his door, she fingered the beads of her rosary in her pocket. Pulling it out, she blessed herself with it and opened the door.

Three hours later, Meg and Tom lay in the great big bed that filled their tiny bedroom. She had just finished reading him the last of her grandmother Wynn's entries in her diary while the children supped in the manor kitchen with Sharon and the other servants.

Tom wasn't sure what to say. Meg had told him before she started to read it that she had already spoken to her father about it. The words of that tormented woman certainly explained a great deal of his father-in-law's hatred for the Irish, but that understanding wasn't enough to simply wipe away years of his own suffering and Meg's. Just because he knew why Jeffrey took a whip to his own daughter simply because she chose to love him didn't help Tom feel better.

Echoing the words his own da had asked him that terrible night, he turned to Meg and asked, "What did he say?"

Meg hesitated for a second and took a deep breath.

"He wept with such abandon I had to call George to dose him. I was terribly frightened that he would die from the shock. But he calmed down after a few moments and actually refused the laudanum when George offered it. George was also very upset. He kept telling Father that he wasn't the one who told me. My father finally reassured him that I had found out from the diary. Once Father relaxed, he told me the whole story, much the same as his mother told it."

"I asked him if he could ever forgive his mother and he began to weep again. He said he had tried right up until she died, but he had never been able to say the words. He told me how she had begged him with her eyes as she lay dying but he was so filled with hate at that time he just walked away. He said he felt so sorry for his father, whom he adored, that he could never get over his mother betraying him."

"That was when he grabbed me and pleaded with me to forgive him. He sobbed and apologized to me over and over again. At times I think he was speaking to my mother. He even begged me to forgive him for hurting Maureen. Oh, Tom! It broke my heart to see him like that. I know you have every reason to hate him and I never expect you to forgive him but he's nothing like the man who hurt us. He's just a pathetic little shell waiting to die."

"I'm so glad Uncle Robert and my mother decided to stay on another week. I'm sure his time is very near and I pray she at least tries to see him before he dies. Forgiving him has given me a freedom I never thought I'd ever have. I can't bear to have her carry the weight of her own hatred for the rest of her life. She deserves to be rid of that burden."

Tom took her hand in his and raised it to his lips. He said no more, mulling over in his mind just what he might do. After awhile, he heard Meg get up and put the kettle on the iron crane to boil for tea. He rose from the bed and took his cap from the second hook.

"I'll be seein' t'th'horses."

He touched Meg's shoulder and left the house by the kitchen door. He was greeted by a stiff wind as he turned toward the stable. He needed to talk to Old Ben.

Ben was snoozing in his rocker when Tom rapped on the door. Waking with a start, he called for him to come in.

"Tom! I niver expected ye t'come so soon!"

Ben and Tom had made plans to share a shorty that evening to celebrate Tom's new property.

"'Tis not the drink that brings me, Ben. I've got somethin' on me mind."

Much like the night they plotted Meg's escape, Ben, now a grizzled old man, puffed on his pipe and listened to Tom as he poured out his heart. When his friend was through, Ben shook his head.

"He really believed that fer all these years? Shoo, that's th'greatest tragedy of all, Tom."

Tom looked hard at the old man.

"Why?"

"Because it isn't true!"

"What are ye sayin', man? Not true! 'Twas right there in his mam's own writin'."

"Suren' she thought 'twas true. But I knew Christian Quinn well before he ever came to Henry Wynn's. When I first came to Ireland, me mam was dyin' and Mrs. Quinn, his mam, nursed her until she passed away. Chris wanted me t'be his partner in a smithy shop up near Ballinisloe but I had a gift fer the animals and really loved horses. Lord Wynn had seen me handlin' horses at the fair in Ballinisloe that year and had already asked me if I would come and work fer him."

"At the time Chris Quinn had been married seven years and no children t'show fer it and his wife had left him fer a travelin' tatie hoker. Within a month she's back braggin' about havin' a bun in the oven and doesn't she show up the next year with twins!"

"Quinn had so many women after that he said he lost count but none of'em took his seed. And most of'em had babies already! But not a one by him. By th'time he met Lady Wynn, he'd tried every tonic and potion and even a fancy Dublin doctor told him it would niver happen. He jist had somethin' missin'. He had been awful sick down there, ye know, as a boyo and th'doc told him that made his seed weak. So, he was right when he denied Lady Wynn's little boy was his son. Lord Jeffrey is Henry Wynn's son as sure as ye're the son of old Thomas Phalen."

Ben shook his head again.

"Ye know Tom, I stopped countin' birthdays years ago but I must be more'n ninety years upon this earth. I know a thing or two. And I know Lord Jeffrey Wynn is not Chris Quinn's son!"

Tom stood up and went to the cabinet where Ben kept his whiskey.

"I think I'll be havin' that drink now."

After several drinks with his old friend, Tom returned to the little stone house. He could hear the children's voices as

417

Meg and Rose put them to bed. He waited outside until he saw the candle go out in the little loft window indicating that Rose herself had gone to bed.

He stood in his da's yard, leaning against the pigsty wall like he had countless times before. His hand ran over the rough stones as he looked up at the stars. He remembered like it was yesterday the night he thought Meg was lost to him and how it had felt to smash those stones and grind them with his bleeding palms wishing he was beating in her father's face.

Even God hadn't wanted Tom that night. How different things were now. Tom knew God was with him tonight. How could the sky be so alive if He were not?

He watched a shooting star fling itself across the sky. Mam used to say that meant someone was dying. He felt very, very small and very peaceful looking at the night sky. He pulled his hand away from the sharp stones and felt something leave him. A burden he had carried ever since that night had been lifted heavenward and taken flight with the shooting star. Slowly he walked the worn path and opened the kitchen door.

Tom sat by the hearth and quietly shared Ben's astonishing revelation. Meg said nothing for a long time. When she finally spoke, her words were soft and measured.

"I'll not tell my father. He has lived with so much pain knowing since he was ten years old that his mother had betrayed her wedding vows, thinking for all that time that he was the son of her lover and finally letting her die unforgiven. What possible good could it do to tell him that it was all so much dust? How could I ever be the bearer of such devastating news? I can't do it! My father will die soon and now that we have finally come to an understanding of our hearts, I will not open such a terrible wound."

Tom looked at his wife with compassion. Perhaps he should not have told her what Ben had said but he felt she had a right to know and a right to decide for herself what to do with the knowledge.

"I respect your decision, Meg. I've made a decision meself."

Meg looked up at him, her eyes unfathomable green pools.

"I've decided to speak t'yer da in the mornin'. I will tell him I forgive him and hold nothin' against him."

Meg rose from her seat and threw herself into Tom's arms. Sobbing, she thanked him over and over as she covered his face with her kisses. Tom was taken aback by this display. He had never thought his decision would have such an impact on Meg. Now he was grateful for the moments he had spent in the yard praying.

They went to bed and slept deeply. In the morning they were awakened by a knock at the door. George had walked over to tell them that Lord Wynn had died peacefully in his sleep. He himself had not been there but when Meg asked, he reassured her that her father had not died alone. Lord Wynn had called for his wife late last evening and it had been Lady Beverly herself who had asked to sit with him through the night. By the time George had arrived to wake him, she had bathed his body with her own lavendar soap and dressed him in his old riding clothes for the wake.

Epilogue

T he story of the Phalen family is, in many ways, everyone's story. Any one of us born into the twentieth century in the United States had ancestors from somewhere else in the world. Even the native peoples who were here when the first Europeans arrived had family who had migrated from somewhere else.

The story of human survival is filled with people and peoples; individuals and nations. We often see throngs of people celebrating, protesting, migrating, fleeing. There are enormous masses of humans on the move everywhere. Their story needs and deserves to be told.

I chose to tell the story of humanity through the lens of my own family history. This one man and one woman defied social convention, risked all that was dear to them, even their very lives to pursue that which has been the driving force for everything good in human history: love.

Most of the words in the three books of The Extraordinary Love Trilogy are not even true. The characters are primarily fictitious. Yet what compelled me to write them and the reader to care about them is their universal quest for what the human race was created for in the first place: again, love.

The story is not over. This family, comes to the shores of America, as some members of the cast of characters in the books already have. Like millions of footsore, burdened, hungry and hopeful others, my ancestors put their boots on this shore in anticipation of a new and better life.

The Phalens will be among them and when they arrive, I'm sure the readers who follow them here will recognize in their stories the most important legacy left them by their own ancestors: extraordinary love.

Non-Fictional Characters Disclaimer

The creation of the fictional Blackthorn Brotherhood and its presence in County Mayo was the author's response to the irresistible urge to include the real presence of political unrest in the lives of her ancestors and treat the reader to some of the suspense of this gripping Irish reality.

While the Blackthorn Brotherhood never existed, there were indeed very brave freedom fighters of the time woven into the story of Duffy McGee and Tom Phalen. These real fighting men, nine members of the Young Irelanders, did in fact stage a rebellion in July, 1848 in Ballingarry, County Tipperary and were sentenced to death for treason against the Queen.

Despite the defeat at Ballingarry, the greater victory lay in their future. Originally sentenced to be hanged and then drawn and quartered, the men, in response to world-wide protests against the harsh sentence, were instead, exiled to a penal colony in Australia, from which they all escaped. All nine rose to great heights in the free world. Of those men, included in *White Dawn Rising* are: Thomas (D'Arcy) McGee, John Mitchell, Morris Leyne (fictitiously nicknamed Sea Snake) and Terrence McManus.

D'Arcy McGee became a member of the Parliament of Montreal, Minister of Agriculture and President of Council Dominion of Canada.

Terrence McManus became governor of the State of Montana.

Morris Leyne became Attorney General of Australia.

John Mitchell became a prominent New York politician. His son, John Purroy Mitchell was mayor of New York at the onset of WWI. He wrote extensively on the 'Irish Holocaust', clearly defining the political intentions of the British to annihilate the Irish through starvation.

The other men involved in the failed rebellion of 1848 were: Pat Donahue, Charlie Duffy, Tom Meagher, Richard O'Gorman and Mike Ireland. While they are not written into *White Dawn Rising*, each and every one of them left their mark on history.

Other recognizable Irish names associated with the Irish cause for freedom include Wolfe Tone, long regarded as the father of Irish Republicanism and an historic leader of The United Irishmen, a political organization of the 18th century that sought the liberal goal of Parliamentary Reform. Daniel O'Connell is also mentioned in the conversation overheard by young Denny. Daniel O'Connell, for whom the famous O'Connell Street in Dublin is named, was a legendary Irish patriot with an uncompromising quest for total independence for his people.

Much credit must go to Ivor Hamrock who compiled and edited *The Famine in Mayo 1845-1850 A Portrait from Contemporary Sources*. Mr. Hamrock gathers together in one book, published by the Mayo County Council in 1998 and reprinted in 2004, articles from multiple sources, mostly newspapers of the time that were invaluable to the research necessary for the second and third books of the Extraordinary Love trilogy.

In *White Dawn Rising* we again meet the evil Mr. Robert Gilchrist, first introduced in *My Tears My Only Bread*. Mr. Gilchrist is a fictional character representing the very worst of class elitism and the terrible bias against the Irish that ruled the English aristocracy in the 19th century.

There were men whose behavior toward the Irish during the potato famine was nothing if not reprehensible. One of the names, still loathed by many an Irishman, is Charles Edward Trevalyan. Trevalyan was the Assistant Secretary to the Treasury in the 1840's. While direct reference to Mr. Travalyan is limited to *My Tears My Only Bread*, the devastation wrought by his cruel social policies continues unabated in *White Dawn Rising*.

In response to a report of people dying from hunger, history quotes him as saying,

"We must not complain of what we want to obtain." This would seem to sum up Mr. Trevalyan's regard for the Irish.

The name Nassau Senior is also found in *White Dawn Rising*. Nassau Senior was a lawyer, economist and a member of the Poor Law Inquiry Commission of 1832. He is (in)famously quoted as saying, that the Great Irish Famine "would not kill more than a million people, and that would scarcely be enough to do any good."

While Lord Jeffrey Wynn is fictional, Lord Lucan is not. He is a factual character known to have employed the wreckers known as the Crowbar Brigade from 1846-1850, evicting extensively and ruthlessly. In an 1881 report in "Landlords and Tenants in Ireland" by Finley Dunn, his style is described as "terse and incisive" and he is quoted as saying that [he] "would not breed paupers to pay priests". Lord Lucan's marriage and relationship to Robert Gilchrist is entirely fictional as is the development of criminal behavior associated with them.

The Marquis of Sligo is also a real character of history whose reputation for fairness and generosity is well documented. The Marquis of Sligo, a descendant of the Browne family, lived at Westport House. Browne's Inn is fictional but the building where the author places it still stands on Clew Bay at the entrance to the woods that lead to Westport House on the Browne property. His relationship to the Cushing family and his purchase of Meg's jewels is entirely fictional as is his nephew Albert Browne

The law firm Hollister and Cooke is fictional and any similarity in name to the esteemed narrator of Masterpiece Theater, Alistair Cooke is an intentional nod in the direction of one of the author's favorite television personalities.

Lord Richard Arbuckle and his father Lord Roland are fictional characters, as are Lord Comfrey, Lord Jasper the Earl of Bennington, and of course, the Brothers Ross. The great and glorious spectacle of Dan Donnelly's arm is very real and still resides somewhere in a private collection in Ireland. For a delicious peek into the macabre story, read Allen Abel's feature in Sports Illustrated, February 20, 1995 or Irish writer, Patrick Myler's piece in The Ring, May 1998.

All of the Roman Catholic priests are fictional and based on the many wonderful priests of the author's acquaintance. The Church of Ireland minister, Reverend Edward Nangle, did have a mission on the northern side of Achill at Slievemore and did indeed have a printing press. His presence in Dooega is purely speculative and the characters of Rev. and Mrs. Trent and Rev. and Mrs. Smythe of Killarney are fictional.

Glossary of Terms

ACHILL CURRAGH: (SEE CURRAGH) ACHILL CURRAGHS WERE CONSTRUCTED WITH A SPECIFIC REINFORCEMENT IN THE HULL MADE OF OVERLAPPING RATHER THAN SINGLE RIBS. BECAUSE OF THIS, ACHILL CURRAGHS BOASTED GREATER FLEXIBILITY AND SEA-WORTHINESS DURING STORMY WEATHER

AVES: PRAYER HONORING THE VIRGIN MARY, COMMONLY RECITED USING PRAYER BEADS (ROSARY BEADS)

BANSHEE: A FEMALE SPIRIT WHOSE MOURNFUL WAILS ARE BELIEVED TO FOREWARN A FAMILY OF IMPENDING DEATH

BARM BRACK: A TEA BREAD MADE WITH BARM, A YEAST-LIKE LEAVENING MADE FROM OATMEAL JUICE

BAROUCHE: OPEN, FOUR-PASSENGER, FAIR WEATHER VEHICLE WITH HALF HOOD FOR BAD WEATHER

BASTIBLE: A COOKPOT SIMILAR TO A DUTCH OVEN NAMED FOR THE VILLAGE OF ORIGIN: BARNSTABLE, DEVON

BEESTINGS: HIGHLY VALUED YELLOW-COLORED MILK OF A COW RECENTLY CALVED

BELTANE, (FESTIVAL OF): MAY FESTIVAL FROM ANCIENT GAELIC TIMES, SURROUNDED BY SUPERSTITIONS, CELEBRATE THE SURVIVAL OF THE PEOPLE THROUGH THE HARD WINTER AND EARLY SPRING.

BLACKTHORN BROTHERHOOD: FICTIONAL LOCAL BAND OF REFORMERS

BLATHERSKYTE: ONE WHO IS FULL OF TALES, PRIMARILY UNTRUE

BOG FIR ROPES: VERY STRONG HANDMADE ROPES MADE FROM SHREDDED BOG TIMBER

BOG FIR STICKS: SMALL SCRAPS OF BOG TIMBER USED TO IGNITE FIRES

BOG TIMBER: FOSSIL OAK AND PINE OF THE BOGS, USED BY THE IRISH FOR CONSTRUCTION AFTER THE FORESTS WERE STRIPPED IN THE 1600S.

BOOLEY: SMALL STONE OUTBUILDING THAT DOT THE WESTERN IRISH LANDSCAPE BOOLEYS DATE BACK TO ANCIENT TIMES WHEN THEY WERE OFTEN USED TO HOUSE DRUIDS.

BOXTY: RAW, GRATED POTATOES MIXED WITH MILK, FLOUR AND EGGS AND BAKED ON A GRIDDLE. TRADITIONALLY SERVED ON ALL SAINTS DAY

BOYEEN: LITTLE BOY

BREAD PEEL: A WOODEN PADDLE DESIGNED TO PLACE LOAVES OF BREAD IN THE BACK OF AN OVEN

BRIAN BORU: HIGH KING OF IRELAND IN 1002-1014. POPULARLY BELIEVED TO HAVE OVERTHROWN THE VIKINGS IN THE BATTLE OF CLONTARF IN WHICH HE WAS KILLED

BROGUES (BROGANS): HEAVY SHOES WORN BY PEASANTS FOR WORKING

BROUGHAM: ORIGIN, ENGLAND 1837. ELEGANT, BOXLIKE 2 PASSENGER COACH

BUTTER-COOLER: VENTILATED, DOMED CONTAINER USED TO STORE BUTTER UNDERGROUND DURING HOT WEATHER

BYRE: A COVERED MANGER USED TO TETHER COWS AT NIGHT

CAIONE: FUNERAL DIRGE SUNG AT THE GRAVESIDE

CATHOLIC DEFENDERS: 18TH CENTURY IRISH REVOLUTIONARIES, ORIGINATING IN ARMAGH; JOINED WITH THE UNITED IRISHMEN IN A 1796 FAILED ATTACK AGAINST THE BRITISH AT BANTRY BAY

CEAD MILE FAILTE: AN IRISH GREETING LITERALLY MEANING: "A HUNDRED THOUSAND WELCOMES"

CHAMBERSTICK: A CANDLE AND HOLDER DESIGNED TO BE CARRIED TO BED

CHANGELING: A FEEBLE CHILD OF THE FAIRIES BELIEVED TO BE SWITCHED IN THE NIGHT WITH A HEALTHY NEWBORN; USED TO EXPLAIN DEFORMITIES

CHEROOT: A SLENDER CIGAR FAVORED BY THE UPPER CLASSES

CHUCHULAINN: ANCIENT, MYTHICAL IRISH WARRIOR SAID TO HAVE SLAIN "ONE HUNDRED AND THIRTY KINGS"

CLAGHAN: THE CLUSTER OF DWELLINGS BUILT TO HOUSE MEMBERS OF A CLAN IN A SPECIFIC AREA

CLAN: THE EXTENDED MEMBERS OF A FAMILY

CLARENCE CARRIAGE: A DOUBLE BROUGHAM CARRIAGE, LARGE, ELEGANT, WITH A COLLAPSIBLE HOOD, THE CLARENCE, LIKE THE BROUGHAM WAS DRAWN BY FOUR HORSES

CLYDAGH GLYN: FICTIONAL VALLEY BETWEEN THE CLYDAGH RIVER AND DERRYHICK LOUGH

COMPLINE: MONASTIC PRAYER BEFORE RETIRING

COUNTERPANE: LIGHT BEDSPREAD

CRAITHER: VAR. OF CREATURE, REFERRING TO THE DEVIL

CRANE AND HAKE (CRANE AND POT-HOOK): LONG, HINGED, IRON CRANE DESIGNED TO SWING IN AND OUT OF THE HEARTH; HAKE, A NOTCHED ROD THAT OFFERED VARYING HANGING HEIGHTS

CREEL: LARGE UTILITY BASKET, OFTEN WITH A WOVEN STRAP FOR CARRYING ON THE BACK; ALSO CALLED A PARDOG

CREEPIE: THREE LEGGED HEARTH STOOL, KNOWN FOR BEING UNABLE TO BE TIPPED

CROAGH PATRICK: MOUNTAIN WHERE ST. PATRICK IS SAID TO HAVE PRAYED AND FASTED FOR THE CONVERSION OF IRELAND

CROAGHAUN: ANCIENT QUARTZITE MOUNTAINS FORMING MUCH OF THE WESTERN SECTION OF ACHILL ISLAND

CROWBAR BRIGADE: HIRED BY LOCAL BAILIFFS TO TEAR DOWN THE HOMES OF THE EVICTED, THIS MIGRATING BAND OF THUGS WAS MUCH FEARED BY THE POOR IRISH TENANTS

CRUASACH: A DISH MADE UP OF LIMPITS AND VARIOUS SEAWEEDS, COMMONLY FOUND IN FISHING VILLAGES OF THE WEST COAST

CURRAGH: LOW, WIDE FISHING BOAT; RIBBED AND COVERED IN HIDE

DASH CHURN: HAND OPERATED BARREL AND PLUNGER STYLE CHURN

DONNEGAL LONG HOUSE: USUALLY STONE HOUSE WITH A SLOPING FLOOR (FOR EASIER CLEANING) USED TO HOUSE ANIMALS WITH THE FAMILY IN THE WINTER

DRESSER: COMMONLY KNOWN NOW AS A HUTCH; THE MOST IMPORTANT FURNITURE IN THE NINETEENTH CENTURY IRISH KITCHEN

DEMESNE: FROM "DOMAIN", THE LAND OWNED BY THE VERY WEALTHY

DEVIL: CURSE WORD COMMONLY USED INSTEAD OF DAMN

DRUID: A PAGAN PRIEST OF THE ANCIENT CELTIC TRADITION; CONVERTED BY ST. PATRICK TO BECOME THE FIRST BISHOPS OF IRELAND

DULSE: ONE OF SEVERAL KINDS OF SEAWEED HARVESTED FOR HUMAN CONSUMPTION; OTHERS INCLUDE CARRAGEEN, SLOKE, LAVER AND DULAMEN

EAR LOCKS: LONG CURLS OR THIN BRAIDS WORN IN FRONT OF THE EARS LOOSELY LOOPED; SOMETIMES FASTENED AT THE BACK OF THE HEAD.

EEL SPEAR: ANCIENT FLAT TINED, PRONGED SPEAR USED TO IMPALE EELS

FAERIES (FAIRIES): INVISIBLE CREATURES BELIEVED TO HAVE THE POWER TO INFLUENCE DAILY LIFE FOR GOOD OR ILL

FALLING LEAF TABLE: HINGED TABLE, HUNG ON A WALL, UNDER A WINDOW. HUNG FLAT WHEN NOT OPENED FOR MEALS

FARL: ONE QUARTER OF A ROUND, FLAT BREAD BAKED ON A HOT STONE

FARL TOASTERS: WROUGHT IRON RACKS OF VARYING SHAPE USED TO TOAST A SINGLE FARL

FOOD ARK (ALSO MEAL ARK): SINGLE OR DOUBLE COMPARTMENT. USED TO STORE FLOUR AND GRAIN MEAL

GAOL (JAIL): PRISON

GALWAY HEARTH: WITH TWO STONE BENCHES BUILT IN ON EITHER SIDE OF THE FIRE

GARROTE: STRANGLE; NOOSE-LIKE

GROVES KITCHENER STOVE: ONE OF THE EARLIEST CLOSED RANGES KNOWN FOR ITS VERSATILITY

HALF-DOOR: HORIZONTALLY SPLIT DOOR ALLOWING BOTH FRESH AIR AND PRIVACY

HANSOM CAB: A CLASSIC, 2 PASSENGER CAB WITH THE DRIVER'S SEAT HIGH IN THE BACK

HARNEN STAND: WROUGHT IRON STAND FOR TOASTING (HARDENING) A ROUND, FLAT LOAF OF BREAD

HAY BOGEY: HORSE OR DONKEY DRAWN CART USED TO DRAG HAY INTO STORAGE

HAYCOCKS: MOUNDS OF HAY PURPOSELY SHAPED TO WITHSTAND REGIONAL WEATHER

HEDGE SCHOOL: SECRET OUTDOOR SCHOOLS CONDUCTED IN DEFIANCE OF ENGLISH LAW, USUALLY BENEATH THE SHELTER OF HIGH ROADSIDE HEDGES

HEDGEMASTER: HIGHLY REVERED TEACHER, OFTEN RISKING HIS LIFE TO TRADITIONALLY EDUCATE IRISH CHILDREN

HOB-KETTLE: MADE OF CAST IRON OR COPPER, DESIGNED WITH POURING SPOUT

HOOKER: FISHING BOAT

HUNDRED-EYE-LAMP: PRIMITIVE, HANDLED LANTERN WITH HOLES PIERCED ALL OVER TO SHED LIGHT

JENNY LIND: SMALL HARD TOPPED BUGGY COMMONLY USED AS A CAB TO TRANSPORT 1 OR 2; NAMED FOR THE BELOVED SWEDISH SINGER

KEEPING ROOM: SMALL, MULTI-PURPOSE ROOM OFF THE KITCHEN. OFTEN USED TO GIVE BIRTH

KOHL: TRADITIONALLY USED IN THE MIDDLE EAST, EYE PAINT MADE OF SOOT OR ASH

LANDEAU: FOUR WHEELED, SPLIT HOODED CARRIAGE WITH TWO SEATS ACROSS FROM EACH OTHER, DRAWN BY TWO HORSES

LIMPITS: SMALL PLENTIFUL FISH REPUTED TO GIVE GREAT STRENGTH WHEN EATEN

LIMBO: ACCORDING TO ROMAN CATHOLIC TRADITION, PLACE WHERE UNBAPTIZED BABIES WERE ONCE BELIEVED TO GO WHEN THEY DIED

LUCIFER: NAMED FOR THE DEVIL, WOODEN MATCH REPUTED TO LIGHT WHEREVER IT WAS STRUCK

LUMPERS: LUMPY, WATERY, POOR QUALITY POTATOES

MACINTOSH: RAINCOAT

MALARKEY: LOOSE TALK

MAY MORNING: THE FIRST OF MAY; SURROUNDED WITH FOLKLORE AND SUPERSTITION

MEAT-SAFE: WOODEN BOX WITH WIRE-MESH DOOR TO KEEP FLIES OFF OF MEAT AND OTHER PERISHABLES

MICHAELMAS: SEPTEMBER 29, TRADITIONALLY THE FEAST CELEBRATED AROUND THE SLAUGHTER OF THE "BARROW PIG" THE LARGEST OF THE HERD. IT WAS COMMON TO HAVE A GOOSE ON MICHAELMAS FEAST

MOBCAP: SMALL, LACY BONNET WORN AT HOME, OFTEN TO BED

MORGAN LE FAY: POWERFUL SORCERESS OF THE KING ARTHUR LEGEND, AN ADVERSARY OF THE ROUND TABLE DUE TO HER ADULTERY WITH ONE OF THE KNIGHTS

MORNING ROBE: HOUSECOAT, USUALLY WORN BY UPPER CLASS WOMEN DURING MORNING DOMESTIC ROUTINE

MORUADH: A LEGLESS FIN-TAILED WATER NYMPH; A MERMAID

MOSES CRADLE: HOODED, BASKET-WOVEN CRADLE

MUSHA: EXPLETIVE DISMISSING SOMETHING AS NONSENSE

OATCAKE: FLAT HARD CAKES MADE OF OATS, WATER AND BUTTER, AND BAKED AND DRIED

OLLAV: TITLE OF HONOR GIVEN TO A TEACHER

OMETHON: FOOL

PACKAGE BOAT: MAIL BOAT

PALAVER: LOOSE TALK

PANNIE: CAST IRON FRY PAN

PANTECHNETHICA: FORM OF ASSEMBLY LINE MANUFACTURING DESIGNED TO PROVIDE TAILOR MADE GARMENTS IN ONE DAY

PAROXYSM: SEIZURE OF VIOLENT COUGHING

PATTONS: RAISED, OPEN PLATFORM SHOES OFTEN MADE OF IRON AND LEATHER THAT STRAPPED ONTO THE FOOT, ELEVATING THE WALKER ABOVE SLUSH AND MUD

PELISSE: FULL-CUT WOMAN'S ROBE DESIGNED FOR LEISURE WEAR OR IN HEAVIER FABRICS, AS A LIGHT COAT

PHAETON: SPORTY FOUR WHEELED CARRIAGE DRAWN BY ONE OR TWO HORSES, REPUTED TO BE VERY FAST. DRIVEN BY THE OWNER, FAVORED BY PHYSICIANS AND WOMEN

PISEOGS: LOCAL SUPERSTITIONS

POKER OVEN: DEEP BREAD OVEN REQUIRING THE USE OF A POKER TO PLACE AND RETRIEVE LOAVES

POLL COW: A RED COW REPUTED TO PRODUCE EXCEPTIONALLY GOOD MILK AND CREAM

POMATUM: A SETTING LOTION VERY SIMILAR TO MODERN HAIR GEL; MARACHEL POMATUM WAS POMATUM CONTAINING DYE, USUALLY MADE FROM HENNA

POOKA: AN ANIMAL SPIRIT WHOSE UPPER HALF WAS OF A MALE HUMAN AND WHOSE LOWER HALF WAS OF A STEED; THE POOKA IS SAID TO COME AROUND THE FIRST DAY OF NOVEMBER

POTATO BASKET: FLAT ROUND BASKET WITH A WELL IN THE CENTER FOR SALT; USED TO SERVE POTATOES AT THE TABLE

POTEEN: HOMEMADE LIQUOR; MOONSHINE, HOOCH

PRATIES: REGIONAL COLLOQUIALISM FOR POTATOES

QUAY: HARBOR, DOCKSIDE

RACING FOR THE BOTTLE: A WEDDING CUSTOM WHEREBY THE SINGLE MEN FROM BOTH SIDES RACE ON HORSEBACK FROM THE ALEHOUSE TO THE BRIDE'S HOUSE. THE FIRST TO ARRIVE WINS THE BOTTLE WHICH IS FIRST GIVEN TO THE GROOM AND THEN PASSED AROUND THE WHOLE GROUP

REEK SUNDAY: THE LAST SUNDAY IN JULY WHEN PILGRIMS COME FROM ALL OVER IRELAND TO CLIMB CROAGH PATRICK IN HONOR OF THEIR PATRON SAINT.

RETICULE: SMALL PURSE

ST. BRIGET'S CROSS: A TALISMAN MADE FROM RUSHES BELIEVED TO PROTECT A HOUSEHOLD FROM EVIL SPIRITS. ST. BRIGET, WHO WAS A COWHERD, IS AS BELOVED IN IRELAND AS ST. PATRICK. HER FEAST FALLS IN THE SPRING AND IS SURROUNDED WITH SUPERSTITIONS REGARDING LIVESTOCK

ST. DYMPHNA: LEGENDARY SAINT, THE DAUGHTER OF A 7TH. CENTURY IRISH KING, EXILED TO ACHILL FOR REFUSING TO MARRY HIM AFTER HER MOTHER DIED, SHE BUILT THE CHURCH THAT BEARS HER NAME. SHE WAS FORCED TO FLEE TO GEEL, BELGIUM WHERE SHE WAS EVENTUALLY MARTYRED. SHE IS REVERED BY CATHOLICS FOR HER INTERCESSION FOR EMOTIONAL AND MENTAL DISORDERS.

SCULLERY: SMALL AREA ADJACENT TO THE KITCHEN OF WEALTHY HOMES USED EXCLUSIVELY FOR WASHING DISHES

SETTLE BED: WOODEN BENCH BY DAY; OPENED UP TO BECOME A BED AT NIGHT

SHITE: EUPHEMISTIC PRONUNCIATION OF A COMMON EXPLETIVE

SHITEGOB: A MOUTHFUL OF THE ABOVE MENTIONED EXPLETIVE OR ONE WHO SPOUTS SUCH MATTER

SLANE: NARROW SHOVEL USED TO HARVEST TURF

SLIDE-CAR: HORSE OR PONY PULLED CART MADE OF TWO WOODEN POLES CONNECTED BY WOODEN RUNNERS FORMING A PLATFORM FOR BUNDLES

SLIP-BOTTOM CREEL (SLIP-CREEL): BASKET WITH A BOTTOM THAT OPENED FOR DUMPING THE LOAD

SLOKE: A VARIETY OF SEAWEED

SOOT-HOUSE: SMALL HUTS MADE OF SOD AND STONE DESIGNED TO BURN TURF ALL WINTER TO FORM ASH FOR FERTILIZING THE SPRING POTATO CROP

SOUTANE: (FR.) PRIEST'S BLACK CASSOCK

SPALPEEN: MIGRANT WORKERS WHO FOLLOWED THE HARVEST OR HIRED ON TO HERD LIVESTOCK. OFTEN USED AS A DEROGATORY TERM BY THE UPPER CLASSES TO DESCRIBE A YOUNG MAN OF QUESTIONABLE CHARACTER

SPANCEL: ROPE USED TO TIE THE LEGS OF COWS FOR SAFE MILKING

SPONC: POOR MAN'S TOBACCO MADE OF HERBS AND GRASSES

STONE: WEIGHT OR MASS EQUAL TO 14 POUNDS?

STORM LANTERN: CLOSED GLOBED LAMP FOR OUTDOOR USE

STRAW BOBBINS: PEGS USED TO SECURE THATCH ON THE ROOF

SULTANA: DRIED FRUIT COMPARABLE TO A RAISIN

SWISS COTTAGE: FANCIFULLY DESIGNED COTTAGE USED BY THE VERY WEALTHY AS A SUMMER RETREAT. THESE RETREATS WERE FOUND IN IRELAND AS WELL AS CONTINENTAL EUROPE

TATTIES: REGIONAL COLLOQUIALISM FOR POTATOES; SOMETIMES POTATO CAKES

TATTIE-HOKERS: DEROGATORY TERM FOR MIGRANT POTATO PICKERS

TENANTRY: TENANTS

TESTER BED: DESIGNED WITH CANOPY BUT NO SIDES, LOW ENOUGH TO BE COMMONLY USED IN A LOFT

TIN OVEN: A BASIC BOX OVEN MADE OF TIN THAT WAS SET IN THE FRONT OF AN OPEN HEARTH

TINNIE: TIN MILK CAN

TOWNLAND: AREA OF AROUND 325 ACRES OR ½ SQUARE MILE WITH ABOUT 50 INHABITANTS. THE SIZE OF A TOWNLAND IS BASED ON THE FERTILITY OF THE LAND RATHER THAN ACTUAL ACREAGE AND A TOWNLAND NAME IS A LEGAL TITLE CHANGEABLE ONLY BY AN ACT OF PARLIAMENT

TRUCKLE BED: A RAISED BED OFTEN USED IN AREAS OF FLOODING. COMMONLY WHEELED UNDER A CONVENTIONAL BED FOR STORAGE

TURF: FUEL DUG FROM THE BOGS OF IRELAND. CALLED PEAT IN THE NORTHERN COUNTIES

TURF-CREEL: A BASKET USED FOR CARRYING TURF, OFTEN WITH A SLIP BOTTOM FOR EASE OF UNLOADING

TURF-CUTTER: ONE OF THE LOWEST CLASSES OF IRISH PEASANTRY, TURF-CUTTERS LIVED IN THE BOGS THEY HARVESTED, CARVING CAVES IN THE WALLS OF THE BOGS AND LIVING BELOW GROUND

UNDERTAKER: AN ADMINISTRATIVE ASSISTANT TO WEALTHY LANDED GENTRY. AN OVERSEER OF AFFAIRS

WATTLE AND DAUB: BUILDING MATERIALS MOST COMMON IN THE MIDLANDS. WALLS WERE OUTLINED WITH WATTLE, (INTERLACED RODS AND TWIGS) AND COATED WITH DAUB (MUDDY CLAY)

WORKHOUSE: A POORHOUSE WHERE PAUPERS WERE TO BE HOUSED AND FED UNDER THE POOR LAW ACT OF 1838

YELLOW MAN: A HONEYCOMBED, STICKY TOFFEE, SERVED HARD AND BROKEN INTO CHUNKS WITH A HAMMER; POSSIBLY THE ORIGIN OF THE CHOCOLATE COVERED TREAT CALLED SPONGE CANDY

About the Author

Mary Ellen Feron is the maiden name and pen name of Mary Ellen Zablocki, who lives in Buffalo, New York with her husband, Ed. She has two married sons, Francis and Paul. Her writing is done in her 1911 living room on a roll top desk surrounded by over fifty antique family photos spanning three centuries and two continents.

Ms. Feron began writing in high school and has primarily published essays, poetry and spiritual works. She was first published in 1985 in New Covenant Magazine followed by articles and poetry in Franciscan publications The Cord and Tau USA. Her short story, *"Sweet Gloria"* took second place in The Buffalo News first annual short story contest in 2005. Her most recently published poem, *"Night Psalm"*, can be found in Prayers from Franciscan Hearts, by Paula Pearce, SFO (St. Anthony Messenger Press, 2007)

Mary Ellen Feron presents *A Tent for the Sun* as the first novel of a trilogy. Books two and three: *My Tears, My Only Bread* and *White Dawn Rising* will be available in early 2013.

Email the author
maryzablocki@roadrunner.com
Find her on Facebook
http://www.facebook.com/mary.feronzablocki
On the Web
www.maryferonzablocki.com

Made in the USA
Charleston, SC
15 August 2014